Tempest

Tempest

Brennig Jones

For every author I have read, every person I have met, every place I have visited, and for my long-suffering family. You have all helped produce this book. Thank you.

Preface. Attempt 1
First Words/Last Words

Week 51. Monaco

Muffled noise outside.

The seatbelt had done its job. I was strapped in behind the steering wheel, upside down.

I shook my head, trying to clear the impact fuzz, the sensation of my head jarring as the car had somersaulted. The windscreen had crazed but held in place. Blood dripped from my face down/up on to the car roof. I blacked out; could have been a few moments or a few minutes.

Woken by noise outside.

'Are you OK in there?' shouted a distant voice.

I didn't answer. Through my bleary vision, I could see upside-down feet running towards me.

'Hello?' A little clearer.

The blood continued to drip upwards from my nose, and my chest hurt. She dipped down and put her head through the open window.

'Are you… Jesus Christ!'

I tried to tell her that I wasn't the Son of God, but my tongue wouldn't work, and I realised that the blood dripping from my nose was originating in my mouth. I'd probably bitten my tongue off.

There was more noise outside, and another pair of feet jogged towards the car. A man's voice shouted something I couldn't make out.

The passenger window was kicked in. She was still leaning in my side when a gloved hand reached in from the other window. It held a gun fitted with a short-barrelled suppressor. The gun spat once, and her face disintegrated.

The gun turned towards me; just before it fired again, I thought I was going to have to do things differently next time.

The gun spat again, and I died quicker.

Chapter 1. Attempt 2
Start. Again

Week 1. London

I woke.

Curled, foetus-like. Shaking. Cold but sweating. Every muscle aching. Stomach pain. My brain was working, but my body was doing its own thing. I puked over myself. I lay in my vomit and shivered for what seemed like days while my muscles did what they wanted. I soiled myself. Twice.

Each time I fell asleep, my spasming body shook me awake again. It was dark before I had some muscular control. I tried to roll on to all fours. The effort made my every fibre scream. I screamed. I dry heaved. I cried. I cried a lot.

When I next woke, daylight was starting to peep through

the tattered rug nailed across the window. I slowly rolled over and up on to my knees. The pain in my legs and ribs made tears run.

I hated coming off drugs. I've done it so often that I'm probably the world's leading expert. That could almost be funny if it wasn't true.

The air in the squat smelled stale and rank and most of that was me. I made it to the bathroom; the mirror was unkind. Thin-faced, sunken-eyed, pale-skinned, bloodshot eyes.

My vest was filthy, stained, and looked like Bruce Willis had worn it when he threw Alan Rickman off the Nakatomi Building. My running shorts were beyond recovery. My legs had bruises and scabs from recent bleeds. I looked at my arms: badly bruised needle marks, a not good thing to see. The shower was cold but made me start to feel human. I had a long way to go with rehab, but at least I'd begun. Again.

My rucksack yielded a change of clothes, not clean, but not as dirty. In a side pocket was a mobile phone that showed one voicemail. I knew what it was; I wasn't strong enough for it yet. I dressed and stood in front of the mirror. At least now my hair didn't look like a matted mess. I knew from previous cold turkeys I wouldn't be able to eat yet, but my stomach hurt, and just moving around these two rooms made my limbs scream with the exertion.

It was seventy-two hours since my last hit, and according to the experts and past experience, I was over the worst. But because my body and its systems were shot, I had a long haul in front of me. I was going through opiate withdrawal without the help of any meds. No methadone, no diamorphine. And no support.

I sat in the badly stuffed armchair and fell asleep.

Mid-afternoon, I woke and had another crying spell. It seemed to last hours but was probably just a few minutes. As soon as it was dark, I picked up the rucksack, carefully went downstairs and crept outside, like a mouse expecting a cat around the corner. There was no cat. It was cold and it had rained. The streets and buildings smelled wet, but after being in the flat, the damp south London air was fresh and clean against my face. That first walk was not much more than a few hundred yards to the corner shop. Every muscle in my legs and chest ached as I climbed back up the stairs to the flat. I unpacked the rucksack. A tin of soup, some paracetamol, and a bottle of anti-diarrhoea medicine because I knew what was coming. Told you. I am probably the world's leading expert at going cold turkey. I've pretty much tried every method. I ate three spoonfuls of soup and slept fitfully.

On the second walk, in the very early hours, I completed one lap around the small park. I felt as if I was close to death when I returned; I had a little more soup and cried myself to sleep.

Every hour that passed I improved a little. By the end of the third evening, I was able to walk one mile twice a day; I could now eat meals of boiled rice and soup; all I could keep down. On the morning of day four, I started gentle sit-ups, just three on the first attempt, and stepped up the pace of my park laps to a slow, intermittent jog. I continued to push myself, worked hard to improve.

Nine days later, I took a fork from the kitchen as I left the flat for my night exercise. This time I strayed off course and cut through the park. As I was slow jogging past the bandstand, he came at me from behind, out of the bushes. I was still slow and weak, but I knew where he was waiting, and I knew his moves before he made them. As he reached an arm across my throat, I stabbed backwards with the fork, through his open raincoat, into his naked groin. He shrieked; I turned and pushed the fork home hard and twisted it with all my kitten-like strength. He squealed like a wounded animal.

As he doubled over, I reached into his raincoat pocket, removed his car keys, and walked briskly from the screaming wreck I had created. His car was near the park's north entrance; the key fob unlocked it. I opened the door, using my t-shirt to keep my prints safe. As I knew it would be, his wallet was under the driver's seat. I took it, touched nothing else, and walked to the flat.

I stayed in for the rest of the night, continuing my push-ups and sit-ups. I knew the risks of going out again that evening. I worked hard on building my exercise routines; getting fit was everything.

———————————

Three weeks after cold turkey, it was time to leave the squat. I walked around the corner to a newsagent, selected some numbers, and bought a lottery ticket. Then, because I needed some immediate hard cash, I put a small amount on an accumulator with the bookies next door. And went to the library for a few hours.

At 4 pm, I smiled nicely as the cashier counted out my winnings. The horses had been generous. I took a cab to a quiet hotel where I booked a full spa session for the next day. They weren't sure about me, but I paid in hard cash, and they liked that. Once I'd checked in, I walked around the corner and bought a change of clothes and a decent bra.

Later in the evening, after the draw had been made, I dialled the lottery claim line and started the process that would put a serious number of zeroes into my bank account.

I suppose, by now, you're wondering how I knew these things? The attacker in the park. Which pocket his keys would be in. Where to find his car. And his wallet. When to stay in the flat. Which three horses to back. And which numbers to pick for the lottery? And also, probably wondering what was behind my resolve to kick my opiate habit?

Those are easy questions. I've lived it all before. Not the moment. Not the day. I've lived this year before. Many times. More than two thousand times.

Each time the year starts, I've been at the end of a cold turkey session that should have killed me. Or the OD before that should have. I don't know how. I don't know why. I just know something happened somewhere. Somehow. I don't even know if it happened to me because of the drugs, or if living the same year on permanent repeat was a side effect of something someone else had done. I just don't know.

Sometimes the year lasted a year. Sometimes it lasted much less. If I died, the year ended, and the cycle began again with another helping of cold turkey. It didn't matter how I died, my death took me back to Go, and I didn't collect £200. If I didn't die and lived out the full year, I woke up in the South London squat on cold turkey day three. Again.

So I learned things. And I learned from my mistakes. The first time he raped and beat me, I dragged my broken, bleeding body back to the squat, sat in the bath, opened a vein, and started the cycle all over again.

For the next few cycles, I avoided the park on that night, but the newspapers told me he carried on; young girls, older women, the only thing he changed was where he was doing it. One year, after reading about his most violent, vicious attack, I decided to stop him. It took me three cycles to learn his moves and to get my fitness to where I could beat him. But I stopped what he was doing. He lived on, but I'd ended his activities.

As I lived each cycle on repeat, I didn't learn just about the attacker in the park. I learned about things. Numbers. People. Events. I learned how to live through drug withdrawal. And after that I learned how to live. I learned what to do with my life. For a year, at least.

Chapter 2. Attempt 2
Learning

Week 3. London

For a couple of days, I kept a low profile; stayed in the hotel room, ate small amounts of plain food as often as I could, and slept as much as my damaged self would allow. I used the hotel gym to take my twice-daily workouts to my mental and physical limits. The biggest fight I had was overcoming the near-unending tiredness.

My psyche wanted to shut down, regroup, make order of everything, recharge. But I'd learned that a year is a very short time and losing days 'recharging' was wasteful. My out of shape body needed an upgrade, my central nervous system needed a clear-out, and my mental and physical reflexes needed a reboot.

Somewhere around my nineteenth cycle, as I came to call these year-long lives, I began looking for answers to the big questions. Why? How? When? Where? What?

For three years, for three entire cycles, I became a compulsive full-time student. I read fact and fiction, studied academic papers, and poured over-educated hypotheses. I wrote my own papers and sent them to scholarly experts and published my thoughts in various places. I emailed authors and people who were authorities on Einsteinian equations and related theories. I even attended talks and conferences.

Eventually, in the face of almost no facts and supported by a lot of conjecture, I came up with my own theory for what was happening. I was trapped inside a bubble that created a new branch of time every time I died.

Each time I started a new cycle, the place I'd just left carried on as an alternative timeline, running in parallel to the one I'd just created by starting anew; the previous one just continued on without me. If I had saved someone's life in the previous cycle, the timeline just carried on and that person went on to live the rest of their life in that world. And perhaps I did too? Perhaps my 'unreset self' continued if my death hadn't been the cause of the reset?

But with every reset, I woke up on Day Zero, going through the same opiate withdrawal at the start of another year-long cycle. At least, that was my theory. I still had no answers as to how or why this was happening.

I learned to accept my new life, learned to live each and every new year. The possibility of unlimited years of self-indulgence stretched before me, and I grabbed each and every opportunity in every cycle.

I tried every thrill, every sensation. I did drugs, and alcohol, and sex. I travelled the world, saw all of the sights, lived in exotic places, sampled exotic tastes. I associated with nice people, and nasty people, with honest, selfless people, and with sly, cunning, selfish bastards. And if a cycle got too much for me, I pressed the reset switch and had another go. But, eventually, the years of self-indulgence began to lose their flavour.

Where do you go? What do you do when you've had everything your heart, mind, and body can desire, and you've had it all on demand for decades, and you have become tired of your own existence?

I drifted for a few years, tried to find myself again, looked for my place in life, and in the early part of one new cycle, I did something different, I turned left instead of right, and I stepped into a different life. I found myself at a week-long music festival, surrounded by young people my family would never have approved of.

I joined them, these new friends. I become a caravan-dwelling hippy. I lived a happy, harmonious life in a small, sleepy commune, played an active part in our little society, and contributed almost nothing to anyone outside it.

Nevertheless, after a dozen cycles, it became difficult to stay. It was tough watching the same people, the people I loved, making the same mistakes, year after year, learning nothing. When I couldn't bear it anymore, I switched tracks again, but I took many of the values from that small community with me.

For another decade, I moved in the business world. I

revelled in my easily won financial successes. I lived high and flew higher; I acquired insider knowledge on repeat cycles, which yielded more wealth than even my contemporary corporate peers could imagine.

But late one night, after a celebratory party in Hong Kong, when two guys who decided that 'no' meant 'yes' were sleeping it off, I dragged my battered body off the bed and killed them.

It was messy for me and not painful enough for them. I stabbed the short one through his left eye with a fruit knife taken from the room service dolly. I doubt he knew anything about it. I angled the knife into the space I thought his brain would be most vulnerable. Blood splashed up across my torn blouse, and I felt it spatter on my face and watched it pump over the side of his head onto the bed.

His colleague was passed out drunk on the bathroom floor. I fetched a large tin of cleaning fluid from the service cupboard at the end of the corridor, poured the contents over his chest and set fire to it. His screams were loud and awful, but I took great comfort in the knowledge that neither would do that ever again. As I opened the sliding door onto the balcony, I decided I needed to learn serious skills. And then I stepped out.

In the next cycle, I started to get some of those skills. I hung around with good people and bad people. I learned from people for whom controlled violence was second nature. And as I learned, I committed crimes, some small, some large; one or two were very large. I started doing things for fun but quickly realised there was more fun in doing things for a reason.

Prime Minister Robinson dying in that terrible head-on

crash with that lorry? That was me. He was nasty, and he deserved to die. Then there was that Saudi Prince, murdered by a hooker in his New York penthouse? That was me too, and the world was a better place for his loss. Or maybe these things didn't happen in your timeline?

One cycle, after getting hopelessly out of my depth and, as a result, dying a bloody and painful death at the hands of an insanely angry Russian drug lord, I decided my skills needed another upgrade. I switched tracks again.

For twenty years, I joined the armed forces; I spent cycles in each of the British forces, and every one of the US forces. Army, air force, marines, arctic warfare, desert warfare, groundcrew, aircrew, weapons specialist, unarmed combat; I did and learned everything. I used my past experiences to position myself as an up-and-coming hotshot. I got fast-tracked into field intelligence, overt operations, tactical supply, special forces, and, best of all, covert projects.

I went on to work military liaison with civilian counterparts. I worked deep cover in unfriendly places in unofficial wars. And I worked at the sharp end of hot conflicts, where staying alive was a bigger challenge than the media back home would have you believe. Those twenty cycles taught me well. Along the way, I learned languages; when I had finished updating my abilities, I could pass as a native speaker in any one of a dozen mainstream tongues and a bunch of regional dialects.

Then I spent ten cycles in civilian police and intelligence organisations on both sides of the Atlantic and in Central Europe. After that I went freelance. I went to Eastern Europe and fought for a cause I believed in. I was good. I was brutal. And I was efficient as I continued to perfect my skills. I spent two cycles in the Middle East and fought on both sides for no particular belief, but I got ruthlessly effective at what I did.

Over the next thirty-five cycles I learned from the people I was with, from the cultures they lived in. I learned from organisations, clubs, and groups. I learned from the experts and enthusiasts, and I learned from their critics.

It was a hardcore time of learning, yet I rarely achieved happiness or contentment. The drive to get good at everything became a psychosis that over-rode enjoying myself. I was likely the most capable killer in the world, but mentally, just before cycle forty of this skills-upgrade phase, I began to fall apart.

I started to go completely insane somewhere around my ninety-third cycle, and I stayed that way for many, many years, none of which ended well or pain-free. For a handful of years, I lived on the streets. I slept in doorways. I ate out of waste bins. I felt wretched and worthless. I did drugs; I punished myself.

And then one year, one month, one night, early in a new cycle, in a dingy park, in a run-down area of south London, I turned the wrong corner and encountered the wrong person, and events started me on the road to becoming a different me.

A healthier me. A determined me. A balanced, focussed me filled with a cold, hard drive. With ambition. With fire in my belly, and ice in my heart, and with a goal in my life.

Over the next dozen decades, I pulled myself out of that dark place and began to put all of my accumulated skills to good effect and evolved into an avenger and a vigilante. When I learned about a terrible crime, I tracked down the cause, and I became judge and jury. And executioner.

And on one cycle, when I was working as a military contractor in the Middle East, in a place that doesn't exist, I learned of the most terrible crime of all. A crime so large, so horrible, it changed me forever, and changed my direction. I turned to hunting much bigger prey than a sex attacker in an inner-city park. I stopped him for the benefit of his future victims, but he was just my springboard out of there.

Chapter 3. Attempt 2
Regroup

Week 3. London

I started rebuilding my life. I joined a boxing gym and booked a ten-week course with the trainer. I wouldn't use all the weeks but that was fine. I liked this guy. His ex-army, no-nonsense attitude matched my needs, the punishing goals he set me were almost unattainable. I joined a rowing club and trained on the river every day. After a few days the zeroes landed in my bank account; I now had the ability to make things happen.

But the persistent sense of loneliness followed me around like a dark shadow, even though my fitness was improving every day. I changed my diet, and within two weeks my body started loving me for the goodness I was feeding it. Around week six, I stopped waking in cold sweats and began sleeping soundly. Dreams still bothered me, but I was now sleeping well enough that they didn't wake me. I trained even harder; never to the point of collapse, but always to the limit of what was sensible.

Eight weeks after I'd checked in to the hotel, it was time to move on. I had a body that was still too skinny but at least it had the makings of muscle, strength, and power. And I had a target and a tight timescale. I used the hotel business suite to buy a ticket to Madrid, with a return flight of the following week that I wouldn't use. I packed my belongings into the rucksack, checked out, walked to the terminus, and caught a bus to the airport.

As I sat on the bus, I ran through things I'd thought about a hundred times in the last few weeks. I needed to be different this time. Something big had to change. I'd had one very serious, well-planned attempt at this target and had been stopped too easily. I needed a new plan, and this time I needed a backup plan to go with it. Getting shot in the face while I was hanging upside down in a car in a Monaco ditch was disappointing, and I wasn't doing this for the disappointment.

Like all of my targets, I wanted to get close enough to see his face. This time he wasn't going to see me coming. This time I was going to succeed.

Chapter 4. Attempt 2
Flight

Week 8. London/Andalusia

The weekday evening flight from London to Madrid is quiet, three-quarters full of business travellers and almost no holidaymakers or families. I took my seat in business class, two rows in front of the emergency exit, one row behind the guy in a fluorescent pink shirt. I settled in and slept for an hour.

In Madrid I checked in to a business hotel near the airport and paid for two weeks. An hour later I slipped out and took a taxi to a shopping mall, where I walked randomly through the crowds. After a while I slipped out through a side exit, walked three blocks and caught a bus. Five stops later I hopped off, and walked half a kilometre to a family-run B&B I'd emailed while I was in the mall. I wasn't evading anyone yet. I was just putting my training into practice and not leaving a direct route for anyone to follow.

The next day I joined a small martial arts gym nearby and continued daily training. My stay at the B&B was what I needed; quieter than a hotel, the owners treated me like family. Jesus flattered and Louisa fed. My time with them was everything a recuperation should be. My training at the gym was punishing and pushed me hard. But the days were passing, and I had targets to hit.

I dipped into my lottery winnings and used the Internet to put some chess pieces on the board. I bought a ten-year-old Toyota truck. I rented an empty cortijo, a remote shepherd's cottage in the south, and took a lease on an apartment in the coastal town of Motril, an hour from the cottage.

For something new, I used an Internet real-estate agent and watched countless virtual viewings of properties. Halfway through the second week, I bought a house in Rio de Janeiro, Brazil, and engaged a consultant to get it decorated and furnished to my taste. Using another app, I rented a lockup two kilometres from the house in Rio. The Brazilian photographs made me realise how much I missed the sea; another website fixed that by selling me an elderly but serviceable seventeen-metre sailing yacht in Argentina. Another website arranged for an Australian skipper to sail the boat north to Rio for me.

Three weeks after I'd arrived at the B&B, I packed my few belongings into the truck, kissed Jesus and Louisa goodbye, and headed south. Five hundred kilometres later, on the outskirts of Granada, Andalusia, I filled the truck with food, bought a couple of LPG canisters, some lanterns, candles, and then continued the journey, keeping the nose of the 4x4 pointing high into the mountains.

A few kilometres later, after passing through a sleepy-looking one-mule village, I turned off the tarmac road and drove up a dusty, potholed track that climbed even further - to the highest levels of the Sierra Nevada mountains.

The late afternoon sun glared low in the rear-view mirror when I eventually pulled up outside the single-storey, stone-built cortijo. I eased out of the truck; the engine ticked as it cooled, the quiet of the mountain made a stark contrast to the hours of engine noise. I looked around what was to be my backyard for the next three months. The sight awed me.

The high peaks still wore their late spring caps of snow,

though the temperature here, just under three kilometres above sea-level, was a cool 12c compared to the 28c it had been in Granada. I had chosen this place for the next stage of my fitness training because it was isolated. There would be no distractions and no interruptions. My plan was to use the mountains as a personal gym. No radio, no TV, no newspapers, and no people. I was going to push myself close to breaking point every single day; the road to recovery and full fitness was going to be hard and painful.

Inside, the cottage was spartan, rustic, and spotless. I threw open the windows, unpacked my clothes and the boxes of food I'd brought, and laid out my sleeping bag and pillows on the bed. I connected the gas canisters to the cooker and water heater and set up the lanterns. There is no such thing as mains gas or electricity in the high Sierra Nevada.

The next day I started my new regime, I worked six hours a day, seven days a week, and pushed myself to near exhaustion. I ran up mountains, ran across the tops of mountains, and ran down mountains. I chopped down trees and chopped those trees into logs and ran those logs from the woods to the cottage I shadow-boxed, I practised martial arts, and when I had reached my limits, I cooled off in the ice-cold streams of snowmelt.

By the end of the second month, my period started as my body recovered from the cold turkey terrors. Although my build was still slight and a little underweight, my speed, strength, and stamina were increasing. My reflexes were sharpening, and I felt clear-headed. The fitness regime wasn't easy, but physically I was coping. Mentally though… Some nights I just fell into bed, having barely eaten, and cried myself to sleep. A person to love, even just someone to cuddle up to, would have made a huge difference to my emotional state.

I made fortnightly trips in the truck down the long, alpine-like track to the nearest village to buy food and water and pick up a new gas canister. Even seeing a handful of people in the village felt odd after the isolation of the mountain. This small contact reinforced my loneliness; the sense of emotional and physical isolation was getting worse with each new cycle. The comfort of another's touch would have been good, but a person I could relax with would have been wonderful.

In the evenings I sat outside the cottage and refined my plans; I started by reviewing the last attempt, and then I added in everything I'd learned during two years of detailed research. This cycle my target wasn't just one person. This time I was going to destroy four people, and their demise would take down an international corporation. The chairman, his head of security, the head of strategy and the company's military liaison were my primary targets. Anyone who got in the way… well, that was their problem.

Thing is, I wanted them to know it was me. I wanted my moment of revenge. I wanted to see their eyes; I needed to watch their dawning understanding that they weren't going to be able to buy or bully their way out of this one. And I wanted them to know that this was personal. I got my phone out and listened to the voicemail for probably the hundredth time. It made the fire within me burn.

Slowly I began to figure everything out. After a couple of weeks, I had a new Plan A and the makings of a Plan B. I looked at my notes; a draft plan to wreak terrible revenge on four people. It seemed out of place in that beautiful mountain idyl. I got up and walked around the table. This needed more work than any other plan I'd put together. I was going to spend the next few weeks getting fitter and refining my thinking. I wanted to line up all the components I was going to need. It was like planning a game of 3D chess. But this time, this cycle, I was determined not to fail.

Chapter 5. Attempt 2
Identities

Week 17. Andalusia

Six weeks after I arrived at the cortijo, halfway through my planned stay, I drove down to the apartment on the coast. I had to show the concierge the rental agreement to prove I 'lived' there. Begrudgingly, he let me in. The full-length mirror in the bedroom showed me why he had been reluctant. Staring back was a straggly-haired skinny waif, with filthy hair and dirt-encrusted, broken fingernails.

My clothes were almost threadbare though they were less than two months old, and my boots looked like they were about to fall apart. I knew that beneath my clothes, my arms and legs were covered with scratches and bruises. I had been at the cortijo for a month and a half. In that time, my body had stopped feeling pain and started developing real muscle, but I had stopped looking like me, or at least how I used to look.

The apartment mailbox held a book-shaped parcel and a

small package the size of an eggcup. I'd ordered both items a few weeks ago. I opened the parcel, unwrapped the book inside, and filled in the cover details with a name that wasn't mine. The eggcup-shaped package held a self-inking rubber stamp. I overstamped what I'd written in the cover of the book, and the USAF crest gleamed when I held the book up to the light. I'd fill in the rest of the details and age the book when I returned to the cortijo. A couple of weeks baking in the sun would help, but just putting a name inside the cover was a start that made me smile. I packed the book and the stamp away.

Then I spent two hours in the bathroom and three-quarters of an hour in the bedroom. When I emerged from the apartment, I felt like a brand-new person. In my best clothes (a clean pair of faded jeans, suede ankle boots with enough of a heel to put a sway into my walk, and a pale t-shirt beneath a light linen jacket), hair tied in a ponytail, and with some tactfully applied makeup, I felt terrific. The concierge gave me a double take as I left the building.

I walked out of the old town, down to the marina, and sat outside a small restaurant where I enjoyed a leisurely meal. Old Motril is a small, densely packed, and ancient walled town crammed with traffic looking for parking spaces that scarcely exist. It was once used as a major seaport by the Moors when Andalusia was part of their kingdom.

A kilometre south of the old town is a modern working port. The port handles commercial, fishing, and ferry traffic to and from North Africa. Motril lacks the laid-back air of a typical Spanish Mediterranean town. Industrial and engineering units to the east of the port complete the new town's urban sprawl.

From my seat outside the restaurant, I could see the tops of yacht masts, could hear the occasional metallic clang of halyards against masts as boats rode the gentle evening swell. Idyllic. But on the way to the restaurant, I'd walked past graffiti in Spanish and Arabic. The youth of the area had much to say, and they were saying it angrily and in tongues.

The man I had emailed arrived respectably late. After introductions and some small chat, we agreed on my proposal. He would meet me outside his workshop early tomorrow morning, would give me unrestricted access for the day, and I would pay a decent rent. For an additional fee, his cousin would allow me a couple of hours use of his printing equipment in the unit next door. We shook hands and agreed to meet at 6am.

At 6.15am he showed me how the forge and metal presses worked and hung around long enough to make sure I wasn't going to break anything or blow the place up. By 8.30 I had fashioned the templates I needed. By 10 I had the finished articles in the palm of my hand. I turned them over inspecting them for flaws. The four small stainless-steel oblongs shone under the harsh neon lights, what I'd made was perfect; so too were the heavily impressed details on them. I put the tags in my pocket, fired up the induction furnace, gathered up the raw materials I'd worked from and burned everything.

In his brother's print shop, I Googled, designed, and then constructed the printing templates I needed. When all three sets of templates were perfect, I added a headshot I'd taken in the apartment that morning. I placed an NFC chip into the recess in the heated printer, and then ran the first finished article onto the plastic card they used. The chip was a blank, but the front and rear barcodes on the printed article were genuine, and the details on the ID card would get me into the places I wanted.

Then I repeated the process and made a slightly different printed template and inserted another blank NFC chip. The third template also got the heated printer treatment; it looked perfect. Then I made up some details onto a single sheet of paper and printed that. An hour later everything was complete.

I had made a pair of US Marine Corps dog tags, a matching US Marine Corps ID card, and a pair of US Air Force dog tags and an accompanying US Air Force ID card. The last two things I had made were a genuine-looking NATO Travel Order, and a US Pilots Licence.

Then I collected all my waste and threw that in the induction furnace too. I checked my email. The purchase of the house in Rio was progressing, so I started looking for a gym nearby. I avoided the glossy websites and eventually decided on an out-of-town gym that had the most rudimentary website, it had text only in Portuguese.

By 5pm, I was at the cortijo, ready to recommence my fitness training. Despite the progress I'd made in Motril, the loneliness enveloped me again that night, and I fell asleep with tears on my face.

Six weeks later, I packed my clothes into the truck. I had completed three punishing months of fitness training. I had a new body, I had sharper reflexes, stamina and strength that my cold turkey self would not have believed possible. It was time to go.

Chapter 6. Attempt 2
Home?

Week 23. Andalusia/South America

I drove north from Andalusia to Madrid; dumped the truck in a parking lot and checked into an hotel a twenty-minute bus-ride away. The next day, I took the noon flight from Madrid to Argentina, VIP class.

We landed punctually at Ministro Pistarini International Airport in Buenos Aires, Argentina. As befitted my status, I was checked in to the VIP lounge because my connecting flight to Mexico wouldn't be ready for another three hours. Except I wasn't going to Mexico in three hours. I used a courtesy phone to call an air charter company and then looked for the best way out of the airport.

VIP security in airports is largely all about protecting the VIPs; it's not really there to stop them from escaping, because why would they want to? Ministro Pistarini is no exception. I helped myself to a glass of orange juice and scouted the lounge. Some of Argentina's finest airport security operatives stood outside the main door, but they were looking at the people who walked past the lounge, and not keeping tabs on the VIPs. I walked around, picked up a magazine, smiled at the hostess and asked for a coffee. She tapped my request onto a keyboard.

A few minutes later a white-jacketed steward brought me a tray. I watched him walk away from me, back through the swing door with the overhead emergency exit sign. Half an hour later, when the status of a flight to Paraguay switched to 'boarding' and the hostess began to shepherd an elderly couple towards the gate, I walked through the emergency exit the steward had used. It led to a short passageway where another double door took me down a staircase to the catering area on the ground floor. Instead of turning right into the kitchen, I turned left, and walked outside through a goods door.

In the catering dock, I got in the back of a truck that was filled with empty trollies and hid away from the rear doors. Less than an hour later a driver got in, started up and the truck left the catering dock. It stopped after ten minutes, the smell of aviation fuel and aircraft noise told me we were still near the airport. I heard the driver get out, close his door and walk off. I crept forward, let myself out, scurried away, and hid behind a large truck.

Confident I was undetected I stood and followed the direction of the exit signs. I found myself in a small business park outside the airport. I walked onto the street and was able to hail a taxi to the main bus terminal. I bought a ticket for neighbouring Uruguay. Eight hours later, my fellow passengers and I stepped out of the bus and into the early morning Montevideo sun. Passport control on the border between Argentina and Uruguay had consisted of the bus being waved through the checkpoint.

In the centre of Montevideo, I found a slightly run-down hotel that wasn't too fussy about checking my passport. If there was anyone tracking me, I was confident they'd believe I was still in Argentina.

The next day I walked a few blocks from the hotel and hailed a taxi. At a private airport on the outskirts of the city I boarded the executive flight I'd chartered in Buenos Aires.

An hour later we landed at a small flying club airfield, just south of Rio de Janeiro, Brazil. The flight was met by the chauffeur-driven limo I'd booked. We didn't even slow down for the airfield customs post; it was shut. The driver dropped me at a smart hotel in the centre of Rio where I had lunch, relaxed, and casually people watched. After an hour I was satisfied I wasn't under observation; I took a taxi home. Home, but not yet my home; the house I had bought a few months ago, while I was still in Madrid.

I opened the front door and walked through the house. It was spacious, light, airy, beautiful, quirky, and I felt I could probably live comfortably here for the rest of my life, or for the rest of the year, whichever came first.

Although it had been decorated and furnished to my instructions, the house didn't feel properly like 'home'. It had everything I wanted, but I hadn't yet formed an emotional attachment. I figured the house wouldn't feel properly mine until I'd lived there for a couple of months. I told myself to give it some time, and anyway it was only going to be home for the remainder of this cycle.

In the evening, I spent an hour looking up commercial investigators; I made a list of three to call. Then I dropped an email to a legal practice based in the corporate centre of Rio.

I stood, stretched, and walked through the house again, gradually feeling the subtle nuance in every room. Yes, this would be a good place to live while I was in Rio. I went downstairs, switched on the outside lights, opened the glass doors, undressed, and dived into the pool. I swam a slow and gentle twenty lengths, just to unwind and to celebrate my first day in my new home. But that night, after spending even more time in every room, soaking up how the house felt around me, I went to bed exhausted and desperately lonely. I cried myself to sleep again.

The next morning, I spent two hours on the phone finding a solicitor and investigators, then walked down the track and caught a bus into the centre of Rio. Nobody else got on the bus at the same stop, I was sure the bus wasn't followed.

In the centre of Rio, I went shopping and how! I bought things for the house and things for me. A few soft furnishings, healthy, fresh food, clothes, and a selection of shoes. In an electronics store I bought security equipment for the house and the lockup. I also bought a camera and an expensive lens. And later, on a motorpark on the outskirts of Rio, I bought a sports motorbike, and a small Fiat car.

That second night in the house felt less empty, but I still felt teary. The dull ache of loneliness sat inside me like a cold brooding mood. I knew I could handle what lay ahead, but I was craving some company; someone to talk to, someone to laugh with. Someone to share my time with, and someone who would share their time with me. I'd stayed away from attachments for so many years, but in this cycle the loneliness was hitting me hard.

The next morning, I went into Rio and had meetings with the solicitor and then the representatives of the commercial investigators. I engaged them all but set them different tasks. I knew what I needed to know; the investigators were going to do the legwork for me.

Chapter 7. Attempt 2
Nesting

Week 23. Rio de Janeiro

The house was a five-year-old, upside-down (on the inside), one/two-storey structure. It was this quirkiness that had attracted me. Built into the side of a hill, twenty kilometres south of the centre of Rio, the house was a kilometre from the Avenida Niemeyer coastal road, up a steeply wooded private track. The hill was covered with pine trees which gave welcome shade against the sun and some protection from the sea wind when the ocean turned nasty. I loved that when it rained the hill smelled of pine and freshness and of salty sea air.

A visitor would drive up the track and park outside the front door. Inside the house, the open-plan reception/living space led to a large lounge, and beyond that to the outside balcony which overlooked the pool on the level below. The kitchen and dining room were off the reception/living room.

Down the spiral staircase was the sub-ground floor which you wouldn't know existed from the front of the house. From here, another lounge led out to the pool. Off this lounge were two double bedrooms, their bathrooms, and a guest changing room. Opposite the bedrooms was the study, which I'd had converted to a gym.

I loved the huge airiness of the rooms and the upside-down-ness of the house. I loved the location, and I loved that down the track and on the other side of Avenida Niemeyer was the private beach. There were a dozen or so other houses in this twelve-hectare estate, but the layout was designed to isolate each house from its neighbours. The comings and goings of the wealthy were kept discrete.

Two kilometres further up the track, over the crest of the hill, was a large reservoir. One full lap on the footpath around the lake was eighteen kilometres but, according to the agent, few of the inhabitants from the estate ventured up there.

On the far side of the reservoir was the slowly decaying township of Pedra da Gávea. If a town could have DNA, the genes of Pedra da Gávea would contain rust and agriculture in equal parts. Once a thriving farming town with some light industry on the side, Pedra was now a shabby, crumbling settlement with almost no employment and fewer prospects.

On the town's lakeside stood half-a-dozen warehouses, most empty now, but those still in use were the main employment in Pedra; light-industrial units, small manufacturing plants, and agricultural specialists. Judging by the decay, Pedra was near the end of her life, and it was coming at her a lot quicker than it should.

Two warehouses stood out against the shabbiness of the town, though one was much smarter; expensive cars in the car park, a neat, tidy front, and a sign outside indicating it was the head office of a company called Pedra Steel. On the opposite side of the road was my destination, a brightly coloured, hand-painted building, doing its very best to avoid decay.

I pulled open the metal door and walked into the cavernous boxing gym. Two young lads were sparring in the ring. The trainer was standing behind one of the boxers, slapping his elbows to encourage him to keep his guard up. A few young men were using gym equipment across the main room.

Large skylights threw sunlight into almost every corner. I made the eighth person in the gym; I walked into the centre and took a ringside chair to watch the sparring. I knew the trainer had seen me, but he didn't break off with the two young boxers until the end-of-session bell. He climbed out of the ring and walked over, disguising a slight limp.

'What do you need?' He had a strong Gaúcho accent.

In the same dialect, I replied, 'I need a trainer, I need a place to train, and I need regular use of some equipment.' My accent surprised him; he expected a more polished high-Brazilian inflection.

After almost two beats, he said, 'I don't have any women here.'

'Good, I'm not looking for any women.' There was a laugh from one of the boxers.

'What are you looking for?' the man asked.

I repeated myself but kept my response unpatronising. 'I need a trainer, I need a place to train, and I need...'

'Some equipment, yes, I got that. But what do you want from me?'

'I would like Rico Oliveira to be my trainer, and I would like to use his gym and that equipment.' I indicated the sets of hardware on the far wall.

'Why? Why do you need these things? And why here?'

'I have been unwell. I'm getting fit but I can't do it all by myself; I need your help.'

'There are gymnasiums and trainers in the city. I can recommend one or two.'

'I don't want to go into the city. I can run here from my home. I want to stay local. Pedra is local.'

'Is that the only reason for coming here? Because it's local?'

'There is another reason. My father watched you fight in Manaus. He came home and told us what a great fighter you were.'

He paused for a moment and then said thoughtfully, 'Manaus. That was against the Argentinian. That was a difficult fight.'

'In Manaus,' I corrected him, 'you fought Hector the Uruguayan. My father said you schooled him every round for almost the whole bout. But Hector lost his temper, and my father said you ended it before he hurt himself.'

'Ah yes,' he said. 'I forget so easily.'

He hadn't forgotten and we both knew it.

'What stage of fitness are you at now?'

'I can run a sub-three-hour race, but it kills me. I need to build my endurance and increase my body strength. And for that, I need a gym and a trainer.'

'A three-hour race is very good. You should be happy with that.'

'I'm not. And I need to improve my stamina.'

'You said.'

'And my body strength.'

'Yes, you said that too.'

He paused and then said, 'You would be the only woman.'

'I would be very lucky then.'

He ignored the humour. 'I have no women's facilities.'

'I don't need women's facilities.'

He scoped me out carefully and then said, 'Walk with me.'

We walked around the gym. He introduced me to each

piece of equipment and asked if I was familiar with it; I said I was, so he asked me to demonstrate each one.

At the end of the tour he said, 'Be here tomorrow morning. Six o'clock,' he was obviously trying to intimidate me. 'I shall give you forty-five minutes every morning for a week, and we shall see how you get on.'

I said, 'Six o'clock is fine, but I would like one hour every other morning for two weeks, and we shall see how we both get on.' It wasn't a question.

'So? That is very specific.'

'I shall swim and run on the days I'm not here.'

'Good, good.' He was genuinely pleased I had a diverse approach to training, and that I was taking it seriously.

At the doorway, I shook his hand and slipped out of the Gaúcho dialect to formally thank him in Brazilian-Portuguese.

Rico and I hadn't discussed money, but for his degree of personal training and a gym this far off the beaten track, I'd pay whatever he asked.

The door closed behind me as I set out along the path, past the expensive cars parked outside the Pedra Steel building opposite. An attractive young woman was parking a bright red convertible, roof down, radio playing. I watched her pick up a laptop bag and walk into the building; I wondered what kind of life she led.

Although the sun was still climbing, it was already hot and humid. I picked up the pace and slow jogged to the house. At the poolside I stripped and swam hard for fifty lengths.

I spent the afternoon arranging for the installation of security devices and researching my target's operations in Brazil. I wanted a lot more information. I also needed to find some

31

special suppliers, one of the investigators was working on that.

Chapter 8. Attempt 2
Routines

Week 21. Rio de Janeiro

The Cagarras are a collection of uninhabited, rocky outcrops, five kilometres off the Brazilian coast. The islands are a nature reserve that stretch to over 400 hectares.

Earlier that morning, I had boarded Musa, cast-off from the mooring, and set out on a north-north-easterly course for the Cagarras, thirty kilometres distant. When I was a quarter of a kilometre east of them, I began a turn around the outcrops and then raced home on a fast run, the sails full of wind, driving the yacht hard.

Sailing a seventeen-metre yacht (fifty-five feet in English) singlehanded can be a challenge, but Musa's previous owner had been a singlehanded sailor. He had spared no expense and had fitted her with every aid for short-handed sailing. Now flying a Brazilian standard instead of the Argentine flag of her previous owner, Musa spent her non-sailing time on a deep-water buoy, a kilometre offshore from the private beach near the house.

As a break from my weekday workouts, on weekends I would take Musa out for a different type of exercise. Early on Saturday mornings, I would catch the tender from a small beachside jetty, putter out to Musa, pack away the box of supplies, cast-off from the buoy, and sail hard for the weekend.

Sometimes I would head for a specific place (usually southwards to São Paulo or north towards Vitoria). Other times I'd make for a waypoint out in the South Atlantic and try to beat my previous round-trip sail-time.

I loved getting the boat balanced, her sails so perfectly trimmed that Musa vibrated with wind power as if she was being driven through the waves by a powerful engine. I suppose she was, really. Occasional spray from the wave-tops spattered onto the deck or into the cockpit, but nothing ever slowed us up as we carried on, focussed on our destination.

After a weekend sailing, I'd get home around 10pm Sunday, shower off the salty spray, climb into bed, and fall into a relaxed but exhausted sleep. Sailing on weekends was the perfect break. Weekdays alternated between beach days and gym days; both were hard work in their own way.

On beach days, I would leave the house at 6am, bag under my arm. I'd walk briskly down the track, beneath the pines, through the access tunnel that ran below the Avenida, and out onto the private beach that served the exclusive hill community.

I chose the same spot every time, spread out my beach mat, got out my towel, book, and water, and pitched my sunshade. A lifeguard would wander over to check I was allowed on the private beach, but they soon stopped bothering me after I'd flashed my permissão card at them a few times.

I divided my mornings, running hard for ten kilometres, sunbathing to rest up, swimming a hard and fast four kilometres - out to sea for two and then back - and, just before lunchtime, jogging a gentle wind-down of twenty-five kilometres. I was still pushing hard but didn't want to destroy myself.

My swim would take me a kilometre out to the line of moored yachts, where I would ease up and offer a cheer-ful 'Olá!' to the folk above decks. I'd usually get a wave or a shouted greeting in return before I powered a further kilo-metre out to sea; I'd tread water for a while and then sprint-swim the two kilometres back to the beach.

In the late afternoon, I would walk to the main road and have a light salad at a roadside café. After lunch, I would return to the house, where I would slip into the pool for fifty lengths. In the evenings, I would drive into town and browse the streets before eating in one of the restaurants off the Avenida das Americas. Beach days were hard but fun.

Gym days were harder. On gym days, I would leave the house at 5am and sprint up the track. When I got to the reservoir, I would ease my pace and jog around the huge lake to the gym. Rico would have me do forty-five minutes of mixed workout on the equipment, and then we'd spar in the ring.

He pushed me hard. Sparring sometimes came close to breaching the limits of politeness, but we were good enter-tainment for the young men. I knew one of them - Fredo - was taking bets on which of us would crack first and deck the other. After sparring, I would take a sauna, followed by a slow walk to the house, enjoying the coolness of the breeze as it gently blew over the water and through the trees.

At home, I would have a long, gentle ride on the bicycle machine, take a break, fix myself a snack and, afterwards,

I'd relax with some yoga. In the early evening, I would swim forty comfortable pool-lengths before changing into casual clothes and driving up into the mountains, where I would eat farmhouse cooking at one of the village restaurants.

After a weekend of sailing, my routine would begin again on Monday morning. But beach day, gym day, or sailing weekend, I missed the company of another. The longing for a person to be with was even stronger this cycle. Did I want a person to love? Unusually I thought that perhaps I did. I knew - to my cost - that although my time in each cycle was precious and love sometimes got in the way, the ache of the first few weeks in the next cycle, when the person I'd loved was no longer with me, was a hammer blow to my heart.

But this time there was no doubt that I was missing a nameless, faceless someone who could make me laugh, make me feel loved, who I could give my love to, and who would share the time I had left to live. I tried not to dwell on it. I needed to concentrate on my goal. But this nameless, faceless person, distant like a squall across the sea, this person who didn't exist… haunted me.

Time, though, was precious. While I had been working on my fitness, the clock had been counting down. It was almost time to put my plan into action. Next week I would begin setting traps for my prey. But first I needed some shopping.

Chapter 9. Attempt 2
Rochina

Week 31. Rio de Janeiro

The negotiations were careful, it had taken two months to set up this meeting and neither of us wanted to walk away empty-handed. We spoke Brazilian Portuguese.

'Are you happy with this arrangement, Pappi?' I used the verb for father, the nickname he was known by across the favela. The airless heat in the large tin-roofed workshop was almost stifling. In the distance, his chickens clucked.

'I have been more miserable than I am today.' He was being cautious.

'It's not every day you do such business,' I offered as neutrally as I could. A smile flitted across his face.

'That's true, menina, but also I am not miserable every day.'

This time his pause was long. The chickens clucked. The suffocating heat in the workshop smelled of dust and chicken feed and engine oil. The two trailers at the far end of the workshop seemed to waver in the invisible heat haze.

Pappi was the second name on a list I'd been given by one of the investigators. He had an expensive reputation but was mostly reliable and, unlike the flashy Angelo who operated from the warehouse in the docks, Pappi kept most of the work to himself or his family.

'And you want these things by Thursday?'

'I would be happy with Thursday, yes.'

'And you will pay me on Wednesday?' he chanced.

'Pappi, I will pay you half on Wednesday. Half on Thursday,

with the shipment.'

He knew my offer was generous, but he still paused as if considering the arrangement again. Half of the money in his hands, yet he still had the whole consignment.

'Good,' he said. The chickens clucked their distant agreement. The blend of smells seeped around me, and the oppressive Brazilian heat felt like it could make steel sweat.

'Seven o'clock Wednesday,' he said and reached a large, calloused hand towards me. We shook on the deal. The old woman who had been standing by the laying boxes walked towards the door and undid the catch. The steel door opened soundlessly on its hinges, letting a wall of fresh heat in.

Walking down the narrow alleyway felt like being in an oven; the unrelenting dry heat radiated off every surface. Below us in the distance, against the deep blue background of the South Atlantic Ocean, I could see the white skyscrapers of the rich and powerful. This moneyed goodness was a few miles from the cramped poverty of the Rocinha favela yet was a world away from the people who lived up here on the mountain.

At the end of the alleyway, I nodded to Pappi's guardian, the soccer shirt-wearing twenty-year-old who stood atop the alleyway wall. He gave me a stern glare so I would know how dangerous he was. I smiled at him because my private investigator informants had told me that the upstairs window on the fifth shack on the left, one row up the hill from Pappi's workshop, was even more dangerous. I walked down the hill and took public transport to the car park at Lago a-Barra, where I'd left my car.

I filled the five days until Wednesday by continuing with my training. In the two months since I had arrived in Brazil, things had progressed.

The house was decorated, furnished, and electronically protected. My yacht was moored out in the harbour, the storage unit was secure, I had my own transport. And I was fit. My healed body, now tanned, looked in better shape than I can ever remember. I was building new levels of stamina and endurance. Not only was I feeling good, I was also feeling confident.

On Wednesday evening, I went back to Pappi's workshop and left the brown paper parcel filled with cash with the old woman. There was no sign of Pappi or his guardian; I guessed they were at the Arsenal de Marinha, the navy base at Ilha das Cobras, doing my 'shopping'.

'Seven o'clock,' she said. Seven o'clock tomorrow. The second payment and consignment handover.

At 5pm the next day, I drove a battered rental van up the mountain to the Rocinha favela but drove past the end of the lane that led to Pappi's workshop.

The door to the shack was unlocked. I eased in with the cover of the radio playing in the kitchen. Pappi's nephew sat in the next room, a stripped-down M4A1 rifle spread across the table in front of him. He froze when he saw me. The suppressor-fitted Glock pistol that pointed from my left hand at his stomach must have seemed huge.

A couple of hours later, Pappi and the old woman helped me load the last of the metal boxes into the back of the van. I closed and locked the rear door and gave Pappi the rest of the money. He handed the parcel to the old woman who took it inside to count the contents. Pappi shook my hand;

mine small in his large, labourer's paw. He held the grip for several beats longer than normal.

'He's not there.'

Pappi looked confused.

'Your shooter in the shack. I let him live, but he will need to be freed.'

He looked up the hill to the shack.

'How did you know?' His dark eyes were filling with sorrow and a little anger at what might have been.

'I didn't know,' I said. 'I suspected.'

'You saw him?'

I put my hand on his shoulder.

'Let's not make enemies today. We don't need to build bad things between us. We will see each other again. Let's not have a feud where none needs to be.'

For a moment, he looked broken, but I knew he would recover; the shock of almost losing a family member was like running in to a brick wall. They would learn from today; would become more dangerous, and that was fine by me. I got into the van and drove through the slums.

Just before the junction that turned on to the main highway, I drove onto the service road and pulled over next to the black Citroen that was parked at the bus stop. Even though their windows were open, the two men in the car ignored me, because strange women parking next to you in a service road in Rio happens all the time, apparently. I picked up the suppressed Glock and pointed it at the passenger.

'I think you should throw the keys to me.'

They didn't move, so I angled the barrel downwards, the Glock did its apologetic cough and the front tyre of the Citroen popped and hissed loudly.

'Now look what you made me do.'

I kept the Glock trained on the face of the passenger as the keys were quickly passed over. I laughed as I drove off and left them to change their tyre. One of the private investigators said that Pappi would try and have me followed and I should look out for two of Pappi's relatives on the road. By the time they got their car running, I'd be long gone.

I silently thanked the flashy Angelo for the Glock and my private investigator for letting me know what I should expect. I drove back to my rented garage on the outskirts of town. After unloading the boxes into the lockup, I took the rental van into Rio, exchanged it for my car, and drove home.

The next four evenings, I dispensed with my normal routine and worked in the lockup. I selected the two best-looking L115A3 rifles and two M18 SIG Sauer pistols, stripped them down, examined them carefully, cleaned every part, then oiled, and reassembled them. Then I hand-sorted the ammunition, inspected and weighed each bullet, rejecting the shells that were either too light or too heavy or out of shape. Some military suppliers aren't too fussy about quality, and some military armourers are less than perfect in their housekeeping. Then I repeatedly stripped and reassembled the rifles and pistols until I knew every component by touch.

At the end of the week, I set aside the better L115A3 and M18. I had chosen two of my tools for the job.

Chapter 10 Attempt 2
Snap

Week 32. Rio de Janeiro

I am not a superhero. I am not immortal. I am not impervious to pain. I just have the ability to come back, time after time after time, until I figure out how to get it right and get what I want. Get what I'm aiming for. Like right now. I put the stock against my shoulder and settled down.

I've done the waiting and aiming routines so often, and with so many different tools, and in so many different lives, my technique with any device was arguably the best in the world. I relaxed behind the crosshairs, my face nestled gently into the stock, and waited for the impeccably dressed convoy to emerge from the hotel in the far distance.

I focussed the telescopic sights on the doorman; the smartly uniformed front-of-house hotel concierge to his customers. One of my investigators had identified him as a gun-carrying, ex-member of the elite military Carregueira Rapid Reaction Force. That made him the kind of guy you'd not want to mess with. I should think street crime near this hotel was at an all-time low.

The revolving door to his right shimmered in the haze as it began turning. A skinny dark-haired woman walked out, bright yellow dress, gold accessories, miniature dog in the crook of her arm. The doorman ushered her in to a cab. Was she going shopping? Was she on her way to meet her husband's best friend for a day of sex? Or was she just going to meet a girlfriend for drinks and a gossip?

Next came two Japanese men. They looked like off-duty bankers might look, uncomfortable in their casualness but determined to have a good time so far from home. A taxi was summoned from the rank to take them downtown.

A few seconds later, the door began to revolve again, a text alert from my investigator in the hotel told me this was my party. Deep breath, close one eye and merge the other with the view down the sniper scope. One by one they walked out of the hotel and into the crosshairs. Part exhale and count them out.

One. The well-turned-out, tall, tanned, blonde-haired surfer-type who walked with the easy, lithe grace of someone comfortable in their body.

Two. The crewcut in the expensive Italian suit. Tall but stocky, yet apparently charming to talk to. An erudite Eurasian capable of strangling your mother but smiling apologetically while he did it. A permanent member of the security detail. Another part exhale; lungs nearly half-empty now.

Three. The local hardman in his expensive two-piece. He had been brought in as a signal to everyone in Brazil not to mess with this party. Scarred face from a knife fight ten years ago. Part squeeze on the trigger, just enough to take up the pressure on the spring.

Four. The beautiful Sandy. I remembered spending quality time with this gorgeous, tanned, and ever-smiling twenty-four-year-old in Dubai in the previous cycle. I released the rest of my breath and completed the squeeze on the trigger as if the two movements were joined in time.

Despite the distance and the heat haze, it was a perfect shot, Sandy's face centred in the crosshairs as the trigger clicked against its stop. I waited one beat, then rolled over, staying flat on the rooftop; disconnected the camera cable from the sniper scope, dismantled the rifle and scope, packed them in the carrying case, and walked across the roof to the stairway, then took the elevator to my car in the basement.

There was no rush. I would email Sandy's cross-haired photo to his father when the time was right. I could only imagine his rage-filled horror when he learned that I had found his youngest son and exposed a fatal security vulnerability so easily.

Brazil was the centre of his Latin American operations, and when I began to expose the weaknesses in his operation, he would send someone to destroy me. I was going to enjoy that. I always enjoyed someone coming to get me.

Chapter 11. Attempt 2
Pipes

Week 32. Northern Brazil

I told Rico I needed to take a week off from our gym routine for a family matter. He didn't quite look at me as if I were a quitter.

Just over 2,500 kilometres north of Rio, perched on the windswept north-eastern equatorial coast of Brazil, sits a small fishing town on the Baia de São Marcos. The town hasn't much changed its way of life in a few decades.

In the late 1980s, the government built a small airport to

connect the town to the capital. With the airport came a trickle of tourism; not enough to make the townsfolk rich, but the visitors brought sufficient money to supplement the local fishing industry.

A year after the airport was completed, work started on building a communications station a few kilometres outside the town. The flights that supplied the construction were routine events of little impact. When the work was completed, flights dwindled to weekly supply trips and to rotate the few specialists needed to maintain the base and its equipment. Things soon settled down, and the town and the communications station largely ignored each other.

A day after I'd taken Sandy's photograph, I took the three-hour turbo-prop flight from Rio to the Baia de São Marcos, picked up a battered hire car at the small airport, and drove to the Pousada farmhouse bed and breakfast, fifteen kilometres outside town. Patricia and Eduard welcomed me into their B&B home. My room was rustic but comfortable, and the smell of fresh coffee and cooking seemed to be piped everywhere.

On the first day I walked down to the dock and arranged to hire a small sailing dinghy. After he'd satisfied himself that I could handle his four-metre boat and that I knew how to reef a sail in a changing wind, Ramon, the semi-retired captain of a ramshackle fishing boat, and I, agreed on a rate.

The next day I walked to the bay, paid Ramon his rental, and took the dinghy out. The wave tops were white, driven hard as the current worked against the wind; breakers formed early, pushed shoreward in front of the near gale that was ripping in from the sea. I tacked the little dingy against the wind until I was about five kilometres away from the estuary mouth.

On the starboard side, I could see the northern shore rise steeply up a tall rocky cliff. The communications station is built on top of the granite plateau. Approached from the land, the only signs that something is there are the long private road, the warning notices, and the guard hut.

But from the sea, the southern perimeter of the fifty-hectare compound was unmissable. Four large golf ball-type domes, the accommodation block, and two single-storey windowless buildings all caught the morning sun. Hidden by the contours of the land were five large radio and microwave masts and a number of smaller antennae arrays.

When I'd got to the estuary midpoint I turned about, and ran the boat hard before the wind, making fast progress towards the foot of the cliff. Just before the shore, I lowered the sails and dropped the sea anchor (a large metal bucket secured to the stern). The well-timed scrunch of wet gravel and hard sand brought the boat to a stop. I jumped over the bow, secured the dinghy with a land anchor, and walked to the foot of the cliff.

Rising up the rock-face were six black, twenty-five-cm-diameter pipes that sucked water up to the communications station. This water was used to cool vital equipment in the base.

I opened a collapsible spade, cleared away the rocks, and dug at the foot of the pipes. When the hole was deep enough, I took two M18 Claymore anti-personnel mines, part of the consignment Pappi had delivered, from my rucksack. I placed one mine between the second and third and the other between the fifth and sixth pipes.

I attached a remote trigger to one Claymore and bridged

it to the other with a length of insulated wire. Then I took a spool of ultra-fine copper cable from my rucksack, attached one end to the bridged Claymore trigger and ran the other end up one of the pipes and down the rear of the other, and secured it to the first trigger. At the top of the copper cable, I fastened a small sealed-unit mobile phone circuit board and impact-glued it to the back of the third pipe. Then I filled in the hole.

The next high tide would remove any sign of my visit to the beach, and no routine inspection would ever find the copper wire or the circuit board. I stowed the collapsible spade, loaded the land anchor, pushed the dinghy into the water and headed back to the port. With the strong wind behind me, I was soon moored in the harbour, stowing the sails.

At the end of my week at the Pousada, I flew to Rio feeling healthy and relaxed. The trick was going to be staying that way.

Chapter 12. Attempt 2
Introduction

Week 34. Rio de Janeiro

Back in Rio, a week after my trip to the north of Brazil, it was a gym day. Rico and I were sparring when one of the lads called his name. As he had done the first time I'd walked into the gym, Rico didn't let up and made sure we finished our practice bout.

I picked up my towel from my corner as he climbed out of the ring and watched him walk over to the athletic blonde surfer-type who had been in Sandy's entourage at the hotel a week ago. They talked for a while, with Rico occasionally gesturing towards the ring, as I began taking my gloves off and unwrapping my hands. I could see the conversation wasn't flowing easily.

I towelled myself off, left the gym, and began the walk home. The smart red convertible was parked outside with the attractive driver leaning against it, waiting. 'Excuse, the man inside said you come here also. Can I ask you? Is it a good place to be at?'

I tried not to laugh at the horrible Portuguese.

'You are not a Brasileira,' I said, deliberately fast. 'Are you Espanhola? I speak Espanhol.'

She looked relieved and switched to Latin American Spanish. 'Spanish is better for me, but I am American.'

'Or we could try English?'

'That would be better again, thank you. How did you know I wasn't Brazilian? Was my Portuguese that bad?'

I kept my accent light, but my syntax stiff, as if I were unused to speaking English. 'Let's say you are good but could do with some practice. How may I help?'

'I work over there.' She pointed to the converted ware-house across the road where I'd seen her park weeks ago. 'But I am looking for a good gym. The owner said you were the only other female to come here. But he said you kept coming back, so I wanted to ask about the place.'

'It's a good gym. The facilities are sparse - it's not a smart gym - but it's here and not in the city where you can never park. I enjoy the workout. I come here to work hard, and Rico pushes me as much as he can.'

'Rico? He's the owner?'

'Yes, the man I was sparring with.'

'He said you had more grit than any of the men who come here.'

'He only says that to make the men work harder.'

'Ah, I see. Do you live far from here?'

'Over there.' I pointed across the lake at the opposite shore.

'Wow, that's some distance. Did you drive here?'

'I run and walk.'

'Well, I don't start work for another hour, I'd be glad to give you a lift? We could talk at the same time?'

I thought about it for a moment. 'OK, that would make a nice change, thank you.'

She drove out on to the main road and began the anti-clockwise loop that would take us southwards towards the sea.

'Will you join the gym?' I asked.

'I'm considering it. How often do you go?'

'Every other day. I need the training.'

'Wow, that's some dedication.'

'It's good for me.'

We talked as she drove. I offered course adjustments with a 'left here' and a 'right there'. She said she was an accountant, working on a contract for an American, and was based in the steelworks head office.

I asked if she was enjoying Brazil. She said she hadn't seen much of the country, living in a hotel room and only seeing her office. She only knew the building next door was a gym because someone had put a flyer on the cars parked outside her building yesterday. I nodded, understandingly, and made a mental note to pay Fredo a little extra for distributing the flyers I'd had printed.

'You can drop me here,' I said, as we neared the turning up the hill to my house.

'If you like. When will you be at the gym next?'

'The day after tomorrow. I'll be there just before six.'

'In the morning?' She looked horrified.

'In the morning,' I confirmed.

'Well, maybe I'll see you there sometime.'

'That would be nice,' I said, and gave her my most inviting smile. I walked up the track with a spring in my step. I didn't want to pin too much hope on just one meeting, but it looked like I might have found a gym buddy. My smile lasted through the fifty-kilometre ride on the exercise bike.

Chapter 13. Attempt 2
Ping

Week 34. Rio de Janeiro

The next day was a beach day. I'd swum out to the yachts moored a kilometre offshore. I exchanged 'Ola!' greetings with the few folks who were above decks.

As usual, I swam the length of the line. This time, though, I uncoupled a small package from a thigh strap, and fixed it below the waterline of a tri-deck superyacht. I'd swum close to it for the last few weeks, so this didn't look unusual. Then

I powered out to sea for another kilometre before turning and swimming back to the beach.

In the afternoon, after lunch, I was walking up the sandy track towards the house when I felt my watch vibrate. I checked my phone as I walked. The house had a visitor.

I didn't change my routine; I walked through the pine trees to the house, up the stone steps on to the patio where I dropped my beach bag, towel, t-shirt, and shorts, and dived into the pool and swam the first length.

As I reached the shallow end, a well-shined pair of black shoes walked into view. I touched the end of the pool with my fingertips and, keeping my shoulders just below the water, and looked up.

'Ola, linda Senhora.'

'Angelo. To what do I owe the honour of this?'

'I've come to pay you a customer service visit.'

'Really?'

'I hear you have used the Glock. I would like to make sure you're happy with the purchase?'

'Do you do this with all of your customers, Angelo?'

'Just the ones who may have more requirements than a single piece of hardware.'

'And what makes you think I have such requirements?'

'I hear you have been shopping at the Arsenal de Marinha?'

'I haven't been anywhere near the place.'

'Maybe not. But I hear your agents have.'

'Really? Is it possible that you have been misinformed?'

'My source was clear that you were the purchaser. The same source that told me you have used the Glock.' Despite their family relationship, one of Pappi's men from the black Citroen had told tales. Pappi would be furious to learn of such disloyalty.

'Really? And what would you offer a customer who was looking to make additional purchases?'

'Generous terms, Senhora, very generous.'

'In that case, perhaps we may have some business to discuss.' I held up my right hand. 'Help me out.'

Angelo reached down a hand and pulled me up on to the side of the pool. As I landed beside him, instead of letting go, I pulled him close, he tried to recoil from my wetness, but the Sukui-nage Judo hold prevented any movement.

'But promise me, Angelo, that you and your people will stay away from my house?' I said quietly in his ear as I ran a fingernail firmly along his ribcage. 'It would be a great disappointment to me if I felt that anyone was ever snooping around my home without my knowledge.'

With impressive calm Angelo said quietly, 'Senhora, if anyone trespassed in your house, I would want, as your trusted supplier, to take action against them myself.'

I relaxed the hold and stepped to the side. 'Thank you, Angelo, that is a generous sentiment. We should arrange a formal discussion; I'm hardly dressed for business now.'

He glanced down at the creeping wetness on his clothes. 'Would you like an evening meeting? We could discuss this over dinner. This evening, if convenient?'

'It would be a change to my schedule, but I can meet you.'

'Perfeito,' he said. 'At the Fogo de Chão? Eight o'clock?' We agreed on eight o'clock. I felt sorry about the water stain on his beautifully fitted suit.

Fogo de Chão is an old-school Brazilian-Portuguese

restaurant in one of the quieter areas of Rio. I parked at the end of the block and walked up the street. The receptionist took my name, and I was escorted to Angelo, seated at a private booth. He stood to kiss me on both cheeks. 'You look beautiful.'

'Thank you, senhora, so do you.'

'I hope I didn't get your lovely suit too wet?'

'I have more than one suit.'

'I'm sure that they too are beautiful.'

'I shall tell my tailor. I am sure he will be pleased to hear your words.'

'Italian, I think?'

'You have a good eye for suits, senhora. I hear you also have a very good eye with a Glock?'

'Shall we eat before we talk shop, Angelo?' He sighed like a small child and simply said 'Si,' but I could see he couldn't wait to talk business. We small-talked while we ate.

'Where are your family from, senhora?' I avoided the trap of his carefully worded question.

'My grandparents emigrated to the north of Brazil. My mother was born in Manaus in the Bahia region. She married a local man from the next town. I only moved to Rio a couple of months ago.' The lies came so naturally.

'And your marksmanship?'

'I grew up on a rubber plantation, and Bahia is very remote. There were always firearms in the house.'

He looked thoughtful for a moment. 'How does Rio compare to your farm?'

'Rio is lovely, but the animals walk on two legs, not four. Though the food is better here.' I indicated the table in front of us.

'Do remote farms often have 9mm Glocks to keep the wild boar at bay?'

'I should think not, but before he retired, my father was an instructor at the Combat Training School and served in the 1st Parachute Battalion. We had his service revolver and a long-barrelled weapon.'

'We?'

'My mother, father, sister, and me.'

'Is your sister as skilled as you with firearms?'

'She died last year.'

'Oh. I'm sorry.'

He tried to change the subject. 'How was your steak?'

I looked at the remains on my plate.

'It was delicious. And your fish?'

'To be honest, I wish I'd had the steak now.' After the waitress had cleared the main course away, Angelo changed tack, and the conversation sharpened.

'Senhora, may I know your name? Your real name, not the Alicia name you gave me when we discussed your purchase.' Just as he knew where I lived, Angelo already knew the name of my Brazilian identity, but at least he did me the courtesy of asking for it. He might be flashy, but Angelo had class.

'It is Laura, Laura Guerra.'

'It is a pleasure to meet you, Laura Guerra.'

'And you, Angelo.'

'Laura, I wonder how I may be of service to you? I would like to keep your custom and stop you going to my competitor, the mad chicken man in the favela.'

'Pappi? But he's so sweet.'

'He has been known to play both sides of a deal. I'm

impressed you left the favela and did so with all of your purchases?'

'I did.'

'But why didn't you come to me for the rest when you bought the Glock?'

'I didn't think you were taking me seriously.'

He gave me a sad look. 'It's true that I thought you were just one of the wealthier carioca, shopping for a little protection in these troubled times.'

I took his use of the word for a native of Rio as a compliment for my local accent. 'But now,' he said, 'I think you are a serious buyer. And I wonder what else you might be looking for that I could help with?'

'Angelo, for now, I have all I need. But in a month or two, I could need some special services.'

'I would be happy to oblige. Could you indicate what you might be considering?'

'I may need five or six reliable people here in Rio to watch and report on someone. But the big-ticket item I might need would be an aircraft pilot in the United States. And perhaps a special tool and the right person to use it, also in the US. Can I count on you for these things when the time comes?'

'Could you let me know the size of these transactions?'

As coolly as I could, I said, 'My budget is two million American dollars.'

For two heartbeats, Angelo became most impassive. 'That is a very big number, Laura.'

I wanted to tell him that some of the work would be risky, but all I could think about was how much I was going to have to work on my fitness for the next week. The lemon cake at Fogo de Chão is legendary.

Later, before I went to sleep, I accessed an encrypted VPN and sent the crosshair photograph of Sandy to a private email address which would be picked up almost immediately.

Chapter 14. Attempt 2 Review

Week 36. Rio de Janeiro

Four days later, she arrived at the gym as I walked into the car park, the roof of her bright red convertible already folded down, music blaring out.

'I thought you'd given up on the idea?'

'Not really. I just lacked the motivation. The idea of working my way through blood, sweat, and tears this early in the day needs a lot of commitment to the cause.'

I pulled the gym door open for her. 'Shall we go and get committed?' She smiled as she walked in front of me. Two hours later, after neither blood nor tears but a lot of sweat, we were back in the warm sun, leaning against her car.

'Well, that was fun in an "I'm completely wasted" kind of way. Now I've got to get over to the office and get ready for work. What do you normally do now?'

'Walk home. Ride a slow forty kilometres on the exercise bike. Have lunch. Swim forty lengths in the pool. Rest, meditate. And this evening I shall go out for dinner in the mountains.'

'Actually, you make that sound quite nice. And you go

through the same regime tomorrow?'

'No, I'll be at the beach tomorrow, swimming and running. I'll be here the day after. Anyway, I saw how hard you worked. You're tremendously fit.'

'A long way short of you. I was wondering if I could join you?'

'Tomorrow, you mean? At the beach?'

'Or this evening? I can't do tomorrow. I have to work.'

I paused to give the idea some consideration. 'Some company tonight would be very nice.'

'I think I can remember the directions,' she said. 'Shall I pick you up?'

'OK. 8.15?'

'8.15 would be good.'

'Can I give you my number? Just in case?'

'That's a good idea.' She held out her hand and said, 'Charlie. Charlotte really, but only my parents call me that.'

'Laura,' I said. I got out my phone and we exchanged numbers.

'This time don't stop at the bottom of the track. Drive up the track about 2 kilometres. My house is the first turning on the right.'

'Terrific. I'll see you there. Can I give you a lift home now?'

'No, thanks. I'll walk. I need the exercise.' She laughed and shook her head as she got into her car.

So how does it work, you're probably asking yourself by now?

How can you (or to be more correct, how can I) go through the same 365 days, meeting the same people, having the same conversations, and getting exactly the same outcomes from everything, every single time?

The simple answer is that's not how it works. No day is precisely the same. I have 365 days, and I can make each one my own. I can do different things on every day. I can go to different places, and I can meet different people. But more important, I can change events through how I interact with people. It's a sort of butterfly effect. The potential variations are infinite.

The difficulty is keeping relationships feeling fresh and new if I've been through them before. That takes a lot of practice, but a lot of practice at relationships is something I've had. Away from relationships I could decide to stay in bed tomorrow. Or get on a bus and go somewhere I've never been before; meet new people, learn new things. And as I interact with people, not only is it new to me, I can make changes to their day. I can shape people's thoughts; I can change things in their world.

I can also change what people think of me, and I can change how they think about you. Or, if I wanted, I could totally mess everyone's day up by doing something really extreme. But I didn't do anything extreme today. Today was a quiet day in my plan. Today I went to the gym, and later I had a dinner date, and we talked about things we've never talked about with strangers before, and that easy conversation with this beautiful American woman is how our friendship started.

———————————

'Another glass?'
   'I don't think so.'

'Good, I'd like to be navigated across Rio by a sober co-pilot.'

I laughed. 'I'm as sober as a judge.'

'How would I know that?'

'Well, put it this way, how many drunken judges have you been seduced by?'

She barely missed a beat. 'Is that what you have in store for me? Seduction?'

I found myself saying, 'Maybe. Eventually.'

She picked up her glass. 'Well. I didn't expect the conversation to go this way. And so fast! Let's take things carefully. I'm fragile like glass.'

'I didn't expect the discussion to go this way either. Carefully it shall be.' The conversation paused while we evaluated where we were. The other diners carried on with their meals and conversations, not noticing the detonation of the small emotional bomb between the two of us.

She could have fiddled with her glass or flicked her gaze nervously around the room, but she met and held mine for what seemed an age while we thought our private thoughts. 'You live a nice life,' she said.

'I know, but it wasn't always like this.'

'When was it not nice?'

'When my family died. That was the start of a very bad time.'

'Is that when you became ill?'

'Not long afterwards. We were a close family. The grief hit me hard. At that time, I, too, was made of glass.'

'I'm sorry for your loss. That's such a cliché thing to say, and I don't mean to sound as shallow as saying it makes me sound. I'm genuinely sorry it hit you hard and that it made you unwell.'

'That's OK. I wasn't in a good place. I broke. I have started putting myself together again. And now I have a nice life, as you say.'

'And tomorrow you will be on the beach. And the next day back in the gym.'

'I will.' We both knew we'd just made a silent commitment for the day after tomorrow.

'Do you have a nice life?' I asked.

'Mostly nice. I don't like being away from home, but that's what being a contractor is like. You go where the work is.'

'No job security, but high income? Isn't that contracting?'

'In any industry, yes, that's exactly how contracting is.'

'How did you get into your work?'

'I was working for a US oil company, mainly moving between central Europe and the Middle East. After ten years, they had a reorganisation and offered me a move to Saudi Arabia.'

'And you refused?'

'No, I jumped at the opportunity.'

'Oh. And?'

'After a year on the job, I had a problem with a senior person in another division. Things started getting difficult, so I left. A couple of months later, a guy I had worked with a few years before called me up and offered me a six-month contract. That was five years ago.'

'No regrets?'

'I miss my home, but over the last few years, I've been away so long that 'home' is just a label for the place where I keep things I haven't seen for ages.'

'I suppose living in hotels means you leave so much of

your life behind? Family? Boyfriend?'

'I see my mom and dad when I go home, but they live a long way from me anyway. And no other family. And no boyfriend.'

'Girlfriend?' I asked.

'I had a girlfriend in college, and there have been a few boyfriends since, but it's been so long since I had any love interest that I don't really miss it.'

'And your home life? What about that?'

'Now that I do miss, such as it is. I'm going home after this job and plan on spending six months doing nothing except returning to peak idleness.' She drifted off for a few moments, probably thinking about doing nothing for six months. Then she came out of her dream.

'Do you always hit so hard?'

'I don't hit hard.'

'Yeah, right. The trainer you were sparring with, Rico? I saw him wince even behind his padding. You nearly knocked him off his feet a few times.'

'He's just making it look like I hit hard to shame the lads in the gym. He wants them to work more, so he pretends I'm giving him a beating.'

'What does 'Aborascar' mean?'

'I think the word is 'a borrasca'. It means a storm, a tempest. Why?'

'The guy I was standing next to used it to describe you.'

'The tall blond guy?'

'Yes.'

'He's got a lot of rage in him. Watch him fight. He's all energy and muscle, and very little brain.'

'Right. And you're a thinking tempest?'

'I was only working out. It's just part of my exercise.'

'I liked watching. You were a dynamo, a machine. You kept moving and hitting, moving and hitting. You never wait, you never stand still, you're always on to your next move as soon as you've landed your last one. And your approach isn't very orthodox.'

'Well, if we're comparing notes, I've never seen anyone spar like you. You use your whole body. Your use of balance is lovely to watch.'

'Ha. I had no balance left for sparring after the workout. I was just lurching about.'

'Back for more the day after tomorrow then?'

She laughed, finished her glass of wine and said, 'Definitely.'

We hardly spoke on the trip back to my house, but before I got out of the car, I held out my hand, which she took, and I leaned forwards and kissed her on the cheek. I slept very well that night.

Chapter 15. Attempt 2
Message

Week 36. Rio de Janeiro

The next day one of my target's men arrived in Rio; the photograph of Sandy in my crosshairs had stirred things up. He was met at the airport by the local hardman, part of the original detail at the hotel. My private investigator had reported the local guy had left the hotel for the airport, so

I changed my beach plans to cause a little ripple in the day.

From where I stood, on top of the highest bridge in Rio, they were too far away to see. But I knew the black Mercedes would have to pull away from the airport and drive down the ramp onto the Via Expressa, the eight-lane highway that carries traffic to and from the airport island and onto the mainland.

I had parked my motorbike in the service bay at the north end of the bridge and kept my dark-visored helmet on for the short walk to the hollow service leg. The rusting lock on the steel door offered no resistance, but a couple of months ago, the climb to the top of the bridge would have been impossible for me.

The L115A3 was broken down and nestled in a bag slung over my shoulder. On top of the bridge turret, I unpacked the rifle components, assembled the freshly cleaned and lubricated parts, and attached the sniper scope and the bipod barrel rest. The 7.62mm ex-NATO rifle was in better condition now than when it stood in its rack in the Brazilian Navy armoury.

I knew their destination; I knew the road they'd take. I had chosen the perfect place to flutter a butterfly wing. I had a clear 360-degree view, an easy route in and out. I'd done my prep. I lay on the service platform on top of the support leg. This bridge crossed over two highways: my own four-lane road and the eight lanes of the Expressa far below that. I felt the wind vibration against the structure of the bridge but couldn't hear the road noise.

I rested the end of the barrel on its bipod legs and focussed through the military-grade telescopic sight. One kilometre distant, through the noon heat haze, I could make out the cars driving down the entry ramp. A shot at this distance would theoretically be possible, but at this height the wind effect on the bullet would be too difficult to compute.

I tracked the car's approach. At three-quarters of a kilometre I could see what I needed, but I had to be patient; the heat haze was messing up my vision, and my sweat trickled uncomfortably into the eyepiece.

As the Mercedes passed the half-kilometre marker - the red t-shirt I had tied to the Expressa exit sign earlier - I focussed on the car and went into my routine. A routine I had used thousands of times in hot wars, in cold wars, as an insurgent, and as a counterterrorist.

I took a deep breath, merged myself into the stock, and began to live through the sniper scope. I part exhaled as I tracked the target. When I had the movement pattern of the car locked in, I exhaled a little more. With my lungs nearly empty, I took up a partial squeeze on the trigger, just enough to take up the spring pressure. And then, as if the final two movements were joined, I slowly released my remaining breath and completed the gentle squeeze on the trigger.

The L115A3 shouted its loud, harsh, flat 'crack', and I temporarily lost sight of the target through the recoil; I quickly brought the scope back to the Mercedes. The windscreen had blown in, demolished by the high-velocity round; the car was beginning to veer off course, it over-corrected, and side-swiped a motorcyclist who somersaulted through the air. As the Mercedes attempted to pass behind a truck for cover, I put the next round through its hood and blew the engine block apart.

With the engine dead, the car had no servo-assisted brakes or power-assisted steering. The Mercedes nose-dived into the safety barrier, spun around, and rolled slowly backwards into the path of the following traffic. Nobody travels fast on the Expressa. Today everybody would be travelling much slower than normal.

I knelt, broke down the L115A3, removed the telescopic sights, put the components in my rucksack and walked to the hollow service leg. The 7.62mm bullets lodged in the Mercedes would be closely scrutinised but would yield no secrets.

I hadn't killed anyone, and the motorcyclist would recover to tell the tale. But putting a couple of holes in his man's car would enrage my target. His increased anger would push him ever more to the edge. His sense of invincibility, fuelled by the isolation of his wealth and the surrounding comfort of all his staff, would drive his rage onwards.

I was going to stop him, but he didn't know that yet. He thought he had all the cards. He just didn't know that we weren't playing a card game. In the meantime, a lot of people on the Expressa would be late home this afternoon. I felt sorry about that. A little bit.

I climbed down the service leg, put my helmet on, and walked to the bike in the pull-in. Less than an hour later, I was on the beach. It was a hot afternoon, but even as I swam and ran to my physical limits, I wore a big smile.

Chapter 16. Attempt 2
Scooter

Week 36. Rio de Janeiro

The next morning, I worked out at the gym without her. I missed her company, but the message she had sent told me something was up:

Hi Laura, sorry I can't make it today, something urgent has come up at work. Maybe tomorrow evening if you like? Charlie.

I replied:

Hey, C. I'll miss you today but won't pull any punches. No worries about being busy. I could pick you up at 8 tomorrow night if that works? Lx

The reply that arrived soon afterwards just said, Awesome! x

'Would you like anything else?'

'Seriously? I couldn't. I just couldn't.'

'Are you sure I can't tempt you?'

She laughed. 'That's a different question. But no, I'm done for food.'

I tried to catch the eye of the waitress who had served us.

'The kitchen staff probably think we're official tasters. We've eaten a little of almost everything.'

'I've never had a Chinese meal quite like it. Thank you for picking me up. I realise eating in the city is a change in your routine.'

'It's a pleasant change.'

The conversation paused, but her gaze held my eyes.

'I hope you aren't working too hard?'

'What? Oh, not being able to make the gym? No. A guy who flew in yesterday had a problem with another project, so all plans were ditched. My day was put on hold, and I could have been told to pick up my work with just a couple of minutes notice.'

'Were you?'

'No. I was kept on hold all day. A waste of time.'

'Frustrating?'

'Very. I'm nearly at the end of my work. I reckon two more weeks.'

'And then back to the US?'

'A holiday. Some time at home, yes, but maybe some travel before I think about another job.'

'Where would you travel to?'

'I don't know yet. I'll get back home before I decide. But I was sort of thinking of staying here for another couple of weeks. You know, see some of Brazil. See some more of you. If you didn't mind too much?'

Time to tell her. 'That sounds really lovely, I'd love you to be here on holiday for a couple of weeks. But also, I have some travel of my own coming up in about six weeks. That would be about a fortnight after you go home.'

'Oh?' she seemed surprised and a little disappointed. 'Where would you be travelling to?'

'The US.'

'Oh really?' she drawled in a pretend Valley Girl voice. 'It's a big place. Where might you be heading, stranger?'

'Has anyone told you your cowgirl impressions are

rubbish?'

'I usually string those people up, pardner. Come on, give. Where?'

'Don't whine, dear. It's very unbecoming.'

'Wow, could you sound any more English?'

'I used to live there. I've got actual qualifications in being condescending.'

'I'm genuinely surprised at that. I thought you were a pure Latin American girl.'

'I've been around.'

'I'm intrigued. But let's come back to that. Where in the US?'

'I need to be in SoCal.'

She grinned.

'You look pleased with yourself.'

'Well. I happen to live in Southern California. So tell me, is this trip business or pleasure?'

'That depends on us, really. But right now, it's business. Just keeping tabs on a project.'

She gave me a shrewd look.

'Depends on us?'

'Well. Depends on you.'

'We'll return to that. I need to think. So tell me about your business. Is this business as in the mob, like the Godfather or something? Or is this business as in narcotics, and that's how you keep up your nice life?'

My turn to grin.

'This is business as in legitimate business interests. Perfectly legal investments. There's no organised crime in my life.'

'How about disorganised crime?'

'None of that either.'

'And someone special?' she asked quickly.

'There's nobody else in my life.'

She paused before saying, 'You just made me realise despite how much we've talked, how little I know about you.'

'Why don't you stick around? Learn more. I'm a fun person and, according to someone I like -' I pointed my finger at her '- I live a nice life.'

She sipped from her glass before saying, with a hint of a smile, 'You do. You live a very nice life. And today was a beach day, and tomorrow is a gym day.'

'Tomorrow is a gym day.' I agreed. 'And will you be able to join me?'

'Yes, I would like that. And perhaps we could have dinner again?' she asked.

'Yes. That would be lovely. If your colleague's issues don't work against us again?'

'I think they over-reacted. He had a rush job, ran into a problem, and everyone else's work went off track.'

'What sort of thing are you working on?'

'I don't know what he's working on, but my project is a re-finance for a manufacturing plant. Not very exciting, but we need to make sure the guy who pays our wages isn't going to catch a cold on his investment.'

'That sounds like a lot of responsibility.'

'Yeah, sort of. That's why I was in that small town where the gym is. The steel manufacturing plant has an office there. They own most of the town, so it's where I'm based.

'Normally, my job is spreadsheets and more spreadsheets and due diligence. Then some more spreadsheets and reports. Nobody wants to take a hit, but the investor has a long-term view for this investment.'

'I find that comforting,' I said. 'So many investors seem to be fixed on short-term gain. I prefer the long-term view.'

'Not one for turning a quick buck?'

The waitress came with the bill; I gave her my card.

'Not really my philosophy. There's too much potential for creating harm in short-termism. You know, understand the price of everything but the value of nothing.'

She gave me a long, appraising look.

'Stop staring. I'll drop you at your hotel and then head home.'

'I don't want you to go out of your way.'

'I want to.'

The waiter brought the card machine.

'Do you do everything you want to?'

As I tapped in my PIN, I said, 'No. Sometimes I know what I want might be nice, but it wouldn't be good for me, so I don't.'

'Oh?'

'I like what's good for me.' The waiter gave me my card. We stood and walked to the cloakroom.

'One day, you must tell me what you think is good for you.' she said as we left the restaurant.

They came for us as we were descending the building steps. The scooter came fast down the sidewalk. The black-clad passenger reached out for Charlie's shoulder bag. I hip-checked her half a pace sideways, which made the scooter passenger reach further for her bag. His overbalance my second goal.

In one movement, I grabbed his arm and twisted it as his momentum tried to take him past us. I felt at least one bone break. The moped rider failed to keep the machine upright, without losing much speed it wobbled and fell onto the sidewalk; I completed my pivot using the passenger's forward momentum to swing him around me.

The moped slid forward, the rider struggling to his feet as I released the passenger into the rider's chest with the full force of the circular movement.

In a fraction of a second, the soundscape of the quiet Rio street had changed. The attacker was screaming in pain, his badly broken arm at a crazy angle from the rest of his body. The rider, less affected by the collision, was hunched over, gasping for breath. The moped was on its side on the sidewalk, engine still puttering.

Charlie was staring wide-eyed at the scene that hadn't existed a few seconds ago. The concierge ran down the steps. I gestured to the pillion attacker and said, 'Mantenha a ponta.' He smirked at being told to keep the tip and gave the scooter rider a kick in the knee to stop him from running away.

I ushered her inside a cab and told the driver to move. Charlie settled into the seat, but she looked shocked. 'What just happened?'

'A moped mugging. It happens. Are you OK?'

The taxi-driver seemed immune to what had just happened. I checked behind us as the cab pulled out. I couldn't see any followers.

'I think so. It was so quick. And you were so... Oh my God, you were so fast.'

'So were you. Getting out of the way was the perfect move.'

'You took them both out. Both of them. Instantly.'

'It was a simple move. Besides, a girl could always do with a good stopper.'

'A girl doesn't need a stopper with you around. You were brutal. What was the word... 'a borrasca'? You were like they described at the gym. A tempest.'

'I'm actually a gentle person. Keep me around. I'll surprise you.'

She gave me a wan smile. I put my hand on hers. She was shaking.

Chapter 17. Attempt 2
Change

Week 36. Rio de Janeiro

I woke in her bed just before 5am. I was still spooning her; we'd hardly moved since she fell asleep. I didn't want to move. I revelled in the deliciously soft contact of another human. For the first time in years, I was close to a person who had shown me nothing but good humour and companionship, and who had made no attempt to use me. I listened to her soft breathing, closed my eyes, and quietly inhaled her scent. I felt like I was healing a part of me that I'd ignored for so many years.

I dozed for a few minutes before nature got the better of me. I eased back the covers; a slim shaft of daylight through the thick heavy drapes guided me to the bathroom. I stripped, managed to keep my hair dry while I took a shower, and then brushed my teeth using her toothbrush. I slid into bed and spooned her again.

'Cold.'

I nuzzled into her shoulder. 'You're warm.' I said.

'Mmmmm. Get warm.'

'For a while. I should go soon.'

'Stay.'

'You have work.'

'Get warm first.'

I kissed her shoulder and slid a hand from her hip across her stomach. She shivered but it wasn't from the cold. 'I am warm. You're warmer.'

'Mmmm.' She said.

'We haven't moved since we came to bed.'

'Mmmm.'

'I'm glad I stayed. You needed company after last night.'

'Mmmm.'

'I only stayed to have my wicked way with you.'

'Mmmm.'

'I love how talkative you are in the morning.'

'Sssshhh. Get warm.'

I spooned her some more. An age later, she said, 'You didn't, though.'

'Didn't what?'

'Have your wicked way with me. I fell asleep before you could.'

'You were exhausted.'

'Mmmmmm.'

She fell asleep again. I took it as a compliment and dozed as well. An hour later, she said quietly, 'Are you awake?'

'No. Are you?'

'Yes. I really need the bathroom!'

'Well, go. I'm not stopping you.'

She slid out of bed and dashed to the bathroom.

While she was gone, I starfished in the middle of the bed, then propped myself on my elbows and took a good look around. The hotel room was good quality; not sumptuously luxurious but very comfortable. Expensively decorated and furnished in a hotel-chain way.

Charlie had very few personal items. It was easy to see why she wanted to get home. This was my first night away from my house since I had moved to Brazil, and even now I found myself missing the familiarity of home. For someone like Charlie, who had to be away for months at a time, it must be a wrench.

She came back; hair brushed, last night's makeup removed, the faint smell of peppermint on her breath. She sat on the bed, looking a little self-conscious.

'I'm sorry I fell asleep.'

'No need to be sorry. I wasn't going to seduce you. Not yet.'

My flippancy was ignored.

'I felt safe. In your arms. I felt completely safe. I fell asleep instantly.'

'Well, that's a good thing, isn't it?'

'Yes, it's very good. But it's all a bit… unusual.'

'What is?'

'You are. We are. You, me, us.'

'Why? What do you mean unusual?'

'Well, look at us. You're barely five feet tall.'

'I'm five-feet-one-and-a-half!' I protested.

She rolled her eyes. 'And you're so slender and small and petite. I'm almost six feet.'

'And in most of your shoes, you're way over that.'

She continued, 'You just look so delicate and…' She groped

for the right word, 'Fragile. You look so fragile.'

'This is unusual, how?'

'Because I felt so safe in your arms. When you spooned me, I felt… comfortable? I felt enclosed. You felt strong. I was protected. And safe.'

'I'll stick around to keep protecting you then.'

She put her hand on top of mine. 'I'd like that. It's ridiculous to say it, but I'd like that a lot.'

'Why is it ridiculous?'

'Because I'm six thousand miles from home, I'm in a strange country, I'm with a girl and I'm truthfully telling her, because of her actions last night, that I want her to protect me.'

'To me, this sounds good. I like this. There's something else I'd like.'

'What?'

'I'd like this not to change. This,' I gestured towards her with our joined hands, 'This thing between us. Whatever it is. I would like this to carry on.'

'So would I. But how can it?'

'You mean because you're so tall and I'm not?'

She ignored my levity again.

'I think we have a lot to talk about.'

'So do I.'

'Shall we start tonight?'

'I'd like that a lot.'

'Your house then?'

'Yes, My house. Eight?'

'I'll be there.'

I separated our hands, slid out of the bed, walked over to the chair, and pulled last night's dress over my head while she sat on the bed and watched.

'There's nothing to you,' she said. 'Just nothing at all.'

'The art to winning in any conflict is to use your opponent's strength against them.'

'That sounds like a quote.'

'My Dad. Also Sun Tzu, a Chinese military strategist, from his book "The Art of War", published around 500 BC. There.'

I straightened my dress over my hips.

'Do I look like I've spent the night having amazing girl-love?'

'No. But you haven't anyway.'

'You look like you looked last night.' I said.

She gave me a quizzical look.

'You look lovely.' I explained.

She actually blushed.

'I look like rubbish, and I'm wearing last night's underwear.'

'I liked it then, too.'

She held a long, looking at me and thinking pause.

'Let's talk tonight.'

Chapter 18. Attempt 2
Dinner

Week 36. Rio de Janeiro

'Your house is gorgeous.'

'Thank you. I like it,' I said, as I put a cup of coffee on the table beside her.

We were on the poolside patio. The sun was starting to sink behind the hill. The trees surrounding the house were full of evening birdsong. The air was lightly laced with the scent of the pines.

'What have we just eaten?'

'The salad was all local vegetables; the fish was a grilled linguado. It's a type of sole, with some seasoning, but it was caught this morning.'

'I miss proper food. The hotel restaurant is good, but it's not the same as eating homemade meals.'

'Maybe you'd like to eat here more often?'

She looked at me with a wry smile.

'Seduction attempt? Already? And over food too. That's a low blow.'

'A girl's gotta do what a girl's gotta do.'

She picked up the coffee cup and quietly inhaled.

Over the brim, she said, 'Have you made many seduction attempts?'

'Just the one.'

'How did that turn out?'

'I'll let you know.'

There was a pause before she said, 'So you're new to this?'

'Never done it before.'

'So why? And why me?'

'I've had my heart broken more times than most people my age,' I said truthfully. 'The definition of madness is to keep doing the same thing and expecting different results. So, I'm trying something that's not the same.'

'And that would be me?'

'That,' I said, 'Would be you.'

'You haven't said why me, though.'

'Oh, that's easy. I saw it the first time we met at the gym when you spoke horrible Portuguese.'

'I'll ignore the comment on my Portuguese for now. It? What "it" did you see?'

'Vulnerability. You have the air of a person who has been damaged. I want to know why. And I want to do what I can to help.'

She said nothing for five beats, just looked right at me, so I broke the ice again.

'Well, that was a conversation killer. Can I get you anything else to eat?'

'No, but you can tell me things because you seem to know me, and now I want to know you.'

'In that case, I will tell you things. And you can tell me things too.'

'I shall too. Who is going first?'

'You are.'

'You're chicken.' She took a sip of coffee. 'This is nice.'

'Thank you. In a minute, I'll tell you how I used to spend my weekends grinding coffee to earn my allowance.'

'Really?'

'No, it would be untrue, but we can run with it if you like?'

'Would you be in a dusty warehouse, turning a large handle on a machine that ground up the coffee beans?'

'Yes! Every Saturday and Sunday to help my father...'

'Grandfather,' she corrected.

'To help my grandfather, I would slowly turn the wooden handle on the coffee grinder in the old, dusty warehouse on the outskirts of town.'

'I can see it now. You're wearing a pair of faded denim dungarees and a large t-shirt. Your long hair is tied in a ponytail. Your face is full of concentration as you keep a steady rhythm on the big wheel.'

'You're making me work hard.'

'The smell of roasting coffee is heavy in the warehouse air,' she continued and took another sip.

'Do you really, really like your coffee, by any chance?'

'Can't stand the stuff,' she said, taking another sip. 'I'm just enjoying the sight of you working so hard for your grandfather.

'One of you is a slave driver. I can't work out who it is yet.'

'It's him. He's making you work while he sits outside, dozing in the sun. I'm just drinking the fruits of your labour.'

'I sweated hard to make that coffee; can you treat it with some respect, please?'

She cupped the mug in both hands and said, 'In that case, I shall treat this coffee with the total respect it deserves.'

'Thirteen-year-old me thanks you.'

'Why aren't you drinking any?'

'Coffee doesn't agree with me. I breathed too much coffee dust into my lungs as a young girl.'

'Ha! So, what is that you're drinking?'

'Guaraná soda.'

'Can I try it?'

I passed her my glass. She sipped and pulled a face.

'It tastes like bubble-gum!'

'Yeah, I can see why you'd say that. It sort of does.'

'And that's better for you than coffee?'

'Not really. I just didn't work at the Guaraná soda factory for long.'

There was a pause in the conversation. The wind blew gently against the surrounding pines, but the breeze barely got to us.

'What did you really do?' she asked.

'When?'

'As a young girl. How was your life?'

I began slowly, but this time I told her the truth. 'I didn't do anything out of the ordinary. My father was a career diplomat. My mother was a diplomat's wife, which was a career in itself. We would spend five years in one country and then move to another.'

'That's not out of the ordinary? Is that what you're saying? Really?'

'Well, no. For a diplomat's daughter, it was very ordinary. School. Homework. Extra schooling on weekends; learning about the country we were living in, trying to make friends.'

'Wow, that sounds tough when you put it like that. How long did that go on for?'

'As long as I can remember. The first home I can remember was in Madrid, I was about five.'

'Is that why you speak so many languages?'

'Mostly. When we went to local schools, we had to speak their language. And it was expected of us to be able to talk to people in their language. I have also learned other languages since then.'

'This is fascinating. I've never really thought about what being a diplomat's daughter meant.'

'It was harder for my mother, I think. But for my sister and me, it wasn't difficult. Going to school in a new country immerses you in the culture of that place.'

'I'm jealous. You must have seen a lot of the world.'

'I've first-hand knowledge of many classrooms in so many countries,' I said lightly. 'And I can tell a joke in a dozen languages. That brings you up to my eighteenth birthday. Now it's your turn while I finish my drink. The lives, loves, and times of Charlie. Go.'

'Really? That much detail?' Before I could answer, she went on, 'Well, you asked for it. My first home was on the outskirts of Rochester, New York State. Dad worked for Kodak. When I was nine, Dad was moved to Watford in the UK.'

'I should imagine that Watford was substantially different from Rochester New York?'

'Very different. Also I hated it.'

'Why?'

'I love the way you tilt your head when you ask a question.'

'Well, answer the question then.'

'You're like a puppy.'

I rolled my eyes but couldn't help smirking.

She sipped and continued, 'The accents were difficult, and so were the people. The school I went to didn't work for me. It was all so different from being at home.'

'But you made friends? And settled?'

She ducked the question.

'We were in the UK for six years. Then Dad was transferred back to the States, to Los Angeles this time. We stayed there as a family for another ten years. When he retired, he and Mom headed to White Plains in Westchester County, in New York.'

'But you stayed in LA?'

'Yep. I was at UCLA by then. We decided it would be best if I finished my degree.'

'Degree in?'

'Oh. Economics. I had started working on the theory of Applied Microeconomics and...'

'Did my eyes glaze over?'

'They did not. So, to continue from where I was rudely interrupted and, because I know you're going to ask me all about Applied Microeconomics, it's the study and application of economic theories and methodologies on individual behaviour and through that individual behaviour to societal outcomes.'

'Fascinating.'

'You said that with a straight face. Remind me never to play poker with you.'

'And from UCLA?'

'I completed my degree and got offered a post with the faculty. After a few months, it became obvious that wasn't working out for either UCLA or for me. I hit a few jobs in a couple of years. They all paid the bills, and then I got the opportunity to work as a contractor. So, I went freelance.'

'And pitched up in my house.'

'Eventually, and after a lot of jobs like this one, and a lot of travel, yes I did. Everything I've done in my life has been leading up to this moment.'

'Well, that's a big build-up. Let's not waste the moment, shall we?'

She smiled nervously.

'What do you have in mind?'

'You look too gorgeous to get messed up, so going for a swim is out.'

'So? And thank you for the compliment. But so?'

'Let's go for a walk.'

'What? In these shoes?' She indicated her heeled silver slingbacks.

'OK, not in those shoes. Nice shoes, by the way,'

'Thanks.' She crossed her leg to emphasise the glittering footwear, or perhaps to emphasise her long, perfect legs.

'But I've got a pair of trainers that would fit you.'

'No.'

'And it's a lovely evening.'

'It is a beautiful evening, but I'm so comfortable here.'

'Come on.'

'And I'm so full of lovely food.'

'I'll bring the trainers to you.'

'And the coffee has made me drowsy.'

'Coffee doesn't make anyone drowsy. Come on, let's get those trainers on you.'

A few minutes later, despite her gentle protestations, we were walking down the hill. It felt awkward not holding her hand, but even though we'd both seen each other in our underwear, the time wasn't right for that yet.

'It's nearly dark,' she said as we neared the underpass.

'I've got a torch. And besides, we're only going to walk along the beach.'

'Why are we?'

'Because do you want to waste the whole evening sitting by the side of the pool?'

'That sounds like a pretty good idea to me right now.'

'We're almost there. I think you'll like it.'

We walked through the underpass, I put the code into the security gate, and we walked onto the freshly raked sand.

'Wow,' she said. 'Your own private beach?'

'Not really. It belongs to all the houses on the hill.'

'And how many houses is that?'

'Not too sure. Maybe a dozen?'

'Yeah, your own private beach because I bet none of those

other houses are lived-in full time.'

'Mine is,' I paused. 'But you're right. I don't think I've ever seen any other cars use the track up the hill.'

'Maybe nobody else is crazy enough to get up at the crack of dawn.'

'Yeah, could be, wait… Did you just call me crazy?'

'Well, you're the person who gets up at 5am to go to the gym when she doesn't need to!'

'I need to.'

'You don't. You look fantastic. And anyway, why?'

'Why don't you take your shoes off?' I interrupted.

We had been walking towards the shoreline, where the sea was lapping quietly against the sand. In the distance, we could see lights shimmering offshore. The bright moonlight shone the gently shoaling water into liquid silver in the half-light.

'OK. Wow, the sand is still warm!'

'The beach soaks up the sun. In this bay, it's sheltered from the cooling breezes. The sand will stay warm for another couple of hours. Dip your fingers into the sea.'

'I'll get my feet wet!'

'I said, dip your fingers into the sea, not go wading.'

She reached down.

'Oh my, the water is warm.'

'That's why neither of us is cold. We have warm water, warm sand, and a sheltered beach.'

'And wet feet.'

I smirked.

'You have wet feet. Mine are dry because I still have my shoes on.'

'I don't want to ruin your trainers,' she said. 'I'll walk

barefoot.'

'Why don't we walk over to the fence by the underpass.'

'OK.'

When we got to the fence, I said, 'Now hold on to the fence and give me your left foot and left shoe.'

She handed me the shoe. I bent and took her left foot in my hands. I brushed the sand off her feet and cleaned the grains from between her toes. I slipped her shoe on and did the laces up. Then I did the same with her right foot.

'Better now?' I asked as I stood.

'Yes, thank you. That was … sensual.'

'Really? It wasn't meant to be.' I lied slightly.

We walked up the track to the house, talking about everyday things in our past and present lives, sharing what we do and think and how we feel about stuff. Deepening our friendship, exploring our common ground, defining our differences. I was enjoying her company; I was loving not being alone and being with someone I genuinely liked made me feel so happy.

As we walked into the house, I said I would go down to the pool to get her shoes. When I brought them upstairs to her, she was leaning against the stair-rail looking around.

'You know I said you had a lovely house?'

'Yes.'

'Actually, it's gorgeous.'

'Thank you. Your shoes?' I said as I handed them to her.

'Can I stay?'

'What?'

'Here, with you. Tonight. Can I stay?'

'Umm. OK. If you'd like to, I would like you to.'

'Good. Stay right there.' She went out to her car and came

in with a holdall.

'Change of clothes?' I asked.

'Just something for tomorrow, and so that I don't have to do the walk of shame past the hotel staff.'

'I like your foresight,' I said, then added, 'It's Saturday tomorrow.'

'I know.'

'Perhaps you might like to stay for the weekend?'

'Oh, I may have brought just enough things for that.'

'You smirked!'

'You smiled first.'

'Are you cold?' I asked.

'No.'

'Come here and let me warm you up.'

'But I'm not...'

I moved closer and gently, with every fraction of soft tenderness I could find inside me, I kissed her.

Chapter 19. Attempt 2
Ignition

Week 37. Rio de Janeiro

She complained when I woke her at 5.30 the next morning. She grumbled at the amount of makeup I didn't give her time to put on. She mumbled beneath her breath as I drove us to the jetty. When the tender arrived, she stared hard at it.

'A boat?'

'Yes.'

'We're going in a small boat? A small boat with an outdoor engine?'

'It's called an outboard engine, but yes.'

'Oh, God, please tell me we aren't going fishing. I had a boyfriend who took me fishing once. I hated it.'

'We are not going fishing,' I reassured her. We clambered into the boat, and granite-faced Marco helped me load the food and clothes we had packed.

'You know I'm not awake yet?'

'I'd guessed.'

'But I'm awake enough for you to tell me why we're motor-boating along the open seas at 5am.'

'It's so much later than 5am. And we're not really on the open seas.'

'You're very good at not giving answers.'

'OK, I'll tell you. Do you see those boats there?'

'The ones we're heading for?'

'Those would be the ones.'

'Yes,' she said. 'I see them.'

'We're going there.'

'You're infuriating.'

'And fun.'

'Yes. You're infuriatingly fun. Why are we doing this?'

'We're going on a boat trip.'

'We're already on a boat trip.'

'We're going on a bigger boat.'

'Oh.'

Marco throttled back as we approached Musa's stern. He held the tender against the rear platform. I stepped out and offered her my hand. She took my hand and climbed out beside me. Marco passed the boxes which I lifted over the stern guardrail into the cockpit.

As we stood in the cockpit, I put my arm around her to steady us, or so I told myself, as we watched Marco putter back to shore. I nuzzled her shoulder, then said 'Let's get going. I want to be moored up by teatime.'

'Where are we going?'

'Paranabi.'

'Where?'

'It's an island south of here, near São Paulo. Sort of.'

'Why are we going there when we could still be asleep?'

'Let's get underway, and then we can talk.'

She looked about the cockpit for a moment while I un-locked the hatch into the galley.

'What do you want me to do?'

'Have you sailed before?'

'No.'

'Can you swim?'

'Not to your standard.'

'I suggest you put a lifejacket on for now. They are under the navigation table seat.'

She stepped through the hatch and reverse-climbed down the steps. I went forward, unhitched us from the mooring. Back in the cockpit I unfurled the foresail just enough to put a little wind behind the boat and start to move us under power. A few minutes later, we were under full canvas and making a steady six knots. I set the autopilot and slid down into the galley; Charlie was tying on a lifejacket.

'Is this yours?' she gestured around the cabin.

'Yes. Is this all right? Are you going to get seasick on me?'

'This boat?'

'Yacht,' I said patiently.

'This yacht is yours?'

'She is.'

'Are you a good sailor?'

'Are you nervous?'

'A little.'

'In that case I'm the best singlehanded sailor you have ever met.'

'You might be the only singlehanded sailor I have ever met.'

'I like that I appear on such an exclusive list then.'

Three hours later, we were well on our way. I sat in the cockpit, one hand on the tiller; she reclined against me. We talked quietly over the gentle swish of water as it passed beneath the hull. Just being close to each other was relaxing; light chat, occasional sips of wine, and basking beneath the sun as it beat down from the clear blue sky.

When she went below to refresh our glasses, I picked up my phone and keyed in a number. Thousands of miles away, in the north of Brazil, the two Claymore anti-personnel mines detonated around the base of the communications station's cooling pipes.

It wasn't a killer blow. When their monitoring systems identified the problem, the few onsite and the many remote staff would fight the rising temperature; they would shut down some non-critical systems, and the facility would stay operational. But my target would see this as another attack on his empire, and he would take it personally, especially after the photograph of his son and the shot from the bridge.

He was going to be furious when he got the news, and he

was going to send a security specialist to review the communication station. I put the phone away as she came up from the galley, and we continued spending quality time together.

Chapter 20. Attempt 2 Coastguard

Week 37. Rio de Janeiro

We moored off the island of Paranabi in the early afternoon and spent a restful, self-indulgent couple of hours swimming and dozing on Musa's deck. In answer to our radio call, the tender picked us up in the early evening and took us to a beachside restaurant. The fresh fish was lovely.

The vines that surrounded the restaurant spilled over the veranda into the dining area. The bushes were lit with thousands of little lights; the light scent of wildflowers added to the occasion. And the company was gorgeous. Truly lovely.

Later, when she went to the bathroom, I took out my phone and pressed another couple of buttons. Back on the moorings in Rio, the limpet mine attached to his million-dollar, tri-deck motor-cruiser detonated. If putting two bullets into his man's car on the way from the airport got him annoyed, and if almost disabling his communications station had got him angry, sinking his prized motor yacht was going to get him furious. That was fine by me. I enjoyed the thought of him being furious.

The next morning, I felt a little regretful as we weighed anchor. We weren't just leaving Paranabi, where we'd had a beautiful, and restful afternoon and evening. We were heading back to Rio. Going back to my goal, back to the uncertainty, the 'will I get him/won't I get him' question. It was unusually selfish of me, but I wished the weekend could continue.

And there was Charlie, in my sight and in my head. It was clear that she was becoming special, and our relationship was worth something I couldn't have foreseen.

For the last 30 nautical miles we slow-tacked to Rio, and although we were fine together, there was a slight feeling that it was the end of the weekend, that we both had school in the morning.

With the statue of Christ The Redeemer looking down on the bay from the peak of the Corcovado mountain, I lined up on the buoy, wound in most of the canvas and went forward to pick up the mooring with a boathook. I stowed the sails and walked to the cockpit where Charlie was reclining. She looked fantastic; I got a case of butterflies when I looked at her, and I loved looking at her.

'You should look pretty smug. I've loved every moment of this weekend.'

'Oh, I'm so glad. I really wanted you to enjoy it.'

'I feel relaxed and ready to go, and also I feel ready for a good night's sleep.'

'That's the sea air. It has a knockout effect.' I resisted the temptation to say that she looked knockout. I stepped down the ladder into the galley and began putting things into boxes to take back with us.

'What are you doing tomorrow?' she called down to me.

'Beach day for me. How does your plan look?'

'I'm starting to wind up. I'll be in the office beginning to close down my part of the project.'

'All finished?' I asked.

'Almost. Unfortunately.'

'You'll be glad to get home, though.'

'I will. I won't.'

'Huh?'

'My house, my things. It will be good to see them again. Not seeing you. Well, that would be… sad. Difficult even.'

'When will you be heading home?'

She said nothing straight away, so I bobbed my head out of the hatch to look at her. She seemed anxious.

'My original plan was to leave at the end of next week, but I'd like to stay for a while. If you'll have me?' I stayed on the ladder. I loved looking at her face, and I wanted to see her expression.

'I would love to have you stay. And also, how would you like a visitor? Arriving a week or two after you settle in back in LA?'

'Oh my God, yes! That would be - what the hell is going on there?'

She was looking off our starboard bow. I climbed into the cockpit and followed her gaze. A Coast Guard patrol boat, flanked by two Brazilian Marine Rescue rigid inflatable boats, were three hundred metres further up the moorings. It looked like a busy scene. The people onboard the RIBs were tending lines that ran off their boats into the sea: there were divers in the water.

'Someone's having a party?' I suggested.

'Hmm, that's some dull party crowd. Oh. Looks like we're

going to have visitors.'

I glanced over; the Coast Guard patrol boat had lifted her bow and was now heading in our direction.

'Well, they're not going to get a coffee; I've packed it all away.'

'Maybe they're not coming over for some of your legendary hospitality?'

'Are you being rude?'

'Oh, no. Not me. Not ever me.' I gave her a look of disbelief.

'As we're about to have visitors,' she said. 'I'm going to spruce myself up.' She gracefully stepped down the ladder into the galley. The patrol boat pulled up alongside, and a tannoyed voice asked for permission to board. Two police officers came aboard, uniform fatigues, uniform shoes, uniform side-arms, uniform close-cropped beards, and uniform scepticism in their mid-thirties uniform brown eyes.

'Is the master of the vessel aboard?'

I gave him both barrels of a stare.

'Lieutenant, this is my boat. I am the master. How can I help you?'

'Apologies, Captain.' At least he had the grace to apologise and give me some rank. 'There has been an incident. We wondered if you might have seen or heard anything you could tell us about?'

'What happened?'

'A cruiser sank.' Careful choice of words.

'Did someone ram it? Some people on cruisers make a lot of noise. I wouldn't be surprised if someone rammed it.'

'We are still trying to find out what happened.'

'Was anyone hurt?' But I knew the answer before I'd asked.

'No. There was nobody aboard at the time. So have you

'seen anything you can tell us about?'

'We've been to Paranabi for the weekend. I'm sure this anchorage was intact when we left. I would have noticed a sinking cruiser.'

'We?'

I called Charlie. She came up into the cockpit, her bright red swimsuit a magnet for two pairs of uniform brown eyes. While he continued to talk to me, his eyes were fixed on her.

'When did you leave for Paranabi?'

He already knew the answer. He would have radioed Musa's name to his colleagues at every port because we had, after all, left the scene hours before the sinking had occurred.

'We came aboard from the tender about 6.15 Saturday morning. We would have left the mooring about 6.30. When did this happen?'

'It was reported to us at 9.45 Saturday evening.'

'Ah, we were at the restaurant. Our reservation was for 9.30.'

He didn't use pen and paper, but I knew he had made a note and would call every restaurant in Paranabi to check.

'Gas explosion?' I asked. 'People are sometimes careless around gas bottles.'

'At the moment, we don't know,' he said, eyes still fixed on Charlie's swimwear. 'I would like your address. Just so we can ask you any more questions if we need to.'

I gave my address, and he gave me an appraising glance. He knew how wealthy you had to be to live on that hill.

'And your friend? Where may I find her?'

'With me,' I said. 'We live together.'

He gave me another appraising look.

'Do you have your papers, please?'

I opened the side zip on my rucksack and gave him my driving license. He glanced at it and handed it back.

'If we need you for a statement, can we contact you at your house?'

'Of course. We're not planning on going anywhere. Except weekends, when we'll be on the boat.'

'Thank you.'

With an 'a despedida', and a 'tchau', they climbed into the patrol boat. It powered away with a throaty roar and resumed patrolling. Charlie put her hand on my arm.

'My Portuguese might not be very good, but I know what "Nós vivemos juntos" means.'

'I didn't want him to be bothering you at your hotel.'

'Would he?'

'He was practically drooling from his eyes. He would have been at your hotel by early evening.'

'Would that have been so bad?' she teased.

'For his wife, yes. It would have been bad for her.'

'There was always the other one...'

'Yes, but his girlfriend would also be upset. So would his boyfriend.'

'You're pulling my leg!'

'Maybe I am. Yes, maybe I am. But you could do so much better than either of them.'

'How?'

'With me, of course.' I kissed her.

Chapter 21. Attempt 2
Stripfire

Week 37. Rio de Janeiro

Eight that evening.

Charlie had gone to her hotel an hour ago, saying she needed a good night's sleep; I was getting ready for an early night before hitting the gym tomorrow. That's the picture that our last texts painted. And that's what didn't happen.

I left the house at 1am and walked an off the track path beneath the pine trees, angling down the hill towards my lockup two kilometres away. I stood outside the rented lockup and pushed some magic buttons on my phone. The locks disengaged, the well-greased doors opened silently, and a small internal light came on when I walked in.

I changed into my leathers, pulled on my boots, gloves, and helmet, and rolled the bike outside. I locked the door behind me, started up and rode slowly down the track to the main expressway. Santos Dumont is a small airport south of Rio. While the main airport handles huge volumes of commercial and passenger traffic, Santos Dumont is a quieter place; its main focus is airfreight, private aircraft, helicopters, and almost no commercial passenger aviation.

In normal road traffic, Santos Dumont is thirty-five minutes travel, southeast of my lockup. On the motorbike at one in the morning, I got there in fifteen minutes. Earlier this evening, my target's private jet had landed at Santos Dumont. I had watched the plane come in on my phone. It had left the Middle East a few hours after the communications station cooling failure. It would have still been en-route when his tri-decker was sunk. He would have been in immediate radio contact, and the ether would have burned with his fury.

I guessed that at the very least, his head of security would have been on the flight, and probably his senior engineer. And now I wanted to make life very embarrassing for his head of security. After all, how secure is the man at the top when his head of security has issues as soon as he hits the ground?

Santos Dumont might be a small airport, but security was still tight. The combined cost of all the winged hardware on the tarmac and in the hangars ran into billions of US Dollars. From the top floor of the car park on the Avenida Alfred Agache, just outside the airport perimeter, my view of the executive jet parking area was unobstructed.

I settled against the place I'd selected as my firing point, pulled the night-vision binoculars from my rucksack and, for twenty minutes, I studied all movement to my front and left and right flanks. The night was quiet, the air was warm, and the limply hanging windsocks told me these were perfect conditions. I mentally checked everything again and then started running the calculations one last time: distance, target, height, drop, wind, and drag. I had to get all of these factors right.

I took out the components of the carbon fibre hunting crossbow and assembled it. The final piece I added was the sniper scope. Next, I took out the reel of micro-thread and the bolt it was epoxied to. The bolt was a thing of beauty; a perfectly balanced, aluminium-tipped carbon fibre rod set with brushed peacock feathers.

I unwound the reel of micro-thread and carefully coiled it loosely on the car park wall. I was using a two-ply strand. Strong, but flexible enough to be used in sewing machines. It weighed a fraction of polyester or cotton thread. I crawled into position, nestled the crossbow stock against my shoulder, and lined up the scope.

Although a modern crossbow can shoot a bolt up to five hundred metres, the effective hunting range of such a weapon, in perfect conditions, is around two hundred metres. The distance from my firing position on the roof of this car park to the six square inches of my target was two-hundred-forty metres, the length of two full-sized football fields. And it was dark. But I had the advantage of height.

The executive jet was buttoned up for the night. In the amber backwash of the airport perimeter light, it didn't look like a gravity-defying thing of beauty. I pulled out the targeting calculator and entered the figures: distance, firing point height, the height of my target and a small allowance for wind. The display told me where I needed to aim to hit the target zone.

I cocked the crossbow, put the bolt in the chamber and aimed the scope at the wing/fuselage joint. Then I raised my aim until the display inside the scope told me I was aiming correctly.

I was about to send him his third message in seventy-two hours. I went into my long-distance shooting routine. When I had no breath left to disturb the course of the bolt, I completed the trigger squeeze. The bolt left the crossbow at three hundred feet per second, and the coiled micro-thread rapidly unwound.

At this distance, there was no sound of impact. The

night-vision binoculars confirmed a good hit; the bolt was embedded in the fuselage joint, halfway across the width of the wing; the business end of the bolt was deep in the air-craft fuel tank.

I gently began to wind up the micro-thread. When I was satisfied with the tension, I tied the thread to the safety rail on the wall and opened the half-litre bottle of gasoline from my rucksack. Then I brought out a veterinarian's large animal syringe, filled it with gasoline, and slowly squirted the liquid onto the micro-thread.

I estimated it would take twenty minutes to discharge the full half-litre through the syringe. And I reckoned I should allow an additional three minutes for the liquid to flow along the thread once I'd finished. Twenty-three minutes. I gave it half an hour, just in case.

While I waited, I dismantled the crossbow, tidied every-thing away, put on my helmet, started the Ninja, lit a match, and put it to the micro-thread. A small blazing flame flick-ered into action and began to burn its way down the light-weight thread. Time to go.

I'd just hit the main road outside the car park when the fuel tank of the executive jet detonated. In my mirrors, the sky exploded into bright light. And even over the motor-bike's engine and inside my full-face helmet, I heard the deep rumble of the explosion.

By 2.30am I was in my bed. Getting up at 5am was going to be difficult, but for two and a half hours, I had a deep and dreamless sleep.

Chapter 22. Attempt 2
Shopping

Week 37. Rio de Janeiro

The next day I met Angelo for lunch. We sat on a bench in the pull-in, overlooking the sea. He tucked into his bauru sandwich.

'I'm sad to say this, but I had forgotten how good it is to get outside for lunch.'

'You should make a habit of it.'

'I rarely get outside at all these days.'

'You must be busy.'

'I need to keep moving. It's important.'

'Ah, I understand.' I wondered how many enemies he had. His black suburban with the blacked-out windows was parked behind us. Inside were two of his henchmen and probably enough hardware to start, and finish, a gang war.

'And you?' he asked. 'You are busy too?'

'Not really, Angelo. But I want to get busy, and this means we need to talk about what I want and when I think I'm going to need it.

He hunched forward intently.

'Would you like another?'

'Oh, God.'

'Is that yes?'

'Oh. My. God!'

'Are you getting religion now?'

'Jesus…'

'If your next words are "Mary and Joseph", I'm going to reconsider this relationship.'

After a long pause, she said, 'I've just never…'

'Never? Never ever?'

'OK. I have. But never like that.'

'This is good, yes?'

'This is good, yes.' She put her hand over mine, on her breast.

I waited for her to say what she felt anxious about saying. 'Can I ask you a serious question?'

'Of course.'

'Stop smirking. I mean it. A real serious question?'

I unpeeled my body from hers and propped myself up on an elbow.

'You may. Ask away.'

'When you come to California, would you come and stay with me?'

'Umm. I thought we had agreed that I would?'

'No. I mean, stay with me. Be with me. Live with me. Or I'll move to Rio and live with you.'

'Wow.'

'Is that yes?'

'First of all, that's just a wow.'

'Oh.'

'Is this how fast you move in your relationships?'

'I haven't exactly had many relationships to compare. And haven't had any like this.'

'Like this means…?'

'This focussed. Of this intensity. Of such passion, such extreme… feeling.'

'I thought you liked me feeling?'

She closed her eyes. 'Can you cut it out and be serious for a minute?'

'Yes. Sorry. I will.' I paused for a couple of beats and then asked her the biggest question of our relationship so far. 'So do you want us to live together? Like permanently? Like a couple?'

'Yes. Well, no. Well, sort of. Look, this is really fast, and I'm trying to get my head around where my heart is. But right now, this moment, I love you and I want us to be together. I don't think it's the sex talking. I really don't. What else I don't know is where "together" might be or what together might look like.' She took a deep breath before continuing.

'Whether it would be in California or somewhere else in the US, or in Rio de Janeiro or somewhere else in Latin America. Or maybe even in Europe, or anywhere. Right now, I just want us to be together. I like this. I like us. I want us to be a couple.'

'I would like that too.'

She hurried on with her outpouring.

'I can get a job just about anywhere. I would stop travelling for work. I would sell my house and buy somewhere we could live together if it wasn't in LA. I wouldn't ask you to give up your lifestyle, Laura. I'm just telling you that I would change mine so that we could be together.'

'I said I would like that too.'

'I heard you,' she said, rushing onwards. 'But I don't know if you realise just how much I'm willing to change my life for us. I've given this a lot of thought.'

'I can tell.'

'I just wanted to tell you how strongly I feel about this.'

She paused for breath. I knew she needed to unburden herself, and I knew it was the right thing to do. She had baggage that she hadn't told me about yet. And neither of us had been in a relationship of such burning intensity before. I knew she meant every word. I knew she was literally giving herself to me. And I was willing to give myself to her, for the rest of my life, however long I had left.

I worked it out and felt the first tear wet my cheek. Four months. If this cycle went the full 365 days, we had just over four months left together. My heart was breaking because at the end of four months, it would be over, but I was also very happy with this moment. I'd never get this feeling, this person, this second back again. I wouldn't be able to start the relationship again, only to know I'd lose her.

'Oh my God, don't cry! I didn't mean to make you feel sad.'

'I'm not sad.' I said, being joyfully happy and terribly sad at the same time.

Chapter 23. Attempt 2
Airflift

Week 39. Rio de Janeiro/California/Nevada

Two weeks later, she left. We enjoyed those two weeks. We lived, laughed, and loved, and then we lived some more. But now it was the end of this job for her, and she had a house in a different country. For however long she needed to be there, she was drawn to her home and her possessions, just as I was drawn to mine.

I drove her to the airport, kissed away her stern face, and told her I'd be in LA in just as soon as I'd closed down the house, put the boat to bed, and covered off a few other things. Five hours after her flight had taken off, I drove to a small airport on the northern outskirts of Rio. The executive jet I had chartered took me directly to a regional airport in southern Spain where customs formalities aren't much observed. My blacked-out limo was waved through the gate and onto the road.

The driver dropped me in the centre of Seville, where I had a light lunch, browsed through the main shopping centre and made sure I wasn't being followed. Over a Cola Cao I emailed an air charter company at North Las Vegas Airport. Then I spoofed an email address and emailed a USAF Transportation Team. I had a final walk around town to make doubly sure I wasn't being followed, then headed to a car rental agency where I picked up a medium-sized saloon.

Just outside Seville I pulled over and changed clothes in an autopista restroom. Sixty kilometres later, my perfectly forged USMC credentials got me admittance to the Morón Airforce Base. I dropped the car at the on-base hire office, picked up my kitbag and the canvas rifle case, and walked to the air terminal check-in.

I didn't much look like me. I was wearing US Marine Corps fatigues, standard-issue boots and my long hair was tied up under my cap; I looked like any other USMC Captain in transit.

The email I'd sent to the Transportation Team at USAFB Morón was perfectly spoofed. It looked like a legitimate travel order. I was accepted onto the flight roster, and my name was checked off the list. The first leg of the journey was to Germany on an elderly C-130 transport. I shared the flight with US military personnel on reassignment, redeployment, or on recall to the USA.

In Germany we had a five-hour layover before we were boarded onto the flight to the US. I spent most of the waiting and flying time dozing, this is usually the only inflight entertainment on military transport. Eighteen hours after departure, the giant Boeing C-17 Globemaster III landed with surprising grace at Edwards Airforce Base in the early Californian evening.

The C-17 taxied to the disembarkation point on the northeast side of the main airbase. There were a lot of tired, irritable military personnel onboard, but being tired and irritable is part of the job description in any service. I made myself small in my seat so my fellow passengers could easily pass by and disembark quickly.

When the huge aircraft was almost empty, I retrieved the M18 SIG Sauer and the canvas rifle case from the secure onboard store, shouldered my kitbag, and walked down the ramp into the Californian evening. And in that short distance, I had walked straight into the red zone.

Rio had been easy. I felt that I'd held all the cards in Brazil. But now I'd gone mobile and changed everything. I had moved into the US, where my enemy could call upon a massive range of official and unofficial resources. This was the danger zone; this was my all-or-nothing attempt to achieve my goal.

The last shuttle bus, engine running, was waiting for stragglers to get aboard. I could sense everyone wishing that we would just get the hell going. Most of the passengers were members of a US Army civil engineering division, returning home after building a bridge in Italy. There were also a dozen members of an electronic warfare group. And me.

With the last of us on board, the bus pulled away and began its rounds. Most got out at the married personnel accommodation on Fitzgerald Boulevard, which left me and a half-dozen others. The airman driver checked where we wanted to go, and a couple of us said High Desert, the on-base inn on Honts Drive.

Reception at High Desert Inn checked my ID and assigned me a room on the third floor. The room was large, comfortably furnished, had two double-beds, and was blessed with arctic-level air conditioning. I spent a long time in the bathroom, letting the shower ease me into full wakefulness.

An hour later I walked the short distance to Club Muroc where a cold beer and a large burger reinforced that I was back in the USA. I had travelled from Latin America into the heart of the US. I hadn't shown my real passport once and I knew I hadn't shown up on any flight systems or passenger manifests. It was a good evening for a walk.

At nine the next morning, dressed in jeans, trainers, and a colourful t-shirt, I checked out of High Desert Inn and got a lift from the Edwards AFB transportation section across the state line to Las Vegas International Airport, where I hired a black sedan.

I drove north out of Las Vegas and headed for Nellis Air Force Base. At the gate an eager MP checked my pass, gave me crisp, helpful directions to the on-base Nellis Inn, and a salute so sharp it cut air. I booked in for ten nights. The young guy behind the desk looked hopeful and said there wasn't much to do in the evenings, but he could show me some of the sights. Despite the unwanted come-on I was nice to him; he looked about twelve years old but probably wasn't.

I settled into the room and called Charlie; she sounded so happy to hear from me, I nearly cried. We had a long call where neither of us said much but spoke volumes. It was good. For the first time in so many cycles I felt loved and wanted. After the call I set a ridiculously early alarm and fell asleep thinking nice thoughts.

At seven the next morning I was parked outside a tall wire perimeter fence in the Mojave Desert. The early morning heat was already easing upwards from hot and heading towards stifling. Even so many hours before noon, the intense, dry, desert heat felt like I'd stepped into a sauna. The sun seared from the blue, cloudless sky; the air was unmoving.

The site was a disused USAF base that had been con-structed on a rocky plateau a hundred feet above the desert plain. I had already walked around the fence, checking for tyre tracks and footprints. I had found none; total distance walked: eight miles. The base was mostly unoverlooked, except for maybe a mile to the southeast, a small bluff of dis-tant hills. The only route onto the former airbase was a track that led off a single-lane asphalt road a few miles north.

While I was waiting in the air-conditioned car, the air charter company I'd emailed called. I flattened my accent into Midwest USA and arranged an appointment at their office for the next day; one more piece moving into position on the chessboard.

About an hour later, a distant dust cloud started growing down the desert track. The black truck that eventually pulled to a halt in a cloud of dust was one of those manly 4x4s that hardly seem to get dirty. This one was no exception; the only dirt on it was from the dust it had raised on the way here.

The Realtor eased out. He looked as smart as his telephone manner had suggested; immaculately groomed, casually dressed, and enveloped in a personal cloud of gorgeously masculine scent.

'Laura?' he asked.

I held out my hand and kept my accent American. 'Uh-huh. And you're Brad?'

'Good to meet you, Laura. Brad Samms.'

'Hey, Brad. Thanks for being here.'

He flashed his most winning smile. 'Absolutely no problem. So, you were very positive about this place in your emails. Let's get in and look around?'

'That would be great, thanks.'

He opened the passenger door of his truck for me and walked to the wired gate set into the fence; despite the earliness of the morning, I took a torch out of my car and ungracefully clambered up into his truck. Brad unlocked the gate, got back in behind the wheel, and we drove onto the site.

'That's one of the stores over there,' he said, indicating the former aircraft hangars. 'There are three more exactly like this one. They're all the same inside and out. Do you want to see them all, or just the one?'

'I'm sure they're as you describe, but if I don't check them out, I'll get into trouble with the unit director. But we're only looking to use three of the four stores, so we don't need to see them all.'

'Three of the four it is. And these are all for your film company?'

'Yep. The production we're working on has a lot of fabrications that we need to put away temporarily. This location is perfect for us.'

'Where are you filming?'

'The town scenes are going to be shot in and around Barstow. We'll be shooting in the desert and up in the mountains as well.'

'That's great. You'll like Barstow. It's a nice town.'

We pulled up outside the first store. 'Let's look around.'

Brad walked ahead of me, took a key out of his pocket, and unlocked an access door set into a full width sliding door. There was limited light inside; no windows or clear panels, but from what I could see, the former aircraft hangar looked perfect.

'Do you want me to open the main door instead of this little one?' he asked.

'Nah, no need.' I flicked on the torch. 'I'll just walk around a little.'

The torch gave me a good idea of what I was standing in. The hangar looked great. There was a light dusting of fine desert sand up against the external walls, but there were no large holes in the structure, no signs of weather damage. Dry and sound; it was perfect.

'I think we're good here, Brad. This looks like it's been

built to last.'

'Yeah, these old US Air Force bases were put up properly. You can't see much from the ground except these hangars, but from the air, you can see the old runways.'

'Really? Wow. Let's look at two more.'

I waited in his truck while he locked up; it was getting really hot now.

Forty-five minutes later, we'd seen the inside of three of the four hangars. I looked around at this almost intact, former military airfield.

'When it was a military base, what was this place called?'

'Cuttle. Air Force Base Cuttle.' And then, anxious to close the deal. 'So, what do you think, Laura? This will be good for you guys?'

'I think it's great, and this,' I gestured around me. 'This is a handy location. How do we move this forward?'

'There's a rental agreement to be signed, an upfront payment for the first six months. And then I need to give you the keys.'

'Great. Do I need to come to your office, or can we do this over the Internet?'

'Internet is fine. I can email you the documents with the payment details.'

'Terrific,' I handed him the film production company business card that I had created and printed out by a machine at the airport. The website address on the card was of a well-known studio, but the email with my name on it came straight to me.

'Email me the forms and payment details. I'll get my people to do the paperwork, send it back to you and make the payment.'

'That sounds sweet,' he said. 'I'll post the keys to you?'

'Your office is in Bakersfield, right?'

'Right.'

'I'll pick them up. I'm still scouting locations in the area with the crew. Better the keys get straight into my hands than get bounced around on redirect.' I knew I could have the rental paperwork completed tomorrow, and the place would be mine the day after.

'That's excellent, Laura. It's good to do business with you.'

I said it was good doing business with him too. We shook hands, he went his way, and I went mine.

I drove up the desert track, then onto the asphalt access road. After a few miles, I turned north and headed towards Las Vegas. Just outside the suburb of Seven Hills, I stopped at a construction supplier where I rented a heavy-duty power generator, a water tanker, a forklift, a spare tank of diesel, and two lighting arrays. I arranged to have it all delivered to the storage unit in a couple of days. Then I headed to my accommodation at Nellis.

I spent the rest of the day going over my plans, going through my lists, and thinking about what/if scenarios.

Before I fell asleep, I called Charlie. She said she missed me. I missed her too.

Chapter 24. Attempt 2
Nevada

Week 39. Nevada

The next morning, I drove to North Las Vegas Airport. I pulled up beside a single-storey office that proclaimed it was 'Sunny Helicopter Charters'.

The efficient young receptionist took my name and asked me to wait while the owner finished his call. I could hear a muffled voice through a partition wall. After a couple of minutes, the call ended, and a door opened.

'You're bright and early, Ms Clay. I'm Anthony (call me Tony) McCall.'

Late middle-aged, lean, tanned, dark cotton pants, and a crisply starched white shirt.

I stayed American. 'Nice to meet you, uh, Tony. Laura.'

We shook hands.

'Why don't you come through to my office, and we can talk about what you need?'

Along one wall of Tony's office were a dozen framed photos of him shaking hands with past and present celebrities: various helicopters in the background of most of the shots. From Internet searches, I knew that Tony McCall was the chief pilot and sole owner of Sunny Helicopter Charters. In the world of aviation, most aircrew were pretty straightforward, trustworthy people. My instincts told me that Tony McCall was no exception. I took a seat.

'Laura, coffee?' he asked.

'Erm, glass of water?'

'Got it,' called his receptionist from the open doorway.

'So, where are you from, Laura?'

'I was brought up in Texas. I live in LA now,' I lied. 'But I'm staying at Nellis for a couple of nights; just going over old times with some friends.'

He looked interested when I mentioned Nellis. 'And your job calls for you to fly an EC155?'

'Well, no, not specifically. The choice of helicopter is mine. I just have a soft spot for the EC155. And the one you're selling is within budget.'

His receptionist walked in and put a liveried mug in front of him and a tall glass of iced water in front of me.

'How long have you been flying, Laura?'

'I got my licence when I was sixteen.'

He raised an eyebrow.

'It was no big deal. Dad was a pilot. He didn't exactly hold me back.'

'What were you certified on?'

'Robinson R22.'

'Sturdy little machines.' He took a sip of his own drink, thought about something for a moment and then asked, 'So what did you do with your daddy's R22?'

'I flew standby, for when he needed a pilot. I didn't fly too much because only the regulars felt comfortable about letting a young girl pilot them around.'

'Who did you fly?'

'Oilmen mostly.'

'Right?'

'Senior execs. The grunts and workers got ferried about in commercial lifters, but the seniors used us. The very senior people had their own helicopters – or they used helicopters that belonged to the oil companies.'

'Yeah, I understand. We get some of that traffic out here too, but not as much as we used to. The State of Nevada is cleaning up its oil industry.'

'Is that a euphemism for shutting it down?'

'Yep,' he paused again and then asked, 'So what after R22s?'

'I left home and started flying for a living.'

'And where was that?'

'AETC.'

He leaned back in his chair and held my gaze in a long, cool stare.

'AETC,' he said, savouring every letter.

'Uh, yeah. Randolph Air Force Base, San Antonio.'

'You didn't get far from home then?'

'I didn't get to see much of my family. The first three months of Air Education and Training Command were pretty hostile. After that, I was sent to Fort Rucker, Alabama, where it just got tougher and tougher.'

'What did you graduate on at Rucker?'

'I flew a few different types, but I spent most of my time in a Sikorsky HH-60G.'

'Pave Hawk?'

I nodded.

'And after Rucker?'

'After Fort Rucker, I bunked at Fort Campbell for a little while. Then I flew operational Pave Hawks.'

He sat impassively for five beats.

'I was impressed before, Ms Clay. Now I'm really impressed.'

'Thanks, but it was nothing. They practically fly themselves.'

'Yeah, right,' he drawled, but we both knew that he'd fixed on Fort Campbell, the home of US Special Forces.

'How long did you serve?'

'Ten years. I've been a civilian for eighteen months, but I'm still on the reserve list.'

'So you're what… Twenty-nine?' He didn't mean to be rude about my age; he was just checking his arithmetic.

'I'll be thirty next birthday.'

'And you've kept your hours up?'

I nodded.

'And, according to our conversation yesterday, you now fly for a film studio?'

'I do. Been with them since I left the service. It's not hard work, and I get to see more things better than sitting in the multiplex.'

'How many hours do you have on the EC155?'

'I haven't flown one for three months, but I've got 500 hours on the EC155 B1.'

'I'll need to see your licence and certifications.'

'Sure.'

I pulled a folder out of my rucksack and put it in front of him.

'Where are you planning on flying?'

'On location, mostly west of Coyote Springs; the ridge mountains of Hayford Peak and Sheep Peak. Off-location flying will be around LA for the studio execs.'

'Coyote Springs is some countryside. You know Hayford Peak is one of the Ultras?' he said, referring to the ultra-prominent peaks of the USA.

'The shooting list the studio gave me had Hayford Peak as one of the locations.'

'That's an awesome place. It's great to see the snow on the mountains in the winter, but in the late spring, at night, the air is so clear up there, the skies are just fantastic.'

'You a stargazer, Mister McCall?'

'I used to go camping there with my daughter.'

My turn to raise an eyebrow.

'Don't look at me like that. She always told me she liked it.'

'But not so much now? Grown out of it?'

'She died,' he said bluntly. 'I was in Iraq; she died before I got home.'

'I'm sorry for your loss, Mister McCall. I'm really sorry for your loss.'

'Thanks, Laura. I'm on the way to being over it now.'

He picked up the flight folder and started going through my documentation.

'When did she pass?'

He paused his reading but didn't look up.

'Fifteen years ago.'

I let that sink in for a moment.

'I'm sorry,' was all I could say again.

I broke the silence while he studied my papers. 'Which service? In Iraq?'

He looked up from my perfectly forged paperwork.

'Marine Corps.'

'You flew?'

'Vipers. I flew close air support for the Chinooks.'

'Now I'm impressed.'

He brushed aside my pilots' licence and certification and went straight to the military flight log I'd forged in Spain.

'It says here,' he said, changing the conversation, 'that you made captain?'

'Dead man's shoes. I was waiting for someone higher up the chain to die or retire. Nobody did, so I got stuck at captain.'

'Captain's a good rank, and you got there really fast looking at your flight record.'

'Where did you get to?' I kept the conversation going

'O-3.'

'So? Another captain.'

He grunted as he continued to read. 'According to this annotation, you got a lot of these certifications in Afghan?'

'They were short of manpower; I was keen to learn.'

'They didn't bring you back for flight training in the US?'

'Things were hot. And we were running out of options.' I meant we were running out of pilots, and he knew it.

'How long were you over there?'

'Three tours, back-to-back.'

'Three operational tours in a war zone is a lot of action. Three tours back-to-back is more than most career officers see in a lifetime.'

'I worked with terrific people. I liked them and I liked the job.'

'Get shot at?'

'Which day?'

'Yeah, so you got shot at a lot then. And Fort Campbell… So, based on what you've told me I'm guessing you flew combat for Special Ops?'

He let that dangle and I didn't take the bait.

'What I want to know is,' he went on, 'Are you the kind of pilot who is going to break my baby out there?' He nodded over his shoulder. 'Or are you a good sensible pilot who doesn't take risks?'

I noticed he referred to the helicopter he was selling as 'my baby'. This was a man who liked what he owned.

'Three ops tours in Afghan and you're asking me if I take

risks?'

'Good point, but I know about battlefield flying, and I know you don't get through three tours without taking the occasional risk.'

'Calculated. Always calculated.'

He tried to look as if he was reading the two different parts of my flying record at the same time. Then he put them back in the folder.

'I suppose it's time we went and saw the bird and see how you feel about her. You good for a trial flight?'

'Sure. When?'

'No time like the present.'

'OK, but I need to change my shoes.'

'The what now?'

'My flying shoes are in my rucksack.' I patted the bag.

After a pause, he said, 'Yeah, I get it. With me, it's my sunglasses. I've never flown without these,' he patted his shirt pocket. 'Even though they're broken, and I've gone through so many wearable pairs since they broke, these are the shades I got my flying training hours in.'

We both understood. Combat pilots have their superstitions. I changed my shoes, we left his office, and walked around the corner to a helicopter pad where a dark blue-liveried Eurocopter EC155 B1 sat.

These machines don't look like most civilian helicopters. The EC155, or the Airbus Helicopters H155 as they're now called, have sleek, streamlined lines that show their military heritage and just shout that in the wrong hands they can be formidable machines. When they are flown hard, with their landing wheels retracted, the EC155 is one of the fastest helicopters in the world. This one carried none of the military hardware, but she was still one of the quickest rotaries on the block, and that's what I was shopping for.

'Hello baby,' I said, quietly, as I stroked her nose. I did a quick walk around and then had a look inside the rear and fore cabins. She was pristine, looked and smelled factory-fresh even though I knew she had some serious flying time on her logbook.

Without either of us speaking, I began a detailed walk-around. I made sure the parts that were supposed to move did move and did so correctly, and I checked that the bits that were not supposed to move didn't. I checked the fluid levels, and I checked the external panels and the control surfaces.

I checked the landing gear, and I opened every inspection hatch and put my head in for a good look around. I pulled a mini flashlight out of my pocket to check that all seals were dry and that the lubricated components were wet. I asked for the service record, and Tony passed me his clipboard. No corners had been cut, and no expense had been spared to keep this machine in peak airworthiness.

'Shall we take it to the next level?' I asked.

'You're the pilot, you tell me.'

'In that case, I'd like to try it on for size.'

He nodded his assent. I opened the pilot's door and slid in; Tony got into the passenger's seat on the opposite side. We put on and adjusted the helmets and seatbelts and did a comms check between us.

Tony handed me a narrow clipboard with the pre-flight checks, put another on his knee, took out a tablet, and began making notes. I fired up the control panel and watched all the lights and indicators come to life. It was like breathing life into another part of me; I got the familiar feeling that this machine and I were about to become a team.

I checked the touchscreens were good, then teased the hands and feet controls to make sure everything moved correctly and that I got the correct feedback from the moving parts. Everything felt perfect. Without even thinking about it I scanned out of the cockpit forwards, sideways, and over my shoulder.

'Clear right,' I said.

'Clear left,' he replied after checking his view.

I flipped the master switches to 'On', started both engines, brought them up to half power and began to work through the checklist while the blades began to chop the air. Tony contacted the tower to tell them we were on a short familiarisation flight. Three and a half minutes later, we'd completed the checklist, both engines were up to temperature, and the blades were spinning at ninety percent of idle speed.

'You good to go?' I asked into the intercom.

'Yep, let's take her out.'

I increased the revs to slightly above normal lift-off speed but held the helicopter on the ground eight seconds longer than most pilots would, then, in one graceful movement, I smoothly lifted this other part of me four feet into the air and held her there. The still Nevada air made the static hover impressive.

We received tower clearance to move forward. I counted to five, checked over my shoulder again and then, keeping absolutely level with the ground, moved her forward, then turned right.

We were granted permission to leave, so I increased forward speed, still keeping the EC155 parallel with the ground, lifted her up to forty feet and then quickly banked upwards and to starboard and away from the runway and out, over the airport threshold.

Thirty-five minutes later, I landed us gently on the same pad. The engines spun down as I went through the shutdown procedure and then, in the relative quiet of the airport, we walked back to Tony's office. I couldn't help looking over my shoulder as we walked away from her.

'What do you reckon?' Asked Tony, as he settled into his chair.

'I like her a lot. She's as good as your advert said. If you can knock ten percent off the price, I can pay you a holding deposit right now. I'd like an independent flight engineer check her over before we do the deal. How does that sound to you?'

He leaned forward in his chair. 'Three percent.'

'Let's call it five percent, and we're both winners.'

He said nothing for three beats.

'I like that you don't screw around, Laura.' He offered me his hand across the desk.

Just under an hour later, he walked me out to the car. We'd completed the transfer of ownership and registration forms and I'd paid a hefty deposit. Tony was going to hold onto everything until I'd got the EC surveyed and had paid the balance of the price.

I spent most of the rest of the day on the road. First, I drove to the real-estate office in Bakersfield. As I drove east, I called flight engineers and got lucky on the second call. I rang Tony McCall to let him know an engineer would look at the EC in the morning. He was pleased, I was thrilled. I was still a little high from flying that wonderful machine.

Once upon a time, in the Middle East, I'd almost lived in the pilot's seat of a similar helicopter. I'd missed the excitement of it.

After I'd collected the keys to Cuttle I drove back to Nellis. The young guy on the desk tried his luck again. Jesus loves a tryer. Probably. In my room, I lay on the bed and called Charlie; we giggled and flirted for an hour. She said she missed me, and I said I missed her too, and we both knew we were telling each other the truth.

I went to the base gym and pushed myself harder than usual. Closing on my prey was no excuse to let up on my fitness.

Chapter 25. Attempt 2
Shopping Again

Week 39. Nevada

A few miles north of the centre of Las Vegas, is a shopping mall that has something for everyone. The ground floor is a combination of fast-food areas and trendy clothes shops. The first floor has serious retail outlets and household items. The second floor is the geek level.

The morning after I flew the EC155 with Tony, I drove to the mall and bought some clothes. I picked things that looked pretty and colourful and comfortable to wear. I also got some shoes. And a couple of suitcases.

Then I went upstairs to the geek level where I bought a

laptop, a powerful pair of field glasses, a lightweight pair of binoculars, a jogger's headtorch, a radio signal amplifier, some hardware called HackRF Mayhem, a small toolkit, a laser rangefinder, a night sight with infrared, and a device called a software defined radio. I was going to use these things to capture a military aircraft. I said the mall had something for everyone, right?

I had a decent meal in an Italian-ish restaurant, then packed everything into the sedan and drove to the Inn at Nellis Airforce Base.

It took me a couple of hours to set up the laptop, the HackRF Mayhem, and the SDR. By 4pm, I had downloaded everything I needed. I installed and configured the files and ran a couple of small-scale local tests which, in three quick GPS jumps, showed me to be in Paris, Texas; then Paris, France; and finally in Paris, Arkansas.

As I was packing everything away, I got a call from the flight engineer; the EC was solid gold and had passed every check. I called Tony McCall. He said he'd transfer ownership as soon as I paid him the balance. I told him to check his account. After a pause, he said the EC would be good to go from seven tomorrow morning.

When I called Charlie that evening, we billed and cooed like a pair of teenagers, and I told her I loved her, and I really meant it. When I said I'd almost finished up in Brazil and that I'd be flying to Los Angeles in two days, she shrieked with joy.

At 6.30 the next morning, I drove to Sunny Helicopter Charters at North Las Vegas Airport and filled in a final release form for the EC155.

Then I filed a 'for info' flight plan. Although I was keeping below the 18,000-feet mandatory flight plan ceiling and wasn't crossing any restricted airspace, I wanted Tony to have some confidence in how I was going to look after his helicopter. Aviators get attached to their machines, even ones they're selling.

As I was doing the pre-flight checks, Tony walked over from a maintenance hangar.

'What's the plan for today?'

'A quick trip around some desert locations. I'd like to bring her back here this afternoon and leave her here overnight, if that's OK?'

'Sure, that's fine. I'll even fill her tank on return. Maybe we could have a coffee and a chat when you get back?'

'That would be good. I'd like that.'

He held out his hand again.

'Just don't bend her, OK?'

'I'll treat her as if I owned her.'

He smiled at my joke and left me to do the pre-flight checks by myself. I flew the same flashy but safe lift-off, then held the helicopter static at four feet off the ground, contacted the tower, and received clearance to leave the airport. I knew that Tony would be watching through binoculars from his cabin and listening on his airband radio, so I left the airport threshold in exactly the same way.

My technique made the helicopter look good, and we both knew it.

When I reached the former USAFB Cuttle in the Mojave, I

descended to thirty-five feet, circled the site, then crossed over the perimeter and flew slowly up the length of what had once been the main runway. I landed, tucked away to the side of what Brad had called Storage Shed 1; I mentally renamed it Hangar One.

After shutdown, I got out and opened Hangar One's large sliding door, then I walked to the perimeter fence and opened the main security gate.

I had plenty of time to spare, so I walked the length of the main runway, inspecting it as I went. It had been made out of thick layers of concrete on a deep bed of rock, stone, and sand. Despite signs of decay on some of the concrete edges, the runway was in good enough condition to take light aircraft, but its days of being up to heavy bomber landings were long over.

From the midpoint of the runway, I stopped and looked around. The dry desert air had helped preserve the base; the hangars had been built for the maintenance of medium-range bombers intended to fly in a war that didn't happen. There were no other buildings here. This base, one of a half-dozen in the region, used to be a satellite airfield to a much larger installation fifteen miles northwest. That larger airbase was still operational but was now in the hands of a shadowy US government agency with deep pockets and tight lips.

I walked into the hangar, hunkered down in the cool dark and waited. Half an hour later, the distant sound of a heavy engine brought me out of my reverie. The huge truck rolled in through the gate and, with hissing airbrakes, pulled to a stop outside the open hangar. On the back of the truck were the two lighting gantries mounted on trailers, a powerful electricity generator, and a forklift truck. Towed behind was a filled-to-capacity five-hundred-gallon water tanker.

The truck guys uncoupled the water tanker then unloaded the flatbed. I signed the delivery note, thanked the driver and his mate, gave them twenty dollars each, and locked the main gate behind them as they headed back to civilisation.

I started up the forklift and towed one of the lighting gantries into Hangar One. I put it near the left wall, unhitched it and lowered the stabilising legs. I repeated the process with the second gantry, except I set it up opposite the first one. Then I towed in the generator.

I ran the power cables from the generator to the gantries, connected them, and started it up. The noise was loud in the enclosed space, but the light from the gantries threw the inside of the hangar into a well-lit monochrome. Satisfied that everything had worked as it should, I shut off the generator, towed the water tanker inside, then walked into the scorching desert sunshine and locked up.

I flew the EC to North Las Vegas Airport and landed on the pad outside Sunny Helicopter Charters. I was working through post-flight checks when Tony McCall walked out, accompanied by a twenty-something, overall-wearing dude.

'Good flight?'

'No thanks, I've just had one. But if you're offering, I'd go for a cool drink?'

'I bet you were a laugh a minute with Special Ops.'

'It's a talent,' I said.

'How was she?'

'You are one proud dad, right?'

'Yeah, guess I am. So how was she?'

'She's perfect. I picked up the DP, and we checked out

three of the four film locations from the air. I put her down to look at a long straight line in the desert. We figured it's an old road, so we may need to work on that because old roads in the desert aren't in the film.'

'DP?'

'Director of Photography.'

'He's the guy who calls the shots?'

'Literally.'

There was a pause in the conversation.

'So, TJ here is going to brim the tanks for you.'

'Thanks.'

'You want that coffee?'

'I'll take a glass of water.'

'Yeah, let's go get that.'

Back in his office, I sat in a comfortable armchair while Tony's receptionist sorted out the drinks.

'Where was this desert road?'

'Southern Mojave, near Fenner, just north of I-40.'

'Don't know the area, but the Mojave has a few old gol-drush townships that don't exist anymore. Could be you picked up a track to one of them.'

'It's not a big deal. I'll tell the crew. There are ways around problems like that.'

'It's an interesting line of work.'

'The industry has its moments, but what I do is fly. The studio stuff is good at first, but the constant repetition with filming just gets dull. But flying for the studio? That's the best job.'

'Yeah, flying is the best job.' He took a sip from his mug.

'So why aren't you?'

'What?

'Flying. Why aren't you?'

'Oh, I do. I've got a Jet Ranger and a Bell. I bought the EC for a tech company contract, but they folded after eight months, so she was just an expensive overhead. I fly the Jet Ranger and the Bell as lead pilot. There's a guy over in Spring Valley I use when I need extra cover. He's a good pilot, but he's not going to be around forever.'

'You're light on flying staff then. Who are your main customers?'

There's a local TV company and a radio station. They both use us when they need a pilot. I get some holidaymaker business out of Vegas. People want to see the Grand Canyon or Hoover Dam or go out and see the desert from six thousand feet, but there's a lot of competition for the tourist market lately.

'There's a bunch of celebrities who use me as a taxi service, and I'm on the list of eight or ten regulars. Then there are the folk who fly in from LA, spend a few days in town doing whatever they do, then want to be flown home again.'

'They don't use charter 'planes?'

'They prefer to avoid the public and like to be piloted straight to their front doors; these people have serious acreages.'

He stopped when the dude in the overalls tapped on the window and gave him a thumbs-up.

'But business is OK?' I asked. Because keeping a Jet Ranger and a Bell on the ground was a lot of equipment burning through money.

'Yep, business is doing really well. I need to expand, but I can't find the right fit.'

'Helicopters?'

'Pilots.' He held my gaze. 'Good pilots. Steady pilots. Pilots who aren't out chasing tail all night and drinking all day.'

I got the inference.

'How do you know I don't?'

'Do you drink?'

'I like a glass of wine.'

'See, that's what I thought. Didn't have you down as a big drinker.'

'How do you know I'm not out chasing tail all night?'

He paused.

'Your eyes don't tell that story, Laura.'

'Don't offer me a job.'

'I won't. But I'd like you to think about it. I've seen you fly twice, and I know an exceptional pilot when I see one.'

He gave me a straight look, so I picked up my glass and sipped my iced water. I'm several thousand years old, and still uncomfortable getting compliments.

Chapter 26. Attempt 2
Angels

Week 40. Nevada/California

The next morning, I drove to North Las Vegas Airport, pulled up outside Sunny Helicopter Charters, and unloaded my two suitcases into the Eurocopter.

I walked into Tony's office; his receptionist said he was flying a survey crew over powerlines, so I filed a 'for info' flight plan to LA and left a message thanking him for his help. Then I sent Charlie a message saying I'd be at her house in an hour and a half.

I had never felt so excited as when I sent that message. Her reply simply said 'Squeee!'

I flew the EC to Long Beach Airport in California and landed on a pad outside Long Beach Aviation Services. I powered down, went into the office, and arranged for the EC to be refuelled and looked after. Then I picked up a hire car. Half an hour later I pulled up on the driveway outside Charlie's house. I'd popped the trunk and was getting my first suitcase out when I was hit by a tall, skinny, childlike ball of energy.

As soon as we were in the house, she scattergunned me with fast-paced nervousness. 'Welcome to my home, I mean our house - that's the garden, this is the living room, through there is the kitchen, that's the bathroom, and this is the bedroom.'

And that's where we stayed for a couple of hours.

Eventually she said, 'I've been very rude.'

'Yes, you have. But we can be rude again once I've got my breath back.'

'That's not what I meant!'

'Oh?'

'I mean I pushed you right in here and you haven't even had a chance to unpack.'

'I'd like to brush my teeth...?'

'Oh. I'm so sorry. I'll make us a drink and you hit the bathroom?'

'Yes please. To both.'

'And later we could go out? To dinner?'

'Well, that would be lovely. And maybe while we're out, we could look around for some gym action?'

'I have some gym-related information for you.'

I stopped rummaging in my case for my toothbrush and gave her a fake stern stare.

'Oh, really?'

'Yeah, I took a liberty. Sorry. But I wanted to do something for you. So I looked at a family gym over at Penman, which is a mile and a half away from here. It's got all the equipment, and it isn't very busy. And if that's no good, there's a boxing gym near Venice Beach that has women members. Not that you're bothered about that but still...'

'You have been busy. Thank you. Can we go and look at them tomorrow?'

'Tomorrow?'

'Yes,' I leaned against the bathroom doorframe. 'We're going out for dinner tonight. You said so.'

Charlie had booked us into an Italian restaurant in Santa Monica, a short walk from the beach. It was good to be beside the sea again but hearing the waves shush against the shore and watching the distant boats made me miss Musa. Brazilian life and my structured, self-centred daily routines seemed so far away, though it had only been just over a week since I'd left.

We walked arm in arm along the seafront, watching beach life start to shut down for the evening; the chilly evening air beginning to make its presence felt.

'What would you like to do tomorrow?' she asked.

'Tomorrow, I shall sit around the house watching you.'

'That's going to be dull.'

'Why will it be?'

'Well, first, I'm going for a run. Then after breakfast I'm going to take you to that gym I found and sign us up, but only if you like it. And in the afternoon, I'm going to swim a couple of miles.'

I tried to keep the surprise out of my voice.

'I'll come with you!'

'Wonderful. Which part?'

'All of it.'

'Up at five-thirty and on the road at six?'

'I'm in.' I said.

'Are you sure? You don't have to?'

'I'm in. I still need to keep getting into shape.'

'I want to get into the kind of shape you're in.'

I smirked and kissed her on the cheek, and we went into the restaurant for what turned out to be an Italian American dinner. All through the meal I couldn't take my eyes off her. I was falling hard.

Chapter 27. Attempt 2
Protector

Week 40. California

Early the next morning we ran, I pushed us, and we ran hard. That's when I discovered Charlie hadn't been holding back on her training since getting back from Rio.

After showering, we sat in her back yard and ate a fresh fruit breakfast and just talked as if we'd known each other for years. We were fitting together mentally, and sexually. Emotionally something was passing between us, I have never felt so comfortable with anyone before.

Mid-morning, we walked to the gym, which she said felt odd. I said it would be odder if we drove; she said I didn't understand LA, where everyone drives everywhere, even to the gym.

We were shown around by a serious-looking trainer who had the most startlingly white smile. The gym was half-full of glamorous people with similarly lightning-white toothy grins. For a serious amount of money, the gym could provide us with all the facilities we needed. Rico would have sneered.

We signed up, and I said we'd be in at six the next morning. Surprisingly, they said that was approaching their peak time. I said we'd fit in somewhere.

Instead of heading straight home, we walked through Oakwood to Venice Beach, which looked gorgeous in the morning Californian sun. I eyed the immaculately clean sand and the sea beyond.

'Shame we didn't bring our swimsuits.'

'We could come back this afternoon?'

'I'd like that,' I said. 'But there's something I'd like better.'

'What's that?'

'Well, I didn't get much sleep last night. So I think I might like to go to bed for a couple of hours?'

'And sleep?'

'Eventually.' I smirked. Charlie smiled back, linked her arm through mine, and we walked on, looking at the people on the beach, and browsing the stalls selling various items of clothing.

'You've changed me. I want to add "already", but you have changed me, and yet it feels like we've known each other for years.'

'Maybe we have.' I said.

'How do you mean?'

'Maybe in past lives...' I let the sentence trail off.

'Do you believe in that?'

'No. Yes. Sort of.'

She raised an eyebrow at me.

'I don't disbelieve it.'

'What sort of person do you think you might have been in previous lives then?'

'Younger, naïve, innocent, carefree.'

'Why aren't you those things now?'

'I've seen too much, learned too many of the wrong things.'

'Are you talking about having your heart broken many times, again?'

'That and other things.'

'Tell me?'

'I will. But not here. This isn't the place for deep, sad conversations.'

'You're right,' she said. 'This is the place for people watching.'

We sat on a low wall like a couple of children and watched the Venice Beach people doing what Venice Beach people do. I think we turned people watching into a high art-form that day.

The early evening sunlight slanted through a gap in the drapes. We were in that half-sleep state that steals over you when your appetite has been satisfied and you are drowsy from exertion. The duvet draped around us like a cocoon of goose feathers wrapped in a soft, crisp, cotton shell. My head on her breast, her quiet breathing amplified in my ear. I was floating away and she spoke so quietly I almost missed it.

'I can't have children.'

Wait. What did she just tell you? Say nothing. No, say something. Say the right thing. Quickly, say the right thing. And don't be funny. Quickly!

'Have you been trying?'

There was a long pause before she whispered her reply. 'No.'

I tried to sharpen my thoughts. 'Did something happen?'

Another pause, longer this time. 'A long time ago.'

I was almost fully awake now. 'And because of that you can't have children now?'

She murmured her response. 'It's related.'

I leaned back onto my elbow, reached up a hand and brushed her cheek. It was wet. 'Is that why you haven't married?'

'No. there hasn't been the right one for me, that's all.'

'Do you want to tell me what happened?'

'Not now.' She tightened her arm around me.

'What do you want to talk about now?'

'Everything and nothing.'

'Can I say one serious thing to you?'

'No.'

'Good. So here it is, my one serious thing that you don't

want me to say. Whatever happened, it wasn't your fault. Nothing you did caused it to happen to you. And I love you.'

I paused for breath and then went on softly. 'I'm glad you felt comfortable telling me about this. You can tell me as much or as little as you want. I'll listen to you, always. No pressure. But whatever it was, however you felt then, however you feel now, you need to know I will not let bad things happen to you ever again. I will protect you.'

She rolled onto her side away from me, I moved in and spooned her, her body heaved gently as she quietly wept.

Her movements eventually slowed as she drifted into sleep. I stayed awake for a while, wondering if this was the vulnerability I'd seen the first time we met. I vowed never to let anything happen to this beautiful person who had brought me such joy. I had failed to protect others close to me in the past. I wasn't going to let anything happen to her.

Eventually I dozed. It was pitch black when I felt Charlie leave the bed. When she came back from the bathroom, she slid in behind me for a change.

'What time do you call this to come creeping home, young lady?'

She hugged me.

'Erm, is it late? I only went to the bathroom.'

'Are you sleepy?'

'Not really. Tired but not sleepy.'

The darkness felt snug around us, it encouraged me to talk.

'Can I tell you things?'

'If I say "no", are you going to say them anyway?'

I ignored that.

'Did I tell you about the very bad thing I did in Italy?'

'No. Tell me.'

'We were at Convent school in the centre of Rome.'

'We?'

'My sister Hana and me. Anyway, the nuns were very strict. One was very tough on Hana in particular. One day I overheard Sister Maria Cristina telling her off, she was so harsh that poor Hana burst into tears.'

'Oh no!'

'So I did what any self-respecting big sister would do, I opened a window on the first floor. The sisters had to walk beneath the window to get to chapel.'

'Uh-huh!'

'When Sister Maria Cristina walked beneath the window, I poured a 2-litre bottle of fountain pen ink all over her.'

She snorted with laughter.

'Did you get into trouble?'

'Oh yes. My parents had to go to the school for an interview with the Headmistress. I lost all my privileges at home for three months.'

'That's such a long time.'

'When they asked me why I'd done it, I didn't tell them. Nobody knew I did it to punish the person who made my little sister cry.'

'I like that, very protective of you.'

'It's what I do.'

She hugged me hard.

Chapter 28. Attempt 2
Trip

Week 40. California

We woke early the next morning, a bit groggy because of our disturbed night. Something had passed between us while we had cuddled and talked our way through the early hours, and our relationship had moved to a new level.

We ran to the gym, did prolonged exercises on the machines, and then sparred with the in-house trainer. While we were changing after our workout, Charlie said she wouldn't speak to me for a week.

'Why not?'

'You hurt me.'

'I didn't touch you.'

'I tried to keep up with you on the machines, and you hurt me.'

'And because of that, you aren't going to speak to me for a week?'

'And you almost killed the trainer.'

'She's only used to puny Californian women.'

'You put her on her ass, knocked her clean off her feet. I think she's not used to short, slender Asian women with muscles of steel and the stamina of a racehorse.'

I shrugged. 'I told her I had boxed a bit.'

'Yeah, you've boxed a bit like I've travelled a little. And you hurt me.'

'You already said that.'

'So because you hurt me, I'm not going to speak to you.

For a week.'

'Do we still have kisses and cuddles and sleep together?'

'Yes.'

'Well, that's good. Do we still have sex?'

The changing room door swung open, and a Pilates body walked in; designer everything including sunglasses.

'Of course, we still have sex.'

The Pilates body gave us a cool look and took herself into a private changing room.

'So the only real penalty of you not knowing when to quit is that you won't speak to me for a week?'

'That's right.'

I shrugged. 'Well, it's a cross. I'll just try to bear it.'

'Good. You do that.'

I pulled on my trainers and stood.

'What do you want to do next?'

'You seem to be speaking to me.'

'Well, obviously. Otherwise, we can't communicate.'

'But you said…'

She stood, picked up her gym bag, and hung it over her shoulder.

'What did I said?'

Even under the harsh neon in the antiseptic changing room, she looked beautiful.

'Nothing. You said nothing. I was imagining it.'

'Good. I'm glad we've cleared that up. What would you like to do with the rest of the day?'

'Can we walk along the beach while I listen to you not talking to me?'

'That would be nice.'

'OK, then.'

It took twenty minutes to walk to Venice Beach; so good to see and smell the ocean for the second time in twenty-four hours. The last couple of weeks had felt odd being so far inland.

'It's really lovely. I've lived here for years but never slowed down enough to enjoy this.' She gestured at the beachfront.

'For someone who isn't talking to me, you're doing a reckless amount of talking.'

'Who said I'm talking to you?'

'Who else might you be talking to?'

'Me. Maybe I'm just talking aloud to me.'

'Oh.'

'But you should feel comfortable about joining in.'

'Oh!'

'So what was I saying?'

'You were just thinking about asking yourself if you'd like to have an early lunch here instead of going home for something to eat.'

'Yes, that's right. And what was I thinking?'

'I think you were thinking it would be a lovely idea.'

'Correct. How well you know me.'

We stopped and leaned on the boardwalk railing.

Southern California beach life was happening in front of us. Not quite a scene from Baywatch, but there were plenty of clichés strutting their stuff.

'I like people watching.'

'I like people watching too.'

'You're supposed to be people watching when you say that.'

'I am people watching.'

'No, you're watching me.'

'You are people,' I protested.

'You're being selective with the facts. I'm a person. I'm not a group of people. Let's find food. I'm famished.'

She pushed off the railing, looped her arm through mine, and we walked northwards up the sidewalk.

'What food would you like?'

'Something that's not going to sit too heavy. I'd like to swim later. Noodles? Or a rice meal?'

'Tapas?'

I thought for a moment.

'Tapas would be really nice.'

'Great. I know a place on Third and Ashland.'

The restaurant menu offered us a peculiar mix of Spanish and Mexican dishes, but the food was worthy of the better tapas bars in Granada, Spain. Over the meal I asked the question that had been on my mind for a while.

'I was wondering if you'd like to have a trip out, a few nights away once I've got used to being in the US? What do you think?'

She considered it for a moment. 'That would be lovely. Is this a road trip, or is there somewhere specific you want to see?'

'Not really somewhere specific. I just want us to keep having some quality time together.'

She looked at me, and I felt as if I were being cross-examined.

'What?' I asked.

'You. Are you up to something?'

'Not really up to something. I want us to talk. I want us to keep getting to know each other. I think we would be more relaxed if we went away somewhere.'

'OK, I like this. Shall we talk about where we are going?'

'As long as it's quiet...' I let the sentence trail off.

'Can I choose? As a surprise?' She suddenly became animated.

I reached across the table and held her hand. 'I would like that. Surprise me.'

Later, I was sprawled on the couch while Charlie did a lot of keyboard-tapping from the table. Eventually, she said, 'There is a place, and there's a but.'

'Uh-huh? But?'

'Well, it's over five hours away.'

'That's a problem because?'

'Because it's a ten-hour round trip. We'd be losing a day on the travel.'

'Is there good accommodation there?'

'Yes. It's rural but comfortable.'

'Is it available for the nights you want?'

She tapped for a moment.

'Yes.'

I eased my credit card out of my jeans and flipped it onto the table.

'Book it.'

'Are you sure? It's such a long journey.'

'I'll do you a deal. You book it, and I'll get us there. And back.'

She smiled. 'That would be lovely. If you're sure?'

'Just do it,' I said. And then asked, 'Where is it?'

'It's about three-quarters of the way between LA and Sacramento. A quiet mountain town, Mariposa, in the foot-hills of the Sierra Nevada mountain range.'

I suddenly remembered the three months I'd spent training

in Spain's Sierra Nevada mountains and smiled. 'Sounds perfect,' I said.

Chapter 29. Attempt 2
Butterfly

Week 40. California

Three days later, we loaded up my rental car and left before seven.

'I'm sorry we're a bit late getting away, it'll be after one by the time we get there, and oh, you're going the wrong way. We need to go north on Venice Boulevard and then north on the I-45.'

'Charlie, this is going to be lovely. I'm looking forward to it.'

'It will be if we ever get there.'

I ignored the gentle snark and carried on.

'But it's also going to be us talking and sharing things about our past.'

'This sounds heavy.'

'Talking sometimes is.'

She sighed. 'Yeah, sometimes it is. But you're still going the wrong way.'

'Trust me.'

'That's your new name.'

'What is?'

'You are now called "Trust Me Laura". I've decided.'

'Is that meant to be harsh?'

'No. Just accurate. Oh. I see what you've done. This is the San Diego Freeway where we need to go north. Turn left here.'

I turned right and continued south.

'Don't sulk.'

She did a pretend pout. A little while later I turned off the I-405 onto North Lakewood Boulevard and then left into Long Beach Airport.

'An airport? We're flying to Mariposa?'

'We are.'

'You're kidding me!' She looked incredulous.

'Would I? Trust me, we'll be in Mariposa in ninety minutes.'

'That'll be before ten!'

'Yeah, that's about what I figured.'

'This slightly crazy bunch of nights away idea just got way crazier.'

I drove through security and parked outside Long Beach Aviation Services.

'I'll be back in a moment. Or you can come with me?'

She came with me; eyes lit with excitement. At Long Beach Aviation Services reception desk, I signed off the hangarage, paid the bill for the ECs stay and told them we'd return in a few days. We walked to the car, popped the trunk, and got the cases out.

'This doesn't look like a proper airline to me,' she whispered.

'It isn't,' I whispered back, even though there was nobody else around. I led the way towards the pad where the EC stood waiting patiently. 'This is an aviation services office. They look after aircraft.' I pointed at the helicopter in front of us. 'This is the airline.'

'Oh, my God.'

'You've been in helicopters before? When you worked in the oil industry?'

'Yes, but that was for work. That was different.'

I opened the luggage compartment, slid the suitcases in, and closed the hatch. 'How is it different?'

'I don't know. It just is different.'

I opened the front passenger door and said, 'Would you like to take a seat, madam? The cabin crew will be around shortly to take your drinks order.'

She climbed in. I shut the door behind her and did my walk-around. Everything looked good to go. I opened the pilot's door and slid in. Charlie looked horrified.

'It's going to get noisy in a minute. If you put that headset on, we'll be able to speak to each other.'

'You are going to fly us?'

'Yep.'

'You?'

'Me. Now put the headset on.'

I showed her how to adjust the microphone and volume, and then I took the pre-flight checklist from the overhead compartment. Under my fingertips, the control panel came to life; all the lights and indicators flickered and settled to normal.

'Is there anyone or anything outside, on your side of the helicopter?'

She looked. 'No.'

I checked over my shoulder and said to no-one in particular, 'Clear right, clear left.'

I flipped the master switches to 'On', started, and began to bring both engines up to sixty percent power and worked through the checklist as the blades began to beat the air overhead.

A few minutes later, I asked, 'You good to go?'

'Oh, yes!'

I increased the revs, held the EC on the ground for a couple of beats longer than strictly necessary, then smoothly lifted her four feet into the air. The tower gave us permission to leave. We took off, left the airport, headed northeast and levelled off at 15,000 feet.

Charlie had been in enough helicopters to recognise we had reached cruising altitude.

'Can I talk?'

'Of course.'

'How long have you been flying?'

I checked the chronometer on the control panel. 'About five minutes now.'

'Did someone once tell you that you were funny?'

I looked at her. Too early for the whole truth. 'I started flying when I was fifteen. I got my licence when I was sixteen.'

'So you've done this a lot?'

'I have more flight hours than most aviators three times my age.' That massive understatement was at least true.

'And is this yours?' She gestured at the control panel in front of us.

'This is actually mine.'

'Oh. And we're flying to Mariposa?'

'Yes,' I said. 'We are definitely flying to Mariposa.'

'Good,' she said. 'I like that idea.'

———————————————

Local control at Mariposa-Yosemite airport asked us to

track in over Runway 2-6 and land in front of the main terminal. I followed their instructions over the threshold and touched down in front of the single-storey airport operations building with the gentle kiss of a feather landing on a blade of grass.

When the EC was powered down, I completed the post-flight checks, got our luggage out and locked up. We walked to the main building where the keys to the pickup I'd rented were waiting with the airport operator's enquiry office.

'You can drive,' I said, passing Charlie the keys.

'Want to look at the town and get some supplies?'

'Yeah, that's a great idea. Maybe find somewhere for a sandwich and a hot drink?'

'I don't think they have that English tea you drink up here in Yosemite.'

'I'd settle for a kiss and a hot chocolate?'

She leaned over and gave me a passionate kiss.

'You can have more of that later.'

'Mmm, I'm looking forward to that already.'

She smiled, started the truck, and pulled away from the airport. We parked in the centre of what turned out to be a cute rural town; the place felt honest and natural, and everyone smiled at us as we walked down the street. I could see why Charlie had chosen Mariposa. It was a nice place to come and relax. At this altitude, in the foothills of Yosemite, the air was crisp and clear and just a touch chilly.

In a homely diner we had orange juice, eggs, toast, and a hot chocolate each. We talked about what we were going to do during the days we were here, and I knew she was wondering what we'd do for the nights.

We decided to make it a real break; eat out, walk a lot, talk a lot, and be totally honest with each other. We had a lot to talk about.

Chapter 30. Attempt 2
Will

Week 40. California

'I've never stayed in a log cabin before.'

'That's OK. I have.' She unlocked the door into a large sitting room, kitchen/diner, and bedroom. 'The bathroom will be through there.' She pointed at the only other door.

I looked around the cabin. 'Actually, this looks really nice.'

And it was. The furnishings looked showroom-fresh, the kitchen well-stocked with utensils, and the temperature inside was comfortable.

'It's going to be lovely,' she said. 'No TV, no radio, no Internet. Just you and me.'

'No Internet?'

'No Internet,' she repeated. 'I'm going to confiscate your phone and put it with mine.'

I raised an eyebrow.

'Where are you going to hide them?'

'Well, der. If I told you that, they wouldn't be hidden, would they?'

'Can we at least keep our phones while we're out walking? You know, in case of accidents?'

She considered this. 'All right. That's a good safety

precaution.'

'Thank you.'

'Get unpacked and get your walking boots on. We're going hiking.'

'You know, you're a different person up here. Is it the altitude?'

'No, it's this place.' She waved a hand at the outside to make her point. 'It's the mountains, the forests, the peace and quiet. It's a bit like being in your house in Rio, but with more mountains and taller peaks.'

'You Americans have to have the biggest and best of everything.'

'Yes, that's right, we do.'

'There's just one thing missing from this bigger and better picture.'

'What's that?'

'The sea.'

'Yeah, you've got me there. It's a long drive to the coast. And you love your boat.' She laughed. 'I love the way you did that.'

'Did what?'

'Winced when I called Musa a boat. It was deliberate. I'm sorry.'

'I'll make you pay for that.'

'How?'

'We're not going for a hike.'

'We're not?'

'No. We're going trail running.'

'What? But that's not fair!'

I laid out my shorts, t-shirt, and trainers and started to get changed. 'Oh, shush. Get changed. The air is fantastic up here. Let's get some lungs full of the stuff.'

She began to change her clothes.

'You're a hard woman, you know?'

'I think you've said that before, beautiful.'

She looked like she'd been splashed by cold water.

'What now?' I asked.

'You called me beautiful.'

'Yes. Yes, I did. Now get changed because I'm going to kick your cute little backside all over this mountain.'

'Something about short people overcompensating.'

'And for that, my tall girlfriend, you can pay for dinner just as soon as I've finished kicking your little backside around.'

'Wait, what? It's not even noon yet!'

'Tie your laces tight. We're in for the long haul.'

She groaned unenthusiastically.

'It's at moments like this I think smokers only have a cigarette because they have nothing to say to each other.'

Silence.

'You know you just made my point?'

More silence.

'Are you OK?'

'To be honest, no.'

'What's up?'

'My body still feels broken and aching after this morning's trail run, and I've just had a meal intended for giants.'

'The quantities were massive.' I conceded.

'Should we sit here until they throw us out?'

'Maybe not that long. But can we stay for a while? I'm stuffed too.'

The restaurant had a rustic feel but was comfortable, and the staff didn't seem to be rushing us out of the door.

'I think we'll both sleep well tonight.' She said.

'Mmmm. What time do you want to get up in the morning?'

'I have to think about that right now?'

'No. I suppose not. I'll go for a run early; I'll try not to disturb you when I get up.'

'Oh, Jesus. We're on holiday, don't you ever switch off?'

'I just want to hit the trail while the air is cold.'

She reached forwards and put her hand on mine. 'You do that. As strongly as I feel about you, you are in a different league of fitness to me.'

I turned my hand over and held hers.

'I love you.'

'I love you too. Scary stuff.'

'I am?'

'It is. We are. It feels like we're moving at hundreds of miles an hour. We're covering ground in this relationship that, before you, would have taken me months or years.'

'Would it surprise you if I said it was the same for me?'

'I suppose it would.'

'Why?'

'You are confident, self-assured. Nothing gets to you. Nothing seems to upset you. And you have an answer for everything.'

'Hmm. Maybe. But those things don't mean I'm not having my breath taken away by the pace of you and me.'

We paused the conversation to reflect on how we felt about us.

'How did you find this place?' I asked.

'This restaurant?'

'Mariposa.'

'Oh. I was going to come here a few years ago. It sounded like a nice place, and I was really looking forward to it, but it didn't happen. So I wanted to see if it was as nice as I thought it might have been, and I wanted to see it with you.'

'That's lovely, thank you.'

'I'm glad we're here.'

'So am I. Was it a boyfriend?'

'What?'

'Who you were going to come here with.'

'A sort of boyfriend. We haven't talked about past relationships.'

'No.'

'Do you want to?'

'We came here for a break and to talk. We can talk about anything we want.'

'OK, let's not do relationships this evening. I'm feeling possessive, and I don't want to think of you with anyone else.'

'Possessive? You? Really?'

'What, you think American girls can't get deeply passionate about who we're with?'

'Oh, I know you're deeply passionate. I'm just surprised you're feeling possessive.'

'I want to know everything about you that I don't already know, but I don't want to know a single thing about your past loves and lovers. Not yet.'

I looked at the tall, willowy, blonde Californian sitting opposite me and wondered just how much I could tell her about my past without freaking her out. 'I have no family left.'

'I'm sorry to hear that.'

I paused for a few moments before continuing. 'I got an email from my solicitor in Rio yesterday.'

'Yes?'

'It's an updated copy of my Will.'

'Oh?'

'If something happens to me, I'm making a series of donations to some animal rescue centres across Latin America and Europe.'

'Oh, that's sweet.'

'I have a thing about animals. In their domesticated form, they're totally dependent on us. We owe them a duty of care.'

'Yes, I see that.'

'And I'm giving some donations to some children's charities.'

'Hmm. Would that be for pretty much the same reason?'

I smiled. 'Pretty much the same reason, yes. The house in Rio and Musa and whatever money is left after those donations, that comes to you.'

'What? I mean, that's amazingly generous, but why would you do this?'

'I have no family.' I repeated and shrugged my shoulders.

'But wouldn't you want them to be sold to raise money for your charities?'

'If that's what you want to do, you can do that. I want them to come to you because they, like you, are part of my life.'

'Well. I don't know what to say. That's lovely. Thank you.' She clasped my hand.

'You don't need to say anything.'

'But nothing is going to happen to you, right? You're not ill? You were, but you're not now?'

'I'm not ill now, no.' I smiled to reassure her of the long life that stretched far ahead of me that I knew I didn't have.

'Think of this as an insurance policy. Like car insurance, or life insurance, or something.'

'OK. Well, if you're sure.'

'I'm certain.'

'So are we going to get any animals?'

'I would like that.'

'Should we decide where we are going to live first?'

'Maybe we should. We have the whole world to choose from.'

'Let's talk about this some more later.'

'That would be cool.'

'Are you ready to return to the cabin now?'

I was. She paid. I was glad I'd raised one of the things we needed to talk about without distressing her.

Chapter 31. Attempt 2
Charlie

Week 41. California

At 3am we started talking again.

We'd been awake for an hour. Uncharacteristically, Charlie had fussed and fidgeted herself into wakefulness and, because I'm a light sleeper, I spooned her as we came to full consciousness together.

'I'm still full.'

'Dinner was massive,' I conceded.

'Do you want to go back to sleep?'

'Eventually, but I'm happy holding you. And if you want to talk that's fine too.'

'I want to talk a bit. This is cozy but I'm not sleepy.'

I understood what she meant. There was something about the darkness and the perfect peace and quiet that surrounded us. It was as if we could share our thoughts with each other, like being in some kind of an anonymous confessional.

'I've never enjoyed anyone's company as much as I enjoy yours.'

I nuzzled her shoulder. 'Thank you.'

'That's not a sex thing. I mean I enjoy being with you. It doesn't feel like I need to make any compromises around you. We fit; we just are.'

'Mmmm.'

She wriggled around to face me. 'That's a big deal to me.'

'I understand.'

'Do you?'

'Yes.' I kissed her cheek. 'No matter how much you love someone, how devoted you are to someone, even little compromises can cause a ripple. And sometimes those little ripples, those minor relationship changes that we're happy with and we accept for today... Well, sometimes those minor changes can get to be a little bruising after a while.'

'Wow, that's deep.'

'But accurate?'

She sighed. 'Too accurate. Not accurate enough.'

'Have you been bruised much? Before us?'

She said nothing for what seemed a long while, but I could sense she was thinking. Eventually she spoke.

'I haven't really fitted into any relationships, not a single one, ever. Even the best ones have bruised me. The worst have almost broken me. And you came into my life and you were just so... lovely. You were so wonderful to me, you took me at face value, you haven't asked me to change a single thing, and you were gorgeous and different and interesting and clever and, and, and you were so interested in me.'

'I cared.'

'What?'

'From the first moment I saw you. I saw vulnerability in you. I saw the hurt behind your eyes.'

'I've never had anyone pursue me because they wanted to make my life better. People have said that before, but nobody meant it. Not genuinely.'

I lay my head on her breast and listened to her heartbeat. 'What hurt you so much?' I asked.

'Bad things. Bad relationships, some with good people, some with bad people. The last one was an affair. I loved him, I didn't think he'd ever leave his wife for me, but I loved him. He said he loved me too, but for him it was just a game. The thrill of the chase. The capture.'

There was a long gap before she spoke again. 'The thing is with emotions; you end up owning them and you own everything they touch, everything that happens to you. It's great if the things that happen to you are good, but when they're shitty things you just end up owning a big pile of shit.'

I kissed her breast in the most non-sexual way I could.

'I'm sorry,' I whispered.

She ruffled my hair. 'We fucked up. I got pregnant. He was going to leave his wife. In the end he didn't. He ended it, cut me out of his life and left me with nothing except our unborn child. I cried every day. When I lost the baby, I almost didn't stop crying. It was like the last thing from our relationship had been taken away from me and all I ended up owning was shit and regret and guilt. Guilt I've been carrying around with me ever since.'

I felt my eyes get salty. My lovely woman didn't deserve this pain. 'When,' I cleared my throat and tried again. 'When was this?'

'Eight years ago.'

'I want to help you; I want to cushion you and wrap you up so you're safe from hurt.'

'I know you do. Crazy, but I know you do.'

I brushed my hand softly against her cheek, wet from her tears.

'I can't have children now.'

For a different reason, neither can I, I thought. 'I love you, Charlie.'

Her arm held me in a soft hug. After a while I rolled over so my back was toward her, she took the unspoken invitation and spooned me. It felt wrong; my natural instinct was to protect, but I now knew what her pain was, and had figured out she needed to love the baby she was still grieving for.

While I waited for her to sleep, I thought about the nature of relationships and how they aren't just about lust, hunger of all kinds, fear of love, fear of not being loved, and really, really fucking up. Relationships are sexy, sweet, sad and skewering. They are a tug-of-war between wanting to get lost in the feelings but not wanting to be wholly devoured by them. No relationship should have gone the way any of hers had, yet too many do.

Eventually I heard her breathing deepen and become rhythmic. I felt I could relax; I fell asleep in her embrace, not wanting our relationship to ever end. The next morning, we didn't discuss what had passed between us in the night, but there was a new 'us', we had a deeper connection and I loved her more than I did yesterday.

We spent the days exploring our area of the Yosemite National Park. The magnificent mountains were imposing, but the trails made them easy to hike up. The waterfalls looked cold and clear, and we easily convinced ourselves to stay out of them. Despite the surprisingly large number of cars and campers on the roads, we rarely encountered anyone else on our hikes.

At the end of our third day, I was sad to be leaving our rural retreat, but Charlie was getting anxious for home - her home, her belongings, and her possessions - and I understood her anxiety. We drove to Mariposa-Yosemite airport and dropped off the hire car keys with the office in airport operations. I paid the charges for having the EC looked after; we took our cases out and stowed them inside.

The Eurocopter sprang into life beneath my fingertips. With the engines running at temperature, I got permission to leave and performed my customary take off. Ninety trouble-free minutes later, we arrived back at Long Beach Airport. I arranged for the EC to have another check over and have its levels topped up.

Half an hour later, we were at Charlie's house.

Chapter 32. Attempt 2
Recording

Week 41. California

'What's the plan, Batgirl?'
 I raised myself up onto my elbows and looked at her.
'Who?'
 'I've decided you need a nickname. I want to call you by a name nobody has ever used.'
 'You called me a few names yesterday evening.'
 She looked at me deadpan. 'Yes, but I can't repeat any of those when I'm not in the throes of lust.'
 'Batgirl would be on the list of things I've never been called, then.'
 'I'm not sure we're sticking with Batgirl, but for now it'll do. Now answer the question, what's the plan?'
 'I thought we were going to stay here, on the beach today?'
 'This is good. And tomorrow?'
 'Well, there's a little trip I want to take. We could do that tomorrow? You could come and we could make it into a picnic?'
 'Oooh, I like! Where are we going?'
 'The desert. And then maybe the mountains.'
 She lay back on the sand and said, 'Well you, Batgirl, are just full of surprises.'

At eleven the next morning, I touched down the EC outside Hangar One at Cuttle, in the Mojave Desert.

'This is nice,' said Charlie as she looked out of the forward canopy. 'If you like Desert Chic, I guess this is the place to come.'

'We're not getting out,' I said, holding the EC on the ground. 'Behind your seat is my rucksack. There's a laptop inside. Can you open it up and switch it on?'

A couple of minutes later, she said, 'Good to go.'

'Great. There's a red icon on the desktop called 'Record', can you trigger that?'

After a pause, she said, 'Yep, done that. it says 'recording'.'

'Just hold the laptop on your lap, we're going to be about ten minutes.'

I lifted the EC twenty-feet off the ground, rotated one-hundred-eighty-degrees, and at 20 feet, flew the length of what used to be the main runway. Still flying forward, I lifted to one hundred feet, flew out over the threshold and, still climbing, flew increasingly large circles of the former air-base. The last lap around Cuttle was over three miles from the centre, and 5,000 feet above the ground.

'You can switch off recording now.'

'Done. Would you like to tell me what just happened?'

'You've just recorded the entire GPS coordinates for a six-mile radius from the point where we began recording.'

'Well, that's nice. I always wanted a six-mile radius of GPS coordinates for a place in the desert I've never been to before.'

'This isn't for you. This is for me.'

'Are you going to tell me why?'

'Of course, I will. Lunch?'

'Yep, I could do with lunch.'

I flew us west for five minutes, then circled a large flat

outcrop just below Edgar Peak in the Providence Mountains State Recreation Area. Landing gear lowered, we slowly descended onto the outcrop, where I powered down the EC. We stepped out on to the mountainside and into the full force of Californian desert heat; I unpacked the two folding chairs and the folding table we'd brought from Charlie's garden.

'We can do this?' she asked. 'We can stop wherever we like and camp or picnic or whatever?'

'Yep. As long as we don't stray into any military zones or restricted airspace, we can just do this.'

She unpacked the picnic while I spread out a rug.

'If anyone had told me we'd just fly onto a mountain and have a picnic… Well, I wouldn't believe them.'

'It's a new level in 'getting away from it all', isn't it?'

'And then some more. Check out those views!'

I checked them out. The impressive Fountain Peak due south, the Mescal Range to the north, and far below us, the floor of the Californian desert to the east and west. Despite the height of the peak we were on, there was almost no freshening wind, just the near-relentless heat percolating up from the desert floor.

'Would you like to be sitting? Or lying down?'

'Let's sit first?'

'Sitting first it is. Now would you like to tell me why we did what we just did? That recording GPS thing?'

'Yes. I've got a lot to tell you. Many things. Try not to get freaked out, OK?'

She looked puzzled. 'What could you have to tell me that might freak me out?'

'I need to talk about me and my past and I have a lot of

past to share with you. And then I need to tell you why I'm doing things, and why I live what you call this nice life.'

She just sat there, beginning to look a little uncertain. 'And then I need us, both of us, to talk about you and me. And that's really important to me. To us.'

'OK.' She said, drawing the syllables out. 'This sounds like a lot of deep conversation.'

'It is. And when I've finished you need to remember that what I'm doing is my fight. I don't want you to take part in any of it at all, right?'

'Right. So now this sounds criminal.'

'Well, yes. It is. Sort of.' I took a deep breath. 'I'm going to steal an unmanned aerial vehicle, a UAV, from the US Air Force.'

She looked at me sceptically.

'And then I'm going to use it to destroy one man, the man who killed my family.'

She dropped the butter.

Chapter 33.
Nebak

Previous cycles. Saudi Arabia

Two hundred kilometres south of the desert town of Nebak, in the Kingdom of Saudi Arabia is, according to all the maps in the world, nothing at all, except for lots of Saudi desert.

But all the maps in the world are wrong.

Stretching thirty kilometres in all directions is a well-guarded, heavily disguised compound. The base is kept safe and secure by an army of military contractors who are backed up by electronic sensors and real-time aerial and satellite surveillance.

Hidden inside this enormous enclosure is a small town. There's a military airfield and extensive hangarage for offensive, transport, and refuelling aircraft. There's a fleet of helicopters; a dozen heavy cargo lifters and ten smaller, nimbler, highly armed seek-and-strike helicopters. None of these would be out of place in any modern air force.

The compound's ground defences include batteries of ground-to-air missiles, and several hundred armoured vehicles of all shapes and sizes. Every single piece of equipment means the deadliest business. And there are thousands of personnel to service and operate this military hardware. In the armouries are enough weapons to start - and win - a small war. At the northern edge of the base, on top of a rocky outcrop overlooking a dry wadi is a set of communications antennae and five large, camouflaged Radome golf-balls.

But you wouldn't know these things existed if you weren't actually there. The airfield, its buildings, and all other signs of life are designed to avoid detection. The entire compound is hidden from the sharpest prying eyes and satellites.

Deep underground is a multi-storey installation. The first sublevel contains living quarters and social amenities for the personnel. The military contractors based here have more home comforts than the real military have on their postings in the region.

Sublevel two contains the working areas; offices where analysts carry out their supply and intelligence roles.

Below the offices are two sections that are - literally - the powerhouse of the organisation. The solar power generated on the surface is stored and distributed around the compound from this section. There are also backup generators which, in turn, are themselves backed up by vast banks of emergency batteries.

In an adjoining hall are the computers. Aisles of rack-mounted servers handle data collected from real-time sources around the world. The data is processed, analysed, and presented for action to a team of intelligence analysts and planners who work in a special section up on sublevel two. That section is known as The Bridge.

The Bridge is where strategy meets tactics. The hot decisions of conflict and the cold choices of intelligence operations are made here. The outputs of such decisions are transmitted to military contractors on the ground and to intelligence assets in the field. All comms are channelled through a network of relay stations around the globe, and a string of private satellites.

The instructions might be small, such as to an intelligence asset 'Go to that place at this time. Meet this person. Say or do this. Pay them that. Report back.'

Or they might be large instructions, such as to an unmanned aerial vehicle - a military drone - to 'Fly to this height, acquire this target, fire missile one, fire missile two, and then return to base.'

Such instructions used to be communicated directly to the UAVs by remote pilots. US Air Force drones are flown by pilots based in the US, no matter where in the world the drones are operating. But that's old school. New school is better. Cleverer. Cleaner.

The UAVs of Whiteland Security Company are formidable. These UAVs are directed not by humans, but by artificial intelligence. No matter where they are, no matter what their role, no matter what weaponry they're carrying or what job they're intended for, the huge fleet of Whiteland UAVs is controlled by humans, but flown by AI.

This is the direction that military conflicts have moved in. It's cheaper than using real troops or real aircraft. It's a PR win, because it's a form of warfare that doesn't put the real military in harm's way, and it removes personalisation from death and destruction. AI is the way forward in 21st Century warfare.

It's beautiful when it works because everybody wins. Except the enemy. The next time the military shares a video of a target being destroyed, and the accompanying press release says, 'We've just taken out an insurgent and his entire rebel force in the desert. Yay!', remember these things happened through AI, because this is how war is increasingly being fought. Defence contracts all round. And it's great for everyone.

Except when a human makes a terrible decision. Of course, there are safeguards built into the system; processes designed to prevent mistakes from happening. Data is continually assessed. Signals get sent and received and analysed.

The updated picture is run through many scenarios; information is continually tested for accuracy. And when it can be tested no more, and it's still 'anomalous', the data is presented to a human for oversight. So yes, there are procedures that prevent accidents from happening. Except humans do make terrible decisions. And sometimes those terrible decisions are not accidental.

Like, for example, when an intelligence analyst takes a tablet to his CO on The Bridge and says, 'This looks like our UAV is lining up on the wrong target', and that goes up the chain to another human, and then further up the chain to a different human, and then a call is made to the human at the top of the chain who listens and says 'Our intel isn't wrong. Take it down', and the UAV and its missiles are allowed to carry out their AI-directed actions of death and destruction… Well, that's when two hundred and twenty-seven civilians are put to death.

That's the moment when my mother, my father, my sister, and two hundred and twenty-four other people have their lives ripped from them. One moment they were sitting in their aircraft, maybe awake, reading or watching a film. Maybe asleep. Ordinary people, flying to their destination at more than six-hundred miles an hour, 36,000 feet above the Indian Ocean. One minute alive, the next moment dead or dying, as their aircraft plummets downwards, destroyed by an air-to-air missile, because a man at the top of a chain of command said, 'Take it down'.

I often wonder how they died. Unconscious or awake and screaming in fear. My sister, if she were conscious, would have tried to figure it out. Her brain was always working; she was the intelligent one in the family.

There would have been no cabin oxygen at that height, but she would still have been trying to figure it out, right up until the end. She would have been tossed from floor to ceiling by the explosion as the plane plummeted downwards. She never wore her seatbelt unless she had to. Did she try to hold my mother's hand? Or my father's? Did she try to protect them?

If they had survived the missile detonation, they would have been horribly injured by the depressurisation; the in-cabin shrapnel would have killed people. I hope my family died instantly. It would have spared them a terrible death.

The impact with the sea would have been brutal. The plane would have split into millions of fragments. Survivors would have lost limbs in the force of the crash. Their insides torn about; their brains almost mashed to soup by the terrible force.

Please let my family have died before the sea. Survivors would have drowned. It was dark when the plane was shot down in an area of the Indian Ocean that has almost no shipping traffic. We know the aircrew didn't get a distress call out. We know that very little wreckage has been recovered. We know that the flight recorders never will be.

We know that some horribly mutilated bodies have been discovered thousands of miles from the aircraft's last known position, carried far by the sea currents. We know that my sister was amongst those souls. But there has been no trace of my mother. No trace of my father. So few bodies have been recovered. There have been many tributes to the missing. Tributes to those brothers, sisters, mothers, fathers, uncles, aunts. Married people. Singletons. Young. Old. Retired. Students.

Two hundred and twenty-seven people blown out of the sky. Just like that. Because one man, on the end of a phone, said so. Nobody is ever going to charge him with his crime. Hardly anyone knows his role in this.

Maybe six people knew about the missile attack; a couple of intelligence analysts, the duty officer on The Bridge, and his CO. Outside of the compound there would have been the man on the end of the telephone. And, later, there would have been the CEO. Some of those six people have been involved in unfortunate fatal accidents, instigated by his head of security, whose aeroplane I blew up in Rio. The head of security is more dangerous than any of them.

But the CEO of Whiteland Security Company; he's coming out of his desert hiding place and will be in the US soon. That's why I'm going to steal a military UAV. To pay him back. For my mother. For my father. And for my sister.

And the final man in the chain? The one who gave the order to shoot the plane down? I'm going to deal with him separately.

Chapter 34. Attempt 2
Words

Week 41. California

The trip back to LA was in conversational silence. We continued not speaking on the ride back to Charlie's house.

I pulled into her drive but sat in the car, hands on the wheel, as Charlie got her stuff out. I'd really fucked this relationship up by being honest, perhaps more honest than I should have been. I wondered if honesty has degrees, like the acute angles of a circle.

I was pulled out of my daydream by the sound of the car closing. Not a slam, but a definite hard push. She leaned in through the passenger window.

'I've never known anyone like you.'

'I don't think there is anyone like me.' I said, truthfully.

'You don't care, and yet you care so much.'

'I care a lot; I care deeply. But I choose the things I care about. I only have so much caring to go around.'

'I don't understand.'

'What don't you understand?'

'It. You. What you have said. What you're doing. Really, Laura, I just don't understand. It's so…' She looked for the word.

'Different?' I offered.

'Alien. Your world is unlike anything I've known.'

'Does that make me a bad person?'

'Yes. No.' She paused. 'Actually, I don't know… Maybe not a bad person. But a different person. I thought I knew who you were. I thought I knew you. I thought the differences between us just made you exotic. I thought you were a flavour of life that I could get used to. Wanted to get used to.'

'And I'm not what you want to get used to?' I tried to keep my words even. I didn't want to lose her. I didn't want her to think I wanted this to end.

'Yes. No. I don't know.' She picked up her rucksack.

'Laura, I want you to know that I… I love you. I love the you that I thought you were. But right now? Right now, I'm not sure I know who you actually are. I love you but I don't know if I like you. Was that person I love… was that really you? Or was that you wearing a mask? Were you making me love you?'

'I've never been anyone but the person I have always been.' I responded. 'I like to think we've been so honest with each other that I have never been anyone except the person you have always believed me to be.'

She wiped her cheek. 'I hear you. But I don't know if the person I believed you to be could be capable of even talking about the things you say you are going do.'

'Charlie, I wouldn't be me if I wasn't capable. I would be a pale imitation, a shadow. I would be a person who couldn't love to the degree that I do. And I love you. I love you with all of my heart. I love you with everything I have to give. And I have so much love to give you.'

'You can't give me this love if you're in prison for the rest of your life.'

'I won't go to prison.' I said.

'Does that mean you're going to end up dead, shot full of holes?'

'No.'

'How do you know?'

'I don't know,' I said, and I didn't know. I had failed to complete this mission in the previous attempt.

'So it is possible then? You could be caught. And then there would be a trial. And you would be convicted. And I would lose you forever.'

Neither of us spoke for what seemed like an age. It felt incongruous to be outside her house on a hot sunny Southern California day, having a conversation that could end our relationship forever. I wanted to sweep away the dark clouds of emotion that were gathering over us. I looked up through the sunroof into the clear, cloudless, beautifully blue sky.

'I don't want to lose you.' I said.

'But how can there be an us when you're in prison? You are going to lose me.'

'What if that doesn't happen?'

'Laura, it will happen,' she said with certainty. 'People don't do the things you're talking about and get away with them. People get caught doing this kind of stuff. This isn't a film. This is real life. Our real life, yours and mine.'

'We have a real life,' I said, imploringly. 'Our life together isn't going to end here.'

'It shouldn't end here. And also, it shouldn't end in a court-room when you get sentenced for murder and whatever else they charge you with.'

'So why are we sitting here talking about this? If you are trying to change my mind, that's not going to happen.'

'Standing.'

'What?'

'I'm standing.'

'Oh. Right. So why are we having this conversation?'

'I don't know. But you've put a lot into my head, and I have to think about all of it. There's a lot to process. It's going to take me time to get my brain around this. Can you see that I need to think about this?'

'Yes, I see that.'

'Can you see that I don't know if I still like you?'

'But you still love me?'

'Yes. Yes, I do still love you. But it would break my heart to realise that the person I love so much isn't the person that I thought you were. I need to be careful; I need to look after me, and I'm just…'

'Fragile.' I finished.

'Yes, fragile.'

'You've said that before.'

'What?'

'That you were fragile. The first time we went out. Dinner.

In Rio.'

'Well, why the hell didn't you remember that I'm fragile?'

'I did. That's why I have told you the truth. I haven't told you one single lie.'

'That sort of makes it worse.'

'Worse? How?' I asked.

'I don't know. It just does. So let me ask you a question.'

'Go ahead.'

'This thing you're planning to steal?'

'The UAV?'

'Right. The UAV. It's an expensive piece of military hardware?'

'Yes.'

'How expensive?'

'A fraction under $16 million.'

She let that sink in.

'Each?'

'Yes. That's what one costs.'

'And it will have weaponry attached to it?'

'I'm counting on that.'

'So... Maybe it's just your Latin American laidback-ness or your even more laidback Asian heritage, but what the hell is it that makes you think you're going to be able to just stroll into some, presumably well-guarded place somewhere, and then just walk out with one of these things tucked under your coat?'

'I have a plan.'

'Would you tell me what your plan is?'

'No.'

She exhaled and her shoulders slumped. I counted eight beats while she stood motionless. Then she looked up and stared into my eyes.

'Can you find somewhere else to stay tonight?'

'Yes.'

'I need to think. I'm not going to be able to do that with you in the house.'

'I understand.'

'Where will you go?'

'Hotel somewhere. This town is full of them.'

'We'll talk tomorrow.'

'I would like that.'

'You might not.'

'If it means seeing you, I would like that.'

'I'll call you.'

She turned and walked to the back door. I waited until she was inside the house before reversing off her driveway.

Chapter 35. Attempt 2
Rescue

Week 41. California

I had nowhere to go so I automatically headed for the sea where I turned north onto the Pacific Coast Highway. I found an expensive-looking, arty hotel right on the beach, north of Santa Barbara. I checked in for two nights.

Women checking in without any luggage wasn't much of a thing, apparently. I didn't even get a raised eyebrow. I chose the most expensive room available. I lay on the bed, overthought too many things, and started getting annoyed with myself.

I was frustrated with how things had gone with Charlie. I got angry for being so clumsy. I hadn't known how she would react, sure, but I needed to tell her the truth. Or some of the truth. Most of the truth. And I'd gone the full distance and told her everything.

She needed to know what I was doing, and yes, I felt I had to tell her why I was doing it. I wanted to make her understand me and my motivation. And yet I had failed. Or perhaps she was right; that the person I had just shown her wasn't actually the person she loved? Even though I felt I was. Or maybe she loved someone who was almost but not quite me? Even though the me that I am loved her with all my heart.

Despite my anger, I felt certain that I could fix this. Perhaps not in this cycle now that things had gone so wrong, but definitely in the next one. And I wanted so much to fix this. I wanted the relationship between Charlie and me to be right. But right now I had so much rage and frustration growing inside of me because I had truly screwed up.

I washed my face, and went down to the hotel gym, bought a pair of shorts and a t-shirt, and then worked hard. There were no boxing facilities, so my frustrations stayed inside me, and I needed to get them out.

I changed into a complimentary swimsuit, walked on to the private beach and swam. I had nowhere to go; I just swam. Even after about half an hour in the sea, I couldn't relax into my usual easy rhythm. I swam hard and fast, and as I swam the saltwater washed away my tears, but the anger burned inside me.

My fury powered me outwards and onwards through the waves. Eventually anger ebbed and was replaced by full-scale self-directed rage for the first time in this cycle.

Despite years of careful planning and one previous attempt, I had already fucked this cycle up, and I hadn't even got close to my target yet. I swam angrily onwards in my bubble of rage, hitting the waves hard, fuelled by my foul temper. As I swam, I worked over the dialogue we'd been through. The more I played it back, the more I couldn't see an easier or a better way to have that conversation with Charlie.

Frustration made my thinking illogical; I began to revise earlier decisions. The next cycle, I told myself; the next cycle I am not going to tell her. It won't be the same, second time around. But I'll still be with her. I can still love her. The next cycle, against all my better judgement, I'm going to keep secrets. The next cycle it will be different. Next cycle I won't allow this to happen, I won't get myself into this…

Voice. Heard a voice. Couldn't be for me. Nobody knows I'm out here. Keep swimming. Not even feeling tired yet.

Clearer this time. 'You in the water. Stand by. I'm going to come about and pick you up.'

I stopped swimming, started to tread water, and took a look around. Even at the top of the next swell I couldn't see land, but I could see the hull of a large rigid inflatable boat easing towards me.

I lost sight of the boat as the swell dropped me a few feet; I realised I hadn't been aware that the sea had become so choppy. On the rise of the next swell, the RIB was within a few feet, and an arm was reaching down towards me.

The anger was still washing over me, but now, for the first

time since I'd checked into the hotel, I had someone else to focus it on. How dare they interrupt me? How dare they disturb my solitude and my thoughts? How dare they break my concentration and my exercise?

The RIB came close; I raised my right arm, and we locked together; I was skilfully lifted out of the water, over the side of the boat, and dumped onto my back. I pulled myself up into a sitting position and noticed the boat was really rolling about. The weather must have changed while I'd been in the water.

'Are you OK?' Concerned voice. American accent but not from these parts.

'Sure. Why shouldn't I be?' There was a very long pause while we bobbed about on the waves. I was about to ask him if he'd heard me when he replied.

'I thought you might be in trouble, so far out to sea.'

I took a good look. Dark brown eyes. Strong nose that had been broken and set badly. Good cheekbones. Short blonde hair. A pleasant face and a good, honest smile.

'I was just getting into my stride.'

There was another long pause before he spoke again. I wondered if he was controlling a speech problem.

'Really?'

'Yes, really.'

The pauses were unnaturally long. Perhaps he's masking a stammer, I thought.

'Where did you start your swim from?'

I had to think for a minute.

'Las Olas Drive.'

'Where?'

'It's a hotel. Near Hope Ranch,' I said, recalling the signs.

'You swam out here from Hope Ranch?'

I bit back all the smart answers. 'Yes. Where is "here"?'

'We're about seventeen miles out from Santa Rosa Island, in the Channel Islands National Park.'

I must have looked blank.

'You have swum almost seven miles out here.'

I was surprised but tried not to look it.

'Not the furthest I've swum,' I said, truthfully.

'I could throw you back in?' He offered.

I sat in his boat and realised I had got on top of my temper and had no need to punish myself any further.

'Where are you going?'

'Are you still aiming for wherever you're heading?'

'No. I think I'm done. For today at least.'

Although my anger had abated, I felt empty; the kind of emptiness you get when you're burned up inside, the hollowness you get when you realise you might have killed a relationship.

'Cool. I'm heading to Stearns Wharf. No trouble to give you a lift if you like?'

'Thank you, that's very kind. Where's Stearns Wharf?'

'Santa Barbara.'

'Oh.'

He held out his hand and helped me up on to the bench across the middle of the boat. Then he pulled a battered wax jacket from beneath his seat and held it out to me. 'It'll keep the worst of the wind off you.'

I took it gratefully while he put his hand on the outboard tiller and twisted the throttle grip. The powerful engine roared, and he turned the boat one-hundred-eighty degrees. As I slipped into the supersized coat, I noticed the best of the sun had passed below the horizon, and early twilight was setting in.

'How long will it take?'

He said nothing, and I was on the point of asking again when he spoke.

'To Stearns Wharf?'

'Yes.'

'In these conditions, about ninety minutes.'

That surprised me. I had no idea how long I'd been in the water.

After fifteen minutes or so, he spoke again. 'You must be an experienced swimmer. The currents around the islands can be hazardous.'

'Is that part of your safety speech?'

'What?'

'Describing the currents here as "hazardous".'

His smile widened slightly to show he was going to speak again. Eventually, he did. 'It's one of the standard sentences I use when I take visitors to the islands.'

'Is that what you do?'

'It's one of the things I do. A bit of fishing. A bit of diving. A bit of teaching fishing and teaching diving. And taking visitors out to the islands.'

'Do you ever bring them back again?'

'I'm sorry?'

'Your boat,' I gestured around me. 'It's empty.'

'Oh. I'm not doing that work today. I've been over to patch the roof of the old ranch house. One of the visitors said that the roof had lifted on the public bathrooms, so I've been repairing.'

'Do you own the island?'

'No. The National Park Service pays a few of us to do some maintenance. Today it was my turn. It's not a full-time job, but it helps pay the bills.'

'And tomorrow?'

'And tomorrow, I'm teaching scuba diving.'

'That sounds nice.'

'Want to join us? I can fix you up with a special Very Strong Swimmer discount.'

I chuckled.

'I think you made that rate up.'

'I did. But maybe you'd like to join us anyway?'

'That would be nice, but I can't tomorrow. I have to wait for a call.'

He looked disappointed.

'Raincheck?' I offered.

His smile widened again.

'Raincheck.' He confirmed.

After a long comfortable silence that must have been over a quarter of an hour, I asked him where he lived. Eventually, he answered. 'Five minutes from Stearns Wharf. I have a small apartment on Helena Avenue.'

'Nice and close to your boat?' I asked.

'I don't leave the area much. I've got everything I need close by.'

We lapsed into another easy silence. He didn't feel the need to talk, and I didn't feel the need to pry. He headed for the long pier that marked the entrance to the wharf, but instead of turning to run into the harbour, he made for a low-level floating pontoon at the seaward end of the quay.

He turned off the outboard as we smoothly and slowly came alongside the pontoon; he leaned outwards and passed a rope through a mooring eye. I took his hand and stepped out of the RIB; the pontoon felt cold and wet beneath my naked feet.

'Come with me, and I'll sort you out with getting back to your hotel.'

'There's no need. I'll get a cab.'

'Dressed like that?'

'I don't think I would be the first swimsuit-wearing woman who got a cab from Santa Barbara.'

He rubbed his chin. 'You'd be right, probably. But I meant that if you came with me, I'll get you a lift.'

'There's no need.'

'I'd like to.'

'But there's really no need.'

I was getting the hang of his long pauses. 'And I'd really like to.' This was no easy-going Californian.

'You're not from around here, are you?'

'Why do you say that?'

'Never mind. I can get a cab.'

'And I can get you back.'

'What's your name?'

'Mark.'

'Well, Mark. I'm grateful for the lift to shore, but I don't want to bother anyone. I'll get a cab.'

'Fine. But come to my apartment, and we'll call a cab from there.'

I'd already sized him up when he stood on the pontoon; six-foot-three, broad in the chest, athletically fit, and probably weighing two-hundred-ten pounds. Despite his impressive build and obvious fitness, I knew I could take him down before he could complete a threatening move.

'Are you going to give way on this?'

'No. Are you?'

'Maybe,' I conceded.

'Let's walk while you make up your mind.'

We climbed up an access ramp onto the pier and walked towards the shore, passing the restaurants, ice-cream parlour, fish and chip shops, and anglers shacks dotted along the walkway. Seagulls wheeled overhead as fishermen tended their rods or leaned on the railings and stared into the distance. There were few other people around in the early evening gloom.

At the main road, we turned right. After a short walk we took the first left and, a hundred metres later, he said, 'Home sweet home. You wait here. I won't be a minute.'

I stood on the sidewalk outside a slightly shabby restaurant while he jogged up an outside staircase to the first floor. I wondered what the locals thought of a barefoot woman wearing just a wax jacket standing around in downtown Santa Barbara.

After a couple of minutes he came back and said, 'Just around the corner.'

Just around the corner turned out to be the restaurant parking lot. He led me to a battered, unfashionably rust coloured, and well-dented 4x4 truck.

'What's this?'

'Your taxi. Get in.'

I was pleased and unsurprised at his generosity, but it also pissed me off a bit because I can sometimes be awkward.

I put my hands on my hips and tried to look intimidating.

He got into the 4x4, it roared into life with more gusto than it looked like it should, and pulled forward next to me.

'I'll take you to your hotel. Get in.'

'What if I lied about the hotel?'

'I'll take you where you want to go.'

'What if I am running away from an abusive husband and I don't have anywhere to go, and I don't want your help?'

'I'll take you to a refuge.'

'I believe you could be quite an irritating person.'

'I've been called that before.'

'What if I don't want to get in?'

'Do you want to get in?'

'Yes.'

'Well, get in then.'

I got in. He turned the truck towards the coast and then headed north. After a couple of miles, he stopped at a gas station and put fifteen dollars of fuel in the tank. While he was paying, I found a scrap of paper and a pencil, scribbled my name and number down, and put the piece of paper in the jacket pocket. Three-quarters of an hour later, we pulled up outside my hotel.

'This it?' He asked, peering through the windshield.

'Yes.'

'Well then, have a good evening.'

'Wouldn't you like to come in?'

'No, I'm good, thanks.'

'The least I can do is buy you dinner.'

'There's no need. I got you back here is all.'

'How about a coffee at least? Or a glass of lemonade? Or a beer?'

'Naw, I'm going to get home. Thanks for the offer.'

'You're embarrassing me.' I said.

'I'm going to embarrass you more.'

'How?'

'Can I have my coat back?'

I got out of the truck, slipped the jacket off, and passed it through the open window onto the seat.

'My name's Laura.'

'Hi, Laura. Nice to meet you.'

He drove away, leaving me to walk through hotel reception in my swimsuit.

Chapter 36. Attempt 2
Reveal

Week 41. California

After showering, I checked my phone: one missed call from Charlie. I called her back.

'Can we talk?'

'Yes, please.'

'Face to face?'

'Yes, please. Here, there, or somewhere in the middle?'

'Where's here?'

'A hotel up the coast, about an hour from your house.'

'Text me the address?'

'I will. And then?'

'And then I'll see you in an hour.'

'Nice hotel.'

'Thank you. I'd like to stay here with you.'

She gave me a look as if I was bonkers.

'To relax. To get away. To be somewhere different. To be pampered.'

'We could do those things anywhere. My house. We could even go to your house in Rio.'

'I know. But hotel service…'

'Ah, I get what you mean.'

The conversation paused for a while; the silence felt fragile, and neither of us wanted to break it.

'Why not go to Rio? Live in your house? And put all this behind us?'

'By all this, you mean…?'

'Your plan. Revenge. Let's just go and be us and concentrate on our life together.'

'Because one man destroyed my family. Took from me the three people I loved more than anyone else in the world. More, even, than I love you.'

'Tell the police, then. Bring him in front of the law so that everyone will see him, everyone will know the kind of person he is.'

'Charlie, he owns the law. Not even at a local level like he's best buddies with the Sheriff of Saddlesore, Indiana, or somewhere equally obscure. This guy actually owns the police in many countries. He is directly connected to presidents, prime ministers, heads of state. People in very powerful positions owe this man.

'Not debts of money, but debts of gratitude, debts so large that he could actually destroy the people who owe him. He has power over powerful people. He has his own army, and his own air force, and his own navy. This man owns a military power larger, and better equipped than many countries, and he does the dirty work of world leaders.

'He employs people who kill for a living. Even if I could take everything I know to a criminal court, there is no chance a case would be put together. Prosecutors would die, or members of their families would suddenly become unwell. People would unexpectedly resign. Or retire. Or disappear.

'Even if a case could be put together, he owns PR machinery and legal experts who would destroy any hope of a fair, balanced case in any court. There is no way this man would ever face trial.'

'I don't understand how you could know so much about him, about what you say he's done.'

'I worked for him.'

'And that's how you saw the evidence?'

'Hard evidence. With my own eyes. Yes, I saw it all.'

'Why did he do it? Why destroy a civilian aircraft? Why kill so many people?'

'There was someone onboard who was going to hurt him. And this is my whole point. He will destroy anyone who is a threat. And he doesn't care about collateral damage.'

'He would kill so many people because of one person?'

'He would order two hundred and twenty-seven deaths to stop one person on that flight from reaching their destination and passing information that would cripple him. Yes, he would do exactly that. He's done it more than once.'

She said nothing for a while. I sipped my glass of water and looked out of the bedroom window to where the sea would meet the sky, but I could see neither. It was after ten; we had been talking for almost an hour. The armchairs in my room were comfortable, but I really wanted to get up and walk.

Tiredness from my long swim had begun to set in, and despite the importance of our conversation, I was beginning to feel drained.

'I don't understand how you can be positive about two things.'

'Which two things?'

'How you can be so positive that he did it? How you can be so positive he wouldn't face trial? And how you can be so positive that you could do what you say you're going to do, and that you can get away with it?'

'That's three things. Or four. Depends how you're counting.'

'Can you be serious?'

'OK, then. But I need you to put some belief in me.'

'I do believe in you. I think that's why I'm scared. Scared that you will succeed.'

'That doesn't make sense.'

'It does to me.'

'I have spent years working on this.'

'You seem to have spent years working on many things.'

I ignored the true statement.

'I have spent huge amounts of money investigating everything about this man. I can tell you everything about his personal history, where he was born in the US, everything about his professional life. I can tell you about his family, his sons, his daughters, his parents, his wife, and even about his distant relatives.

'I can describe his wealth in detail; I can tell you in which countries his cash sits. I can tell you what assets he owns through anonymous corporations. I can tell you which onshore and offshore banks he owns - and he owns those banks as a cover for his own wealth.

'I could map out his connections across the globe. I have spent so much time in his military bases in the US and the Middle East that I could recite the room numbers in every building and can tell you what goes on in each room.

'I can tell you how his communications network works; everything about his ground stations around the globe, some clearly marked as civilian, some are bona fide military installations, and a lot of bases are neither of those things.

'I can tell you about his strings of communications and tracking satellites. And I have barely started to talk about his military assets. He owns more military might than some NATO countries. This man is a one-man nation. He is wealthier than kings, dictators, and emperors. He is invincible. Unstoppable. Invulnerable.'

I paused for a moment.

'Except that's not quite true. I can stop him. I can end him. I can make sure he doesn't continue.'

'Continue?'

'I am convinced he has done this before. Or arranged for it to be done.'

'This?'

'Brought down other civilian airliners. At least two more, apart from the flight my family were on. I think he's directly responsible for over six hundred civilian deaths. And I think he's also responsible for bringing down four civilian light aircraft, three of those in the US.'

She looked shocked. 'Why can't you prove he did these other things?'

'I have no evidence. It's that simple. He's far from stupid. Everyone who wasn't part of his inner circle who knew about the bringing down of this airliner has vanished. Only he and his head of security know everything.'

'You said you have spent huge amounts of money? Yet you have no evidence other than you've seen stuff?'

I couldn't tell her that evidence didn't come with me when I started a new cycle. 'It's the same every time,' I said. 'I find someone close enough to know what happened, then they disappear. His head of security is efficient and ruthless.'

'How can this head of security do that? And how can he know?'

'Every person who works for any of his companies, or their subsidiaries, is monitored. Without their knowledge or permission. It doesn't matter who, everyone who gets close gets the snooper software installed on their phone. And on their tablets. And on their laptops.'

'But that's huge, that much organisation must take…'

'Almost nothing. It's all automated.'

'And that's legal?'

'It's not illegal. But the downing of civilian airliners full of people is.'

She sat still for a few moments.

'I feel like you're only giving me part of the picture. Your family, the airplane... Are you holding anything back?'

'There is one thing I haven't told you, yes.'

'About you?'

'About my family.'

'Oh!' She was surprised. 'I don't want to pry…'

Keeping my voice as level and emotionless as I could, I gave her the missing pieces of information.

She listened without moving.

Then I played her the voicemail. The voice I knew so well began its terrible narration. I've heard that voicemail so many times in so may cycles, but it's still horribly painful to hear. I sat still and watched as her face began showing curiosity, then horror, outrage, and then sorrow. She was openly sobbing as it ended. She got up, went to the bathroom and I heard a tap running. After a while she came back and stood in front of me.

'Can I get a drink?'

Without speaking I got out of the chair, walked to the minibar and recited what was on offer.

'I'll have the white wine.'

I broke the seal on the small bottle, poured a glass and handed it to her. She downed it.

'Hit me again.'

I refilled her glass which she instantly drained.

'Still thirsty here.' There was an edge, a hardness to her that I hadn't heard before.

'The bottle's empty. There's a bar downstairs?'

'Well, get your things, and let's go.'

I got my things. We ordered drinks and settled in a corner of the bar overlooking the darkened beach. After the second glass of rum, she asked, 'How do you keep a lid on all this? How do you manage to live a normal life?'

'I've done my grieving. My family are gone, nothing I can do will bring them back. Planning revenge is helpful. Knowing I will bring the people responsible for this terrible thing to justice... it's sort of cathartic.'

'Jesus Christ, that's cold.'

I shrugged.

'You aren't drinking.'

I took a hefty belt from my glass and didn't say that Charlie was drinking enough for the both of us.

'I don't know how I feel,' she said, and took another drink.

'I can see.' I could see what she couldn't. Her eyes were burning, she was angry.

'Will you play it for me again?'

I put my phone on the table between us, turned down the volume and pressed play. It was odd hearing it again in that setting, the lower volume made us concentrate harder, which somehow brought it home with more impact. The recording played out. Tears were trickling down her face. She drained her glass in two gulps and signalled the bar staff for more.

'Talk to me,' she said. 'I want you to tell me things about you and your family that I don't already know.'

'I locked myself in an airplane toilet when I was eight.'

'What?'

'It wasn't deliberate. I got in, did my stuff and couldn't get out again. I kicked the door and yelled to be let out. The cabin crew had to unlock the door from the outside. My mother was so embarrassed she apologised to the crew a thousand times.'

'I would have liked to have met her.'

'She was an old-fashioned woman, from a different time. She would have liked you, but she wouldn't have liked us.'

'And your sister?' she asked.

'Younger, obviously. A little taller than me at the same age. Much prettier...'

'I doubt that.'

'Seriously. She was absolutely beautiful. Features like a finely cast doll. And much more intelligent than me. Languages were easy for her.'

'You speak languages.'

'It's never been easy. She could just pick them up. Accents, syntax, regional differences. She had my father's intelligence.'

'And your father was…?'

'Tactful. A strategic thinker. Analytical.'

'You'd expect that in a diplomat.'

'He was a caring, compassionate man, but sometimes his daughters were too much for him.'

She took a few gulps from her glass and chuckled. 'His daughters?'

'Maybe just the older one.'

'And you were? As a teenager?'

'A tomboy. Slightly out of control. And a quiet rebel.'

'What were you rebelling against?'

'Almost everything. Society, rules. Other stuff.'

'I love the rebellious youth. You, I mean.' She took another drink. 'Are there other things you haven't told me?'

'No. Yes. Sortov.'

She drained her glass. 'Well which is it?'

'I haven't told you how much I care. Or how much I love my family. I haven't told you how protective of them I am. I mean was. I haven't told you how much my sister means to me, even now. How much I adore her… And I haven't told you how much I love you.'

She looked surprised and opened her mouth to speak but I cut her off.

'Oh, I've told you I love you, but I haven't told you how much I love you. I haven't told you how much I adore you. I haven't told you that I will use all of my skills and experience to protect you. I can't tell you these things. I don't know how to. I've loved before, but I have never loved like this… like I love you.'

'I don't want to lose you,' she said, and then added, 'Us. I don't want to lose us.'

'You won't.'

'But you are either going to get caught or killed. Or both.'

I realised she was drunk.

'I won't.'

'But that recording…' She left the sentence unfinished.

'It's horrible.' I said.

'It's worse. It's terrible and at the same time it's terrifying.'

Despite the quantity of alcohol she'd put away, I could feel her eyes x-raying my soul, looking for deception and finding none.

'I need to tell you something.'

I held my breath and the stillness in the bar became magnified.

'I missed you. It's been a day, one single day, and I missed the certainty that you were a part of my life.'

'I unders…'

'I'm holding the talking stuck. Stick. I'm holding the talking stick.'

'I think you're dru…'

'Still holding the talking stick here.'

'Sorry, carry on.'

'I don't like what you are planning. And even more than that, I don't like the thought you might not be a part of my life.

'And I'm still trying to understand everything. I understand the loss of your family, but I didn't understand your desire for revenge. Until now. And I don't understand that this one fabulously wealthy individual could exist, and that he could be some global chess-player with all mankind as his prawns. Pawns. I'm still trying to understand that. But that recording… I get your drive, now. But I need you to understand one thing.'

I nodded to avoid being told off again. She carried on, speaking quietly, and it was the quiet focus in her voice that told me things were different now.

'I need you to understand that I love you and also that I am seriously fucking furiously angry. I've never been so angry, so full of rage. You've done this to me. You opened the gate with that recording.'

I held eye contact.

'We need to talk more. I need you to tell me more. I need to think this through more. I need to process all of this. But that's for tomorrow.'

She took another hefty drink and emptied her glass. 'Can I stay with you tonight? Will you hold me and tell me everything is all right? And that we're going to be OK when all this is over?'

I waited until it was clear she was expecting a response. 'Yes. You can stay. And I will hold you. And I will tell you that everything is going to be all right.'

'Good. I need some reassurance that only my personal tempest can give me. Now, take me to bed.'

I did.

Chapter 17. Attempt 2
Money

Week 41. California

My head woke me at four-thirty. I didn't feel like my usual routine, but I unwound from Charlie, slipped out of bed and, not having anything I could go running in, went for a swim. Nothing as adventurous as yesterday's epic, just five miles of hard pushing through saltwater.

Beach life was beginning to wake up as I walked to the hotel. Surfers were in the sea, kites were up in the air, and seagulls were wheeling in the sky, calling noisily to each other. Charlie was in the shower when I let myself in the room.

I tried for a deep voice and said, 'Scuse me, ma'am. I've come to look at your plumbing. Can I get my tools out and poke around inside for a while?'

She replied in a Southern Belle accent, 'Well, I declare. I haven't had anyone look at my plumbing for so long, I'm not sure it works properly. You just get right on and help yourself.'

I peeled off my swimsuit and stepped into the shower cubicle with her, and we inspected each other's plumbing for a while.

'Can we get married?'
  'I don't think so, no.'
  'But whyyyyy?'

'Because that young man is the waiter who has just brought your breakfast. You don't even know each other.'

'But look at this!' She gestured at the breakfast in front of her.

'I agree; it's magnificent. But you still can't marry him because he brought it.'

'You can be a proper grown-up sometimes.'

'I know.'

I turned to the waiter.

'Thank you for this.' I read his badge. 'Simon. I apologise for my girlfriend. She doesn't usually propose to every young man who brings her food.'

'Just the good-looking ones, Simon.' She winked at him. 'Just the very good-looking ones.'

Simon blushed and walked quickly away.

'You made him blush.'

'You made me blush earlier.' She said.

'That was different.'

'Yes, it was. But I feel like I need to share the blush.'

'A sexual blush isn't the same as embarrassing a waiter.'

'It might be for him.'

'Yes, I suppose it might be for him.' I agreed.

She took a spoonful of fruit, looked thoughtful for a moment and asked, 'Are we together?'

'I think so. But it largely depends on you.'

'Does it?'

'Absolutely it does.'

She ate some more, took a sip of orange juice and asked, 'Would you tell me a thing if I asked?'

'Yes.'

'That was bold. You don't even know what I want to ask

yet.'

'I'm going to be even more bold. I don't want to have any secrets from you. So if you have a question, whatever it is, just ask it.'

'Do you love me? Really love me?'

'That wasn't the question you were going to ask.'

'No, it wasn't. But do you?'

'Yes. I love you. I can't imagine being without you. I feel like I've found someone special. And you, this special person I've found, you are mine. And I'm yours.'

'Another question?'

'Go ahead.'

'You said you had spent a lot of money investigating this person.'

I just looked at her.

'What's a lot of money to you? I want to know what a lot of money is to a person who flies her own helicopter and who has, as we've agreed, a very nice life without ever having to work.'

I added up all the money I'd spent tracking my prey, and his organisation, over the last three cycles. Then I added five percent for my own time.

'One hundred and twenty-five.'

'OK, a hundred and twenty-five thousand is a lot of money.'

'Million.'

Her mouth opened, and she dropped her toast on her lap.

'But that's more than twenty million dollars,' she said quickly, converting Brazilian currency to US Dollars.

I sighed.

'US Dollars. One hundred and twenty-five million.'

She sat frozen.

'Shall I ask Simon to pick up your toast from your lap for you?'

She didn't move.

'Are you all right?'

I filled a glass with iced water.

'Drink this, it'll help.'

She took the glass but sat still with it raised in her hand. I was beginning to get worried; shock can do strange things to an unprepared person. Her eyes focussed, and she raised the glass to her lips. She took a sip of water.

'That's a staggering amount of money.'

'Well, you can't take it with you.' I joked. 'Unlike the toast in your lap. You could take that with you.'

She put the glass aside, picked up the slice of toast and began nibbling on an edge, as if she'd taken it from a plate. 'And that money, that hundred and twenty-five million dollars. That's all yours?'

'No. Now it belongs to other people. But it was all mine when I spent it.'

'How? How did you get it? I mean, I don't want to be rude, but I shouldn't think diplomats are so well paid they can leave that kind of money to their daughter.'

'You're right. I got precious little from the demise of my family. I made some risky investments that paid handsomely.'

'Well. I just. Don't know. What to think.' She nibbled some more toast.

'I think you're in shock.'

'You have spent more money than I could earn in a handful of lifetimes.'

'It's a lot,' I agreed.

'Did you get it legally? I mean did you get it honestly? I

mean did you rob a bank or commit fraud or steal something worth a lot of money and sell it?'

'Yes to the first couple, no to the rest. What I've spent is my
money, and I came by it through my own efforts.'

Because scooping a lottery jackpot is actually my own efforts, right? I could do it again, here in the US, right now. I
know the numbers. I could also go to the financial markets
and go short on a handful of stocks. And I could go long on
others. And even in the brief time I have left in this cycle,
the rewards would be unbelievable.

'How much are you worth now? I mean, I don't want to be
rude, but after spending that much, what do you have left?'

I added up the remainder of cash in my accounts.

'About ninety million US.'

'Jesus.'

'Eat your toast,' I said, as I began to tuck into my cold eggs.

'You're a multi-millionaire.'

'I am. Does that change things?'

'In what way?'

'Between us. Does that change things between you and
me?'

'No. Of course not. Why should it?'

'That's exactly my point. It should change absolutely nothing between us.'

'At least I know why you don't need to work.'

'Oh. That's a thing I wanted to talk to you about.'

'What?'

'I've got to fly to Nevada in just over a week.'

'Why?'

'I need to look up some information.'

'Can't you make a call?'

'No. Not for this. I need to check something.'

'You're not going to kill someone?'

'No.' I put my hand on hers. 'Nothing like that. I just need to look up a schedule.'

'The Internet?' she asked.

'This information isn't published on the Internet.'

'And yet you can go somewhere in Nevada and just look it up?'

'Yes.'

'Just like that?'

'Yes, just like that.'

She sat and thought about it for a couple of beats and then reached her logical conclusion.

'Can I come with you?'

I surprised myself.

'Yes. Mostly. You can come to Nevada. We could spend a night or two there if you like. But you can't come with me when I go to look it up. That's probably going to take two hours, and I have to go by myself.'

'I like the idea of a couple of nights away. But why can't I come?'

'Because the information is in a sensitive place.'

'So sensitive that you can get in, but I can't?'

All I could do was nod.

'I'm not sure I like this idea.'

'In view of how you feel about what I've told you, I understand. But I would like you to come. We could have a touristy couple of days away from LA.'

She thought about it some more. 'I'm not sure about coming. You'll be engaged in some kind of activity, and I want to think about whether I want to be around when you're doing that.'

I wanted to tell her that she wouldn't be around, but I needed her to feel comfortable with whatever her decision was. 'Think about it.'

'I will.

'Speaking of thinking about things, I was thinking it would be good if we could get into the habit of having early nights.'

'We could definitely aim for an early night every night. Do we need to go home straight after we've finished breakfast?' She indicated the partially eaten meal in front of us.

'We could stay here if you wanted. Tonight, I mean.'

'The bedroom has a bigger shower than I have at home.'

'Notwithstanding the nice shower, let's stay anyway.'

'But all I've got to wear is what I came in last night.'

'I could say something rude, but I won't. I'd like to go home and pick up some clothes. I don't have a change either. And it would be nice to get my swimming costume rather than use the complimentary one from the hotel.'

'Go home after breakfast then?'

I wondered if there was time to go back to bed for a little while, before we went to LA.

Chapter 38. Attempt 2
Dive

Week 41. California

We decided to take my rental car. Charlie found us a radio

station that played back-to-back rock classics. We sang loudly, and badly out of tune, to songs we didn't quite know all the lyrics for. The seriousness of my goal, the disagreement we'd had yesterday, both pushed out of her mind for now.

As we crested the hills towards Thousand Oaks, my phone rang. A familiar voice boomed through the car's speakers. 'Avon Point, Ohio.'

'I'm sorry?'

There was a long pause before he continued, 'You said I'm not from around here.'

'Ah. I don't know Avon Point, Ohio. What's near there?'

'Lake Erie.'

'I wouldn't be the first person who said to you that's an eerie place to come from, would I?'

Long pause. 'No.'

'Where are you teaching?'

I almost felt Charlie raise an eyebrow.

'East Beach, East Cabrillo Boulevard, Santa Barbara.'

'There all day?'

'Finish at four.'

'See you just before four.' I hung up.

Charlie tried to look out of the car like she didn't care, but her silence said many words.

'Wrong number,' I said. 'Now let me concentrate on my driving, and when we get home, you can give me a private show of which swimsuit you plan on taking to the hotel.'

***

Just before four we squeezed the rental car into the East Beach parking lot on Santa Barbara's East Cabrillo Boulevard.

'Why are we here?'

'Do you know how to dive?'

'Well, yuh.'

'Scuba dive?'

'Der.'

'Sometimes you can be so childish.'

'I'm allowed.'

We got out of the car and walked to the railing overlooking the beach.

'Nice beach.'

She was right, it was. Despite being mid-afternoon, the sun hung high over the kind of nice beach that comes so easily to Southern California; cleaned daily, manicured nightly, pretty to look at.

About two hundred metres offshore, a rigid inflatable boat was motoring slowly around four wetsuit-wearing people who were bobbing about in the water. One would get hauled up into the boat, sit backwards on the side and roll into the water. Then another would be brought out of the water to run through the same process. Then another, and so on.

I guessed from the tired way they moved, they'd been running through backroll practice for quite a while, but they kept getting lifted out with little effort. After a few minutes, all the divers were collected from the water, there were no more backrolls, and the boat opened up in the direction of a canvas windbreak not far in front of us.

'Care for a walk?' I asked.

'Where to?

'Down there.' I pointed at the windbreak.

'If I get wet feet, will you brush the sand off like you did that night in Rio?'

'I will brush the sand off your feet anytime you ask.'

Her eyes held mine for an hour, or a minute, or a second. Her smile widened, I thought she was going to throw back her head and laugh at my seriousness, but instead, she leaned forwards and kissed me on the mouth.

'I love you.'

'I love you too.'

'OK, let's go. And you can tell me why we're going there.'

I talked as we walked. 'I met someone yesterday evening, before you and I spoke, before you came out.'

'Met? At the hotel?'

'No, about seven miles away from there.'

'That's a specific distance. Were you out running?'

'Swimming.'

'The what the where now?'

'In the sea. Swimming.'

'First things first. You were seven miles out at sea? And then you just happened to bump into this person? Really these things?'

'Yes, really these things.'

'Seven. Miles. Out?'

'Uh-huh.'

'Do you know how far that is? Well, obviously you do because you swam it. But seven miles? In the sea? There are ships that far out. You could have been hurt.'

'I was fine. It's California, nothing is going to hurt me here.'

'Jesus, you're so confident. But don't you care? You could have gotten a cramp or been hit by a speedboat like that singer was or been picked up by slavers or anything.' She paused for breath and went on. 'And why? What on earth drove you so far out to sea?'

'Rage.'

'Wut?'

'Rage. I was angry at myself.'

'Why?'

'You. Us. Disagreement. Argument.' I slipped my arm through hers as we walked across the sand. 'I was furious that I thought I had lost you. I was working out my rage.'

'That's a serious amount of rage to keep you going for seven miles. Where would you have stopped?'

I couldn't tell her the truth, that I would have kept going until I could swim no more. And then started the cycle over again. And learned from my mistake. 'I would have turned around eventually. I've swum greater distances.'

'Have you? Really?'

'Greater than seven miles? Yes. A few times. The Straits of Gibraltar is only eight miles wide but has much tougher currents. I've swum the Straits twice.' In two different cycles, to get from Africa where serious people wanted to rape me and kill me.

'Are you in the Guinness Book of World Records?'

I couldn't help chuckling. 'No. There are many people who regularly swim greater distances. There's a Croatian guy who has swum a fraction under a hundred forty miles.'

'Look, that's extremely impressive and everything, but I don't care about some Croatian guy.'

'Let's not fall out again,' I said, as we arrived at the windbreak. 'I'd rather not get that angry at myself again.'

'Wait a minute. I have another question. And also, angry at yourself?' She stopped and turned away from the sea to face me. 'This person you happened to meet a mere seven miles offshore, were they swimming as well?'

'No, I was in a boat.'

She turned and looked at Mark. Today he looked very different. Swimming shorts, evenly tanned torso arms and legs, muscular, and his uncovered hair sun-bleached.

Stringing along behind him were five scuba-suited diving pupils, carrying their cylinders, masks, and flippers up from the boat.

'Hello, Mark from Avon Point, Ohio.'

'Hello, Laura from the hotel at Las Olas Drive near Hope Ranch. You don't look as if you are suffering from your extended swim yesterday.'

'Wait, this is the mermaid you told us about? This is the swimmer seven miles out to sea?'

I turned to look at the tall, late-twenty-something woman. 'Mermaid?'

'Well, that's how he described her. You. How he described you.'

I looked at Mark. He gave me a slight smile and a half shrug.

'It's not every day I meet a woman far out to sea. I needed a name, and with your long, wet hair, well, it seemed like a good description.'

'Huh. How was diving school?' I asked.

'It was good. Betty is the star of today's class. Couldn't dive at nine, and now she thinks she's part dolphin.'

A slender girl, early twenties, bent at the waist and gave a half-bow. A couple of the dive group gave her a round of applause.

Mark turned and addressed his class. 'You've all done so well. Except for Betty, who proved she's completely incapable of following orders.' Someone cheered. Mark continued,

'That, as we discussed this morning, I would like to extend to you the offer of an evening meal and one drink (that's just one drink, Betty) all at a substantial discount for becoming diving course graduates, at the Mesa.'

A few of the group cheered.

'So if you're interested, let me know. I'll book us a table.'

He turned to me. 'You and your friend are invited too. If you'd like to join us?'

'We hadn't made plans,' I said and looked at Charlie.

'Well, I was hoping for an early night...'

'Oh, we won't be late,' said Mark. 'I need to make sure these good folks get home because the gentle streets of Santa Barbara aren't ready for the likes of them.'

'Damn right,' said an impressively muscled mid-forties guy as he struggled into his shirt.

I looked at Charlie. She looked at me.

'OK. An early dinner and then an early night. Best of both worlds.'

Chapter 39. Attempt 2
Table

Week 41. California

Mark drove his truck on to the beach, and we all pitched in with loading the flatbed.

Two of the diving class got in the cab with him. The others, plus Charlie and me, got in the back. We drove off the beach, turned left onto East Cabrillo Boulevard, and then made a right turn onto Helena Avenue.

We pulled up in the parking lot of the same restaurant I'd waited outside yesterday. This time the doors and windows were open, and an older man and woman waited in the entrance. This was starting to feel coordinated.

Charlie and I climbed down first and helped the others off the flatbed. Mark walked the group over to the couple, who he introduced as Mom and Dad. The inside of the restaurant was an unexpected joy; a high ceiling with plastic grapevines growing up the walls, an Italian-style mural across one wall, decorated mirrors, and dining furniture straight out of the book of rustica. I felt homesick for Rio.

A large circular table had been laid up for us; we were the only early diners, but other tables were set for later meals. Dad took our orders for drinks, Mom took our food orders, and no matter what anyone wanted, whether it was on the menu or not, it seemed to be available in the kitchen.

The divers lapsed into an easy conversation, and it struck me that what I was hearing around the table was not just the kind of conversation of random people who have been sharing experiences for one day. There was more to it, a common theme ran through them all. Betty sat next to me. As she sipped her iced water, I tried a guess.

'Where did you serve?'

It got very silent around the table.

'Afghan,' she said.

I took a punt.

'And you, Mark?'

'Iraq.'

'You're all veterans?'

'We are,' said the man who had struggled into his shirt earlier, because half of his left arm was missing. 'That cool with you, lady?' He asked in a gently chiding way, as if he were schooling a child.

'That's cool with me.' I tried to gauge his stature and hazarded a guess. 'Sergeant?'

'Gunnery Sergeant,' he corrected me.

'I'm sorry, Marine.'

I turned to Betty and looked at the person she wasn't wearing; something clicked inside me, and I just knew her history.

'Lieutenant? Army? Air Cavalry? You look like an AH-64 Jock to me.'

Betty sat rock still, but her eyes began to glitter with gently pooling saltwater.

'How did you know?' Mark asked.

'And you, Mister DIY Handyman, who teaches a bit of this and that and picks up poor defenceless women when they're out for a peaceful swim, you're something special. Despite all the time you spend on the water, I'm guessing you had dry feet. So... Army, but a specialist unit. So I'm guessing Fort Benning? Ranger? Rank is easy because you're too pretty to be an officer.'

This got a laugh around the table. 'Corporal. Because you like the hard work?'

'Corporal, because that's as high as I got before I was invalided out. And yeah. Ranger. You're a pretty impressive act, Laura.'

Dad came over with three large pitchers of beer and filled every glass on the table, regardless of what everyone had ordered.

'How did you know?' This time asked by the Gunnery Sergeant.

'I spent a little time in uniform,' I said. 'It isn't that Betty here is missing her lower left leg or that you've had an altercation and your arm came in second best. Or that Mark here...' The penny suddenly dropped.

'Or that Mark here has hearing problems because he couldn't get his head out of the way quick enough. Or that you've all got physical or mental scars. It isn't any of those things.'

'What is it that gave us away then?'

'The way you hang together. It's the brotherhood. It's every day you all wore the uniform, that's what holds you together as a group.'

Betty leaned over and kissed me on the cheek.

'Service?' Asked the Marine Gunnery Sergeant.

'Army.'

'You're too pretty for infantry,' said Betty.

'I flew.'

'Flew what?' asked the Marine Gunnery Sergeant.

'Helicopters.' said Charlie, keen to join in.

I put my hand on hers. 'Sometimes I flew Black Hawks but mostly Pave Hawks.'

The Gunnery Sergeant wasn't impressed. 'A Pave Hawk? That's a mighty big suit to fit into.'

'It's a mental fit, Gunny. You just need to tell them who's boss.'

He looked sceptical, but he was just being sceptical about me.

'Go anywhere tasty?' Asked Betty.

'After I was boosted out of Fort Campbell, when I was

allowed to sleep, I mostly slept in Bagram.'

I could see the Gunnery Sergeant digesting that I'd been based at Fort Campbell, home of US Special Forces.

Mom began bringing out the first course, and the conversation broke up into tall tales and daring feats; about half of which I reckoned were true.

Charlie got a little drunk and flirted with Mark and Betty, but I eased off the booze because either way, I had to drive us to a bed somewhere. After the main course, I cornered Mark at the bar where he was talking to Mom.

'Well, Mister DIY and do a bit of this and a bit of that, you're a dark horse.'

'And you, my mermaid, you're a dark horse too.'

'Mermaids can't be horses.'

'Sea horses?'

'I have legs.'

'I saw.'

'I need to ask something.'

'Ask away. I might not answer, but there's no law against asking.'

'All those things you do, that bit of teaching fishing and that bit of teaching diving. I'm betting that you only teach veterans.'

He took a sip of his beer.

'There a law against that?'

'No law at all. There is a reward, though.'

'A reward? What kind of reward?'

'This kind of reward.'

I put my arms around him, nestled my head against his chest, and gave him the most bearhugingly bearhug I had in me.

'Can't. Breathe.'

'Stop kidding,' I said, as I hugged him some more.

'No. Really. Can't. Breathe.'

I stopped hugging him and stepped back.

'Wow, you're impressively strong.' He took a couple of deep breaths.

'You're just kidding.'

'Really not.'

I decided to ignore him and change tack. 'Tell me about Mom and Dad.'

'They're sort of my adopted parents. It's a long story.'

I looked at Charlie getting on like a house on fire with Betty.

'I have time.'

'All right. I went to school with a guy, Bobby, my best friend. We hung around together, went to school together, sailed Erie together, played sports together.

'After high school, we got jobs together. Moved out of our family homes and into an apartment. Lived pretty close lives.

'About a year later, we both got the feeling that we needed to be somewhere else. Lake Erie wasn't cutting it, so we decided to come out to the West Coast and work fishing boats. Because we knew how to do that.

'We worked inshore for a couple of months, but the money was better offshore, so we moved on to trawlers. We were in the job about three months, that trip we'd been out at sea for three days when we got hit by a storm.'

He took another sip of beer, then shook his head as if it wasn't very nice. 'Man, that was the worst storm ever. Worst storm either of us had ever seen. Way worse than any Lake

Erie storm. Big seas, and I mean really huge swells. White water all around us.

'It was about two in the morning. Bobby and I were on deck on manual pumps in the worst part of the storm when the netting rig broke loose and hit him. And just like that he was gone in the wind and the rain. My best friend. We'd known each other almost nineteen years.

'The storm eventually passed before dawn broke. After a lot of pumping, we made it back to shore. The trawler felt like it was wallowing deep in the swell, she had so much water in her belly.

'I couldn't tell Bobby's parents over the phone. So I flew home. Walked up the path. The look when they saw me was gold. And then they realised I was alone, and they just knew. I told them how he went, and we cried all day and stayed up all night. Just talking.

'They asked if I was going to move back, but I said I couldn't stay. It wasn't Bobby, or his parents. It was the town. Too many memories for me. So, I joined the military.

'I was halfway through my first tour in Afghanistan when a shell detonated right above my head. I lost my hearing, so that was a real good guess of yours. I have limited hearing now, but the army didn't want to keep me around, so I got my disability and left.

'I decided after all the desert I wanted to be by the water again. But not Erie. A guy I roomed with in the hospital in Germany said I could do worse than settle in Santa Barbara. So, here I am.

'I wrote Bobby's parents from Germany, told them what I was planning, and three months later, Mom and Dad rocked up on my doorstep.'

'Wow!'

'Very much wow. They sold their house and bought this place. We all live upstairs. I'm like their son now. And, as you guessed, I work mainly for veterans. And Mom and Dad put all their energy into feeding us. We all get something out of it.'

'What about your own parents?'

'My father died when I was eighteen. My mother followed him less than a year later.'

I noticed the slightly more formal names he'd used, but I could see some pain in his eyes. I put my hand on his. 'I'm sorry, Mark.'

'Thanks, Laura. But we're doing all right. I do what I do. Mom and Dad specialise in feeding veterans at a loss, and what they charge civilians makes up the difference. And we just about manage to pay the bills. Life isn't too bad, you know?'

'Yeah. I know.'

Chapter 40. Attempt 2
Jolly

Week 41. California

After dinner, I drove us to the hotel, put a very drunk Charlie to bed, and lay awake for a couple of hours, just thinking about people and what they do and their motivations for doing them. I decided that Mark was something else; I started thinking about how I could reward him.

In the morning, neither of us had a hangover, but Charlie lacked the get up and go, so I ran and swam by myself. We checked out at noon, drove to LA, and began living our lives again. But we didn't talk about my goal, and we didn't forget about it. We just didn't need to go back there again. Yet.

I fell into my twice-daily exercise routines and turned up the difficulty levels, constantly pushing to be better, fitter. Charlie and I slipped into the routine of a couple of domesticated cats. We lived and loved and enjoyed every single moment of every single day.

After a couple of days, I asked Charlie if she would like to take a pleasure flight in the helicopter, her eyes lit up.

The next morning, we flew the EC out of Long Beach and headed north. We watched the land beneath us change from city to town and then to countryside.

As we flew into the Californian mountains the landscape turned from brown to green. The breath-taking Sequoia National Forest looked stunning, spread over a range of huge peaks in all their natural glory. Then we turned west, flew around Fresno and onwards until we saw the mad hilltop architecture of the Hearst mansion at San Simeon. We turned southeast, keeping the coast passing beneath us at two-hundred-miles-per-hour, the sea to our right and the distant Californian mountains to our left.

As we approached Santa Barbara, I descended to three hundred feet and looped westwards.

The rigid inflatable boat was half a mile offshore East Beach, about where I thought it would be. As we flew over, I waggled the EC from side to side. It looked as if there were a handful of people fishing from it.

When we were a hundred metres beyond them, I banked to starboard, made a large climbing turn and headed back to Long Beach Airport. If the people in the boat had cameras, they would have got some stunning shots of an aircraft in perfect motion.

'That was an awesome move!' The grin on Charlie's face ran from ear to ear.

'If you think it was good for us, it would have looked so cool to the people in the boat.'

Even on a shortish, fun hop like this, the sheer pleasure of flying the EC coursed through my veins. I felt that this beautiful machine, and I were joined, as I controlled everything we did through both hands and feet. All the way to Long Beach, Charlie's smile didn't change once. My love for flying seemed to be infectious.

Later, as Charlie was poking about in her kitchen working out what we could have for tea, my phone rang.

'I've never seen a flying mermaid.'

'Well, let's be honest, army. You've never actually seen a mermaid.'

'Only you. Got a question for you.'

'Go ahead.'

'You guys busy? This weekend?'

'I'd need to check with my social secretary.'

'Do that. Let me know if you're free.'

'Sure. Will do.'

I hung up.

'Mark?'

'Mark.'

'What's he want?'

'Probably you, the way you were flirting with him.'

'Well he can't have me. My heart belongs to another.'

'Good, I'm glad.'

'Who said it was you?'

'It isn't?'

'Well of course it is, I'm just playing it cool.'

'In that case, I shall try to play it cool too. So, back to our important conversation. What's for tea?'

'Umm, in the face of extreme kitchen difficulty and some poor choices, I have decided to invent a Not Waldorf salad?'

'A Not Waldorf salad?'

'It's a salad. But it doesn't have any nuts. But it does have three different types of cheese.'

'I can always get behind a good cheese salad. Let's eat. I'm starving.'

Charlie went into the kitchen, clattered a bit, and then called out, 'Laps or table?'

'Plates instead?'

She walked out carrying two plates. 'Did someone once tell you that you were a comedian?'

'Also forks?'

She sighed noisily, went into the kitchen, and returned with a huge bowl of potato salad.

'A Not Waldorf salad and a potato salad?'

'Do you have a problem with that?'

'No. Both kinds of salad sound delicious. What's for dessert? A fruit salad?'

'You know my earlier question about someone mistakenly telling you you're a comedian?'

'No?'

'Sit and eat and save the gags, they need help.'

We sat at the table.

After a while, she said, 'I've got a question about the future.'

'Go ahead, salad girl.'

'This. This here and now. You and me. This feels like it's not real.'

'Howso?'

'It feels like we're on holiday from the real world.'

'This isn't the real world?'

She put her fork down and counted on her fingers. 'You're a multi-millionaire. You fly helicopters. You plan on killing someone.'

'Which one of these things is not in the real world?' I asked.

She looked exasperated. 'All of it is not in the real world. Normal people have jobs. And work regular hours. And don't plan on killing people.'

'I dispute all of your points. There are much richer people than me who do real work. And people fly helicopters for a living, and as to the last point, I've known plenty of people who would like to bump someone off. Wife, husband, lover, bank manager, boss…'

'You're exasperating sometimes. OK, I'll concede those things. But as far as killing someone goes, almost nobody actually does it. And you are. I can tell. I can feel that you're going to do it.'

'And this feels like we're on holiday from the real world?

'Yes, it feels like we're on a giant holiday from the real world where we don't need to go out and work, and where we don't need money, and where we could live fabulous lives in your luxurious house in Rio and sail your yacht, and we could have sex all day every day.'

She paused for breath and rushed on.

'Take today, our trip out in the helicopter. That isn't what normal people do. Normal people go to work and come home and watch TV, go to bed, don't have sex, get up in the morning and go to work again. But instead, we go to the gym, and we stay in nice hotels and meet interesting people you bumped into while swimming, and then we fly around in a helicopter. It just doesn't feel like the real world.'

'We do have sex almost all day every day, though.'

She did the exasperated sighing noise again. So I said, 'Charlie, the real world is going to catch up with us soon enough. Let's just enjoy where we are in this one.'

I could see she had reservations, but she didn't want to provoke an argument right now; she just needed to get some of these thoughts out of her head. After a few moments, she said, 'OK, you're the pilot.'

After another few minutes, I said, 'I'm quite enjoying my Not Waldorf salad. And speaking of food, Mark wanted to know if we're free for dinner.'

'When?'

'This weekend.'

'Are we free for dinner?' She was curious.

'Might be nice. But if I catch you flirting with him, you're going to be walking to Nevada next week.'

'You can be really harsh sometimes.'

'I can, where you're involved.'

'In that case I'll keep myself to yourself. Now finish your salad. And then eat your other salad. And then I'll go and get you the other, other salad.'

I may have put my hand to my face in mock surprise.

Chapter 41. Attempt 2
Mark

Week 41. California

The next morning, after gym and swimming, we got home, showered, had a light breakfast and, without much persuasion, fell into bed.

While she slept, I reviewed my last few cycles. Despite all my research, the previous attempt on this target had failed. In Dubai I had got close, but his head of security had somehow found out about me and intercepted me; he'd had me run off the road and shot in the face as I hung upside down in a car wreck. Somewhere on the last attempt, I'd revealed myself, or I'd shown enough of my intentions, and he'd seen me coming, and I still couldn't figure out how that had happened. Maybe Dubai was just too much of a tightly wound place to take him out, but Dubai was still easier to manoeuvre in than Saudi Arabia, where he mostly lived these days.

That's why I'd come to the US. I knew my target was going to be hosting a weapons demonstration here, showing off his latest R&D products for the Pentagon brass. I also knew when and where that demonstration was going to take place. This time, instead of keeping a low profile and trying to slide into his inner circle, this time I was going to hide in plain sight; I was going to use all the natural cover around me.

Five weeks to go. My pulse raced. I ran over my plans again. And then I worked through them once more, slowly, step by step. Everything felt good. I was determined that I was not going to fail again. Then it occurred to me that I had less than three months left in this cycle. Five weeks to stop him. Less than three months with her.

I resolved to make every single day count. I decided to take Charlie's criticism, that everything seemed to be a holiday, on the chin. Holiday? I'll show her a holiday. She slept on while I made plans for the two of us.

The next afternoon we drove to Santa Barbara and picked up Mark from the car park behind the Mesa restaurant. Charlie slipped into the back seat so Mark could navigate easier.

'So, where have you booked that has a quaint yet exotic menu for us to sample?'

'Mark, you invited us, remember?' Said Charlie.

'This means you haven't made plans?'

'The only plan we had, army, was that we would pick you up. The destination was your bag.'

'In that case, you'd better take us to the end of this road and then turn left.'

'Where are we going?' Charlie just can't contain herself.

'We, my friends, are going to the very gorgeous, very sexy, four-star rated, In-N-Out Burger.'

'Joking, right?'

'I never joke about food.' He was good. Deadpan face. I guessed he'd played a lot of poker. And broken a lot of hearts. Mark directed us west out of Santa Barbara; the road began to climb into the mountains as Charlie asked him about his day.

'The teaching fishing thing, you mean?'

'Well, what else have you been up to today?'

'I swept the floor and laid tables in the Mesa before I went out on the boat this morning.'

'For some reason, this surprises me.'

'Don't let it. Sometimes I help Mom cook. Sometimes I tend bar. Most mornings, I sweep up and clean.'

'Which nights for the tending bar thing?' I asked.

'The busy ones.'

'Do you have many of those?'

'Some. Now and then. Why?'

'I just wondered. When we ate at the Mesa it was half-full.'

'And the party still managed to drink us almost dry.' He looked over his shoulder at Charlie.

She wasn't having any of his innuendo. 'How much further? I'm hungry.'

'The reason you're hungry is because you hardly eat anything.' I said.

'We don't all have your metabolism!'

'Are you saying I eat too much?'

'No. Yes. No. I mean, I'm saying you eat waaay too much for a short...'

'I prefer "economically packaged".'

'Eat far too much for an economically packaged flyweight.'

'Can I say something?' asked Mark.

'If you must,' said Charlie. 'But I would prefer you concentrated on the 'right here' and 'left there' stuff.'

'Right here.' He spoke quickly.

I swerved onto a single-lane dusty track, past a sign which simply said, 'The View'. We pulled up outside an ordinary-looking two-storey house; there were at least a dozen other cars parked in a row.

'Shall we go in?'

'Is that rhetorical or...'

'Charlie, let's just get inside. I've never been to an In-N-Out Burger before.'

She did a fake pout.

The first surprise inside the house was that it wasn't a house. The ground floor was stripped out, no internal walls, dark wood flooring, the walls were painted bright white. Most of the square footage was a neatly laid out, sparsely decorated restaurant.

The second surprise was that the entire ground floor back wall was glass. Behind the huge window was the most stunning view over the lower green hills, the skyline of Santa Barbara below, and the clear blue of the Pacific Ocean far beyond. To the right, along one of the shorter walls, was an open-plan kitchen. There were about thirty diners seated, and the smell of cooking made me appreciate just how hungry I was.

A waitress asked if she could help us. Mark said there was a table booked in the name of Mermaid. I couldn't help but smile.

We sat and traded small talk while we read the menu and made our choices. Mark asked if we wanted wine and, because we were in California, I picked a Napa Valley Rosé. He ordered a beer, and the conversation turned a corner.

'So, how did you two meet?'

Charlie had obviously been waiting for this one.

'In a boxing gym, in Rio de Janeiro, Brazil.'

'What?' He tapped his left ear. 'This one hears things you don't say, and the other doesn't work too well.'

'You heard right.'

'A boxing gym, you say?'

We both nodded.

'In Rio? In Brazil?'

Charlie nodded again while I took a sip of the wine. It was good.

'In that case, I've gotta ask, what were you two doing hanging around in a boxing gym?'

'Laura was beating the shit out of the gym owner.'

Before he could come back on that, I corrected her, 'I was sparring with him.'

'Lady, I really believe you were beating the shit out of the gym owner. I've felt your hug. I'm guessing you're a hard hitter.'

I shrugged and took another sip of wine.

'How did you get to Rio?' he asked Charlie.

'I was working there. Laura has a house there.'

'Really?'

'Yep.'

'Really Laura has a house there?' He looked at me. I took another sip of wine.

'Laura has more things going on in her life than you would believe.'

I dived in. 'What about you, Mark? What things do you have going on in your life?'

'Just what you know. Bit of fishing, a bit of diving, a bit of teaching fishing and teaching diving. And taking visitors out to the islands.'

He and I said the last sentence together.

Charlie said, 'Jinx!' and I said, 'That's your speech, isn't it?'

'You've caught me out. I'm so dull I have a script.'

'I bet it gives you plenty of action.'

'How so?'

'I bet the tourists you take out to your love-nest on the islands fall over themselves when you flash those big eyes and muscles at them.'

'You have a love-nest on some islands?' Charlie asked.

Mark said, 'No,' at exactly the same moment I said, 'Yes.'

Although we didn't know each other, the three of us relaxed into a comfortable place. Over the main course I probed a little further.

'So how long have you been doing your thing for veterans?'

'A little less than a year. It started by accident, a couple of one-off events. And then it became a proper thing.'

'How do you start something by accident?'

'I was taking people out to the island, one time. And a guy in the party was an amputee. I asked him if he'd served. We talked about all the things he wanted to achieve. I said I could help him with diving. He said he might have a couple of friends who would also be interested. Three others came along, all vets; two were amputees too. And that was how I started something by accident.'

Charlie said, 'Awesome.' But I just looked at him. He sipped his beer and met my gaze.

'So you teach veterans to dive, and you teach veterans to fish and you tend a bit of bar for veterans, and you sweep up in a restaurant for veterans, and occasionally you take people out to the islands, and sometimes you remember to bring them back again.'

He smiled at my joke, which Charlie didn't get.

'That's about it. And you fly...'

'I'm talking about you.'

'Wow!'

Charlie stage whispered, 'She can be a bit assertive

sometimes.'

He whispered back, 'I'm finding this out!'

'What do you want to do? Where do you want to go from here?'

He pulled a little-boy face.

'I'd like to go home from here. If that's OK? In one piece would be good, if that's all right with you, lady?'

'Can you be serious?'

'Now and then.'

'Can you be serious now?'

'Yes, I can. How's your fish?'

'Delicious. So where do you want to go from here?'

He put his knife and fork down.

'I don't have a plan. I used to have big plans. But now... Now I'm just taking it one day at a time.'

I felt there was a lot more to what he wasn't telling us, but I wanted to stay friends, so I didn't push.

After dinner, we sat outside on the balcony, sipped coffee, and enjoyed the free lightshow as the evening descending into dusk and the lights of Santa Barbara slowly populated the hills below.

Mark was enjoyable company. As the evening had progressed Charlie and I had fallen into the rhythm of his hearing delay; it slowed down the pace of conversation, but not the quality of our discussions. He didn't seem to have a single mean or unkind fragment inside him. Despite his size, he was a good-humoured, truly gentle man.

After the meal, we drove him to the Mesa, refused his offer to go in for a drink, and returned to Los Angeles. Charlie slept all the way home.

We brushed our teeth and went to bed. She fell asleep

instantly. I searched for automotive stylists and vehicle modification experts in Barstow. I sent one of them an email.

Then I slept. I slept very well.

Chapter 42. Attempt 2
Chad

Week 41. California

The next morning, as we were walking home from the gym, the automotive stylist called. He was keen to meet up. We arranged to meet at Barstow-Daggett Airfield at four. Charlie didn't look impressed with my side of the call, but I said I'd explain after breakfast.

Mid-morning, I googled 4x4 trucks for sale and with not many clicks of the mouse, I bought a three-year-old truck that looked like it could conquer deserts and mountains. I arranged for it to be delivered to Cuttle. The Internet is truly awesome.

Over lunch, I told Charlie about the call and that I had to take an afternoon trip to Barstow for a meeting.

'A meeting?'

'With some people. Or maybe with just one person. I don't know.'

'Is this a 'Gonna shoot someone very important and get caught and spend your whole life in jail writing me long and soulful letters' kind of meeting?'

I sighed heavily. 'It's indirectly related, so maybe the

answer is yes but also no. And anyway, I'm not going to get caught.'

'You're so convinced.'

'Humour me.'

'This isn't very humorous.'

'In that case, trust me.'

'In as much as you're asking me to trust someone who is planning on breaking the law to kill another person, I do trust you. But that's not the point.'

'What's the point?'

'The point is that even if you do it and even if you succeed, you're going to get caught.'

'I won't get caught.'

'How can you say that?'

'I have a plan.'

'Having a plan does not mean you won't get caught.'

'I won't get caught.'

'You shouldn't even be doing this. You shouldn't be planning this. You shouldn't be considering killing someone no matter what they've done.'

She paused and then asked, 'What if I told the police?'

'Would they believe you?'

'They might take it as a serious threat. Especially if we played them the recording.'

'The recording is evidence of nothing. It could have been recorded by anyone. And anyway, what would you tell them? Your lover, who you met in Rio de Janeiro, is going to try to kill a fabulously wealthy man who has his own army, and she's going to do it somewhere at some time, and you don't know any of the details?'

'I know about the place in the Mojave.' She almost pouted.

'You do. But why would you even consider telling the police?'

'To keep you out of jail, my love. To keep you out of jail.'

'What if I keep an open mind – keep questioning myself and keep checking against my plan? What if I get to a point where it's just too much? What if I panic? What if I have a crisis of confidence? What if I come to realise that I can't get away with it?'

'That's when we stop. And put the idea behind us.'

I loved her use of the word 'we'.

I put my hand on hers. 'I promise then; I truly promise to you that if any of those things occur, I will talk to you, and I will put this idea behind me. I really promise this.'

She looked relieved. I couldn't tell her that her lack of confidence in me and my plan was misplaced. All right, I had never tried to take him down in the US, but I had carried out years of research. I knew almost everything, and the little that I didn't know now, I soon would. She broke my chain of thought.

'Can I come?'

'Huh?'

'To Barstow? If it isn't a top-secret clandestine meeting?'

I thought about it for a moment.

'Sure.'

She looked like that wasn't the answer she was expecting.

I put our rucksacks into the EC, radioed our readiness to leave, and took off from Long Beach Airport into the early afternoon SoCal sunshine. As soon as we had crossed over Mount San Antonio and the Angeles National Forest, the land beneath turned rapidly dark brown from fire damage, and then to light brown dryness, and then to desert.

Air Traffic Control at Barstow-Daggett sounded cheery despite being stuck out in the middle of nowhere. The controller's voice had a firmness that indicated she was on top of her game. Radio chatter told me there was a lot of military traffic in the local system. Some of the voices were crisp, clear, and confident, while others had the uncertainty of immaturity. Instructors and trainee pilots, I thought.

I touched us down in line with a couple of US Army UH-60 Black Hawks and let the engines spool down to stop. I glanced at Charlie, smiled at her, and held her hand for a moment.

The short walk through the breathtakingly hot desert air to the airfield car park made me appreciate the air-conditioned crispness of the EC. Apart from half-a-dozen cars, the car park had an obvious stereotype: the large, expensive Mercedes 4x4 with the blacked-out windows and the broad-shouldered, five-foot-eight, middle-aged, bald-headed, beard-wearing dude leaning against it. Sleeve tattoos ran up both his arms into his t-shirt, and some impressive inkwork showed on his legs below his shorts.

'That's got to be our guy,' I said under my breath.

'Not scary at all,' Charlie whispered.

'Chad?' I asked.

'I am that. You Laura?'

'Sure. Pleased to meet you.'

'You wanna sit inside? It's cooler in there.'

Charlie gave me an anxious glance, but I'd already mapped out his weak areas.

'That would be great.'

He walked to the back and opened the rear door to reveal sofas on both sides, a small cupboard and swivel armchair behind the rear seats. He climbed in, sat in the chair, and opened the cabinet.

'Can I get you a soda or something?'

"Uhhh, yeah. Glass of water?' Charlie was gaining some confidence.

'And for you, Laura?'

'I'll have a glass of water too, please, Chad.'

'Well, come on in, make yourselves at home.'

I climbed in; Charlie followed. As we took our seats, he picked up a remote control and with a whisper of electrical motor, the door closed, and air conditioning kicked in.

He fixed us each a glass of iced water from the fridge. 'Cheers!'

I looked around. The inside of the truck was decorated to a high standard. Well-lit by LEDs, blinds on the windows, nice carpet, and the furniture looked hotel suite standard.

'This is nice.' I said.

'Thank you. I did the fit-out a few months ago. My wife says I should sell it, but my little girl loves being in here.'

'How old is she?'

'Fifteen.'

I could see a fifteen-year-old girl being cool with this kind of transport.

Small talk out of the way, Chad got straight down to business. 'So you want a helicopter transformed?'

'We do. What we want is for you to use the style in the photographs I've emailed you. And a couple of days later, when the filming has finished, we'll need you to restore her to her original condition.'

'No problem to copy those photos. But we'll need a place to work. I don't have anywhere big enough to work on a helicopter.'

'The studio has an aircraft hangar you could use, but it's a little way out from here - about an hour away by road?'

'An hour? We can live with that. Can I see the helicopter beforehand? Take some additional photos? And some measurements?'

'Right now, if you like?'

'Cool. I do like. Let me get my bag.'

We climbed out of the truck. Chad picked up a small, flat bag from inside the driver's door, and we walked to the EC.

'There she is.' I gestured to the helicopter. 'Help yourself. If you need anything just ask.'

'Got all I need here, thanks.'

From his bag, he took an electronic gadget and measured every surface of the EC. Then he photographed her from every angle, going in really close on the hinges and panels.

Five minutes and many, many photographs later, he was done. 'I think we're good to go, Laura. And your email said you wanted us to start a week on Monday, right?'

'That would be good. I can email you directions to the hangar. I'll also email you the tail numbers and the IDs we want on her. And I will meet you at the hangar and make sure you have everything you need.'

'Yeah, that would be great. And like I said on our call, it will take us five days to wrap it. And when you have finished filming, another two days to unwrap and put her back like this.'

'Perfect. Half the payment on the finish of the wrap, the balance when she's restored?'

'Suits me.' He said and confirmed how much the whole job would cost.

'In that case, we have a deal.' I held out my hand, which he shook warmly.

We watched him drive away, then climbed into the EC, and I brought her to life. Charlie, who had been mostly quiet during the conversation, asked where we were going next.

'Home.'

'Until the next subterfuge meeting?'

Even though she hadn't seen the photos I'd sent him, she wasn't happy with the conversation between Chad and me. We climbed to thirty feet and left the airfield, then I pointed the EC northwest, and we headed for Los Angeles.

'We're going home to shower, have a meal, and go to bed. And tomorrow, we're taking a flight to Texas.'

'I don't think this thing is working too well.' She tapped her headphones. 'For a moment, it sounded like you said we were going to Texas.'

'I did.' I may have smirked. I like being mysterious.

Chapter 43. Attempt 2
Prep

Week 41. Texas/California/Nevada

We flew to Austin and for five too short, so precious days we slipped into the 'old us', the 'us' that we had been before I told Charlie my goal.

We laughed, we loved, we cuddled, we kissed, we walked, we talked; we met strange people in bars who turned out not to be so strange. We swapped phone numbers with folk who, a couple of hours before, had been random strangers. We saw live music, we went to a film show, we walked in parks, we went to a gig, we said 'Hi!' to everyone we passed in the street, and most of them said 'Hi!' back; we loved every moment, and it felt like every moment loved us.

Flying to LA at the end of the week, she held my hand the whole way, and that night, in bed, we slept entwined; we just fitted together like a couple of pieces from a puzzle.

The next day, walking back from the gym, I told her I had to go away in the morning and wouldn't be back until mid-afternoon the next day. I felt the darkness start to come between us.

'We talked about this, a week ago? A quick trip to Vegas? You were thinking about coming with me?'

She sighed heavily.

'We did. I'd put it out of my mind.'

'And when I get back, I've got plans for us.'

'Will you have done it? When you get back?' She meant will I have killed him.

'No.'

'I don't know whether to feel relieved, annoyed, or frustrated with you.'

'Can you think of this as if I'm just going away on an overnight business trip?'

'Are you sure you're not going to have done it? Can you promise me this?'

I took her hand in both of mine. 'Charlie, I promise you with everything I've got to give you, this is just a business trip.'

'As in you're going to be taking care of business?'

'No. Nothing like that.'

'Can you tell me what you will be doing then?'

'Just prep.'

'Prep to shoot someone.'

'Just prep. I need to look up some information. Can we leave it at that?'

'No.'

But we did. For now. There was a mood between us for the rest of the day, and neither wanted sex that evening, but I spooned her and told her I loved her. She fell asleep in my arms, but we both had a restless night.

The next morning the mood still hung over us. I was sad and disappointed that I had caused a cloud to appear over us. Sad because it had happened, disappointed that it had happened through being open with her. But I had a conflicting balancing act. I didn't want to be dishonest, and I couldn't let so many of his wrongs go unpunished; I was still focussed on my target.

I kissed her on the cheek, left the house early, drove to Long Beach Airport and flew the EC to Cuttle; I did my usual check that the site hadn't been visited by anyone, then opened the gates.

Shortly after eight-thirty, a dust cloud appeared on the horizon. Ten minutes later, a flatbed semi rolled into the compound. The semi was bringing the 4x4 truck I'd bought. I signed the paperwork, waved the driver off, then put the truck in one of the unused hangars. I locked up, got in the

EC and flew to North Vegas Airport.

Tony McCall was out aviating, I asked the secretary to get the overall-wearing dude to check the EC out and brim her tanks. I got into the hire sedan I'd left there and headed up the I-95 towards Creech AFB. A short distance outside Indian Springs, I pulled up at a diner, took my fatigues and ID out of the trunk, got changed, pinned my hair up, and became a USAF Captain.

I got to Creech AFB just after noon. Security was no problem for my fake IDs. I asked the MP on the gate where vehicle maintenance was and got handed a map with the workshop neatly identified.

I pulled up outside base headquarters to check the layout on the map. As well as the vehicle maintenance section, the aircraft maintenance hangars were also clearly marked; that was what I was looking for.

I drove to a different section of the base and parked in a slot outside a hangar signposted '432nd Aircraft Maintenance Squadron'. The large hangar was open; I could see an MQ-9 Reaper UAV undergoing maintenance. An Airman First Class was working on a weapons pylon.

Now this is the combined strength and weakness of the USAF: compartmentalised security.

The Reaper pilots sit in secure, air-conditioned Flight Operations Cabins on the far side of the base; they fly the UAVs through remote control, no matter where in the world the drones are operating. These FOCs are disconnected from the outside world and, in an emergency, they can be put on a truck and transported to another location. Each FOC is crewed by two flight officers who control the UAVs, a mission controller, and an armed MP responsible for security, but the MP is really there in case anyone goes rogue.

There's no contact between the Maintenance and Flight Operations squadrons: mission security in the FOCs and on-base physical security sit in separate bubbles.

Behind the Aircraft Maintenance Squadron is a two-storey building, the sign outside said it was the 'Flight Planning Section'. Flight Planning's role is to schedule the base's inbound and outbound air traffic. It's their job to make sure that bottlenecks don't happen, and Air Traffic doesn't get overloaded. I walked into reception.

'Help you, Ma'am?' asked a young corporal.

'Hi, do you have a blank flight plan I could fill in?'

'Yes, Ma'am. Just a sec.'

She swivelled in her chair, opened a vertical set of drawers and slid out a triplicate form. While she was doing this, I picked one line out of the rows of information on a display board on the wall.

I took the form from her, said thank you, and walked to the sedan where I wrote down U/250/A, 16.30Z, 36°51'27.3" N 116°00'29.5" W. I wished I could have photographed it, but cameras aren't allowed on Creech, and smartphones are frowned on in sensitive areas.

I drove off base and turned south on the I-95, back towards North Las Vegas Airport. I got changed into civilian clothes at the first truck stop.

Back at Sunny Helicopter Charters, Tony was still out flying, but the mechanic said the EC was good to go; I paid for the fuel and flew back to Cuttle. I landed as the afternoon sun was starting to set. I powered down, got my sleeping bag out of a luggage compartment, unlocked the second hangar, climbed into the rear seats of the 4x4 and settled in.

I called Charlie, but it wasn't a great conversation. I told her I loved her, and I meant it, but she didn't seem to think so. After the call, I hunkered down and successfully tried for a night of fitful, restless, and broken sleep.

Around four in the morning, I had the horrible feeling that something wasn't right. I was beginning to feel anxious. Worried. And normally I don't get anxious or worried. Also, normally, I can sleep anywhere. This felt like a bout of insomnia, and that's not the person I am. My head was telling me I'd overlooked something. My mind spun itself up to full speed, and despite feeling tired, I could only doze restlessly.

Chapter 44. Attempt 2
MapRef

Week 44. Nevada

At five AM, I brushed the crumbs of sleep out of my eyes, splashed some flask water on my face, opened up my laptop, got out the HackRF Mayhem hardware and began to assemble everything that would allow me to steal a fully weaponised US Air Force MQ-9 Reaper UAV.

Less than half an hour later, I had downloaded the latest satellite positioning coordinates, edited the final piece of data, and transferred the new GPS positioning files, along with the coordinates we had recorded a few weeks ago, into the new software package. Then I plugged the HackRF hardware into the laptop and connected the output to the ECs radio transmitter.

I was good to go. I got out the information I'd copied from the Flight Planning Section at Creech and started to break it down. U/250/A, 16.30Z, Mid: 36°51'27.3" N 116°00'29.5" W.

U/250 was the ID for the Reaper. The /A meant it was armed. 16.30Z was a timecheck. All NATO forces around the world synchronise on Greenwich Mean Time, or Z = Zulu. Mid: 36°51'27.3" N 116°00'29.5" W were the flight midpoint coordinates.

So I knew that at 16.30Z, or 09.30 local time, Reaper ID 250, carrying live ordnance, would be at the coordinates of 36°51'27.3" N 116°00'29.5" W.

All I had to do was get to the same place at the same time and steal it. What was missing was the height the UAV would be at, the direction it would be travelling from, and the speed it would be moving at. And filling in those blanks would take every inch of piloting skill I had.

At 8.15, I fired up the EC, disabled her ADS-B Out transmissions, so she couldn't broadcast her ID or whereabouts, then I took off and pointed her at 36°51'27.3" N 116°00'29.5" W.

When I first hatched this plan, I had spent a lot of time calculating the flight characteristics of the Reaper. I had figured that a fully laden UAV would be flying somewhere between fifteen-to-twenty-five thousand feet above ground level. The EC had a maximum ceiling of fifteen thousand feet, but that was OK. I didn't need to be at twenty-five thousand feet; I just needed to be able to hit that altitude with a radio signal.

I reckoned a fully loaded Reaper would likely be moving at around one hundred fifty to one hundred sixty miles per hour, which the EC could comfortably match. Speed was the primary reason I'd chosen the Eurocopter for this mission. The EC is one of the fastest civilian helicopters around. Its ability to rapidly accelerate from stationary hover to maximum speed, and its unrivalled agility made this helicopter an obvious choice.

When I was twenty miles from the target zone, I descended to one thousand feet to adopt a minimal radar profile. There's a lot of secret military activity in the Nevada desert, and some of the sensitive bases in the area probably have super keen radar.

I'd also noticed a place called Sugar Bunker in the centre of 36°51'27.3" N 116°00'29.5" W. My research told me that Sugar Bunker was a top-secret military base, so it seemed like a good place to avoid. Unfortunately, I needed a fully loaded Reaper, and this beggar couldn't be a chooser.

At one-hundred-seventy miles per hour and one thousand feet above the ground, I adopted a grid-based search pattern through the granite mountains that surrounded the coordinates. I also slipped into combat flying mode. I stopped thinking about flying and began flying by muscle memory. My learned reflexes were on the job, reacting subconsciously and seamlessly to the external stimuli my eyes were picking up and sending to my hands and feet at the speed of light. It's a little like learning to speak a foreign language; when you get good at it, you stop translating, you just listen and speak it. At least, that's the best description of combat flying I've got for you.

I flew a grid from west of the Smokey Radio Towers going

south, almost to the secret township of Mercury, then diagonally northeast past the equally secret Sugar Bunker, before looping back to the grid start point.

The Reaper was due at 09.30. At 09.20 I reached over and slapped the spacebar on the laptop; this triggered the broadcast of the amended GPS coordinates. HackRF was now pumping out a set of GPS coordinates that said we were in a different location. I continued to fly the grid, keeping my eyes on every sector of the sky as I searched for a UAV the size of a two-man glider.

09.25 came and went. 09.27. Then 09.28. The timer on the control panel seemed to slow down. 09.29. 09.30. 09.31 and still nothing.

09.32. 09.35. 09.40. Fucking fuck. Who screwed up? Them? Me? Someone else? Am I blown? Has my mission been discovered and they've changed everything? I kept flying the grid. 09.42. 09.44.

09.47 and oh Jesus there it is. There. A glint in the sunlight as it banked a little to port. Maybe eighteen thousand feet above the highest ridge of Skull Mountain.

I could see the Reaper was flying a circle which matched the GPS coordinates my laptop was broadcasting. I don't know how long the Reaper had been in my spider's web, but the plan had worked; I'd caught it.

I reached out and slapped the laptop spacebar again; the second broadcast was transmitted, and the UAV reacted immediately. It broke out of the circle, executed a rolling descent to five thousand feet, changed course westwards, and headed towards Death Valley, except as far as it was concerned, the Reaper thought it was going home to Creech Air Force Base. I followed it, broadcasting the new GPS coordinates.

Sixteen miles north of the enormous China Lake Naval Air Station is possibly the largest airstrip complex in the world. Codenamed Bingo, the runways had been built to test Space Shuttle landings. NASA carved the three long runways out of the desert but, now unused for more than two decades, Bingo was the perfect stopping-off point for the Reaper.

I followed the UAV closely; the spoofed GPS signals I was transmitting guided it onto the second Bingo runway; it landed gently and came to a halt after less than a mile. I landed immediately behind it, picked up the laptop, and ran to the Reaper.

I opened the UAVs primary interface flap and plugged in the laptop. I found the navigation and communications settings and disabled the UAVs capability to transmit or receive any data except mine. I unplugged the laptop, ran back to the EC, got in and climbed to one thousand feet then activated a new GPS setting called 'Home' on the laptop. The Reaper picked up the new heading, accelerated down the runway, took off, and headed on its new course. I followed closely.

Half an hour later the Reaper touched down on the main runway of the former Cuttle Air Force Base. I landed the EC behind the UAV, ran to it, opened an emergency flap and shut down the engine. I walked back to the EC and shut its engines down. The peace and quiet rolled over me like a huge wave. Or perhaps it was the relief that I'd succeeded with this phase of the mission.

I towed the Reaper into Hangar Three. For a while I just stood and looked at it. Then I collected my toolkit from the EC and began opening the UAVs panels. By four o'clock, I had all the components out that I needed.

I locked the hangars and flew the EC to Long Beach Airport. I really wanted to be back in LA. I needed to see Charlie. We needed to talk.

Chapter 45. Attempt 2
Wrap

Week 44. California

'Coffee? Really? You asked me if you could come in for coffee?'

'It was the best I could think of.'

We sat in her kitchen; the afternoon sun beginning to cast long shadows across the room.

'Lame.'

'I know.'

'Must try harder.'

'I will.'

'But I don't want to give you the wrong impression, so I'll say it. I'm pleased to see you.'

'I'm pleased to see you too.'

She paused and took a sip from her cup.

'Have you done it yet?'

I didn't let my funny bone loose.

'No.'

'Are you going to do it soon?'

'No.'

'Would you tell me if you were?'

'No.'

'Do you know how infuriating you can be?'

'No.'

'Have you stolen that drone yet?'

'No.'

'So, final question, would you tell me if you had done any of these things?'

'No.'

She sat back in her chair and looked at me; I couldn't read her mind.

'When are you away again?'

'Tomorrow.'

'How long will you be away for?'

'Just the day.'

'Back tomorrow then?'

'Around one in the afternoon. If you'll have me, yes. Please.'

'Why wouldn't I have you?'

'Because you're not happy with me.'

'I'm not happy with you. But I still love you. I still want you. Even if you're going to spend the rest of your life wearing unfashionable clothes in a Federal Correction Facility.'

'I'm not going to spend the rest of my life anywhere, except with you.'

'Oh.'

'I'm serious about that. I really mean it. I'm serious about something else. I think we should talk about getting married.'

'Oh!'

'And when I say we should talk about getting married, what I mean is that we should get married.'

It seemed like a long time before she spoke again. 'That's

quite a thing you've said.'

'Like I said, I mean it.'

'Have you been married before?'

Several hundred times, I thought. 'No.' I lied. 'Have you?'

'Nearly. Once.'

'Let's make it just the once then.'

There was a long pause before she spoke again.

'I don't want to lose you.'

'You're going to have to scrape me off to lose me.'

She stood and leaned against the table. I could see she was building up to something important; I got anxious she was going to tell me she wasn't ready to make a lifelong commitment. She took a deep breath and started again.

'The thing is with relationships; sometimes they stop working. Sometimes things fall apart. They fall apart so hard. You can't ever just put them back the way they were. You know. It takes time. You can't just come around for coffee and expect...'

She paused and went on.

'There's just so much to work through. Trust has to be built again. On both sides. We have to learn if we're even the same people we were when we fell in love; see if we can still fit in each other's lives. It's a long, important process. And... Can we just skip it? Can you just be kissing me now?'

I didn't know what to do for a moment, what to say. Eventually, my words came.

'You know I love you?'

'Yes.'

'And I'm going to be with you forever.'

'Good.'

'But there's one thing you have to promise me.'

'Say it.'

'Never, ever, quote the Tara and Willow speech from Buffy The Vampire Slayer at me again.'

'Too much?'

I stood and kissed her on her cheek, put my arms around her and hugged. 'Much too much.'

'I'll work on something else for the next time you infuriate me.'

The following day I landed the EC at Cuttle at 8.30am. I powered down her engines, hitched up the forklift and towed her between the lighting gantries in Hangar One.

Then I went outside, unlocked the main gate, opened Hangar Two, and drove the 4x4 truck into the hot desert air. I settled behind the wheel for a cute little daydream. After a while, I saw dust on the horizon.

Chad's expensive 4x4 school taxi rolled into the compound twenty minutes later, followed by a medium-sized truck, a couple of younger Chad-clones in the front.

'You're early.'

'Big job for an important customer.'

'I bet you say that to everybody.'

'Only the important ones. The bird in here?' He nodded towards Hangar One.

'Yep, have a look.'

Although the doors were wide open, it was gloomy inside. I showed him how to start the generator; the twin lighting gantries quickly threw the world into brightness.

Chad walked around the EC, inspecting it from every angle.

When he'd finished, he had a face full of smiles. 'We're going to enjoy this job.'

'Pleased to hear it. You have everything you need?'

'Sure. I've got a folder full of the information you've sent me. Not a problem to replicate that.'

'Good. You still reckon five days?'

'Might get it finished sooner, but let's stick with five days, just to be sure.'

'In that case I'll return in five days. There's plenty of fuel for the generator here, and a tanker full of fresh water. Just help yourself.'

I walked out into the sunlight. It seemed as though I had turned a huge corner and, for the first time, I was looking at possibilities I'd never been close to before.

I drove the 4x4 out of the compound. Ninety minutes later I arrived at Long Beach Airport and switched to my hire car. Just after noon, I pulled up outside Charlie's house.

We were both in that dreamy post-sex state where sleep is almost on you, but you still want to talk or walk about or do something low impact but do something.

'You said home for a week?'

'I said home for a week. But if you want that's flexible. Could be two weeks. Or three.'

'Flexible? That's kinda kinky. What shall we do?'

'We could go to Rio?'

'Wow, really?'

'Really. But for longer than a week.'

She sighed.

'When will you know? How long you've got? Before your

next thing?'

'I'd need to make a couple of calls.'

'Calls to trained killers?'

Be cool, I said to myself. Don't be funny. Leave the sense of humour alone. Don't try to be…

'No.'

Good. Very good.

She filled the silence herself. 'I've got another idea.'

'What's that?'

'We could go anywhere. It doesn't have to be Rio. We could stay here.'

'We could. And as well as staying here we could also do small stays in some really nice hotels, eat very well, exercise gently, work out hard, and have sex in expensive bedrooms.'

'Expensive bedrooms… Mmmm. Or…'

'Or…?'

'Or we could go to Rio and stay in your beautiful house.'

'And we could swim in the sea or the pool. And go to the gym and knock the boys about. And we could sail…'

She put her hand on mine.

'You miss her. Your boat.'

'Yacht.'

She actually giggled. She shrieked when I pulled the duvet off her; I slid out of bed and went to the bathroom to brush my teeth.

'Rio!' She shouted from the bed. 'We're going to Rio. As soon as you can, please.'

I smiled a face full of toothpaste at the mirror. We were going home.

Chapter 46. Attempt 2
Three

Week 41. California/Rio de Janeiro

Later that afternoon, while Charlie went food shopping, I made three calls. Chad said he'd send me photos when he'd finished working on the EC.

The second call was to an air charter company who said they'd have everything ready. And Mark said OK in the third call.

Then I emailed my housekeeping service in Rio, and arranged for the house to be cleaned and aired, fresh bedlinen and towels to be put out, and for a supply of fresh food to be brought in. I also emailed the pool cleaner and asked them to do a tidy up. I was putting my phone down when Charlie breezed in from shopping.

'Well?'

'I'm feeling very well, thanks. You OK?'

She picked up a tin of sweetcorn and threatened to throw it.

'Your ability to scare me with a tin of Jolly Green Giant is unparalleled. I shall tell you everything.'

'This is your famous sense of humour I hear so little about, right?'

'Right.'

'Well come on then, girlfriend. Spill the beans.'

'You mean sweetcorn.'

'Really?'

'We have a taxi picking us up tomorrow.'

'Tomorrow? But I haven't done any shopping or anything!'

'We have shops in Brazil.'

'Yes, but... Things!'

'We also have things in Brazil.'

'You know what I mean!'

For a moment, I wished I could tell her that when I came to America this time, I just carried a US Army kitbag and a rifle.

'The taxi is booked for seven-fifteen tomorrow evening, so we've got plenty of time for packing.'

'And shopping?'

'Is it a defect?'

'Yes. And it runs in my family. My father is just the same.'

'Really?'

'Really truly. Hardware stores, DIY equipment, engineering things, power tools. He just can't say no.'

———————————————

By six the next evening, we were packed and ready to go, in that strange state of limbo where we didn't really have anything to do except sit around killing time.

At seven, she was pacing around the house like an overactive toddler. 'Are you sure we can take this much stuff? The luggage allowance seems generous.'

'It's fine. I paid a premium so we can take as much as we want.'

'It's great, but it seems a bit...'

The doorbell interrupted.

'Taxi's early!' She almost shrieked. I've never known an adult get so excited.

'You go.'

I followed her to the door, she checked the spyglass and said 'Oh!'.

'Mark's coming with us.'

'Really? I mean, nice surprise and all, but I thought it was just going to be us having a quiet time together and you know...'

'It is just going to be us. Mostly. Mark hasn't had a break from what he does for too long. He can stay in the spare bedroom. We don't have to hang out much together, and I think you should at least open the door to him.'

'Oh! Yes. All right.'

She opened the door and said with a deepened voice, 'Come on in, stranger.'

He stooped to come in, and almost had to turn sideways to walk through the door.

'That it?' Charlie pointed at his kitbag. 'That all you're taking?'

'Yeah, I normally travel light, but I thought I'd bring more than usual this time.'

'You're such a funny guy.' She kissed him on the cheek. 'Come on through. The taxi will be here soon.'

She stepped aside to let him into the lounge. He stooped to kiss me on the cheek, but I gave him a big squeeze.

'Stop.' He pretended to gasp. 'Can't. Breathe.'

'Oh, you're such a kidder.'

'Yeah, really not. Are you Supergirl or something?'

'Drat. You've seen through my cunning disguise.'

'Nice house.' He looked around the lounge.

'It's only tidy because we're going away.'

'My apartment at the Mesa is pretty spartan, easy to keep clean. And Mom sneaks in once a week and does a clean.'

'That's sweet of her.'

'She's a sweet lady.'

He changed the subject.

'So Laura, you said you had sorted out flight tickets for me?'

'They're waiting for you at the airport.'

'OK, cool. Just, you know, I'd like to know how much they're going to cost? Because, well, this is a great invitation of yours but, you know, money.'

I tried to cover his embarrassment. 'It's fine. It will be much less than you think. I used some of my air miles.' I lied.

He gave a sheepish grin, but I could tell that money was a sensitive point for him. Before he could speak again there were two blasts of a horn outside.

'Taxi's here!' Charlie, again. This time she was right. I had ordered a large taxi, what we got was a people carrier. It was an easy fit getting all of our cases, Mark's kitbag, and the three of us inside.

'The airport?' asked the driver.

'Long Beach.' I said.

The journey took just over half an hour, Charlie held my hand and squeezed a lot. Mark spent a lot of time looking out of the windows. As we pulled into the airport, I directed the driver into an empty traffic lane that said 'Private'.

At the security gate, I showed the booking to the guard. We were directed to Stand #3. The taxi pulled up at the foot of the executive jet staircase.

'This?' asked Charlie.

'This.' I confirmed.

'Well, this is a thing of beauty.' From Mark.

He was right. In the early evening dusk, the lines of the

Gulfstream did look beautiful. As we were unloading, an air hostess came down the staircase.

'Ms Guerra?'

'Me.' I said and handed over the booking for her to check.

'Good evening, Ms Guerra. My name's Amy. I'll be your hostess for the flight. Captain is just talking to the tower. We'll be ready to depart as soon as you and your guests are comfortable.'

'Thank you. The only luggage we have is what came out of the taxi.'

'If there's nothing you need from your luggage on the flight, I'll have it stowed away for you?'

I checked with Mark and Charlie, and we all agreed our hand-luggage covered what we needed onboard. Amy led me up the staircase, Charlie behind and Mark following. The inside of the executive jet was as beautiful as could be. Amy made sure we were comfortable, that our luggage had been loaded into the hold, and that our onboard bags were put safely away.

She went forward to the flight deck and came back a few minutes later to say we'd been given a take-off slot and would be on our way in five minutes. The engines increased pitch, the staircase was folded into the fuselage, the cabin door was secured, and we were soon on our way.

After a long, steady climb, the aircraft levelled off, and the engine noise subsided. Amy took our food and drinks orders and came straight back with coffee for Charlie, tea for me, and fruit juice for Mark. After a couple of sips, he leaned towards me.

'I can't afford this.' He said quietly.

'You're not paying.'

'Well, who the heck is?'

'I am. The trip's on me. If it helps, you should consider it a reward.'

'Reward for what?

'For what you do.'

He thought about that for a moment.

'How the hell can you afford this?' He gestured around us. 'This is beyond expensive. This trip is costing money I can't even think of.'

'I'm an international criminal,' I said. 'I smuggle coffee into Latin America.'

He didn't blink. 'Why would anyone smuggle coffee into Latin America, where it's grown?'

'And that's why I can afford this flight. Nobody else has thought of doing it this way. Now sit back and enjoy the flight.'

He sat back but continued to look uncertain.

'That's a great story,' Charlie whispered. 'Smuggling coffee into Latin America.'

'Thank you. I thought of it as a career when I was grinding coffee beans for my uncle.'

'Grandfather,' she corrected.

I was pleased she'd remembered the fantasy conversation from our second dinner date. Then I realised that had been just a month ago, and now we had less than three months left together. We'd come so far as friends, as lovers, as a couple. I was emotionally invested in our relationship to a surprising level. I've loved before, but I've never loved so completely. So... unconditionally.

I had made a conscious effort not to count the remaining time in this cycle, but because I'd dived into an emotional bond and had achieved such a tremendous connection, there seemed to be a constant shadow hanging over me.

'Miles away?'

'Yes, sorry. What did you say?'

'I was asking what time we are going to arrive.'

'Umm, we left just before eight, that puts us into Rio around ten tomorrow morning, Brazil time.'

'How long will that be for us?'

'Oh, right. It's a ten-hour flight. So six California time.'

'Got it, thank you.' She put her hand on my leg. 'Why don't you get some sleep? You look tired.'

'Keep your hand there, and I'll soon be very alert!'

She didn't remove it, but I reclined my seat and closed my eyes. Despite the comfort, sleep was fitful. More insomnia? Maybe. I spent the time I wasn't asleep going over my plans. The more I thought about things, the more I thought I'd missed something obvious.

I woke from a long doze to the smell of fresh coffee and warm food. Mark was sprawled out on one of the couches. Charlie was asleep next to me, head resting on my shoulder. The engine noise was normal, the lighting was subdued, the plane felt in level flight, cabin temperature felt good. No alarms. No surprises. And relax.

The display on the cabin bulkhead showed it was five LA time, nine Rio time, and our ETA was an hour away. Amy arrived at my elbow and quietly asked if I'd like to see the breakfast menu. I said that would be nice. While I was yawning and stretching the knots out of my back, Charlie woke up.

'Sorry, I was trying not to disturb you.'

'That's OK. I feel like I've had a great sleep. Oh my

goodness, look at him!'

Mark was still stretched out, his broad-shouldered tallness dwarfing the two-seater couch.

'He looks comfortable.'

Amy brought the menu, saw Charlie was awake and asked if she should wake Mark up.

'Let him sleep. He leads a busy life.'

Charlie and I ate a light breakfast, followed by coffee. For the first time in ages, I was taken by a craving for a cigarette. The seatbelts sign came on, the lighting came up a little, the landing gear was deployed, and the engine noise changed pitch; we were on approach. Mark slept on.

Less than fifteen minutes later, we were on the ground, back at the private airport in northern Rio that I'd left from. We taxied to a private hardstanding. I could see that my little car was still here, but there was no way the three of us plus all our luggage were going to fit. I'd have to return for the car.

I leaned over the sleeping Mark and whispered in his ear.

'Time to go, Corporal. Chow in half an hour.'

He smiled, and without opening his eyes, he replied, 'I'm so hungry I could eat a pair of diving flippers.'

'We'll do better than that once we're at the house.'

The limo I'd rented got us home; I gave Charlie a door key and unset the alarm from my phone as we drove up the track. She unlocked the house while Mark and I wrangled our luggage up the step and into the house.

Mark looked around the first floor.

'Wow! This is some place.'

'We like it.' I said. 'Welcome to our home. For the next ten days, you're our guest. The aim is that you only do what you want to do.'

'I'll give it a shot.' But he looked uncomfortable.

'So here's our routine.' I said. 'Charlie and I will get up early every morning and either swim or go to the gym. We'll be back here by nine. Don't feel you need to get out of bed if you don't want to.

'Your room is downstairs and second left. The pool has been cleaned and ready for use, and at the bottom of the track we've just come up is a private beach which you have access to. I'll give you the code to get you in whenever you want.'

'Great, thanks.'

'I'll give you a door key, and a card with the address and some taxi numbers. Just don't feel that you're stuck here with us. I want you to relax, Mark.'

'Thanks.' He still looked uncertain.

'And I'm not casting you loose either. We're on holiday too, but we'll do things now and then. You should feel free to join us.'

He looked embarrassed.

'And no, you won't be a spare wheel.'

He coloured up. There's something endearing about a grown man blushing.

Chapter 47. Attempt 2
Return

Week 46. Rio de Janeiro/California

A week and a half later, we were on another Gulfstream jet, heading back to Long Beach Airport.

Charlie and I were even fitter, I was a little leaner, and the three of us were nicely tanned. Mark had come to see us work out at the gym one morning, and quickly declared that wasn't the standard of fitness he was looking to carry into early middle age.

I had used a little personal time to rewrite my Will and sent an update to my solicitor. I also spent a handful of hours working on the components I'd removed from the Reaper. And I paid Chad for his work on the EC. The rest of the time I didn't even think about what was on the horizon, but there was still an edge of insomnia in my sleep pattern.

I had rested, worked out, eaten well, swum, and sailed. Mark had surprised me by being a super competitive helmsman, and we informally took on some of the local racing crews for bottles of champagne. Even though Musa was no lightweight speedster, we didn't make it easy for our competitors, but we did end up providing the champagne, which was always shared between winners and losers. Charlie was a willing hand on the ropes and winches, but she preferred to be working on her tan, and that didn't come easily when Mark was challenging strangers to a racing duel.

It had been a wonderful holiday. Insomnia had mostly stayed away. Charlie and I became even more of a couple, and even having Mark around didn't get in the way of our relationship. And now we were descending through three thousand feet on our approach to Long Beach Airport on an early Californian afternoon.

We walked down the steps; I led the way to the pad where the EC was usually kept. After a few paces, Charlie asked the question.

'How are we getting home?'

'Driving.'

'You might be one of the sharpest minds I've ever encountered, my love, but I have to point out there's no car. And pretty soon, our luggage will be on the tarmac.'

'It's OK. Mark's driving.'

'Uh, what? My truck is at the Mesa car park because you told me to get a taxi to your house.'

I could feel their eyes on my back as we walked on.

'Mark?' I asked over my shoulder.

'Yes.'

'What's the plate on that truck in front of us?'

'6GDG486.'

I got the Certificate of Title out of my rucksack and passed it back to him. He looked at it.

'6GDG486.'

'Correct.'

'But this,' he gently flapped the Certificate of Title. 'This says that 6GDG486 is registered to me. It's got my name on it. My address.'

'In that case,' I said, passing him the keys. 'It must be yours. Congratulations, army, you've got new wheels.'

He just stood there for a moment.

'Now you can move your veterans around in a truck that doesn't look like it's held together by rust.'

'I can't accept this.'

'Of course you can. And if you don't want it, just consider this an interest-free loan that you can pay back to me by returning the truck, whenever you want.'

'For a short person...'

'I prefer "economically packaged".'

'She said that to me when I called her short,' Charlie commented.

He ignored my preference. 'For a short person you sure pack a lot of hard punches.'

'Just take the keys and drive us to our luggage.'

He took the keys and got in, made the driver's position fit his frame, and then took us over to our bags. All the way home, he was silent, but he was already treating the truck like he loved it. He pulled up outside Charlie's house and helped us out with our luggage.

'I've got just one question for you, Mermaid.'

'Go ahead.'

'How did you get my signature on the transfer of ownership for the truck?'

'Oh, that's simple. I forged it.'

'You what?'

'I forged it. Well, no, that's not right. I didn't know what your signature looks like. So I made it up. I figured what someone from Lake Erie would write like, and I did that.'

'So I'm an accessory to forgery or something?'

'No. Tomorrow you need to get hold of the DMV and tell them that when you signed the form, it was in the middle of a parking lot and blowing a gale, and you need to provide them with a proper signature. Happens all the time.'

He looked dubious.

'Trust me.'

He didn't look less dubious, but he put the truck into gear, said he'd see us soon and pulled away.

We were in bed; she was laying across my chest; sleep was starting to beckon, but she wanted to talk.

'I've never come home from a long holiday with so many clean, freshly-laundered clothes.'

'Maid service is one of the greatest gifts a family can ever have.'

'Family?'

'Family. You. Me. We're a family.'

She hugged me.

'And you flew us there and back in private jets. That must have cost a fortune.'

'What's the point of hoarding money?'

'And you bought Mark that huge truck.'

'He loves it. You could see it in his face.'

'He does love it. And I love you.'

I kissed her. 'I love you too.'

'Shall we get married?'

'Didn't I say this? Weeks ago?'

'I don't remember.' She bluffed.

'Let's go to the County Clerk tomorrow, after we've been to the gym.'

'OK.'

'Really?'

'Really?'

'I love you so much.'

'I love you more.'

'No, you don't.'

'Yes, I do.'

'You're such a child sometimes.'

'That's just part of my charm.'

'In that case, we're going to take your charm to the County Clerk's office tomorrow morning and see what we can do about making this relationship official.'

Chapter 48. Attempt 2
Plans

Week 46. California/New York

The next night I got hit by insomnia. I was suddenly wide awake at two, as if someone had just flipped my 'on' switch. I lay in bed, trying not to disturb Charlie, my brain running at full speed. I was worried. I was worried about having insomnia, and I felt sure that I had insomnia because my subconscious was worried about the plan. Vicious circle. I spent two hours trying to get back to sleep while my head refused to cooperate.

It had to be my plan. Nothing else felt out of alignment. Over the last couple of weeks, the plan had started feeling good - but now, in the cold light of insomnia, it didn't feel perfect - and I needed perfection. I'd spent so much time, effort, and money on putting together this plan, and now, unexpectedly, my head was telling me it wasn't sure about it. Or maybe my head just didn't like the plan anymore.

I spent much of the next morning's gym session going over the plan. I'd seen his schedule when I worked in his compound in Nebak. The fundamentals were simple. I knew where my target was going to be, and I knew when he was going to be there. I had the right tools for the job, and I'd put together a way of getting in, doing the job, and getting away again.

But it was the "what if?" that was worrying me. I felt sure of that. What if things went wrong? What if it didn't work out? What if I wasn't successful in my plan? What if something behind the scenes changed and I was unaware of it? I felt sure it was the fact that I had no contingency that was bothering me. I had been so certain that my plan would work that I had nothing in reserve. I was blindly fixed on an all-or-nothing plan.

Maybe I needed another plan? No, not another plan, a second plan. A 'plan B' plan. It was a bit late in the day to be coming up with…

'Where are you?'

I finished tying my trainer. 'Clothes shopping.' I said quickly.

'What?'

'I'm wondering what I should wear when we get married.'

'Oh! That wasn't the reply I was expecting.'

'So I've got something for you to think about.'

'What's that?'

'Where are we going to get married?'

'Ah, I have been thinking about that!'

'And?'

'On the beach.'

'OK, that sounds interesting. Umm. Which one?'

'I'm not going to tell you.'

'Oh. Well, that's going to be slightly inconvenient on our wedding day.'

'Well der. Of course, I'll tell you which one before then. I just want it to be a surprise.'

'If we're going to get married on a beach, do I get to wear a swimsuit? And flippers? And a snorkel?'

'If you want to, yes.'

She wasn't in the mood for taunting, obviously. I tried another tack. 'Do you know what you're going to wear?'

'I have a good idea, so yes.'

I was impressed. I actually hadn't given it that much thought. 'Is what you're going to wear influenced by where we're going to get married?'

'Oh. I see what you mean. No. It's what I always wanted to wear when I got married.'

'OK, then. Next question. Who are we inviting?'

'Me. You. Some other people.'

'Riiiiight… I get the feeling that you've given the guest list less thought than your outfit.'

'That might be a fair assessment, yes.'

'We need a list of things.'

'I know we do.'

'Food, guests, venues.'

'Probably several lists then.'

'Yep. Are you inviting your parents?'

'Yes. Marrying another girl isn't what my mother would have wanted for me, but I love them and they will learn to love you too.'

'OK, then. We'll make a few lists. The first list is people we are going to invite, and at the top of that list are your parents.'

Four beats passed before she said, 'Thank you.'

'No problem.' I said, as we walked out of the gym and into the bright Californian sun.

'Who are you going to invite?'

'I don't know.'

I didn't. I hadn't spent any time in this cycle socialising, and I hadn't missed any of my friends from previous cycles. Besides, they wouldn't know me. This time around, I had been so wrapped up in planning and preparation and falling so hard for Charlie that I hadn't mixed with anyone. Charlie was all I wanted in my life. I hadn't needed anyone else. Charlie was my emotional support. And unlike some earlier cycles, in this lifetime, I didn't feel alone. I felt like I'd found my home.

Instead of running, we walked home arm in arm and chatted about everything under the sun. When we got home, we went virtual window shopping; the Internet got hit hard that afternoon.

Later, as I was stir-frying some vegetables, Charlie came into the kitchen and put her arms around me.

'They want to meet you.'

'Who does?'

'Well der, who do you think? My parents, they want to meet you.'

'That's probably a good idea.'

'You OK with it?'

'I'm mildly terrified about it. But I think it's a good idea.'

'Can we go and meet them? Spend a few days there?'

'Of course.'

'Thank you.'

I turned around, and she kissed me, and the stir-fried vegetables became very well done.

White Plains, Westchester County, New York State isn't what I expected from a community just twenty-eight miles from Manhattan. Expensive commuter belt houses tucked away on landscaped, green, leafy avenues; the many trees giving an unexpected illusion of rural isolation, so near to New York City.

There's a small town called Valhalla (no Norse gods were in evidence) which borders the Cranberry Lake Preserve (the lake didn't contain cranberries or preserve). Charlie's parents lived in a two-storey detached house a few miles outside Valhalla. Their home was perfect to look at, a real-estate agent's marketing dream, well-maintained with hardly a blade of grass out of place.

I parked the hire car next to a three-year-old Chrysler. Before we'd even got out of the car, the front door of the house opened, and Charlie's mother walked towards us.

Her mother was a pocket-sized version of Charlie; the same poise, the same way of walking, but her too-serious face lacked the same quick and easy smile that was such a large part of Charlie's character.

'Mom, this is Laura.'

To kiss or shake hands or stand there looking embarrassed? We were in America. We shook hands.

'Call me Margaret, dear.'

I resisted the temptation to call her Margaret Dear.

'Very pleased to meet you, Margaret.'

'Leave your cases. Richard will bring them in.'

Wow, she was brusque! I figured that Richard was Charlie's father. We walked in the front door as Richard was coming up a flight of stairs from the basement garage. The resemblance between him and Charlie was unmistakable; his eyes burned with the same intelligence, and there was an air of mischief about him. I soon found they shared the same sense of humour.

'Hi, Dad.'

'Charlotte.'

They kissed on the cheek.

'And you must be Laura?'

We shook hands while I agreed that I was indeed Laura.

'We've put you in separate bedrooms, that all right with you?'

I didn't know how to react.

'Dad, stop teasing!'

'Well, I have to protect my daughter's honour!'

'Richard, you can play with the girls later. Could you get their cases upstairs first?'

'Have you brought the usual quantity, Charlotte?' he asked. 'Should I get a fleet of elephants to carry them in for you?'

'Herd.'

'What have you heard?'

'Jesus, Dad.'

'Richard. Cases.'

Chapter 49. Attempt 2
Change

Week 47. California/Nevada

Five days later, we were on a flight back to LA. Charlie held my hand, leaned over and kissed me on the cheek.

'Thank you. Thank you so much.'

'What for?'

'For the last week. For being you. For not letting my family get to you.'

'They're sweet.'

'My mother can be a bit fierce, and my father is over-compensating for a lifetime in industry.'

'I think your mother is like that because of your father's sense of humour.'

'They liked you.'

'Really? I'm glad. I liked them too.' And I did. They were Charlie's parents. They gave her life, and they helped shape her character. For those things alone, I liked them.

We got home, unpacked, checked email and voicemail, and the actual mail that had been put through the door. While Charlie fixed us a snack, I checked the schedules. The demo had been brought forward three days. It was no longer early next week. It was now the day after tomorrow.

Insecurity set in. Had they brought it forward as an additional security precaution, or was it just to accommodate someone's scheduling change? I tried not to let this uncertainty show, but I felt my pulse quicken.

We ate, cuddled, went to bed, and fell asleep in each other's arms. Despite being excited by the date change, I fell asleep almost immediately. I still woke up at two though. Worried and stressed. As I lay in bed, I put effort into working up a Plan B. The next morning, I broke the news to Charlie.

'Today?'

'Yes. Sorry.'

'I thought you said it was next week?'

'It was next week. It's been brought forward.'

'Why has it?'

'I don't know. Scheduling conflicts, probably.'

'What am I going to do without you being around for two days?'

'Watch TV and go shopping?'

'Fair point. OK, so, what will I do without you in our bed for a whole night?'

'Starfish?'

'You know me too well.'

I smirked.

'Will you call me?'

'Even in the most inconvenient moments.'

'Good. I'm counting on that then.'

That afternoon I drove to Cuttle, and the first thing I did was call Charlie. She sounded relieved to hear my voice, even though it wasn't long since we'd seen each other.

After the call, I opened Hangar One, fired up the generator, and inspected the EC. Chad had done a perfect job; she looked like she'd come straight from a military paint shop. She was now a genuine military helicopter.

I opened the pilot's door, slid in, and got to work. I connected the laptop to the communications panel. Then I reprogrammed the helicopter's transponder with a new identity and installed a set of selectable squawk response codes. When I was finished, I opened Hangar Two, towed the Reaper out into the late afternoon sunlight, and began upgrading it.

I refitted all the components I had worked on in LA and in Rio. Then I overlaid the EC's software with updates I'd written over the last few days. I ran additional diagnostics through the control panel, which then showed me two rows of green lights; the reprogrammed hardware and software were behaving themselves.

I shut everything down, fastened the panels and towed the Reaper back into the hangar. It was just after seven, and I had a long wait in front of me.

I walked the length of the runway and set up some stones as targets. Back in front of Hangar One I lay down with the L115A3 and put 25 rounds through the rifle. The smell of cordite hung heavily in the still desert air, but when I walked back down the runway and inspected the stones, I felt satisfied with my shooting.

I pulled the sleeping bag from the EC, got into the hire car, reclined the seats, wrapped myself up, and phoned Charlie. She laughed because, true to my word, I was calling at an inconvenient moment; she was in the bath. The swish of water around her limbs was a distraction. I imagined her athletic body, surrounded by bubbles, candles on the shelf, a glass of wine, music in the background. I wanted to be with her. I promised myself that I soon would be.

I had a near-sleepless night, but when the day broke I was ready for the day's challenges. I climbed out of the car, towed the Reaper onto the main runway, and positioned it for take-off. I opened the primary inspection panel and flipped all systems to standby. Then I towed the EC out. I stood and admired Chad's handiwork in the daylight; it was a beautiful job. The sandstorm camouflage indicated she was a working military helicopter and not just a VIPs taxi.

I washed, brushed my teeth, and dressed in USAF flight overalls and a survival vest. I put the laser rangefinder, high-powered binoculars, the Glock, the L115A3 and the tripod into the back of the EC, and then I locked up the hangars. I phoned Charlie and told her I loved her and Oh God I did, I loved her so much. We talked about the future and the present and avoided talking about what I was doing or where I was doing it.

After the call, I sat in the EC, plugged in my helmet, flipped down the sun visor, and started my flight checks. When everything was steady in the green, I took off and headed for the weapons demonstration site: the top-secret Yucca airstrip in the Nevada desert.

I flew a loop eastwards, then northeast around Las Vegas then northwest, tracking along the route of I-95.

At eight thousand feet I flew directly into the danger zone because I wanted to be seen. I figured the huge amount of detection equipment in the Nevada desert, plus the manned towers around the target area, meant a sneaky entrance wouldn't work. So I wanted to look ordinary, not extraordinary.

The approach frequency was busy. I enjoy listening to military air controllers; they're used to dealing with the unexpected. Creech AFB were on to me very quickly.

'Unidentified helicopter bearing 290° this location, Squawk Mode Charlie.'

I reached over and hit the space bar on the laptop which

transmitted the Squawk Mode, a three-pulse response to any crypto-coded challenge.

'Blackjack20 squawking now.' I replied.

The good folk in Creech would be looking up Blackjack on the register of callsigns and would see that it was reserved for the Nellis AFB rangeboss. The suffix 20 meant I was a senior officer. And I'd just squawked an authentic challenge/response.

Five beats later, I got my reply.

'Blackjack20, you are cleared through this area. Be advised there is heavy traffic in the zone at this time, proceed with caution.'

'Blackjack20, caution will be exercised.'

'Two-zero, Roger. Have a good day.'

'Blackjack20,' I acknowledged.

I flew northwards around the main hub of Creech then headed westwards for the Yucca airstrip.

I had one more radio challenge, this time from the Yucca controller, but the same responses I'd given Creech got me cleared for landing. I was advised to park next to a C-130 on the east side of the airstrip.

Maybe it was the sharpness of the military air control-lers, or maybe it was that I was flying in protected military airspace, or that I was back in uniform again, or possibly because the EC was wearing desert colours, but something caused my head to loop back to previous cycles; I flew into Yucca exactly like I shouldn't have.

I made the approach very low, very fast and on an angle to the ground like I was coming in hot and heavy and look-ing to avoid unfriendly eyes. At the last moment, I hit the button to lower the landing gear, flared the EC into a straight and level attitude and just as the control panel showed three greens when the wheels locked into place, I touched down as soft as a new mother's kiss on her baby's chest, and immediately cut the engines.

I shouldn't have done that; despite being a satisfying move, I regretted it immediately. It was a flashy and distinctive landing. I hoped there wasn't anyone around who would recognise the manoeuvre for what it was.

When the EC had spooled down, I took off my flying helmet, put on my sunglasses and walked out into the bright desert sunshine.

On the west side of the black asphalt airstrip were two rows of spectator stands decorated like it was a passing out parade. Red, white, and blue bunting, and strips of US flags added an almost holiday-like air. I looked over my shoulder, the EC didn't look out of place next to the air force C-130, and an army Bell 206.

To the left of the spectator stands was a large marquee with a row of portable toilets behind. I was headed for the latrines, but a First Lieutenant, who looked ten years too old for the rank hailed me.

'Captain, you the pilot who just flew that in?' He pointed at the EC. He must have seen me get out, so I didn't evade.

'Yes, Lieutenant, can I help you?'

'It was an impressive approach. I recognise Special Ops flying.'

'Thank you.'

He held out his hand. 'Craig. Craig Evans, Captain Alvarez.' He read my name tag.

I took his hand. 'Becky.'

'So, I just wanted to check, as I'm liaison here today, is

there anything you need? Anything I can do for our Special Ops colleagues?'

'No, I'm all right, thanks. I was just going to have a look around before the demo starts.'

'Are you an observer?'

The movements schedule flashed into my memory. 'I'm not officially on the roster, but Lieutenant General McAdams asked me to drop by.'

I'd taken a punt that a First Lieutenant and a Three Star General wouldn't be having chummy conversations.

'Ah. Right. Well. If there's anything you need, just holler, and I'll make it happen for you.'

'Thanks, Craig. I guess I'm early, so I was just looking around.' I gestured pointedly towards the latrines.

'Sure thing.'

From his chest pocket, he took a folded piece of paper and offered it to me. 'If you're going that way later, you'll need a security pass.'

'Obliged to you, thanks.'

'No problems. Anything else you need?'

'Yeah. Before you head off, what does the timetable look like? I didn't get the full schedule.'

'The VIPs should be assembled by ten. Couple of speeches. First flyby fifteen minutes later, engagement commences at ten-twenty. Final scenario ten-forty. Last speech ten-fifty. Marquee for the buffet and handshakes at eleven. VIPs due to depart at noon.'

'Thanks, Craig. Good to know. I'll probably get out of town early, socialising with the brass isn't my thing.'

'No worries, Becky. Remember, if you need anything just let me know. Have a good day.'

I checked my watch as he walked away. It was 08.45 now. I reckoned I'd be making my move just before noon. I was beginning to feel confident. I had an hour and a quarter to kill before things started, and I needed to keep a low profile; hanging around the stands or the marquee would draw attention. I could either hide in the latrines or get comfortable in the EC.

I used the latrine, then walked back to the EC, set a timer on my watch, stretched out on the rear passenger seats, phoned Charlie, and then tried to doze.

Chapter 50. Attempt 2
Target

Week 47. Nevada

My alarm woke me. I climbed into the front of the EC and had a good look around.

Yucca had filled up while I slept. Behind the marquee there were rows of trucks, cars, and jeeps; the PA system was telling everyone how loudly it could count from one to two. USAF Security Forces were all over the place; desert camo, pistols on their hips, and carrying M4 assault rifles like they knew how to use them. Their distinctive blue berets marked them out from any other branch of the military.

I watched two helicopters come in over the airstrip and land on the line next to the EC. Neat flying. Functional. Very military, by the book, doing just enough. They were a pair of Leonardo/Boeing MH-139 helicopters in USAF colours, not in desert camo like the EC. Probably bringing some heavy brass. I got the binoculars out and continued scanning.

Ten minutes later, an executive jet circled the mountain ranges, then flew in and landed on the airstrip. That would be my man. It was definitely his jet.

An air force sedan drove out to the jet as it came to a halt at the far end of the runway. Steps extended from the side of the plane, the door opened, two people descended and got into the sedan. I watched them. My target and his head of security, no doubt about it.

The sedan drove to the front of the spectator stands; the same two people got out and began shaking hands with the military and civilian brass. The sedan moved to the back of the marquee.

The speeches started. The first, from a staff officer, was brief, little more than introductions. The second speaker was my target. I watched the cream-suited man who had destroyed my family and many other families. He got to his feet and the PA carried his voice through the still desert air. He talked about cooperation and justice and the future and technology and destiny and right and wrong and good and evil and Oh My God it made my stomach sick to listen to his twisted human being.

When he finished there was no polite applause. It was loud, fulsome. Flattering. They were feting him. He was the bringer of new toys and Lord, how the military loved their toys.

At 10.15 a Reaper flew low overhead, getting ready to show off its latest technology. The crew at Creech would be controlling it remotely and watching everything on their monitors. The distinctive sound of the UAV faded as it was flown higher and began its demonstration attack against an older, slower UAV because nothing highlights fairness and righteousness more than picking a fight with someone older, smaller, and slower, and whose face doesn't fit in the gang any longer.

I pulled out my phone and punched in a number. Back at Cuttle, my Reaper sprang to life. The display on my phone told me when the engine had reached operating temperature and all its systems had come online. When everything showed green, I sent a four-digit code that triggered the Reaper's new programme. The engine would increase power, the brakes would release, the Reaper would gain speed down the runway, take off, enter a climbing circle over the former airbase until it got to fourteen thousand feet, then it would head towards the Yucca airstrip. When it was fifteen miles south of here, the Reaper would descend to seven thousand feet and fly a twenty-five-mile circle around the airstrip. That altitude would keep the Reaper safe from the tallest peaks. The course and distance would put it over territory used to seeing Creech-based Reapers on a near-daily basis, but far enough away from Yucca to raise no concern. The UAV acknowledged my signals.

Somewhere above me, there was a bang as a small charge from the 'enemy' UAV destroyed a target drone. I didn't know what they were demonstrating today, but it seemed to be going down well with the brass in the stands.

There was a sharper bang as the new kid in town showed up. The demonstration Reaper fired an air-to-air missile that took out the enemy UAV. This was toys for grown-ups.

There were more bangs as another enemy drone flew in and began attacking the demonstration Reaper, but it had some kind of defence against air-to-air missiles, which enabled it to evade the attack. The audience clapped this new development. Then the demonstration Reaper launched its counterattack.

The presentation finished with a loud bang as the final attacking UAV was destroyed. After a round of applause, my cream-suited target stood in front of the microphone and fed the brass some more headlines. There was further applause. People rose from their seats, began filing out of the stands and heading for the marquee.

I put some power into the ECs control panel, switched off the transponder, then brought her to life, put my pride behind me, and executed a dull but standard military take-off.

I headed south, towards Creech AFB, an unremarkable route. As I passed over the 4,658' summit of Puddle Peak and lost sight of Yucca airstrip, I put the EC into a contour-hugging dive and followed the terrain to the valley floor. I levelled out and banked south. A few miles later, I looped around a low cluster of mountains and headed northeast. At the foot of a long range of intimidating mountains, I climbed steeply, keeping close to the rocky contours, until I'd reached the summit; this was Hogback, 4,498' high. Hogback overlooked the Yucca airfield.

I carefully set the EC on the flattest, most stable-looking part of the peak, and powered down her engines. My position gave me a good view of the airstrip far below. My phone beeped; the Reaper signalled that it had entered the holding pattern around Yucca.

I stepped out and unloaded the low tripod, the binoculars, and the laser rangefinder I'd bought in LA. I coupled the binoculars to the rangefinder and then attached them to the tripod. I scanned the airstrip.

There were no gaps in the carpark behind the marquee yet, so I guessed the socialising and PR chatter was still in full swing. I shifted my gaze to the end of the airstrip; the private jet was still there, parked at the end of runway 1-9.

I checked out the rest of the airstrip. The C-130 was still there, one of the MH-139 helicopters was starting to rotate its blades, but nothing else had changed. I felt a trickle of sweat run down the side of my face as I watched through the lenses. Hurry up and wait is a well-known military expression. I hurried up and waited. If I added all my waits together, I reckoned I'd waited many years for my targets. Some waits have been more comfortable than others. I've waited in cars, and in woods. I've waited in deserts, on sand dunes and, once, I waited inside the Arctic Circle. I've even waited in beds. Today I waited on a rocky ledge on top of a mountain in the Nevada desert.

I was thinking too much about me and not enough about the job. I tried not to think of Charlie. Tried not to think of our life together, the remainder of my life with her. We just fitted together, and I adored her. My mind wanted to roam through possible lives we could live together while I really needed to concentrate on the view through the binoculars. The stillness in the air amplified my tension. My cramping muscles forgot how uncomfortable the rocks were.

Eventually, twenty minutes behind schedule, there was a lot of movement below. The sedan pulled out of the parking line and drove to the front of the marquee. Through the powerful lenses I saw my pale-suited target climb into the back of the car. His head of security, a face and a posture I knew so well, got in the opposite side.

I sent a three-digit code to the Reaper that would make it climb to 12,000' and turn onto a circle with the norther end of the airstrip as the centre of its turn.

I focussed on the jet; the passenger door opened. I looked back to the car; it was pulling away from the marquee. I quickly scanned the area. Vehicles were leaving, heading off in different directions. An MH-139 had just lifted into the air, the blades on the other were beginning to rotate, the C-130 was warming up its engines. The blue berets were mustering near the marquee. This was check-out time.

I waited until the sedan had pulled up at the foot of the jet's staircase. When the first person, my target, began to climb up it, I switched on the laser rangefinder and focussed it on the midpoint of the aircraft. In the still mountain air, I could almost hear my heartbeat.

I watched his head of security start to climb the steps, the jet's engine noise increased, and a cloud of desert dust hid my view for a few seconds. When I could see clearly, I saw that the staircase had been retracted, and the fuselage passenger door closed. The distant engine noise continued to rise as the jet engines were brought up to full power.

After a few minutes the jet pulled off the hardstanding and onto the clearly marked '1-9' at the far end of the runway. I checked my Reaper's position; it was just beginning its clockwise circle at the southern end of the airstrip.

The jet began to move down the tarmac, gradually picking up speed. My Reaper, half a mile south of the foot of the runway, was straightening out of its turn at 12,000'. The positioning was perfect. I sent a two-digit code to the UAV.

Far above these mountains, a Paveway II laser-guided bomb was released from the UAV and began its silent glide to the precise point I was directing the laser rangefinder.

I had figured the pilot would keep the aircraft running on the airstrip as long as possible; the hot, still desert air wouldn't give much support for a rapid take-off. I'd been right. I watched the jet pass the halfway marker. I sent another two-digit code to the Reaper, a second Paveway missile detached itself and homed in on the same point of the laser beam.

I didn't take my eyes off the aircraft; the front wheel started to lift and then the jet began to fall apart. There wasn't a very bright flash followed by a loud bang. There wasn't an obvious point of explosion; the jet and the Paveway collided too quickly for the type of explosion Hollywood has made popular.

The Paveway struck the jet at the top of the fuselage, halfway along. The combined speed and opposite directions of travel pushed the missile into the aircraft and then it exploded. To me, in my lookout, it looked as if the jet was being peeled from the inside.

The structure of the aircraft just folded back and then there was a blinding flash. The noise took what seemed like an age to reach me. I kept the binoculars and the laser rangefinder on the remains of the aircraft. A wing buckled and rubbed the airstrip causing the already weakened fuselage to split into three. The wing took half the fuselage with it, the nose of the aircraft dug into the surface of the airstrip and the tail section, still attached to the port-side of the fuselage, flipped high and over itself, spiralling away.

The second Paveway detonated on impact with the largest remaining section of the fuselage. The double ba-boom echoed around the mountains, making the explosion seem as if it was never ending.

My binoculars showed a large fireball had engulfed what used to be the fuselage. The jet's nose section had disintegrated into the runway, debris scattered a long way back down the tarmac.

People were running onto the airstrip, streaming from the marquee and from the C-130. I figured the survival chances of my target and his head of security would be nil. I was sorry for Danny, the pilot.

I sent a four-digit code to the Reaper that put it on a ground-hugging, mountain-dodging course back to Cuttle. I stowed my hardware into the EC, strapped in, started up, and put her into a steep dive off the peak that would have got a civilian pilot licence revoked.

At very low altitude I headed westwards out of Nevada and into Death Valley, California. Even though I was flying hard, I loved the thrill of watching the altimeter dip into negative numbers as I approached the desert floor.

I landed the EC in a dried-up riverbed and powered down. For two hours I sat and waited, listening to the air radio, and occasionally scanning the skyline for someone looking for a helicopter. Shortly before 3pm I was sure my trail was clean; I brought the EC up to full power, took off and died.

Chapter 51. Attempt 3
Rerun

Week 47. Nevada

My alarm woke me. I climbed into the front of the EC and had a good look around.

Last time I had missed something crucial, and I'd paid the price with a new cycle. This time I gave my attention to every single detail.

Yes, Yucca had filled up while I had slept. Check. Yes, there were rows of trucks, cars, and jeeps parked behind the marquee. Check. Yes, the PA system was telling everyone how loudly it could count from one to two. Check.

Yes, USAF Security Forces were all over the place; desert camo, M9 pistols on their hips, M4 assault rifles like they knew how to use them. Check. Their distinctive blue berets marked them out from any other branch of the military. Check. I looked harder. This time my senses told me that something wasn't quite right with them. Maybe check. I'll come back to them, I thought.

I flipped my gaze away and watched the two helicopters come in over the airstrip. I didn't take my eyes off them. I scanned down the full length of both machines as they approached the line. I recalled one MH-139 was in the air before I blew the jet. Perhaps somehow it had got on to me? Maybe it saw me leave Hogsback? Maybe it carried enough enhanced equipment to track my diving run across the desert floor?

Or maybe they just got lucky searching after I'd destroyed the jet, and the minute I popped the EC out of the dried riverbed they just hit me with an air-to-air missile and scattered me all over the desert floor?

They landed on the line next to the EC. Neat flying. Functional. Doing just enough. Very military. But no check. I scanned them again. Something was wrong but I couldn't put my finger on it.

I half-watched the executive jet circle the surrounding mountain ranges. Something else here didn't add up. Something else was going on. Or not going on. If the helicopters weren't right, what else was wrong with this picture?

I looked out of the cockpit, deep in thought, while I watched the jet taxi to a stop on the far end of Runway 1-9. The sedan was on the way out to meet it and suddenly I began to wonder about the blue berets because there weren't any large trucks in the parking lot. So how did they get here?

And what if they weren't what they seemed? What if they were part of his security detail? What if the blue berets had arrived in the C-130? But what if they weren't legitimate? I mean, if a bunch of military police turn up at a military installation, and they're wearing the right uniform and carrying the right weapons, and they'd got out of a military transport, who's going to ask them for their ID? And who's going to say, 'What are you guys doing here?' After all, that was pretty much the same logic I was using, right?

And suddenly I had a bunch of complicated things to think about. The more I thought about it, the more it seemed likely I hadn't been detected by a lucky search. The last time I'd tried this, I had gone very low and very fast into Death Valley. And I had waited in a dried-up riverbed. They hadn't known where I had waited. If they had, they would have taken me out immediately instead of waiting for me to take off before ruining a perfectly good Eurocopter.

Even though the ECs transponder was switched off they'd somehow tracked me into the desert. How? I knew where all the desert radar outposts were. I had avoided the footprint of them all. I knew where the manned observation posts were. I'd kept away from them.

Maybe my target had his own UAV? A spotter drone? A Reaper with the right... Wait a minute. They already had a Reaper up there. They UAV they were showcasing. The flight crew back at Creech could have tracked me visually. If it was out of ammunition, and that seemed likely after the demonstration, all the flight crew had to do was tell the troops where I was holed up, and all the bad guys had to do was wait until I popped up out of the dried-up riverbed and no more Laura. This was looking like the likely explanation.

Meanwhile, the sedan had arrived back at the stands, its passengers were out and shaking hands with the brass.

Shit.

There were too many unknowns. Suddenly my whole plan looked uncertain. I had no time for a major replan and I had to think fast. I needed a distraction for the girls and boys who were flying that demonstration UAV; they needed something else to look at. It had to be something really attention-grabbing. I hoped what I'd brought would help with the distraction. And I needed a new way out of here, just in case.

But I had to put the first part of my plan into action. The speeches had started. I watched the cream-suited man get to his feet and talk about money and power, because that's all this was really about. His money. His power.

The demonstration UAVs manoeuvred into position; my Reaper left Cuttle on its way here. Time to go. I fired up the EC, switched off the transponder and flew the same course to the crest of Hogsback, landed, and powered down.

I unpacked a heavy blanket from the luggage compartment, lay down and used the binoculars to check out the scene below. The USAF Security Forces personnel were still on the ground. The C-130 was still there too: I'd guessed, because there was no heavy transport truck in the behind the marquee, it was their transport in and out of Yucca.

I slowly shifted my gaze over the nearest MH-139. These helicopters are beefed-up, militarised cousins of the civilian EC155. They're a little longer in the body, a little heavier in the ass (and therefore a little slower), but they are powered by the same formidable twin engines as the EC. The big differences are the MH-139s are fitted with armour, have built-in weapons systems, and all kinds of super high-tech radio and navigation hardware.

The longer I looked at the helicopters the more I felt there was something wrong. I flicked the binoculars back over both fuselages and the penny dropped. Neither helicopter had tail markings. They had no tail markings! How the fuck had I missed this the first time?

Every aircraft, and every helicopter has tail markings. It's their ID. The tail markings that I'd asked Chad to put on the EC were clones from a genuine USAF EC155. But those mothers out there? No markings at all? That was either careless or ballsy. I mentally kicked myself for missing this.

I focussed in tighter on the nearest MH-139 and slowly moved my gaze around it. Blacked-out canopy, solid passenger doors (no windows). That seemed unusual. I flicked the binoculars back over the fuselage to check I hadn't missed a badly placed marker and yep, this bird definitely had no tail markings, just a discrete '01' painted below its tail rotor. I looked at the other one, it had '02' painted on its tail fin.

If just one of those MH-139s got into the air I was in trouble, this now seemed likely how I'd ended the last cycle. I needed to improvise my way out of this, but I had no ground-to-air or air-to-air weapons. There was just me, the civilian EC painted up to look like a combat bird and, in the luggage bay, the Glock and the L115A3. I went back to the EC, got the long canvas bag out and set up the L115A3 next to the binoculars and the laser rangefinder.

I scanned the scene below once again, and the nagging feeling that something else here didn't add up hit me. If the helicopters weren't right, what else was wrong with this picture?

I looked at the first helicopter, then the second one. Then I looked hard at the C-130, That, at least, had a legitimate tail number. Or did it? I pulled out my phone and searched for it. Two websites said the ID belonged to a C-130 airframe that had been lost in Operation Sharp Edge. So how was it in front of me?

I started to feel outnumbered and heavily outgunned. If the two MH139s and the C-130 weren't legit, those well-armed USAF Security Forces folk down there? They weren't kosher either.

I had no time for a major replan, and had to think fast; I needed to execute the plan differently. And I needed to give those boys and girls down there, and the UAV flight crew back in Creech, a distraction, otherwise I'd be starting a new cycle again in a few minutes.

In the hands of an expert, the MH-139 can get from engine start to airborne in ninety seconds if the pilot is prepared to cut a corner or two. The thought I'd have two of them tracking me as I cut out across Nevada wasn't a good one.

I looked at my watch. I had arrived on the peak at 11.20. My Reaper had entered its holding pattern at more or less the same moment. The small window of opportunity I had was now looking even smaller.

I nestled into the stock of the L115A3 and put the telescopic sight to my eye. There was some activity around the C-130 ramp, and the anti-collision lights on the closer MH-139 flicked on as the pilot ran through the start-up checklist. That had to be my distraction target. The laser rangefinder confirmed the distance was 1,720m, or 5,643', or just over a mile.

In November 2009, British Army Corporal Craig Harrison achieved the record for the longest sniper kill, taking out two Taliban from a range of 2,475m with his L115A3. But Craig had been putting so many rounds through his rifle every week that it felt like it was part of his arm and was wired to his brain.

I was a decent shooter, but I was an amateur compared to Craig. The twenty-five rounds I'd put through the rifle yesterday evening at Cuttle had given me some confidence, but I had only been shooting at 1,500m. Now I needed to be accurate at 1,720m which the L115A3 was capable of, and I'd selected the best ammunition for it. The problem wasn't the rifle; the problem was the person holding it.

I adjusted the sights, checked the windage, and focussed

the crosshairs on the first MH-139, its blades had just started slow rotation. I zeroed in on the main rotorhead and waited as it gradually spun up to full power. There was a slight movement, a moment of almost instability as the helicopter began to lift.

I squeezed and put the first round into the rotorhead, slid the bolt back and forth and put the second bullet into the main gearing assembly. I cocked the third round into the chamber, paused, and watched the complicated piece of engineering fall apart. The rotorhead is a nexus of five blades, but it's also home to the swivel, rotate and tilt mechanisms - the servo-assisted levers that link the pilot's arms and legs to everything that makes the helicopter fly.

Right now there would be alarms in the cockpit; lights would be flashing red, gauges would be returning to zero, and there would be a huge vibration through the airframe. The cockpit would not be a happy place. The MH-139 dropped back onto the ground, the wobble in the rotorhead grew more severe. The blades started to slow - the pilot had cut the power - but the helicopter was becoming more unstable faster than he could stop the blades turning.

Almost too fast to follow, one of the blades rose off its horizontal plane, the tip of the blade flicked high above the MH-139, the mounting fractured, the blade sheared off and buried itself into the side of the C-130, slicing through its armoured fuselage like a craft knife through a sheet of paper.

Unbalanced, and now with just four blades pulling in different directions, the MH-139 began to roll on its axis. The pilot had engaged the clutch and was applying the brake to the rotors. It was a good attempt at slowing everything down.

I flicked my sight to the main marquee; blue berets were now swarming around it, forming a defensive perimeter. Christ, I'd been right. They were his troops. Legitimate Security Forces would have organised themselves then fanned out in all directions looking for aggressors; they wouldn't be forming a tight defensive ring - not unless they had orders to protect someone - and that's not the blue berets bag. That's what bodyguards are for.

I focussed on the far end of runway 1-9; the heat haze told me the jet was running its engines up to speed. Back to the marquee. The sedan was shifting fast out of the parking line. It pulled up in front of the marquee, loaded its two passengers, and sped hard for the jet, raising a shroud of desert dust in its wake.

I signalled the Reaper and put the laser rangefinder on the still unmoving jet; returned my view to the L115A3 sight. The wall of dust that had followed the sedan obscured my vision. When the dust cleared, I saw the jet nose forward onto the runway and begin its take-off, so the passengers must have scurried aboard while I was unsighted. They were in a hurry to get out of town. I sent the first code.

High above the Yucca airstrip, the Paveway detached from the Reaper and followed the invisible beam of light from the laser rangefinder. The bomb glided through the cockpit windscreen and exploded almost immediately. The jet folded from behind the wings like some huge force had pushed it into an invisible wall. The explosion split the front of the fuselage open like a set of aluminium jaws. I sent the second code; the other Paveway detonated on the port wing, breaking the jet into unrecognisable fragments.

I watched the aircraft break apart, blow up, and burn in its tracks on the airstrip. All I had to do now was to get away with my life. And get home to Charlie.

I checked back with the MH-139s. The main engine of the helicopter I'd shot up was smoking heavily. Another blade had sheared off and was embedded in the sand nearby. Despite the rotor assembly spinning more slowly, the helicopter's body was still vibrating. It juddered around on its landing gear, looking like it might topple over.

The C-130 was taxiing forward onto the airstrip, its tail ramp only a quarter closed, the MH-139 blade protruding halfway down the starboard fuselage. The aircrew wanted to get away fast. The undamaged MH-139 was still powered down, so I figured that aircrew had run for it. Time for me to run for it too.

I sent the four-digit code to the Reaper that would put it on a ground-hugging, mountain-dodging course into the centre of Lake Mojave. I doubted it would ever be recovered from such a large body of water. I stowed all my equipment into the EC, started up, and executed a contour-hugging dive off the peak.

This time I decided to head for the cover of a lot of military air traffic. I flew east for sixty-five miles. When I reached Coyote Springs, I climbed to five thousand feet, then headed southeast to Lake Mead where I switched on my transponder, contacted Nellis AFB approach, and requested permission to put down to pick up a couple of passengers.

Nellis was cool about it; permission was granted. Why wouldn't it be? I was just another military helicopter in a sky full of military hardware.

Chapter 52. Attempt 3
Normal

Week 47. Nevada/California

On the ground at Nellis, I secured the EC, booked a refuelling, and got a lift from the Transportation Section to the on-base Air Force Inn on Fitzgerald Boulevard.

The same young guy sat behind the desk; it was almost two months since he'd seen me last. I said I was booking in for just one night and he looked like I'd crushed his dreams. He obviously had a thing for Asian girls in military uniform.

After I'd showered, I called Charlie. Our conversation was light; she didn't press what I'd been doing. She didn't really want to know.

I said I was going to a gym this evening; she said she'd already been. I asked what she was having for supper, and I trumped her chicken salad when I said I was going for a cheeseburger with extra fries. I could almost hear her pout through the phone.

While I was walking back to the Inn after dinner, I went through the whole day. Mission accomplished. Target eliminated. And I was still alive. The only thing I was sure of was that I'd not only taken out his executive jet, I'd also kicked over an ant nest; he'd brought a lot of personal security; two MH-139s, a C-130, and a troop of people pretending to be USAF Security Services.

I got in to bed and reviewed this cycle. I'd changed very little that had gone before. I liked the dynamics that meeting Mark at sea gave our friendship. I loved what Charlie and I had the first time we got together. I worked hard to keep that excitement. If anything, starting again with her made me anticipate every moment even more.

Before I fell asleep, I flicked through the local TV stations. There were no reports of anything at Yucca airstrip. I didn't really expect anything; the place is a highly classified location full of subterfuge and cover stories. Hardly anyone knows what really goes on at Yucca, most of the public think it's a disused nuclear test site and it isn't. News management would be simple for the US Government and for the Whiteland Security Company. They both had reputations and investments to protect. I slept well.

The next morning, I checked out of the Inn at six and got a lift to Flight Operations, where I lodged a flight plan to Edwards Airforce Base, California. Then I walked three miles across the base to the EC. She'd had her tanks filled overnight and was ready to go.

I flew a straight-line course from Nellis. Edwards AFB approach directed me to the visitors landing area where I set down long enough to have delivered a Very Important Passenger. When I took off again, I headed southeast, looped south around Barstow, where I changed transponder codes from fake military to the ECs civilian ID, before turning northwards back to Cuttle.

I reckoned that dodging from Yucca into Nellis, where I'd had a lot of cover from military fixed-wing and rotary traffic, spending the night there, and then flying from Nellis to Edwards under an official flight plan would have thrown anyone looking for an unusual pattern. Flying straight from Nellis to Edwards had given plenty of opportunity for un-friendlies to have a go at me. Nobody had. And there were no obvious signs that I was being followed in the air.

I got to Cuttle at 9.30am. As soon as I touched down, I ran a scan for air traffic. There was nothing in the area, and no signs of anything that could have been following me.

I towed the EC into Hangar One and moved everything from her luggage compartment into the trunk of the hire car. I washed, changed into jeans and a t-shirt, and locked up. I called Chad and arranged for him to come and unwrap the EC; he said he'd start the next day. Then I drove to LA. Four hours later, I pulled up outside Charlie's house.

Less than an hour later I was on the couch using her laptop, she was wrapped around me.

'Have you done it yet?'

'Can you keep quiet? I'm concentrating.'

Yes, of course you are. But have you done it yet?'

'Honestly, I'm going to…'

'Ssssh. Just tell me if you've done it yet.'

I sighed and clicked the mouse. 'I've done it.'

'Really? You've really done it?'

'Really yes, really I've really done it. Really.'

'Are you being mean to me?'

'Would I ever be mean to you?'

'Umm.'

'The correct answer is "No".'

'No?'

'Now try it without the question mark.'

'I'm Californian. We say everything with a rising inflection?'

'You're just doing that to make a point now.'

'No, I'm not?'

I put the laptop beside me, leaned over, and kissed her. Then I kissed her again, properly.

'Wow. Can we go to bed now?'

'I don't think so. Let's go for a walk.'

'But you just made me feel very bad.'

'Walk first. Then shower. Then bad. And maybe PJs and some music later, or maybe a film?'

'Have you forgotten we're in SoCal where people don't walk?'

'Just around the block then.'

'Can we talk about things?'

'What things?'

'The things you've just done?'

'Definitely.'

We left the house and walked up May Street, onto Marco Place, talking as we walked. Almost automatically, we headed in the direction of Venice Beach.

'So we're getting married.' I said.

'We are?'

'Yes, we are. I just booked it.'

'Did you?'

'We're getting married here in California.'

'Really?'

'On the beach.'

'Wow, whose crazy idea was that?'

'Yours. Your idea. Definitely was. Now can you be serious for a minute?'

'I'm so happy.'

I squeezed her hand.

'You're like a giddy teenager.'

'I've never felt like this. I love you so much.'

'I love you so much too.'

We hit Ocean Front Walk and stopped to lean on the railings while we watched the late afternoon activity on the beach.

'I've never had a beach wedding before.'

She punched me in the ribs.

'That's not the sort of thing you're supposed to say to your fiancée.'

'Not even if it's true?'

'Well yes, obviously. But also no.'

'You're not at all contradictory.'

'Thank you.'

'I was being sarcastic.'

'Oh.'

'Who are you going to invite to our beach wedding?'

'I liked the sound of that.'

'I liked saying it. So who?'

'My parents, for sure. They liked you.'

'They've seen me once, and that was less than two weeks ago.'

'They liked you.' She was insistent.

'OK, so your parents. Who else?'

'I don't know. Maybe a couple of people I went to university with. We haven't stayed close, but there have been the usual invitations.'

'I know what you mean.'

'What about you? I mean, Brazil is a long way, and you're in California...' She let the sentence trail off.

'Oh. I've got a few people who are coming.'

She was genuinely pleased.

'I'm so glad. Who?'

'Well, there's Angelo, a smooth-talking gun-running mobster from the better side of Rio's badlands.'

'Oh.'

'And there's Pappi, a sweet murderous crook of a man from one of Rio's most notorious Favelas. He deals in guns and drugs and dodgy chickens.'

'You're pulling my leg now.'

'A little bit.' I said. 'But definitely dodgy chickens.'

She put her arm around me and I rested my head against her. Then after a pause. 'I've had enough walking and talking. Let's go home and get clean and be dirty.'

Deep inside, I was starting to feel exhausted. The last two days had been something else. And I couldn't tell her about it.

Chapter 53. Attempt 3
Truck

Week 48. California

Two days later we were jogging back from one of the toughest gym workouts we'd ever put in; we rounded the corner onto May Street. At the side of the road, outside Charlie's house, there was a telecommunications truck. The sidewalk inspection cover was up, around it was a red and white guardrail.

'Keep going to the end of the road.'

'What?'

'Seriously. Keep this pace to the end of the road and then go left around the corner. Something's wrong.'

'What's wrong?'

'Please, Charlie. Trust me. Something's not right. Keep going. And don't turn your head to look at your house.'

'What? Why?'

'Please. Just do what I'm asking. If there's no problem, I'll just look an idiot.' She didn't say anything but kept her eyes lowered as we jogged to the end of the road and around the corner.

'Now tell me what's wrong.'

I held her hand.

'There's a cable company truck outside your house.'

'I saw that. And the cover is off the hole in the ground. Like they do.'

'The registration on the truck is out of state.'

'So?'

'So it's odd. And there was nobody in the hole in the ground.'

'Maybe they're in the truck?'

'Yeah, maybe they are. Or maybe they're not.'

She peered around the corner while I thought about it.

'Will the trash have been emptied yet?'

'Hold on.' She walked to the nearest bin and peered inside. 'This one's empty.'

'Are your neighbours going to be home right now? The people who live on this side of the house?'

'Not normally. They go to work about 7.45. What are you thinking of?'

I took her hand in mine. 'This might be nothing, or it

might be something bad. I need you to stay here. If I'm not back here in twenty minutes, call the police, and tell them there's an armed intruder in the house.'

'What?'

'It'll get them here quicker. And if that truck moves, film it. Don't be too obvious but try and catch the driver; get their face if you can.'

'Jesus, Laura. You're scaring me now.'

'I'm sorry. I'm really sorry. I won't be long.' I hugged her, kissed her cheek, and jogged back up May Street.

I stopped outside the house next door, wheeled the empty recycling bin up their drive like it was a thing I do every week. I stood in their carport and listened; heard nothing out of the ordinary. I found a stepladder in the carport; carried it outside and put it next to the hedge. I climbed up and peered over at the side of Charlie's house. Everything looked normal; the kitchen door was shut, there was no sign of a forced entry.

I ungracefully climbed into the hedge and rolled through the privet onto Charlie's drive. I ducked behind my hire car. I looked down the drive; still no movement at the truck, nobody in the front of the truck, nobody in the inspection hole. I kept low, moved to the kitchen door and listened again. Nothing. Keeping low, I eased the handle downwards and opened the door a fraction. I wasn't able to see anything through the small gap, but I could hear movement inside, drawers being opened, cupboards being shut.

Suddenly the door was pulled open from inside. I had a flash of an image, a large man in dark blue overalls in the doorway. I don't know what he expected, but because I was crouched low, I punched him hard in the balls, and used my left leg to power myself upright, brought up my right knee fast. As he pivoted forward from the blow to his testicles, my right knee hit him hard in the face; I felt the splintering of bone, but I was already looking for his accomplice because there's never just one. Framed in the bedroom doorway was another overall-clad guy. As the kitchen door guy began to fall backwards, unconscious, I put my hands on his shoulders and used his momentum and catapulted myself over his falling body into the house.

The bedroom doorway guy was already shifting his weight, bracing for a frontal attack, so I didn't give him that; I hit the floor, rolled between his legs, and sprang to my feet behind him. I flipped the nail file off the top of the drawers, and before he'd even half-turned towards me, I stabbed him in his side.

I didn't penetrate far, connected with something hard beneath his overalls, so I used my other hand that was already almost up to the side of his head and smashed his head with all my strength against the doorpost. He went straight down. There was nobody else in the house. The kitchen and the bedroom looked untouched, and the lounge was still tidy.

They'd been looking, not burgling. I turned the bedroom door guy over and undid his overalls. I'd tried to stab him through a Model 638 Smith and Wesson .38 Special Revolver. A classic, as they say. Light, good grips, and an easy concealed carry. I put the gun in my hoodie pocket and gave kitchen door guy a check over. Another S&W .38 Special Revolver. So maybe these were issued, not weapons of choice.

I picked up the phone, dialled 911 and said I'd disturbed two intruders in the house, and I was a lone woman, and they were still in the house. All true. The operator told me to stay calm, and that help was on the way. I hung up and felt pretty calm.

I couldn't drag either one, so I left them where they lay. I called Charlie and said it was safe to come home and thought about things while I waited for her.

Standard weapons? And just looking? I figured that these guys were just foot soldiers doing a job, but I wanted to know who they were working for. I frisked their overalls again, removed a small billfold and a set of tools that might have been lockpicks from one guy, and a larger wallet and the truck keys from the other. I put the truck keys in my hoodie pocket and pushed the wallets, lockpicks, and the two .38s into a kitchen drawer.

Charlie ran breathlessly up to the kitchen door, stopping dead when she saw kitchen door guy on his back. 'What the absolute bloody hell?'

'We've had visitors that I think neither of us invited.'

'What? What are we going to do about it?'

'We could put the kettle on?'

'What?'

'Well, LAPD will be here in a minute, they might like a coffee.'

Bedroom door guy moved. I walked up to him and kicked him in the balls like I was taking a field goal. Then I checked on the kitchen door guy. He was out for the count.

'Jesus, you're taking this pretty calmly.'

'Well, what's the point in having a fainting fit? Break-ins happen all over the world.'

'So that's it?'

An LAPD squad car with the lights on pulled up outside

and parked across the width of the road.

'I guess it is, for now. Do you want to go and invite the officers in?'

She walked out of the kitchen, shaking her head. I couldn't hear what was said, but I heard Charlie and a couple of people talking. Then she appeared at the door, flanked by two of LAPDs finest.

Less than thirty minutes later, we were alone in the house. Officers Steve Embrich and Janet Moran had cuffed the intruders before they were awake, they took some photographs, said someone would arrive in an hour to take some prints and asked us to go to the station to make our statements. They gave us a business card with a crime reference number on it, then crammed our groggy visitors into their squad car. The cops were a couple of professional, no-nonsense people who didn't take too kindly to poor defenceless women catching burglars in their home. They left saying that a recovery vehicle would pick up the truck later.

'So, what do we do now?'

I put my arms around her waist. 'We, my girl, are going to have showers, and then we're going out for the day. And the night.'

'Are you trying to cheer me up? Because I don't think it's working too well.'

'I promise you'll feel better when we've had a shower, and we've got clean clothes on.'

'When are we going to give our statements?'

'Tomorrow. We can ring the nice station commander and arrange to do it tomorrow.'

'OK, then. What are you going to do first?'

'First, I'm going next door to put their stepladder back; I

wouldn't want to get into trouble with the neighbours.'

'Oh. Right. That's considerate. I guess I'll hit the bathroom.'

I put next door's ladder back. Then I tried the truck. All the doors were locked. I unlocked the back door. It was disappointingly empty. The front was clean and tidy and revealed almost nothing, but in the passenger door pocket, there was a small notebook which fitted in my hoodie very neatly.

Chapter 54. Attempt 3
Stakeout

Week 48. California

We packed for a night away; Charlie booked us a hotel in Malibu. Then we went shopping. I drove to the largest mall in SoCal; South Coast Plaza, Orange County's 128-acre temple to the retail gods.

I told Charlie my plan while I drove. She had a million questions, and I didn't have many of the answers. I used the word 'trust' a lot, and that word was doing some heavy lifting.

I parked in one of the in-mall parking structures; we agreed to split up. Less than an hour later, I slotted a rented SUV next to the hire car and transferred our stuff onto the rear seats. You can buy or rent anything in a large American mall.

'Where u at booful?' I texted.

'Sprtng gds lvl 2e'

'K'

Although a little disappointed that 'Sprtng gds' didn't mean spurting gods, the sight of Charlie taking swings at imaginary baseballs with an aluminium bat made me smirk.

'If you keep your elbow a little higher, you'll rock that ball right out of the park.'

'I'm feeling so angry I could take someone's head right off.'

'Are you angry or hangry?'

'Maybe a bit of both?'

'Let's go and eat.'

'But the baseball bat?'

'We'll take two. Now come on, we've got to buy some handcuffs before we eat.'

'I suddenly like the way today's shaping up!'

We checked into the hotel in Malibu early, unpacked, showered, and went to bed. Even though it was only 3pm on the same day, it already seemed like discovering two men in our house was easing into the distance; Charlie was still carrying her anger and there was enough of that in her for both of us.

'Not feeling the love?'

'I just want to be held. Spoon me while we doze.'

I held her while she didn't doze, but I did.

My watch woke me at eight. She was finally asleep. I brushed her hair away from her eyes, and for just a few moments, I loved her so much that I felt I could burst. I slid out of bed and began getting dressed.

'You look good in black.'

'It's sort of my colour.'

'Because you're a ninja?'

'Because of my hair, doofus.'

'What's a doofus? I'm not sure it sounds very nice.'

'Oh no, a doofus is lovely.'

'Are you making this up?'

'Would I?'

'You might do.'

I pulled on my tracksuit top and did the zip half up. 'You don't have to come with me.'

'I'm coming with you.'

'Are you still feeling angry?'

'You bet your cute little ass I am.'

'Will you listen to me and be advised by me this evening?'

'Yes. I've already thought about this. I'll be good. But I still want to be angry.'

'Good. A little anger is helpful. It'll give you some focus. Get dressed, then we'll get some coffee and pick up some food.'

We parked in May Street, a few houses north of Charlie's house. We had a flask of hot coffee, sandwiches, bags of potato chips, a couple of small bars of chocolate, a selection of fruit, and two sleeping bags to put across us if the Californian night got cold. That didn't seem likely, so I rolled the windows down.

'Are you sure someone's going to come back tonight?'

'I'd bet my cute little ass on it.'

'How can you be so sure?'

'There are things.'

'What things?'

I counted on my fingers.

'One. We know this wasn't a routine burglary. Routine burglars don't use phone trucks as camouflage. Routine burglars aren't so skilled that they can enter a property and not leave damage.

'Two. We can guess, because of what we know, this burglary targeted your house. So we can guess that whoever sent the burglars, they would have run a basic background check against you. Even before those guys were despatched, the people back at Bad Guy HQ would have known your name and your address. And your car registration. We can also guess that, by now, they could have accessed your bank details, and likely your credit cards, and they may be able to track your card use in real-time. They may also have access to your phone records.'

'That's scary.'

'Three. We can also guess that losing two operators this morning would have come as an unexpected surprise to whoever sent them. They were professionals not enthusiastic amateurs, and they got taken down. Even if whoever sent them has been able to get the police to release their guys, one or maybe both of them probably needs a stay in hospital. We can guess these things would be embarrassments back at Bad Guy HQ.'

She exhaled deeply and stared down the block. 'What else do we know?'

'Well, we don't know who sent them or why they were sent here. But I have my suspicion.'

'The man you targeted for revenge?'

'Or his organisation, yes. I think the burglary was a fishing trip, they were trying to find out who we are. Somehow, they've connected you with me, and connected me with what happened in Nevada.'

'So that's why you asked me to pay for the hotel in Malibu for the night?'

'Uh-huh. It's not an uncommon thing for someone to spend a night away from home after they've had intruders. And I'd like to bet that whoever sent those guys after me would have seen you book the hotel on your credit card.'

'Us.'

'What?'

'You said "whoever sent those guys after me", meaning you. But that's not it. They sent those guys after me as well. It's you and me and we're an us, so they sent those guys after us, and I hate them for that.'

I reached over and held her hand. 'At the risk of being boring, I love you.'

'At the risk of being repetitive and unoriginal, I love you too.'

'So... we've become a dull, boring, repetitive, and unoriginal couple?'

'I don't think so.'

'Good. I don't think so too. Nothing says not being dull or boring or unoriginal more than staking out your own house at whatever time of the night it is.'

'A little before ten-thirty.'

'When do you think they're going to come?'

'A little before ten-thirty.'

'What?'

'I think they're here.'

'Where?'

'Just pulled up down the road.'

The late-model Volvo saloon was the perfect camouflage for May Street; fitted into the unremarkable neighbourhood in an unremarkable way. It had pulled past us and parked a short distance down the road on the opposite side to Charlie's house. Shrewd. Almost but not quite on target, far enough away not to be considered a threat.

'But nobody's getting out.'

'Let's just wait and see.'

I kept checking the mirrors, back and side. There was no other movement on the street. The only new arrival on the street had been the Volvo; ordinary, amongst the dozen other cars parked on the road. The fact nobody had got out was strange. Might be picking someone up. But might not be.

'I want to get out and see what's going on.' She said.

'We need to stay here.'

'Why?'

'This doesn't feel right.'

'What do you mean?'

'I mean whoever is in that car is being way too cool. They're playing a waiting game. And we need to know if they're just waiting for time to pass, or if they're waiting for someone to come out of the house they're parked outside, or if they're waiting for something else to happen.'

She sighed but sat patiently. 'Do we play I Spy?'

'If you like.'

'I spy with my little eye, something beginning with c.'

'Tell me it's not 'car'.'

'It's not car.'

"It is though, isn't it?'

'Yes, it is. Damn, you're good at this game.'

'I've got a puzzle for you.'

'Go ahead, ten four rubber duck, good buddy, over.'

I raised my eyes towards the roof of the car but carried on with the question. 'In the time we've been running to and from the gym, we've not seen anyone just out for a walk, right?'

'You're in SoCal, baby. People don't 'go out for a walk' here.'

'Maybe you should go and tell those two.'

'Which two?'

'There's a woman at the south end of the street who has just walked across the intersection for the third time. And there's someone at the north end of the street doing the same.'

'Well, that is unusual.'

'So, if these are all bad people, we have walkers north and south of us and whoever is in the Volvo, but nobody actually making a move on the house. I'm beginning to think we've been blown.'

'I'm disappointed.'

'So am I. Let's give it ten more minutes and then call it a day. Do you want to play I Spy again?'

'We could make out?'

I needed that much convincing that we made out. It's really difficult to make out in the front seat of a car and keep a look out, especially when things get heated. Ten minutes came and went. Eventually, she broke the silence.

'Fuck, I want you.'

'Oh, God, I want to do you.'

'Let's go to the hotel and fuck like bunnies.'

'Yes, let's go to the hotel and wait.'

'What?'

I put my finger to her lips.

'Ssssh. Wait.' I said quietly. 'I heard something.'

Our car windows were still open; I'd heard a click out there. It could have been anything, but…

'Have you got the rucksack handy?' I asked quietly.

'Who is Andy? And yes, I've got the rucksack. Why?'

'I can't see anybody in the car. I think we were the reason they hadn't made their move.'

'What does that mean?'

'It either means they were so disgusted by our lesbian making out that they've gone for a walk, or they had night vision on us, and until we started kissing, we were making them suspicious just by sitting here.'

'Well yay for lesbian love then.'

'My money is on them having night vision.'

'Is it a problem if they do?'

'It means we need a Plan B, 'cos sneaking up on them in the house isn't going to work.'

'Why not?'

'They've got night vision. The house will be in darkness. They'll have total visibility, and we'll have none.'

'Oh. What about the walkers at the end of the road?'

'Still there; crossing both ends of May Street every couple of minutes.'

'If we can't catch them in the house, do we just sit here and follow them when they come out?'

'I think I have a better idea. Have you got those apples in our food bag?'

'Yep.'

'Gimme.'

She handed them over. 'Now I need something long and

very thin.'

'There's never a penis around when you want one.'

I got my metal nail file out and stabbed a hole through the centre of each apple.

'Is that something they teach you in the military? How to core an apple with a nailfile?'

'This is a skill I learned in an organisation far more deadly than the military.'

'Really? Which one?'

'Girl Scouts. I'll be back in a minute. If you see anyone coming, sound the hooter.'

'Where are you going?'

'I'm going to set a trap. When I'm gone, can you count to twenty and then call 911 and tell them we've got intruders in the house again?'

'OK.'

I flipped the internal light to 'don't come on', opened the door, slid out, and ran, crouching, to the back of the Volvo. Thankfully it wasn't an electric car; it had two single tailpipes just below the rear fender. I placed an apple to the mouth of the first pipe, then pushed it all the way in. Then I did the same thing with the second tailpipe. I crouch-ran back to the SUV.

'Fuck, I didn't see you!'

'Nothing to see here anyway.'

'I'm being serious. You're like a superninja.'

'I don't think they really exist. No sign of anyone?'

'Nobody at all. So what's the plan?'

'There are at least four people out there, and we don't stand a chance of having any kind of meaningful conversation with four unfriendlies.'

'That's good.'

'So because you've called LAPD I think the two lookouts will vanish as soon as a patrol car rocks up.'

'And the two who were in the car?'

'They're going to get in their Volvo and drive off, maybe they'll do that even before the police get here.'

'And we follow them to their destination, and jump them and beat the truth out of them?'

'I think you've had enough coffee for the evening.'

'Well, what then?'

'We follow them a little way, they stop, we stop, we give them a ride somewhere nice, we ask them some questions.'

'I have so many questions!'

'I hope this works.'

'Wait a minute, Hoss. You don't know this is going to work?'

'I'm not completely sure, no. I haven't stopped a car by jamming an apple in its tailpipe since I was eight. And where does Hoss come from?'

'After some intense making out, you've got me feeling all hot and frisky and I'm sitting here in wet underwear for you, and you're not completely sure whatever it is you've done is going to work? Well, on that basis I think I'm allowed to call you Hoss, Hoss.'

'What do I call you?'

'You can call me whatever you like.'

'Maybe I should call you Betty.'

'You can't, because then there would be one too many Bettys in our lives.'

'True, true. I wonder how the diving crew is doing. Anyway, it's Rio. I'm going to call you Rio.'

'Is that because I'm like a river to you? Long and gently flowing?'

Before I could answer, two shadowy figures ran across the street from the direction of Charlie's house and got in the Volvo. It started up.

'I can't hear any sirens.' She said.

The Volvo pulled away.

'I'm guessing one of their lookouts is listening to the police band. I'm going to follow them. Do you want to stay here and wait for the police?'

'I'm calling shotgun on this ride.'

'OK then.'

The Volvo turned left off May Street on to Victoria Avenue. As soon as they were out of sight I started up and followed.

'They're going to stop really soon. I'll pull up behind them. The driver is probably going to get out and pop the hood. I want you to get into their car fast as you can. Use the driver's door and point the blunt end of your baseball bat into the face of whoever is in the passenger seat. Show some aggression and make them think you're one degree away from remodelling their face.'

'What are you going to do?'

'I'm going to have a word with the driver. Don't let the passenger reach for anything. And don't let them hit the door handle. Whatever they try, they're going to be really fast.'

'OK.'

Traffic was light, keeping the Volvo in sight was easy. Three blocks later, their car showed signs of being in trouble, it stuttered a few times, and then it pulled over onto a vacant lot. The flashers came on, and sure enough, the driver got out and walked to the front.

I put the SUVs lights on high beam, flipped my flashers on, and pulled up behind them. I was out of the SUV really quickly and almost up to the front when I heard the Volvo driver's door open, and Charlie's voice say, 'Don't!'

The driver stepped away from the open hood, towards the passenger side, so I hit him behind his knees with the baseball bat; he went straight down. I hit him hard in the stomach to keep him quiet for a while. I quickly frisked him. I retrieved a .38 Special from a hip holster. I walked back to the passenger window and tapped on it with the end of the bat.

'Open it.'

The electric motor lowered the window.

'If this is a mugging, I have a little money in the glove box.'

She reached forwards, so I hit her in the face with the blunt end of the bat. Charlie cried out, taken by surprise at the speed and violence of my attack. When the woman looked up at me again, blood running from her nose, I dangled her partner's .38 Special on my finger. She wasn't happy with the way her evening was working out. I took the handcuffs out of my pocket and dropped them on her lap.

'Put them on, or I'll hit you again.' She put them on, blood continued to drain from her nose. She and I had worked out we were both dealing with people capable of inflicting great physical harm.

'Look at me.' She looked. 'If you try anything, I'm going to break you. Do you understand?' She nodded slowly.

I left her in the company of Charlie, who was still unsure about what she'd seen. Right up until this moment it had all been a game for her.

I went to the driver, who was trying to sit upright. I kicked him in the ribs, and while he was on the ground, I put a pair of handcuffs on him. Then I gave him a proper body search and took a wicked-looking five-inch blade from inside his jacket sleeve.

From my rucksack, I took a roll of black tape and bound his mouth, then I put a cloth sack over his head and bound that in place. I walked him to the back of the SUV, popped it open, and positioned him so he was sitting on the tailgate. Then I told him to climb in. Even through the sack I felt his stare, but he did it.

I got his passenger out of the car, cleaned then bound her mouth, and put a sack over her head too. Then I gave her a thorough search. Her regulation issue .38 special was also in a hip holster, but she had a SIG Sauer P365, semi-automatic pistol strapped to the inside of her thigh, just above the hem of her skirt. Despite its size, this tiny 19mm parabellum is a real showstopper in the right hands. I had no doubt she was the right hands. I slipped the SIG Sauer into my jacket pocket and put her in the back with him.

'I'm going to give you both a little safety lecture now.' I said. 'Don't move. Don't kick your feet. Don't attempt to kick the windows out. Don't struggle. Don't fight. Don't attempt to shout out. We're going on a little trip, and when we get to our destination, we're all going to have a little chat. Until that time, just be good, and we'll get along fine.' I closed the back then got into the driver's seat.

'Ready, Rio?'

'Ready, Hoss.'

We pulled away, leaving their car on the vacant lot.

Chapter 55. Attempt 3 Questions

Week 48. California

I drove east through Lakewood, then Anaheim, then high into the hills. It was midnight as I pulled to a stop on a deserted track off a mountain road. The distant lights of LA twinkled below us in the distance.

'What are you going to do?'

'Find out who sent them and what they want.'

'Are you going to kill them?'

I knew they could hear us, so I winked at her. 'Maybe. It depends if they cooperate or not.'

I got out, pulled open the hatch, and put the tailgate down.

'Out you get, sweetheart.'

She didn't move, so I pulled one of the .38 Specials from my hoodie, jabbed it between her legs and cocked it.

'Get out. Or I'll not be getting my deposit back on the car rental and you'll never fuck anything ever again.'

She carefully slid out and sat upright on the tailgate; hands still secured, hood still in place.

'Could you remove her hood please, Rio.'

'OK, Hoss.' After a bit of fumbling with the tape, Charlie pulled off the hood and stepped back.

'Could you take the tape off her mouth, please?' She ripped it off.

I tried for a little conversation. 'How are you doing? Everything all right in your world?' Hope the ride up here was OK for you?'

She wasn't feeling too cooperative.

'I have just two questions for you. Answer these and you'll go home tonight. If you don't answer them, you won't be going anywhere ever again. Do you understand?'

She understood but didn't look too convinced I was telling the truth.

'Question 1: Who are you working for?'

I paused.

'Question 2: Why did you break into our house?'

It was clear from her expression she had no intention of answering, and I didn't want to spend all night on a Californian mountain.

'Stay here please, Rio. Keep an eye on the guy in back. If he moves, hit him as hard as you like.'

I pulled the woman's handcuffs forward; she slid off the tailgate and stood. I herded her to a large bush thirty feet away. Out of sight of the car, I put the gun to the back of her neck.

'I never forget a face. If I ever see you again, I will kill you before you can even react. Do you understand?' No response: she was still playing hardball. I pointed the gun at a large tree and fired once.

'Run.' She didn't move but all colour drained from her face.

'Follow the track downhill. You'll get to civilisation sooner or later. If the bears don't get you first. Now run, before I change my mind.'

She ran. I walked into the clearing, Charlie looked a mix of horrified and curious.

'I need to get another t-shirt, Rio.' I said, loud enough for the guy in the back to hear. 'This one's all splattered.'

I gave her another wink and kissed her cheek as I walked

past.

'OK then, you're next, guy. Slide yourself out.' He sat on the tailgate. Charlie removed his hood and mouth tape. I went through the same routine with him.

'I have just two questions. Answer these and you'll go home tonight. If you don't answer them, you won't be going anywhere ever again. Do you understand?'

He nodded.

'Question 1: Who are you working for?'

I paused.

'Question 2: Why did you break into our house?'

He said nothing, so I pulled his handcuffs; he slid off the tailgate and looked at me; he was way bigger in every direction, but I knew I could drop him before he even completed a muscular movement.

'Do you mean it?'

'Yes. Why would I lie?'

'People do. To get information.'

'I'm not lying.'

'I work for a military contractor. Whiteland Security Services, headquarters in Virginia. I'm normally based at a training facility in San Diego.'

That was an unsurprising tick in the box. Whiteland Security had somehow connected me with Yucca, and through me to Charlie.

'And question 2?'

'We were told to go in and look for anything unusual, but not to disturb the place or break it up.'

'And?'

'And plant a device on the router.'

'Thanks for being honest. So I'll be straight with you. Slide in and we'll take you to the bottom of the mountain.'

He looked uncertain.

'If I wanted to drop you, this is where I'd do it. Get in and have a ride down.'

He looked at Charlie and then rolled back in.

At the turnpike I pulled over, got out, and helped him wriggle onto the tailgate. As Charlie removed his handcuffs, I gave him the same words about killing him if I ever saw him again. He looked like he believed me. I did the hatch up, got into the SUV, and pointed the car towards Malibu.

'Are we staying in the same hotel tonight?'

'Yep. But I've booked us another room under false names, and we'll pay cash.'

'That's cunning.'

'Thank you.'

'Did you shoot her?'

I chuckled.

'No. I shot a tree. I set her free. I used the shot to make him think I'd killed her, that's all.'

'Oh.'

'Oh?'

'Oh. As in an "Oh, I'm really quite relieved" kind of way.'

'They're both going to be pretty pissed when she turns up at wherever their local meet-up is.'

'He said he was from San Diego.'

'Yeah, they might be from there, but there were four of them, remember.'

'I'd forgotten about the other two.'

'It's been a bit of a long day. Let's get to the hotel, move our stuff into the other room and get some sleep. We're seeing the police later.'

'OK.'

She was fast asleep before we got to Malibu.

Chapter 56. Attempt 3
Mojave

Week 48. California

The next day we went to the precinct house and gave our statements. The police were sympathetic, typed everything into their system, and asked us to sign what we'd dictated. They were unable to give us any useful information about the people they called "the burglars". Charlie and I knew they weren't burglars, and I'm sure LAPD did too.

We went home and had our first proper shout it out loud argument. Two hours later, I drove Charlie to LAX, kissed away her tears, and put her on a flight to Rio. I messaged Angelo to say she was en route. Then I drove to a sporting goods store, spent a little money, then headed out to the Mojave Desert.

I'd figured that if I'd been traced to Charlie's house, my base at Cuttle was compromised. Driving in the front gate wasn't the best method of finding out.

There are two ways to get into Cuttle; three of you're a nutcase. The front door is the dirt-track that runs onto the base from the imaginatively named 'Old Government Road' a couple of miles to the northwest. The only other way in is to fly. Or, if you were some kind of a nutcase, you could invent a back way in by walking, if you didn't mind carrying yourself and your supplies through the desert and across the hard flinty desert rockfields.

This nutcase walked in, most of the way.

Five miles south and ten miles east of Cuttle the long Nevadan/Californian freight trains pass slowly through the Kelso-Cima railroad crossing.

A couple of hundred years ago this area played a major part in the Californian gold rush. But now the many long-abandoned mines in the Eastern Mojave mountains, and the long-dead ghost towns on the desert flats, are nothing more than a few lines in local history books.

I parked my rental behind the disused Kelso Depot station, got out my rucksack and a roll of carpet, and lay down close to the track. A few yards away was the Chinese Cemetery, one of the few memorials to the many immigrants who gave their lives to build these railroads.

When the early evening freight train from Las Vegas slowly pulled through, I got up, ran alongside, and clambered up onto the side ladder of a liquid tanker. I stood on the bottom rung, hooked my free arm through the ladder and hung on for ten miles.

I felt the carriage pass over sets of points and switches, and saw the single railroad track split into three. I did a controlled roll off the ladder onto the soft desert soil beside the track. I stood and dusted myself off, picked up the carpet roll, and adjusted my rucksack while the train continued its slow pull uphill.

When the last carriage had rumbled away into the late afternoon setting sun, I looked around. This was Kerens.

In the early 1800s the town was no more than a handful of

houses and a livery on the stagecoach route. When gold was discovered and the railway came in, Kerens quickly grew into a busy freight terminal and station stop. The town supplied goods to the ranchers and miners in the Mojave. These days Kerens is just a name on a map; the buildings are gone and the rail spurs that served the town are decaying on their rotting sleepers.

I checked my kit and supplies were OK, and began the five-mile hike to Cuttle. Half an hour after sunset, I arrived at the foot of the bluff of hills I'd noticed the first time I saw Cuttle. In the gathering gloom I hiked up the southern side of the five-hundred-foot outcrop and walked across the top to the northern edge.

Even in the early evening dusk, the former airbase was clearly visible, the shapes of aircraft hangers were outlined against the darkening sky.

I unpacked the binoculars, scope, and laser rangefinder. Then I unwrapped the L115A3 components, assembled and checked the rifle, then set it on the bipod. I put my eye to the sniper scope and inspected the former airbase.

I could clearly see the front and left side of Hangar One, where the EC was housed. I could also see the front and right of Hangar Three. All I could see of Hangar Two was the right-angle of the front. I flicked over to infra-red.

It took me ten minutes to get my scanning pattern established. On the third scanning pass I spotted the body heat of the first unfriendly, lying flat on the dispersal pan in front of Hangar One. A couple of minutes later, I identified the second unfriendly on the roof of Hangar Two. On my next sweep, the heat detector caught rising warmth from behind Hangar Three. There was a lot of it, so I guessed someone was sitting in a vehicle, running the engine.

Just three unfriendlies? If I was the commander, I would have sent five, maybe six, possibly even seven. I resumed scanning.

I found the heat signature of unfriendly number four when he rolled over, probably for a pee. He was just outside the main gate. Shrewd positioning, he could cover action inside and approaching the base.

I thought about the numbers. I would put unfriendly number five inside Hangar One. Maybe even inside the EC. Where would I put number six? The unfriendlies on the air-base were in intelligent positions. But I would still have put another pair of eyes on the ground.

Maybe unfriendly number 6 had dug in, which is why I couldn't see them? Maybe at the end of the runway? But that didn't make much sense. It was a good firing position, but too exposed.

I pulled up the laser rangefinder to check the distance; Hangar One was 2.36Km or 1.47 miles away. That's a long distance, but in my favour, there was no heat haze to mess up my vision, and the early evening wind was minimal.

I settled onto the carpet and was reaching for a sip of water when the cough made me freeze. It was very close. Immediately to my right and maybe three feet away. Perhaps just behind that low rock, or maybe a little lower on the ridge, using the rock as cover?

There was a quiet sniff as the person who coughed wiped their nose on their sleeve. Or maybe on the back of their hand.

This made things interesting. From this distance, I figured that unfriendly #6 was either a long-range spotter or a backup gun. Or both. Someone had used their head. I put the rifle down, eased out of my coat to minimise fabric noise, and slowly crawled towards the noise.

The distance from my position to the far side of the rock was eighteen feet. It took twenty-five minutes to silently crawl over the loose rocks and stones that covered the top of the bluff and to peer around it carefully. There was nobody behind it. I waited, and five minutes later heard another quiet voice. I crawled forward to the edge of the outcrop where I could only hear one side of a conversation and wasn't able to make out the spotter's words. Whoever it was on that ledge below the peak, he was using a throat microphone and an earpiece. I hoped his was using a push-to-talk switch and not a voice-activated microphone.

There were some more hushed, indistinguishable words and then a long pause. I risked a lean out and took a look down. The spotter was well merged into the ledge. I had to admit he was better placed than where I'd pitched up.

I checked my watch, 6.30pm.

I needed to know the routine. I rolled onto my back and began to pick out the stars and constellations in the cloudless Californian dusk sky to take my mind off waiting. I was concentrating on the Milky Way when I heard his voice again. The words were still too muted to distinguish, but from the cadence of how he spoke, it was obvious this was a radio check. After a pause, he spoke a few words again. Another pause, a few more words. And two more times he spoke. I was sure he was checking in with the five unfriendlies.

I checked the time; it was almost two minutes after seven, and that gave me their routine; the spotter was radio checking with each unfriendly every half-hour. I had to have a new plan. I'd only come in across the desert in case the base had been compromised. I hadn't reckoned on a well-organised reception committee.

I quietly crawled to my stash and packed it away. Then I edged back to the ledge. I slipped the rucksack off, put the rifle next to me and waited. The radio check routine started a couple of minutes later. When he'd completed the last check, I gave him two minutes to relax into his own routine while I unpacked a clean sock and the black tape from my rucksack. Then I dropped on him, hard.

I broke my fall with my knee; I literally took all of his breath away. He had no fuel in his engine to fight me with. I stuffed the sock in his mouth, taped his mouth up and hoped he wasn't going to vomit. Then I handcuffed his hands behind his back, taped his ankles together, and ran tape from his ankles to the handcuffs. He was gagged, hogtied, and still fighting for his breath.

I took the radio off his belt, ripped the cable out of the throat mic, and put the earpiece in. There was a push-to-talk switch on the radio; that was a relief, nobody had heard me landing on him.

I checked the time; twenty-three minutes to the next radio check. I slung his rifle over my shoulder and scrambled up to my position above the ledge, made my little nest, set up the L115A3, and switched to night vision. With my left eye I checked the time. Twenty minutes to the next radio check.

My first target was unfriendly #1, on the dispersal pan in front of Hanger One. The night vision showed me his outline, lying prone, a little cover afforded by a camouflaged sheet over him, but his body heat gave everything away. I went into my routine and at the moment my lungs were empty I completed the squeeze. Two and a half seconds later the .300 Winchester Magnum 7.62×67mm round silently exploded his head.

There would have been no sound at Cuttle, there was hardly a breath of sound, the super-suppressor fitted to the L115A3 made sure of that. But I expect the guy on the ledge below me had heard the whispered shot and recognised it.

I cocked another round into the chamber and shifted the sights up to the roof of hangar number two. He would have been hard to spot from the ground, but from the height of this bluff, I could see his outline silhouetted against the light in the night sky beyond. I merged myself into the rifle; we became one semi-organic mechanism. When my lungs were empty, I gently squeezed the trigger.

Chapter 57. Attempt 3
Bugout

Week 48. California

Three unfriendlies out of action, one here on the bluff and two on enemy ground.

I checked the time; nineteen minutes until the next radio check. I cocked a fresh round into the breech, ejected the partially used magazine, put it in my trouser pocket, then slid in a full one. I set a timer running on my watch.

I hurriedly broke camp, scaled down the north side of the bluff, and began running the mile and a half towards the southern perimeter of the former airbase. When I was a couple of hundred metres from the bluff, I dropped his rifle into a gully. My load wasn't too bad, and the L115A3 was light, but I wasn't going to break any speed records.

It was going to take me twelve minutes to run from the foot of the bluff to the southern perimeter fence. I reviewed my estimates as I ran. It would have taken me one minute to break camp, five more to get from the top of the bluff. Add one minute to get comfortable at my destination and start scanning. Nineteen minutes in total.

I put everything out of my head and ran; the night vision threw the green-on-green landscape at me as I put in an extra burst of speed. Not too much. I didn't want to get there puffing and panting; I needed just enough extra speed to take a handful of seconds off my estimate. The night vision got uncomfortable but taking it off wasn't an option.

I ran on, periodically scanning the green horizon for signs of any movement. I kept running, silently talking to myself as I ran. Don't think about anything else. Keep running. Keep upright. Don't fall into any holes.

I ran on. In the last half-mile, I eased my pace a little and regulated my breathing. I reached the foot of the plateau and scaled up the rise to the perimeter fence.

I checked the timer; one minute to go. I was feeling good. Not out of breath, and plenty of fuel left in the tank. I bedded down and started scanning just as a voice whispered in my ear.

'Alpha, this is Echo.'

I checked the timer; thirty-one minutes since the last radio check. They were sharp on their procedures. I kept scanning for any sign of movement. There was no response to the radio call. I reckoned Alpha was the spotter I'd left on the bluff.

'Charlie, this is Echo.'

'Echo, send.'

'Charlie, I'm late on my radio check from Alpha.'

'Roger. Nothing heard here. Take a rollcall, and I'll call it in.'

Shit. I wanted to know who Charlie was going to call it in to, and what pain that could bring.

'Alpha, this is Echo, rollcall.'

There was no reply.

'Bravo, this is Echo, rollcall.'

There was no reply. I kept on scanning.

'Charlie, this is Echo, rollcall.'

'Echo, this is Charlie.'

'Delta, this is Echo, rollcall.'

There was no response.

'Foxtrot, this is Echo, rollcall.'

'Echo, this is Foxtrot.'

'Stations, this is Echo. Tac 3-5.'

They were smart and disciplined, and now they knew they had lost Alpha, Bravo, and Delta. By now, they would have worked out that I was probably on the bluff and that I had a long gun. And calling for a switch to another channel - to Tactical 3-5 - meant they were assuming their communications had been compromised.

I kept scanning the airbase and wondered about the unfriendly outside the entrance on the north side of the perimeter. Would he have kicked himself into action and moved to a new position? Or would he sit tight and wait for orders to move? I knew he wouldn't be able to see me from where he was, but if he moved to somewhere with a better view of the land south of the perimeter, I could be exposed.

There was no more radio chatter. They'd heard the rollcall; they all knew who was up and who was down. I unclipped the radio and earpiece and dropped them on the ground. My scans were telling me very little.

There was a cooling hotspot from behind Hangar Three and no heat coming through any of the hangar walls. They hadn't pulled out; I was sure of that. They'd gone hard to ground somewhere on the base, and were waiting. Waiting for me? Or maybe waiting for reinforcements? Waiting for both? No, I rejected the thought they were waiting for me. I was certain they hadn't considered that I would be at the base perimeter. They thought I was a distant threat. My yomp across the desert hadn't been one of their considerations.

I thought about them waiting for reinforcements. Air or land? I scanned again. They could be waiting for air support. Even as the night darkened, I'd be vulnerable to airborne surveillance and attack. Land-based support seemed less likely; it would take too long to get here across land.

But these guys had gone to ground so hard that doubts began to set in. What if they had land-based backup somewhere close but off base? What if they'd gone to ground until reinforcements rocked up? I remembered the desert maps I had studied when I was planning this mission.

The only place I could figure as a possible location for ground support was the huge US Army base at Fort Irwin, fifty miles north of here. What if Whiteland Security had two or three Black Hawk helicopters, fuelled and ready to go, and thirty or forty combat troops, just sitting around at Fort Irwin, fingers itching to pull some triggers? And what if they'd just had a call from someone called Charlie who had said they should get their asses to Cuttle? None of this was impossible. They'd had enough time to put this together.

Or while I was lying here thinking about all this, they could be putting up a Reaper from Creech; I'd be defence-less against an airborne weapons platform equipped with night vision and infrared.

I had to face facts. This was out of control. My original plan of a simple, surgical strike on his jet at Yucca had kicked up more dust than I'd wanted. I needed to pull this back. I thought about what their intelligence told them. They now knew the EC was here. They also knew I was the pilot. They knew I was responsible for the attack at Yucca. They knew Charlie was a link to me. And they knew I'd repulsed two attempts on Charlie's house. And now they knew that I'd taken out half of their covert force here.

They knew too much, and I didn't know enough. The big thing I didn't know is why this had kicked up so much activ-ity. It should have all gone quiet once I'd taken out the two people at the top of Whiteland Security.

It was time to get control back. I needed to get some hard intel, and then I needed to get the hell out. Plan A had been returning to the bluff. Plan B was to head northwest to the weirdly named settlement of Zzyzx and from there up onto I-15.

I packed my kit, scrambled down to the desert floor, then skirted around the plateau until I was at the eastern perim-eter. I climbed the rocky rise and scanned in all directions; nothing. I unpacked the L115A3 and scanned through its night vision. I could see the rear of a Hummer H1 parked behind Hangar Three.

I switched to infrared and scanned again. The Hummer was the full-on lightly armoured, fast-moving military Humvee utility vehicle, the source of the large heat signature I'd seen from the top of the bluff. But there was nobody home now; the Hummer was almost cold.

Somewhere on the airbase were Echo, Foxtrot, and Charlie, three unfriendlies who were armed and probably very dangerous. Probably two inside the base and maybe one more outside. Where were the two inside? I would probably put one in with the EC, one watching the ECs hangar, and the third unfriendly on watching standby from another position. That's the guy by the main gate.

My mission for the evening had been to check the base was clean and retrieve the EC now that Chad had returned her to original colours. Although I'd been cautious getting here, I hadn't expected a tactical squad to be waiting. Somehow, they'd traced the EC from Yucca to here. I couldn't figure out how they'd done that yet. I needed more intel, and then I needed to get off their radar.

I pushed the rucksack and the rifle under the fence, crawled beneath the wire, picked up the L115A3, and crouch-ran to the back of the Hummer. I got on the ground, crawled underneath the car, and waited.

Chapter 58. Attempt 3
Briefing

Week 48. California

Just under an hour later, I heard trucks entering the base; they pulled up somewhere near the front of Hanger One. There was banging, voices, distant conversations, people calling out. I could see boots walking around. I figured that the bodies were being collected. I felt sorry for the people they had been. After a while, two pairs of boots walked towards the Hummer. The wearers got in either side, their conversation was illuminating.

'You all right?'

'Yeah, I'm OK. Internal bruising is all.'

'Can you give me a debrief? What can you tell me?'

'I was in position on the ledge; I chose the ledge to shelter from the wind. I'd just completed the radio check when I got jumped from above.'

'Above?'

'Yeah, from the top of the bluff. It was a real ballsy move to jump onto another person on a rocky ledge in the dark, but that's what he did. He was small, hard as fuck, and really, really fast.'

'But immobilised you.'

'Yeah.'

'And took out two men from the top of the bluff using his own rifle, so whoever it is, he came prepared'

'Yeah.'

'Was that difficult shooting?

'It's no fluke to hit two people at that distance, both head-shots. This guy, this guy's a world-class marksman.'

'So are you.'

'Two headshots. That's something else. One round per target 'cos I only heard two shots. Goes beyond being just good.'

'OK. Anything else you can tell me?'

'Catch him. I want to shake him by the hand and kick him in the nuts at the same time.'

'All right. We'll do our best. Get out on the next transport and get checked out.'

'I will. Thanks.'

The passenger door opened, and a pair of boots walked away.

There was a pause.

'Sitrep. One shooter. Two of ours down, our long-distance spotter was taken out but not killed. Yeah, he's OK, he'll get over it. But we were sloppy. We shoulda put two men on the bluff, the spotter and someone to protect his back.'

'No. We don't know if it was the chopper pilot. They brought their own weapon, so could be a specialist brought in maybe, tell you why in a minute. No, no idea how he got out to the bluff. Theory is he walked, but from where? It's just desert, there's nowhere to come from. No, no trace of him so far, but he's still out there somewhere. We put a guy on the ridge with IR and night vision, no sighting so far. There's a Reaper due in thirty minutes, but I'm not hopeful. Whoever it is, they're one step ahead of us, but I got one thing for you. I don't think he hit us from the bluff because he knew we were here but couldn't figure out where we all were. I think he knew where we all were. No, I don't know how, but I think he knew where every one of us was. I think he walked into the target zone, sent us a message, and then just ghosted. He knew we were here, and he wanted us to know that.

'No, the hangars have got nothing to tell us. We traced the hire of the lighting rigs and the generator to a construction company in Vegas. They were legitimately rented but the name on the credit card doesn't turn up in our databases. A girl. No, just a girl. Drove in off the street and booked the kit. Good description from the construction company rental office. Short. Asian. Early thirties. Maybe Chinese American. Yeah, apparently the same girl bought the helicopter. Guy who sold the helicopter says she's a hotshot ex-special forces pilot and something special. Nah, he's not involved. Did say he offered her a job. We could break into his office tonight and copy the paperwork, but it's likely just a load of dead ends. We did good getting a lead on the helicopter when the refuelling team at Nellis recorded its airframe number and reporting it.

'What's the news on the house in LA? What? Both of them? There was a team waiting for them? What do you mean not a team? You telling me the same girl took out both of our teams? You've probably got all this on the threat board but let me get this out. Tell me if I'm missing anything.

'At Yucca we got a helicopter pilot, a long gun shooter, and somewhere, but we don't know where, we have a drone pilot who knows how to target air-to-ground missiles. Between these three players they took out our jet, disrupted our security, and got clean away. In LA we've got two of our teams taken out. Then tonight, out here, we have a world-class shooter, who has some serious desert skills? Well, that's why

I say there's no way this can all be the same person. There's someone else behind this, the girl is just the front we're meant to see. We need to know who the other members of her team are.

'How'd the second team in LA get taken out? What? Apples? That's resourceful. If this is all one person, and I really don't think it is, are we chasing our tails all over California and Nevada because of one woman? How likely is that? No, I don't think so either. We got anything on her this Asian chick? Real name? Prints? Anything?

'Hold on. So now I'm thinking something else. Even if it's not the same woman doing all these things, what if it's the same person behind all of this? What we're missing is motivation. Who is behind all of this? Who has the money to put all of this together? And the resources? Who knew about Yucca in the first place? Do we have a leak somewhere? Our side? At the Pentagon? No. I'm thinking there's more to it than this. We're missing something. Maybe we're missing several somethings.

'What about the woman from LA, where's she in all this? Brazil? Really she's gone to Brazil? Is that accurate or is that a blind? Do we have eyes on her in Brazil? No? Why the fuck not? She disappeared in the airport? Jesus fuck, this is starting to feel like comedy hour. We can't keep our top brass safe in the US, we can't track one woman here, and we can't keep track of another woman in a third-world country like Brazil? Who's running the Brazil operation? What? Haven't we got anyone left in Rio after the clusterf… Oh Jesus. Wait. Our losses in Brazil. The relay station, the boss's boat, the photograph, the plane… What if it's tied to all this? What does threat analysis say? Well, get them to run it again. Run it all. I want them to include all of that stuff and everything that's happened here in their next threat model.

'And Brazil? Get him the fuck off the job. Get someone else on it and get them into Rio fast. Jesus, it's like a clown show. We need to take this way more seriously than we are. I'll make calls and sort this. Leave it with me. Yes, I'm angry. This whole operation is a joke.

'What's the news your end? How is he? When? OK. The shareholders are going to want to know real soon, and I want to know before you even think about moving him or telling them. I want to know what the advice is and where the destination is, and I want three experts on the call when you brief me.

'Here? I reckon this place is a bust. The helicopter is back in civilian markings, but it's definitely the same one that got tagged refuelling at Nellis after Yucca. I think this place is done. No, there's no trace of the Reaper here. All we've got out of this is two fatalities and no trace of whoever the fuck we're chasing. I'm going to leave a little something to remember us by, but we're taking our bodies and pulling out. I'll get back to Irwin and make sure everyone gets moved back to Saudi.

'No, not me. I'll come over. I want you to keep running the threat board. Every permutation. When I get there, I want to see a top five of possible scenarios. No, I'll see these guys into Irwin first, then I'll drive to Vegas. Book me a jet out of Henderson, will you? I'll see you when I get back.'

I felt pleased. And I wondered how quickly I could get to Henderson.

Chapter 59. Attempt 3
Reunion

Week 48. California/Nevada

I watched his boots walk away and around the corner. I slid from beneath the Humvee, crouch-ran to the end of the alleyway and peered around the corner; a couple of trucks in US Army colours, motors running, tails open.

I watched two men carry a bodybag to the nearest truck. I checked around and waited for them to walk away. When I was sure I had a clear run, I made a break for it; sprinted across the open ground and slid beneath the tail.

A couple of minutes later, two pairs of boots walked to the tail; I assumed they were putting the second bodybag in. The tail was then lifted and latched into place. I figured with the tail up, nobody else was going to get in. I watched the two pairs of legs walk away and scanned 360°, nobody in sight. I crawled out, slithered up and over the tail, and onto the last bodybag they'd put in.

I silently apologised to Bravo, or maybe it was Delta. I rolled as far as I could towards the truck cab, then crawled underneath the side bench seats. Less than twenty minutes later someone got in the cab, the gears were engaged, and my silent passengers and I began our journey to Fort Irwin.

Tiredness began to set in. I risked a couple of brief dozes but was jolted awake by the movement as the truck pulled off the rough desert track onto the much smoother I-15. I picked up my kit and the roll of carpet, crawled up to the tail, clambered over, dropped onto the concrete, and rolled away as the truck started to pick up speed and move away.

Checked the time. 11pm. I sent an email to Angelo from my phone. I hoped there was enough time to move more chess pieces into place. I put my kit at the side of the road, stood, and waited for the first hitchhiking-attempt to drive up.

At Seven Hills, on the outskirts of southern Las Vegas I climbed down from the cab of the semi and wished Mick, the driver, the best of luck with all my heart. I watched him pull away and wondered at the life that a married man with two children chooses to live, away from his family and loved ones for so many weeks a year.

It was 2.15am.

I reckoned I had four or five hours head start on the guy who had been in the Hummer, his trip out to Fort Irwin worked in my favour. I needed to do some emergency shopping, and I was thankful that most of the big Las Vegas shopping malls are open 24/7.

Four hours later I got out of a cab outside Henderson Executive Airport. I still carried the rucksack, and the rifle, back in its canvas case, but now I was wearing a pair of black heels, nylons, a business-length black skirt, white blouse, and black jacket. I'd gotten a shower in the mall, and my hair was neatly piled on my head. I looked like every other executive jet air hostess.

From the payphone in the airport main lobby, I began to call the charter companies at Henderson and got lucky on the second call. The flight was due out at 8am.

I stowed the L115A3 in a storage locker, picked up the

rucksack, and walked through the staff operations entrance. The thing is, with regional airports, if you look the part, you're not usually challenged. I was challenged, but I had the flight information from the call I'd made.

'Oh, I'm doing the inflight on CVZ217. I only got the call an hour ago; wheels up at 08.00. It's being fuelled, and pre-flighted now.'

He checked his clipboard. I'd given him enough correct information to make it plausible. 'Yep, that's pretty much what this says. Doesn't say anything about you though.'

'Like I said, I only got the call an hour ago. I'm happy to walk around the block and go through the charter company to get onboard if that's best?'

'Nah, you're OK. This manifest was likely sent through before you were allocated.'

'Yeah, that happens often. We're usually the afterthought.'

He slowly eyed me up and down.

'You live in Vegas?'

Of course I don't live in Vegas.

'Yeah. You?' I played my eyes over his face and only saw an open-faced, lonely, late-twenties guy working very early shifts.

'Green Valley.'

'Nice. And close to here for you too.' I didn't want to lead him on, but I needed his cooperation to get onto the airfield. Using the charter company's entrance would be problematic.

'I like it. It's small but quiet. And it isn't so much the town or being here or being close to my other job. Where I live is real close to college.'

'You've got two jobs, and you're going to college?'

'I work part-time at a bar. Just now and then, when they

call. Yeah, I'm training to be a medic.'

'Oh, that's so cool. That's a wonderful thing to do.'

'I was going to try for the full-time college, but... well... money, you know.'

'Sure, I do. Listen, I work out of Henderson maybe twice a month, the rest of the time it varies, but maybe... Oh, hey. You got a pen and paper?'

'Yeah, sure.' He got a pocket pad out.

'Be a sweetie, write your number down for me? And your address would be good too?'

'Sure.'

He scribbled and handed a sheet of pad over.

'Thanks,' I glanced at his badge. 'Terry. You always work the early shift?'

'Uh, yeah.'

I shook his hand. 'Laura.'

'Nice to meet you, Laura.'

I smiled, let go of his hand and walked through the door. I hate loose ends. I'd have to fix that one later.

The Cessna Citation CJ4 stood on a dispersal pad; hooked up to a generator. A fuel tanker was just pulling away. The lower fuselage luggage compartments were shut. The air-craft's boarding ladder stretched to the ground from the open hatchway. I could see movement in the cockpit. I crossed the perimeter to the aircraft, climbed the ladder into the cabin, turned left, and walked into the cockpit.

'Good morning.'

He stopped punching numbers into the navigation computer and turned in his seat. 'Hi. And you are?'

'Laura.'

'Ah. Right. Hello, Laura. I'm Rafael.'

'Pleased to meet you, Rafael. I won't interrupt your checks. We've got some time before wheels. I'll go backstage and sort things out. You need anything?'

'I'm good. Thanks, Laura.'

'Give me a buzz if you need anything, Rafael.'

'Will do.' He turned towards the navigation computer again.

I'd done some research on the charter company's website. This Citation was fitted with four forward-facing and two backwards-facing executive seats. They were mounted on the port and starboard sides of the fuselage, leaving a walkway between them from the stern to the cockpit.

The galley on this jet was a built-up walk-in cupboard on the rear starboard quarter, near the cabin crew seats. I opened a cupboard and found beverages, milk, a built-in water heater, and a dozen half-sized bottles of wines and spirits. There was a low-level cupboard with crockery, cutlery, and some dried microwavable meals. A cleverly disguised microwave was set in the side of the divider. A drawer offered up packets of biscuits and shortbread.

I tucked my bag behind the rearmost passenger seat, sat on the crew fold-down against the aft bulkhead, pulled the aircraft documentation folder and began to read how everything worked.

At 7.45, I heard footsteps on the ladder. I stood up between the two rearmost seats. He came into the cabin, and my skin seemed to freeze. I tried a smile but didn't make it.

'Welcome aboard, sir. I'm Lyra. In the cockpit, we have Rafael. Please take a seat wherever you feel most comfortable, and I'll ask the pilot to get us underway.'

He barely looked at me, but I knew he'd taken in every

detail and could even describe my makeup. 'Let's get wheels up.' He slumped into a forward-facing seat in front of a small table.

I walked forward to the hatch, activated the control that retracted the ladder and then pulled shut and dogged the door. I slipped into the cockpit and told Rafael we were buttoned up and ready to push off the pad. He gave me a thumbs-up sign and got on the radio.

I walked over to our passenger. 'Is there anything I can get you, sir?

'Soda.'

I walked to the rear, put some ice and lemon in a glass and half-filled it from a bottle of soda, put it on a small tray and returned to him. He took it without a word. I felt the aircraft manoeuvring, checked with Rafael, and he held up three fingers.

'Wheels up in three minutes, sir. If you need anything, just press the call button in the arm of your seat. I'll be available until we start the take-off.'

He half-waved a hand in my direction. I walked to the rear of the cabin, stepped into the toilet for a couple of minutes and rearranged myself. Then I sat and tried not to stare at the back of his seat.

He was dead. But he wasn't. He should have been, damn it. He should have died in a fiery explosion on the Yucca airstrip. Somehow, he was sitting ten feet in front of me. He must have stepped off the executive jet before it had started taxiing when my sight of it was obscured by dust, just before I hit it with the first missile.

I'd missed that, and I'd missed him because here he was, untouched by the explosion, completely unharmed. And he'd been the one in the Hummer yesterday evening at Cuttle. This was the man I'd overheard debriefing the spotter and heard on the phone. This was 'Charlie'. This was the guy who had been the unfriendly, waiting for me inside the hangar.

Sitting a few feet in front of me was Whiteland's head of security. Alive, unblemished, and extremely dangerous. But not alive for long.

Chapter 60. Attempt 3
Flight/Fight

Week 48. Nevada

We began to level off, and the seatbelts sign pinged off. I went forward to ask our passenger if he wanted anything, but he was asleep, head back against the headrest. I put my head through the curtain to check on Rafael, who asked for a coffee.

'Sure,' I said. And headed towards the rear of the cabin. I was halfway there when I was grabbed from behind; an arm snaked around my throat, another reached around and punched me in the stomach. Robbed of the ability to breathe and surprised by the attack, the animal in me wanted to curl up and go foetal, but I knew I had to do something different if I was to stay alive.

I dropped straight down. My attacker found himself suddenly supporting all my weight, and he bent forward under the unexpected load. As I dropped, I jabbed my elbow backwards and upwards and felt the soft squash of his testicles. He grunted in pain, and his angle towards the floor became more acute; I reached the maximum drop, reversed direction, and powered myself straight up, the top of my head connected heavily with his chin.

His grip gone, as his upper body snapped backwards, I half rotated and rabbit-punched him in his armpit, kicked a leg from underneath him and helped his journey downwards with a left-handed punch to his throat. I needed to breathe but I needed to keep going to live.

He hit the floor as I completed my half-rotation and dropped on him, the full weight of my body landing through my knee onto his already damaged throat. With my left hand, I punched his groin twice more while kneeling hard on his neck.

The whole exchange took less than three seconds. The only visible blood was a trickle from the side of his mouth where my head impact with his jaw had caused some damage in his mouth. I couldn't breathe yet, but at least I was conscious; he was disabled and dazed but not out for the count.

As I knelt over him, I started to drag air into my lungs in shallow, noisy gasps. I did a quick assessment. He was in a lot of pain, but he'd fight it. He wasn't unconscious, just temporarily disabled. I felt OK, but I could see I'd broken the heel on my right shoe.

It took me a couple of moments to recover my breathing. He started to move, and his eyes looked a little focussed, so I punched him in the groin again, took off my shoes and kicked him in the ribs, stood, and walked unsteadily to my rucksack. I got out the handcuffs and the tape. I walked over to him and kicked him in the ribs again just because those were new shoes, dammit. I rolled him over, cuffed his hands behind his back, taped his ankles together, and put a coffee on for Rafael.

I straightened my clothes, touched up my hair, calmed myself, and delivered the coffee to the cockpit.

'Everything OK?' I asked.

'Sweet. All right back there?'

'No problems.' Well, that was almost true.

'Good. I like quiet flights. We should make Virginia in about four hours, ETA just after noon.'

'Thanks. You need anything before I go back?'

'Sandwich?'

'Rebel didn't provide much food, but I picked up some from the mall on the way in. You got any preferences?'

'I like the way you think. Whatever you've got, please. Leave something good for our passenger.'

'No worries.'

I was going to leave something very good for our passenger.

'I know you can hear me. You can stop pretending to be unconscious.' He didn't move. I lifted up the thermos flask.

'This is a flask of boiling hot coffee. Stop fucking around, or I'm going to pour it in your eyes.' He opened his eyes. I put the flask down.

'Good, we have communication. I want you to stay there on the floor while we have a little chat. OK?'

He didn't say anything, probably because I hadn't removed the tape from his mouth.

'OK, let's do this. First question. Yucca. Apart from the

pilot, who was on the plane? Your boss?'

He slowly nodded.

'Anyone else from the board?'

A careful shake. This made sense; there had still been no public announcement of the crash.

'Anyone else from your company?'

He shook his head, so I kicked him in the thigh. He groaned satisfyingly.

'You were on the C-130?'

He nodded. It made some kind of sense that he'd get out of the devastation with the security detail.

'And he's alive? Your boss?' He slowly nodded. 'He's in Virginia?' Another begrudging half-nod. 'You're on your way to see him?' A nod. 'Are you going to Nebak after Virginia?'

His eyes flared. He wanted to know how I knew about the base in Saudi Arabia. 'Is his second in command still on the Bridge?'

He closed his eyes for a second. I was telling him I knew everything, and he didn't like that. I'd revealed that I knew about the Bridge, the operations deck below the Nebak compound; the underground war room from where every operation is directed and monitored.

'Do the principals know about Yucca?' He slowly shook his head. So the company's shareholders and backers didn't know that the key man had been hit, I guessed that the board did, but the company needed to hold this information back. Without the moneymen the company was toast. I knew it, and he understood that I knew it.

'So just his inner circle knows he's been hurt; you, the second in command, maybe the board, and probably nobody else, yes?' He stared at me. I reached for the flask and started to unscrew the cap. He nodded.

'And finally, is he going to live?' He gave a sort of shrug, and that was good enough for me.

I was tempted to unscrew the flask and pour the contents over him, but it was only cold water, and I didn't want him to know I was sometimes a bluffer.

'Here's how this is going to play out. You're going to stay there. We'll land. You will do exactly as I say.'

He nodded but thrust his pelvis upwards a couple of times.

'You need the bathroom?'

He nodded.

'Soil yourself. I really don't care.' I ended the conversation by punting his thigh like I was a place-kicker for the Giants, stepped over his groaning, writhing form, and walked to the rear of the cabin.

In the toilet, I took off my blouse and checked myself for damage. I was going to be bruised tomorrow, and my stomach was tender, but other than that there was no real damage. I had even managed to keep my ear studs in. I reset my hair, put my blouse on, touched up my makeup, settled on the crew seat and fruitlessly tried to fix my broken heel with black tape.

Chapter 61. Attempt 3
Execution

Week 48. Virginia

Rafael put the jet down on the private airfield very lightly. We taxied to a pad on the perimeter track, a black SUV pulled to a stop beside the aircraft. I put my head through the curtain into the cockpit. 'I need to go offplane with our passenger and run a little errand. Can you be ready to go? I'm probably going to be twenty minutes.'

'Sure, no problem. I'll keep everything warm.'

'Great, thanks.' I released the steps, undogged and opened the hatch, and walked down into the cold Virginia air. The driver's window lowered as I approached the SUV.

'Mister Wilkins asks that you help him off with a large green metal box, please.' My description of a box of munitions did the trick.

'Sure.' The SUVs door opened, and the driver led the way up the steps. As he turned right into the cabin, I smashed his head into the side of the hatch. He dropped like a stone. I secured his hands behind his back with the second pair of handcuffs, opened the flask, and patted cold water onto his face. He slowly came to his senses. I pressed a finger joint hard against the centre of his forehead. It's an old trick but it keeps focus every time.

'You're going to carry Mr Wilkins down the steps and into the car. Then you're going to get in the back with him, and I'll drive us to where we're going. And if you try anything, I'm going to put a hole in your forehead, right here.'

I pressed a little harder and let him see my Glock in its hip holster. His eyes registered the well-used grip.

'Good. Now kneel.' He got up into a kneeling position. I walked through the cabin and helped the head of security to his feet. I noticed he hadn't soiled himself.

'Walk.' I jabbed him in his kidneys. He waddled up to the driver. 'Bend over.' He bent over.

'You, driver, stand up and carry him like a fireman's lift.' They fumbled their way into it; considering neither could use their hands, it worked pretty well.

'Down the steps to the SUV. And if you drop him, you'll be taking a pay cut for the rest of your career.' Unsteadily, the driver made his way down the steps. On the tarmac, I walked ahead and opened the rear door of the SUV.

'Throw him in for all I care.'

The driver slowly lowered his cargo. Because his feet were still taped together, the head of security hopped into the rear doorway and looked at me as if to say, "How do I get in there?"

I pushed him in; pushed him hard with the flat of my hand, a body-slamming blow that would have robbed him of breath for a while. I flicked the safety lock on and slammed the door, pulled the driver backwards by his handcuffs, put him in through the other rear door and flipped that safety lock on. I got into the driver's seat.

'Where is he?' Silence. I unholstered the Glock, fitted the suppressor to it, turned around, pointed the gun into the driver's groin, made firm contact with his family jewels, and repeated the question.

'Building 54, medical centre. Behind the main admin block.'

'Just pretend I've never been here before.'

'Behind the hangar labelled Bravo, the one you're parked in front of.'

I started the SUV and drove in the direction he'd described. Building 54 had a sign outside that said, 'Care Unit' and the Staff of Hermes medical insignia. I pulled up outside and walked straight in. There was a small reception area, a fresh-faced man in a light blue healthcare tunic sat behind a desk, a bank of medical monitors to his left.

'I'm here to see Derek Ray.' I pointed the gun at him, the suppressor must have made the barrel seem massive, but I read his eyes, and they had flicked onto something in front of him. The suppressor did its whispered cough, he screamed, a hole appeared in his tunic's upper forearm and blood began to leak out of him. Whatever he was reaching for remained unreached.

I walked around the desk and pressed the hot mouth of the suppressor against the bloody hole in his arm. He shrieked again. 'I'm. Here. To. See. Mr. Ray.'

I thought he was going to faint, but he managed to say, 'Emergency Care Room. Down the corridor. On the left.'

I pulled him to his feet, pulled his good arm up behind his back and marched him through the double doors and down the corridor. The Emergency Care Room had one occupied bed in it. I pushed the medic in through the plastic curtains.

The naked figure in the bed only vaguely resembled the man I'd worked for. Most of his face was burned off, he had tubes in the bandaged stump of an arm, one leg was missing, and most of his body was burned black and covered with some kind of lotion.

'Why are they trying to keep this alive?' I asked.

The medic didn't answer.

'On whose orders?'

'I don't know. I just do what the surgeons say.' I sighed and shook my head at the obvious futility.

I felt sorry he wasn't going to see this coming, but I didn't think the mess in front of me would ever regain consciousness. I raised the pistol and put a bullet into his forehead. The machines monitoring his condition flashed red and made alarm noises.

'Come on.' I said and pushed the medic in front of me; held by his good arm, I marched him quickly up the corridor. Three nurses were sprinting towards the Emergency Care Room from different directions.

I marched him out of the building and out to the SUV. The two men in the back had been trying to get out, Wilkins, the head of security, was halfway over the driver's seat. They hadn't expected me to be so quick.

I opened the rear door, hauled Wilkins back into position and pushed the medic into the back with them. I got into the driver's seat, turned around, and shot Wilkins between the eyes.

'We had an arrangement,' I said to the other two. 'The arrangement was he behaved himself, and I let him live. He fucked that up and now he's dead. Here's your arrangement: you do what I say, and you get to go home. You fuck with me, and I will end your life. Do you understand?' They both nodded.

I sped the SUV back to the executive jet and pulled to a halt at the foot of the steps. I opened one rear door, pulled the medic out, walked him around the car, opened the other door, and pulled the driver out. Wilkins' body lolled in the back seat, a trickle of blood from the hole in his forehead, a big splash of blood and brains across the headrest.

I herded my two passengers up the steps into the cabin and pushed them into the first row. I stuck my head into the cockpit. 'Are we good to go right now?' Rafael gave me a thumbs-up, and I heard him telling the tower we wanted clearance. I retracted the steps and dogged the hatch shut. I turned to the passengers.

'When we get to our destination, I'll let you go. You're only here for convenience. Buckle up, enjoy the flight, and don't cause any trouble, the cabin crew is antsy today.'

The jet pulled forward agonizingly slowly until we were at the end of the runway. Clearance was given, and we began our forward run.

A moment later Rafael called me into the cockpit. 'Tower is telling us to abort take off and return to the hangar.'

'What did you say?'

'Nothing yet.'

'Let's keep it that way.'

'You're the boss.'

About two-thirds of the distance down the runway, Rafael eased back the controls and the aeroplane climbed steadily.

'Tower has stopped asking us to return.'

'I'm not surprised. They wouldn't want certain information to be broadcast all over the skies. Speaking of which, I've got some broadcasting of my own to do. If you need anything, just give me a shout.'

'Are we likely to get any airborne interference?'

'Stick to the main routes. We'll be safe there.'

'OK.'

'Can I get you anything?'

'A soda would be good.'

'Give me a couple of minutes.'

I turned and looked at the passengers and asked them the same question. 'Can I get you anything?' The medic looked pale; the driver looked furious. Neither replied to my question.

I walked to the rear of the cabin, pulled out my laptop, and typed a press release on a Whiteland Security company template. When I'd finished, I used the aircraft's executive communications to transmit the press release to the Wall Street Journal, the New York Times, and a bunch of European newspapers.

I carried the laptop to the two passengers and let them read what I'd sent. The medic looked like he might faint, the driver looked like he wouldn't believe me if I told him ice was cold.

Chapter 62. Attempt 3
Show/Tell

Week 48. Nevada

I took two sodas from the small fridge, gave one to Rafael, and opened the other for myself. Then I pulled a flight crew seat out of the forward bulkhead and sat facing the passengers. The medic was the first to speak.

'Is it true?'

'The downing of Flight ZJ184 is definitely true. I worked

on the Bridge in the base in Saudi for almost a year. I saw the documents.' I took a sip of soda.

'As to Flight 1816, I think it's true, yes. I was gathering evidence when Wilkins discovered me, and I had to leave in a hurry.'

Actually, he captured me. After four days of interrogation, I was repeatedly raped then set on fire.

'Smaller flights, definitely true. I've seen evidence of three light aircraft brought down over a five-year span; two in Nevada and one in California.'

'I don't understand. Why? Why would they do that?'

'They brought down Flight ZJ184 because there was a whistle-blower onboard, and whistle-blowers are bad for business.'

'A whole passenger plane, an entire civilian flight?'

'My mother, father, and sister were on that plane.'

'Oh shit.'

The driver finally found his voice. 'And that's what this is all about?'

'If by "all this" you mean "is this why I'm taking down this company", then yes, that's what all this is about. I've cut the head off the corporate snake; I'm now making sure the whole organisation goes out of business.'

'What happens next?'

'We fly to Nevada and go our separate ways.'

'Just like that?'

'Just like that.'

'How do we get back to Virginia?'

'You can try and get another pilot to fly you, but before we land your employer's accounts will be frozen, and their credit rating will be worthless. Probably best to get a civilian flight.'

I looked at the medic. 'I'd get that arm patched up when you get back to base. Hospitals in Las Vegas report gunshot wounds to the police, and you probably don't want to be talking to them.'

'You killed him. Wilkins.' The driver was still shocked.

'Yeah, sorry about the mess in your car.'

'Does that mean nothing to you?'

'His death means less than nothing to me. I've exterminated a pest, that's all.'

'Lady, you are one hard bitch.'

I smiled at him, got out of the seat and walked to the rear of the cabin. In the bathroom, I washed my face, cried, and washed my face again.

Four hours later, we landed back at Henderson; we taxied to a stop at the Rebel Air Charters stand, next to a couple of other executive jets. I picked up my rucksack and walked to the front. Rafael was shutting down the aircraft systems.

'What did you do with the pilot?'

'He's tied up in his apartment.'

'Don't forget to let him out before you vanish.'

'An hour after my flight home takes off, the Las Vegas PD will get a call.'

I didn't ask where home was.

'Nice. I like that. There's a little something extra in here for you.' I gave him a bundle wrapped like a child's birthday present.

'Angelo's already paid me half. I'll get the rest tonight when he confirms with you that the job has been done.'

'Call it a productivity bonus. Don't spend it all at once.'

'I won't. About those two?'

'I'll leave the handcuff keys where they can get them. You need to leave straight behind me. They'll free themselves eventually; I expect both of them to just vanish. I'll give them a little something to help get them home. Thanks for everything.'

'No problem. Give my regards to Angelo when you see him.'

'I will.' I shook his hand. He gathered up his flight bag and coat.

I stood in front of the medic and the driver. 'I won't see either of you again.' I handed them a bundle of notes. 'There's enough here to get you both back to Virginia. I'm sorry I had to bring you with me. It got more complicated than I thought. I'll leave the handcuff keys in the microwave. Have a safe journey.'

I walked down the aircraft steps and out of the air terminal into the early Nevada evening.

Chapter 63. Attempt 3
After-words

Week 48. Nevada/Rio de Janeiro

I took a taxi to McCarran International airport in Las Vegas. I had to change flights in Amsterdam, but less than twenty-four hours after leaving Nevada, I climbed out of a cab and walked in through the front door of my house. Our house. Our home.

A tall streak of energy hit me and nearly knocked me off my feet as soon as I'd closed the door. I was hugged and kissed and held tight and told that I was loved and missed and that if I ever did that again I was going to be in so much trouble and she loved me and she was never going to let me out of her sight ever again and can we just be getting back to normal lives now please and let's go to bed and she could show me the new underwear she's wearing and how was I anyway and hello…

'I thought you were never going to draw breath.'

'What?'

'You've hardly stopped talking since you walked in the door.'

'Two things, precious.'

'Yes?'

I counted on her nipples.

'One, I walked in through the door about three hours ago.'

'Oh.'

'And two, you haven't given me a moment to even talk once.'

'Really?'

'You lectured me in the hall for what seemed like ten minutes non-stop, then you whisked me in here, gave me the briefest flash of some new underwear, threw me on the bed, undressed me, and then had your wicked way with me.'

'Did I?'

'Wickedly.' I confirmed.

'This isn't how I remember any of it.'

'Well, perhaps you'd like to explain why my bra is hanging off the TV?'

'You were energetic taking it off?'

'You took it off.'

'Umm, I did?'

'You did.'

'Oh, God. It's lovely to have you home.'

'Are you changing the subject?'

'No?'

'Hmm… I think you are. Anyway, tell me what you've been up to for the last three days. I want to know everything.'

'I went to the gym.'

'Oh, I'm pleased to hear it.'

'Wasn't as much fun without you though.'

'I'm kinda pleased to hear that too.'

'And I went shopping.'

'Oh, your poor credit cards!'

'Well, I figured that if we are going to live here, I should have more clothes than just a bathing suit and an evening dress.'

'You won't get any argument from me about you having just a bathing suit and… wait a minute, you said we're going to live here?'

'I think so, yes. If that's OK with you.'

'But you'll miss the US and the American lifestyle.'

'Give me a chance to get used to the lifestyle here; I think I'm going to like it better.'

'But your friends…?'

'I don't really have friends. I have people I'm in touch with but who I hardly ever see.'

I thought about it for a minute. 'Don't make any hasty decisions. Keep your house in LA. It might be nice to visit once in a while, even if we do decide to live here. Anyway, I quite like California.'

'But could you live there?'

'I could live somewhere there. Maybe not in a city. But Mariposa was lovely.'

'It was lovely. And it was too far from the sea.'

'I could keep Musa on the Californian coast.'

'Would you keep the helicopter to get you there? It would take too many hours to drive to the coast.'

'Maybe. Or maybe I'll buy a light aircraft.'

'What? Are you mad?'

'Just an option worth considering.'

'Do you know how to fly one? Wait. That's not even the point.'

'Yes, I do, and what is the point?'

She rolled off my shoulder, pulled herself up on to her elbow and looked down at me.

'The point is I think I could live here with you.'

'Well, my point is that this isn't a house we chose together. This is my house. Maybe we should look for a house that's ours. Our home.'

'Here? In Rio?'

'Or in California. Or even in White Plains if you want to be close to your parents.'

'Rio's nice.'

'Why are you pushing back on living in the US?'

'I'm not.'

'You are. Is it because of the burglary?'

'No, not really.'

'Well, what really? Tell me.'

'I'm just afraid that it's not all over, and we're safer here.'

I pulled her down and kissed her cheek.

'We're getting married in California, right?'

'Uh, yeah. Right.'

'Also, I tell you it's safe, right?' She just looked at me. 'It's safe. Right?' I said with more emphasis.

'OK.' But she avoided eye contact.

'In four days, we're flying to LA. Two weeks after that, we're getting married. Where we live afterwards is up to us. But one thing I guarantee you, my love, we'll be safe wherever we live. Look at me. We'll be safe. I promise this. I will move heaven and earth to make anywhere safe for you.'

'I don't see how you can.'

'Because I can. Believe me.'

'Let's not talk about this anymore tonight.'

'That's the quickest conversational backout ever. But OK then. What do you want to do?'

'I've prepared us a meal.'

'What?'

'Did you not hear? I've prepared us a meal.'

'No, I heard. It was just… Unexpected.'

'Are you dissing my culinary skills?'

'No. I know you're very capable. I just didn't… I thought we might go out.'

'But I've prepared. And I've set it up in the dining room upstairs.'

'In that case, we'll eat in. Am I allowed upstairs to see?'

'You most certainly are not! It's a surprise. It's my surprise. For you.'

'OK, that's lovely, and I'm already looking forward to it. Is it OK to have a shower and put clean clothes on before I come up?'

'Perfect. It should be ready to serve in forty-five minutes.' She leaned over, kissed me, slid out of bed, into a bathrobe, and out of the bedroom door.

The first thing I did was pick up my phone and do a news search.

The fallout from the press release was significant. The Pentagon was reviewing all contracts with the company. There were some high-profile resignations from the Whiteland board of directors. Governments around the world were working hard to distance themselves from Whiteland Security, and the strongest condemnations were being issued by world leaders. The company's stocks had ceased trading after a rapid fall.

I flipped to my email and pulled up the draft I had started on the flight from Amsterdam.

It was addressed to the head of security and the company CEO. Even though they were dead, their email accounts would be monitored. I copied the email to every member of the board of directors, even those who had resigned in the last twenty-four hours.

The email attachment was brief and blunt. It needed to be. "This message is addressed to every board member of Whiteland Security Company.

"I have destroyed your company as part payment for the innocent lives you have destroyed around the world.

"If you interfere in my life, or the lives of those near me, I will come for every single member of the board; I shall take you, and I shall take every member of your family. No matter how young or how old. Within ninety days of any attempt to harm me, or my loved ones, or our friends, or relatives, you and every member of your family will be dead.

"You, your wives, husbands, mistresses, boyfriends, girlfriends, your children, your grandchildren, your parents, your brothers, and your sisters. They will all die within ninety days of any attempt to harm me or hurt anyone I care about.

"I will not hide. I will not run from you. If you want to find me, you will, because you are resourceful. But so am I. The events at Yucca and in Virginia should tell you that.

"I have levelled your company and damaged your fortunes as a punishment for what you have done. Any attempt to damage me, and I shall bring you down, every single one of you. And I will destroy your families.

"This is not a threat. This is a promise from someone who lost a mother, father, and sister aboard ZJ184 - the aircraft that your organisation destroyed."

I sent the email, shut off my phone, showered, dressed, put some makeup on and went upstairs for a meal that was fit for a queen.

Chapter 64. Attempt 3
Loose Ends/Knot

Week 48. California

We spent the night before the wedding apart; Charlie stayed home with her parents who had gradually been taking over our lives for the past week. I checked in to a hotel on Yale Street, in LAs Chinatown, near my outfitter. What we would each be wearing were closely guarded secrets.

I had a quiet evening; made one phone call, to Charlie, of

course, read a couple of emails and dipped into a delight-fully trashy novel. So much for an early night.

My dress fitter and makeup specialist arrived at eight. At ten, I walked carefully out of the hotel to the waiting limo; I'm out of practice of walking in a tightly fitting, handmade, pure silk cheongsam.

A short car ride later, the limo pulled up beneath the awning we'd had put up; Mark was waiting for me under the canopy. He opened the car door and held out his hand.

In his Mess uniform, complete with medals and battle honours, Mark looked nothing like the man who had pulled me out of the sea.

'You look fucking fantastic.'

'So do you, Laura. So do you.'

'Oh, this old thing? Just something I pulled out of my wardrobe. And look at you with your Purple Heart.'

'Oh, this old thing? Just something I pulled out of my kitchen.'

'If I kiss you, I'm going to mess my makeup.'

'Later then.'

'Later.'

I held out my arm, and we walked down the steps, on to the wooden sidewalk that had been laid across the beach and down to the front of the gazebo. There were about thirty seated inside. As we walked slowly down the aisle I nodded and smiled and got a knot in my stomach. Mark and I sat and had a whispered conversation.

'I'm a bit nervous.'

'Really? I'm shitting it.'

'You're allowed to be, Laura. You're the one getting married.'

'I could have stayed in bed another half an hour. She's going to be late.'

To prove me hopelessly wrong, the priest stood, and the PA played "The Ride of the Valkyries"; I worked hard not to laugh as Charlie's sense of humour washed over us, and I knew everything was going to be all right.

Mark flicked a glance over his shoulder and whispered, 'Now.'

I stood, turned around and looked. And my heart melted.

Charlie was dressed in a white, above-the-knee, chiffon bridesmaid dress; it perfectly complemented her height and shape. She looked... wonderful. Her hair, her makeup, her smile, it was all so gorgeous. She was going to be my wife, and I was going to be hers. Her father walked her down the aisle looking immensely proud. When she was at my side, she held my hand, leaned towards me and whispered. 'You are the most beautiful person I have ever seen.'

It's not often that I'm lost for words, but at that moment I was.

I woke at eight the next day, clear-headed and excited. I rolled over and spooned her. She wiggled her backside into my lap.

'Well, that's it then.' She sighed.

'It is, as you say, it, then.' I said into her ear.

'Married.'

'Yep.'

'To each other.'

'To each other.'

'Any regrets?'

'Not yet. You?'

'Nope.'

She rolled me over and held me down.

'And that thing that you were going to do?'

'Which thing?'

'That thing. That bad person. That killing people thing.'

'Oh. That thing.'

'Can you promise me there's no more stuff like that?'

'I can. I promise you there's nothing else like that. My life is ours to share now.'

'I like that. Your life is ours to share now. My life is ours to share now too.'

'What do you want to do this morning?'

'I want to spend a couple of hours with my family. That's you. You're my family now.'

'Yeah. And you're mine.'

I pulled her face to me and kissed her.

'You've got glitter in your cleavage.'

'I think I've got some up my ass too.'

'In that case… shower and breakfast first? I'll check you over for stray glitter afterwards.'

'I think I'm going to like being married.'

We sat on the hotel restaurant balcony, overlooking the beach.

'Well, Mr Purple Heart. About time you gave us an intel briefing.'

'Well, Mrs Special Forces Hotshot Combat Pilot, I'll begin with the damage.'

'Damage? Really? There's damage?'

'Really. You two broke at least three hearts yesterday. That's a lot of damage.'

Charlie put her hand on mine.

'We will break hearts wherever we go. It's a burden we have to bear.'

'However, other hearts had good things happen to them.'

'What? Tell us more.'

'The young lad you had brought in from Nevada? The trainee medic?'

'Terry?'

'That's the guy. The hot news is that halfway through the evening he and Betty disappeared.'

'I'm sorry? You're telling us what?'

'I'm telling you that they went off to Betty's apartment. Or maybe to his hotel.'

'Well, Betty!' Said Charlie.

'And well, Terry!' I added. For a moment we said nothing, we just sat and thought our thoughts.

'What's the other news?'

'There isn't really anything else. Your wedding presents will be with my parents at the Mesa until you collect them. And your parents will be here in about an hour to spend some time with you both.'

'That's lovely, thank you, you're amazing.'

'I'm just here to help you guys.'

'I bet you say that to all the girls.'

He laughed.

My phone rang.

'Hello?'

'Miss Guerra'

'Yes?'

'We have made a delivery for you.'

I was suddenly chilled.

'I see. Thank you. Where?'

'Three hundred metres north, under a large bush.'

'That's great. Please pass on my thanks to Angelo.'

'A pleasure Miss Guerra. We shall leave the package there until you tell us to remove it.'

I thanked the caller and hung up.

'Anything interesting?'

'Just a delivery. Some tack for Musa.'

'When are we going sailing again?'

'Next month? If that's OK?'

'I would love to.'

'We still haven't decided where we're going to live yet.'

'Let's start next week.'

'Decide where you're going to live?' Mark let his curiosity out.

'Decisions that newly-married people need to make.'

'California? Or the States in general? Or Brazil?'

'Or all of these.'

'How much longer are you going to stay here?'

'Here in the hotel?'

'Yep.'

'A few days. And then to LA. Things to do, places to go.'

Charlie looked at me.

'I've got to get the helicopter back to Long Beach.'

'Ohhhhhh… I'd forgotten that.' She said.

'There's some hired equipment in the desert that needs to be collected as well.'

'So you're going to be away for a while?'

'Overnight only. You could always come with me?'

'Maybe. We'll see how it goes.'

'Fair enough. Anyway, if you'll both excuse me, I need to visit the bathroom. Back in a minute.'

I walked into the restaurant, through the hotel, out of the main entrance and walked up the hill to the left of the hotel. In a bush beneath a large Catalina cherry tree was a dead man. Although most of his head was missing, there was enough of his face left to recognise the driver from Virginia.

They'd probably sent him because he could identify me. And maybe he was naïve enough to think he had a score to settle. He was slumped over an M24 rifle fitted with a day/night telescopic sight. I eased the rifle and sight out from underneath him, put them in the nearby case, walked to my car, and put the case in the trunk.

I texted the number that had called me, thanked them for their delivery, said I was going to keep part of the consignment but wanted to return the rest. The almost immediate response merely said, 'We shall process that order. Thank you for your custom.'

I returned to the restaurant balcony, where I joined in with the post-wedding chat. I loved both of these people.

Chapter 65. Attempt 3
Firefighting

Week 51. Long Island/Virginia/California/Arizona

One week later, a private jet whisked me out of LA and put

me straight into Francis S. Gabreski Airport, Long Island. It was time for the avenging angel to flex her deadly wings again and, as usual, she had to flex and run, and run very quickly.

There had been no further attempts on my life; my bodyguards - Angelo's men - would have notified me. I asked them to continue watching Charlie while I made this trip.

I drove the hire car out to Cedar Point and parked on the isolated end of the spit of Long Island that juts out into Gardiners Bay. I walked deep into the woods and set up on a rocky outcrop beneath the trees. The modern glass-and-aluminium house six-hundred yards in front of me was well isolated in the woods.

I spread the carpet on the rock, lay down, and waited behind binoculars. An hour later, I knew the security profile of this side of the house. Three men patrolling a diamond pattern. This meant there were at least nine men on the ground in a standard box-and-diamond defensive zone. I fitted the suppressor to the barrel of the M24. It felt right to use their own weapon against them.

Just over an hour and a half later, as she said they would, they walked out of the house, across the lawn and into the tennis court, his arm around his very attractive, very socially networked girlfriend. The whites of their tennis clothes so brilliant the handsome couple almost gleamed, the scene looked like a TV commercial.

I got behind the M24 and waited while they took position at each end of the tennis court. I ignored the three security guards for now. I watched him bounce the ball twice then throw it up into the air; his head perfectly still, calculating the trajectory as the ball completed its upwards path and began to fall back towards him.

I completed my exhale and Sandy's head exploded. The brutal 2,580 feet per second that the M24 spits the 7.62mm NATO round out at can penetrate light armour. Almost before the round had found its target, I'd slid the bolt back and forth, refocussed, and squeezed the trigger again. Sandy's girlfriend's face changed permanently mid-scream; her bloodied corpse dropped to the floor as I chambered another round.

A woman ran out of the house, Sandy's mother. I dropped her as she ran down the steps from the house. Reloaded. A security guard started to run in my direction, so I dropped him. A dog ran out of the house. I left it alone. I remained focussed on the door. Sandy's brother ran out and straight into another high-velocity bullet. I ejected the magazine and loaded a fresh one. A flash of white clothing in an upstairs window caught my eye. I focussed and waited. Sandy's sister showed herself again briefly. I dropped her with a chest shot because the angle was tight, and my view was restricted. Then I picked off the two remaining security guards because they were threats.

I quickly packed up, got into the car, drove to the airport, and we took off. It took the jet forty-five minutes to travel the three-hundred-forty miles to Williamsburg International Airport, Newport News, Virginia. I picked up the booked hire car and drove out to the remote, heavily wooded area on the west bank of Deep Creek.

I walked through the woods to the water's edge, set up against a rock and got out the binoculars. I studied the pontoons of the Yacht and Country Club on the east bank opposite. The twin-deck motor-cruiser was still moored there, but the onboard activity suggested she wasn't going to be around for long. I guessed that word had got around about Long Island. I figured that the rest of the board of directors were either making themselves secure or, like these guys, were about to make a run for it.

I waited.

The cruiser soon pulled away from the pontoon and began its turn towards the sea. I got behind the M24 and waited some more.

When the bow of the boat had completed a quarter of a circle and was pointing straight towards me, I put a bullet through the forehead of the helmsman, reloaded, and waited. The boat maintained its course towards my side of the river; everyone must have been below decks having a drink or congratulating themselves on making such an easy escape.

I waited.

The boat came on at me at a steady four miles per hour. When it was less than sixty feet away, it hit ground with a grinding noise and listed to port, wedged by whatever it had struck beneath the water.

Three men appeared on the top deck, one of them dressed in white, maybe the skipper. There was screaming from below decks; I could clearly hear the men shouting about getting help. I brought the M24 to bear, it whispered three times, and they shouted no more. I ejected the five-shot magazine, put another in, and waited. There was further shouting and screaming.

I waited some more.

A young man, maybe eighteen or nineteen years old, crawled over the stern, slid into the water, and began to strike out for the far shore. I waited until I had a clear shot of him in the water, the M24 whispered, and he swam no more. In the distance I could hear the growing sound of sirens. I guessed they'd called the police but that was all right; they'd automatically go to the wrong side of the river. The boat was less than sixty feet away. I reached into the bag and pulled out a fragmentation grenade. I pulled the pin and threw the grenade onto the top deck. While it was in the air, I pulled the pin on a second grenade and threw that onto the foredeck. My third grenade landed on the roof almost immediately after.

The first explosion seemed to cause little damage, but the second blew the foredeck to fragments. The third grenade destroyed the coachroof; smoke began to pour from inside the boat. I got back behind the sights. Two females and an older male were trying to sneak over the stern, but they had no cover left. The M24 whispered death, and they stopped sneaking. The boat was slowly sinking at the stern, the smoke from inside was thinning, but flames were taking hold. I had two grenades left, I decided to keep them for a rainy day, put everything away and left.

After a short car ride, I was back at the jet. While we were in the air, I checked my email. It had been just under two hours since the avenging angel had visited Long Island, but already there were thirty-one pleas. Thirty-one emails imploring me to stop; none of them asking why I'd started.

They'd known. They'd all known about the driver at the hotel. They'd wound him up, made him angry or jealous or a combination of both; they'd put a deadly weapon in his hands and told him where to find me. They'd ignored my threat of retaliation, and they were now paying the price, and they didn't like the fee.

'Cuttle?' Rafael asked.

'Cuttle.' I confirmed. I didn't care if they liked the fee or not.

I stood by Hangar One and watched Rafael fly away into the early afternoon sun

Apart from the broken lock, there was nothing immediately unusual about the Hangar One doors. I slid the main door back. I could see the EC, the lighting gantries, and the generator. I put on the infrared sights and shone the infrared torch at the ground. There was a tripwire just inside the hangar; I disabled it, wondering what it had been connected to.

I got on my hands and knees and crawled in, turned left, and crawled around the edge of the hangar. Under the first lighting gantry was an oblong block of C4 high explosive. I pulled the detonator, put the explosive in my rucksack and the detonator in my pocket. In the far corner of the hangar was another tripwire. This one attached to a flash-bang stun grenade; designed to panic me into making a mistake. I disconnected it, put it in my rucksack and moved on. Fixed to the underside of the generator was another block of C4 explosive. Again, I disarmed it but kept the detonator and explosive.

Inside the ECs luggage compartment, hanging on a thin line, was a grenade. If it was jolted the pin would have got pulled and blown the helicopter apart.

I did three more laps inside the hangar, once with infrared, once more with ultraviolet, and once more with a jogger's headtorch. There were no more booby traps, but I did find the coil they'd cut the tripwire from. I kept that too.

I towed the EC out into the hot afternoon sun and inspected every inch of her. Then I opened the engine cowlings and checked the engine and exhaust. There were no other signs of sabotage.

I stepped back and looked at the EC. Chad had done a brilliant job. The helicopter had been cleaned and polished and looked better now than the day I'd picked her up from Sunny Helicopter Charters.

I loaded my kit and sat in the pilot's seat; it was good to be inside her again, I'd missed her. I brought up the control panel, started the engines, and gradually increased the revs to operating speed.

When everything was 100% and in the green, I took off and headed southeast towards Arizona. It took the EC an hour to cover the one-hundred-eighty-two miles to my next destination. I set her down seventy miles northwest of Phoenix, on a patch of land that was part of thousands of acres of scrubland, in the middle of nowhere. I put my rucksack on, picked up the M24, and jogged across the open countryside. The nearest road was four miles due south, the only nearby house was five miles away. This Arizona wasteland was just miles of open nothingness except scrub and stunted trees. I jogged carefully through the light brown emptiness.

The late 19th Century, two-storey farmhouse was well lit in the evening gloom. I pitched up in a dry hollow which probably used to be an open drain and surveyed the area.

Four steps up to a veranda, a few small tables and chairs arranged along a terrace beside the front door. Upstairs, a balcony that skirted the front of the house. This was nobody around, I couldn't believe it. This was either an elaborate trap, or security had been delegated to a bunch of amateurs.

To the north of the house were two large barns and a stable block. There was a stack of straw bales beside the stables. Further behind was a corrugated tin building that could have been a workshop or a garage.

Four cars were parked in front of the house, a crusty old 4x4, a modern pickup truck, an out-of-place BMW sports-car, and a Chevrolet SUV.

I skirted left through the brush to the stable block. At the rear of the stables was a large water butt. I used it to climb on to the stables roof and crawled towards the house where I set up the M24. I had a good view of the front and near-side, and a partial view of the rear.

I wanted them to think I was where I wasn't. I used the suppressed M24 to put two rapid rounds into the stone chimneystack. Any debris that fell would make them think someone was on the roof.

Two men ran out of the front door, one carrying a rifle the other a handgun. They both half-turned as they ran and looked up at the roof. The man who flashed out of the rear door and immediately went to ground interested me more. The infrared wouldn't show me anything useful yet, so I brought the gaze of the M24s telescopic sights back to the men at the front of the house. Two quiet whispers, two down. I chambered a third round, replaced the magazine, and scanned the rear of the house but could see nothing. He'd gone to ground well. Maybe he was the only pro they had available in Arizona.

I waited.

A cloud of dust appeared along the track. Surely whoever

arranged security for the house hadn't just put three guns inside and left the rest of the security where the track met the road? Maybe they had. Maybe the security detail here really was that stupid. The telescopic sights showed me a pickup racing up the track. This felt like amateur hour; I was surprised the house was so poorly protected.

I zoomed in. Three people in the front seat, four squeezed into the back, six sitting on bench seats on the flatbed, three on each side. It was a fair assumption they were all armed. Thirteen men in the truck and one more out there, somewhere behind the house. Even though the guys in the truck looked like a bunch of hick amateurs, I didn't like those odds.

I reckoned the truck was moving at close to sixty miles per hour. It negotiated the long lazy bend, then straightened to follow the track up to the house. The driver was in his early thirties, blonde crewcut, a cheap tattoo on his neck. The two men next to him looked the same age. Maybe they were out of the same gene pool. Somebody's sons. I stayed on the driver.

When the distance between the truck and the house was two hundred metres, I put a bullet between his eyes, reloaded, and exploded the head of the man next to him who had made a grab for the steering wheel.

The pickup fishtailed but hardly slowed. A couple of guys on the back saw the inevitable and deciding to take their chances, jumped. Their landings didn't look happy. The truck barrelled up the remainder of the track and into the cars in front of the house. It was a big, noisy hit.

The M24 breathed twice and took care of the two men who had jumped. Then I shot three more who had been on the flatbed and had ridden into the crash on the pickup. I replaced the empty magazine with a full one. That left one guy in the front cab, four in the back seat, and one from the flatbed unaccounted for.

Through the truck's rear window, I could see two people on the flatbed; the M24 did its near-silent cough twice, and I could see no heads in the back of the truck. I replaced the magazine with a full one and quickly tallied the numbers. One missing from the flatbed, two unaccounted for from the back seat and one in the front seat; I hadn't seen any of them escape. The odds against me were maybe down to four to one now, if the men still in the truck were fighting fit. I didn't think they were.

Time to go. I swept up everything I'd laid out and crouch-ran across the roof. Halfway along I heard a shot hit somewhere behind me; I didn't stop to see how far behind me. Someone had height. Someone was dangerous.

I dived sideways off the roof onto the straw bales; slid down the stack to the ground, reversed my direction and, under cover of the stables, ran towards the house again. From the corner I could see a rifle barrel pointing out of a first-floor window. It was now aimed at where they expected me to be next, at the far end of the stables, not back at the end nearest the house.

I couldn't see the shooter, just the business-end of the barrel. The upper part of the house looked like it had been built from wood. That suited me.

I squatted and drew an imaginary line through the window frame to where I expected the shooter's head to be. A gentle squeeze on the M24s trigger and the window frame exploded; the rifle dropped inside the house. Even if the shooter wasn't dead, he was probably injured by wood shrapnel. But I was confident I'd hit him. My calculations with a long gun are seldom wrong.

I needed to continue behaving unexpectedly, so I crouch-ran into the red zone, straight to the wreckage pileup in front of the house.

I hunkered beside what was left of the pickup and scanned the house. There were no signs of movement on the ground floor, so anyone left inside was either lying flat on the ground floor, or they'd gone upstairs, or the house had a basement or a storm cellar of some kind.

There was movement and a groan from inside the wreck-age. I crept to the front passenger door and edged a look inside. Three people still alive. One guy in the front, trapped, his leg jammed into the cab floor. His face was a mess, likely impacted with something when the truck hit the cars. I reached in, took the commando knife from his belt and opened his carotid artery. In the back seat were the corpses of the two men I'd shot as the truck had approached the house, plus another guy dead from the crash impact. Another man was dying slowly, so I used the knife to help him out.

I crept round the back. On the flatbed was a guy with a compound fracture of his left leg. He looked scared and far too young to be in a firefight. The commando knife made sure I didn't have to worry about him making a recovery.

I did a quick headcount; maybe sixteen down in total. I knew Whiteland Security could call on an actual army, so being sixteen good ole boys down wasn't going to stop them. Cutting the head off the organisation was the only way I had of remaining safe. I thought I'd done that, but someone on the board of directors had decided to take me down, even after I'd removed the CEO and the head of security.

And now I had to take out the deputy CEO. I crouch-ran around the corner to the far side of the house; there was a double storm-door set in the ground. I gently tested the handle; the doors were locked or wedged.

From my rucksack I took a block of C4. I squeezed it into the handle, inserted the detonator, then retreated into the scrub and took cover beneath some stunted trees. I lay down and aimed; from this distance I couldn't miss.

My shot hit the detonator, which triggered the block of C4; in the split second of the explosion, it looked like the entire frame and the basement doors were lifted out of the ground, the side of the house seemed to buckle inwards but held. I kept still and waited for the dust to settle. And waited and watched.

There was a very slow movement hard to my right where there should have been none. This was the person who had gone to ground from the back of the house; someone more professional than the guys in the truck. I checked my left, just to be certain; it looked clear. I eased the stun grenade out of the bag and rolled slowly onto my back.

I slipped the Glock out of its hip holster. I reckoned he was no more than forty-five feet away. I pulled the grenade pin, released the trigger, then threw it in a high arc to land where I thought he was.

The flash-bang exploded, he broke cover, heading unsteadily away from the threat. I dropped him with a shot between his shoulder blades. I rolled back onto my stomach, picked up the M24, and focussed on the side of the house.

After six or seven minutes, the remains of a basement door

opened, and a head slowly emerged; young, male, maybe nineteen, combat jacket. The M24 whispered, and his head exploded. Two more minutes, and there was a shout.

'Don't shoot. I'm coming out. I'm unarmed.'

I didn't respond.

'Do you hear me? I'm coming out and I'm not armed.'

Said nothing because to answer back would give away my position.

'Don't shoot. I'm coming out. Do you understand? I'm coming out now.'

Slowly he emerged from the basement, late sixties, thin, tall, full head of hair but greying. He was wearing just a pair of shorts to show he had no concealed weapons. He climbed all the way out of the basement, hands high in the air, took three paces forward, looked to his left and right but saw nobody.

'I'm John McCabe.' He shouted. 'Since you killed the CEO, I'm in charge of what's left of the company. I want to negotiate a truce.'

I shot him in the thigh with the Glock; he went down hard, moaning in pain. There was a woman's cry from the basement.

I waited until he'd finished groaning; used the time to scan for the faintest movement. When I felt certain there were no threats, I responded.

'I gave you a truce. I gave you a way out where no lives would be lost. You ripped that truce up when you sent someone to kill me on my honeymoon.'

I left the M24 on the ground, slowly raised myself to a crouch, Glock in hand, and exposed my position to him.

'Don't kill my family.'

'You killed mine. You killed all of my family. And then you tried to kill me on my wedding day.'

'They're innocent civilians, for God's sake. Kill me. But leave my family alone.'

'Didn't you get my memo, John? Didn't you read what would happen to every single one of you, and to all of your family members?'

'Yes. We all read your email.'

'And you all thought I was kidding?'

'One or two did. A couple on the board were convinced they could make you think twice. Some felt they could stop you. When you didn't come for us right after the attempt to kill you in California, the hawks were sure you were bluffing.'

'I was on my honeymoon, John. I wasn't going to break that off just to exterminate a nest of vermin. I'm a busy person. You want my attention; you have to take a ticket and wait in line.'

There was movement at the basement doors; a woman's head slowly raised above ground level. I pointed the Glock at her face. He saw my movement. 'No!'

'Why not, John? After all the civilians you've killed, why can't I?'

'Because there's nothing to be gained.' She spoke from the basement hatch.

'There's everything to be gained. If I eliminate the board of directors, I get to sleep at night without ever having to wonder if they're going to come for me again.'

She'd been crying, but despite her ashen, tear-stained face, she looked as if she was ready to put up a fight.

'Who did it, John? Who decided to come for me?'

He didn't answer.

'Whose idea was it to break the truce and kill me on my wedding day?'

'Wilson. Charles Wilson.'

That was a coincidence, but I wanted to check.

'Newport News, Virginia?'

'The boat you shot up earlier today, yes.'

'Did I kill him?'

He looked up at me. 'You don't know? Jesus Christ.'

'I had to leave in a hurry. Did I get him?'

'Yes; you killed him, and his whole family.'

'Good. Who's left? On the board.'

'Aren't you ever going to stop?'

'Why should I stop? I gave you a way out, and you came for me on my wedding day.'

'You destroyed the company we've built up over the past twenty years. They were angry. All of us were angry.'

I couldn't let that go.

'And you killed hundreds of innocent civilians, on the ground and in the air, John. Any criminal court would find you all guilty of mass murder. I've saved the public the expense of your trials, and I've stopped your highly expensive lawyers from reducing your sentences and getting you some cushy custodial surroundings.'

He closed his eyes and sighed. His wife twitched, thinking he'd died and wanting to be next to him.

'My family were on one of the civilian airliners you destroyed.'

He opened his eyes and looked up at me.

'That was a terrible mistake.'

'Who is left in the house?'

'My daughter. She's thirteen. Please leave her alone.'

'There were thirteen-year-olds on Flight ZJ184.'

His wife openly sobbed.

'There are three board members left, John? Cummings, Winthrop, and Dayton?'

'Yes.'

'I've destroyed the company. But the four of you are wealthy. You could just continue to send people for me, no matter how many I stop. You could keep sending dozens until you get lucky. Or I could just kill you all. That would stop this. Those are my options. Killing you all seems to be the only way I get to have a good night's sleep. Do you understand?'

He nodded slowly. I pointed the Glock at him. His wife sobbed again. I looked at her.

'So why should I let you and your husband and your daughter live? What reason can you give, strong enough to convince me to let your family live?'

'Whatever he's done, whatever terrible crime he has committed; we will stop them sending people after you. We'll stop whatever is happening.'

I noted the "we".

'I was told that once before, Mrs McCabe. By your husband and all the others. And then they sent someone to kill me on my honeymoon. Can you believe that? On my fucking honeymoon? So why should I believe anything you tell me? What's different now?'

'Me. I shall make it different. For the sake of my daughter's life, I shall make it all stop. You stopped the company, and that hurt the people who created it and built it up and ran it. I shall stop those people who used to run it. I know them, and they know me.'

It wasn't her words; it was her complete conviction. This sixty-year-old mid-American mother was convinced she could stop three of America's most powerful, wealthiest men. She looked at me, and I felt her belief.

'OK. I'll let you run with this. With one exception.' She looked up at me, wanting to ask, but not wanting to know the answer.

'Dayton. I won't stop until I've got Dayton.'

Relief visibly washed over her. 'Take him. He's evil. Take him whenever you want.'

Chapter 66. Attempt 3
Dayton

Week 51. Virginia

The house on Leslie Avenue, Alexandria, Washington DC, was an unimposing brick-built two-storey detached. Four steps up to the front door. Two chairs on the porch. A driveway to the right. A single car-width garage. An unremarkable house in a normal DC suburb, but it was only his weekday pad.

His main house, the seven-bedroom mansion just south of Portland, on the Cape Elizabeth Coast, was palatial by comparison. But there were too many people at his other house. Three days a week, he lived here, a fifteen-minute drive from his office, his desk was just two minutes' walk from his reserved space in the North Rotary Road car park at the Pentagon.

A man of habit and routine, he left the house at 6.30 every morning and returned by 7.30pm; he sure put the hours in. I guess that's what two-star generals do.

Sometimes, his wife and two children accompanied him to Washington, but this week his daughter said he would be by himself. Perfect.

At 8.15pm I walked away from the van parked opposite, bounced up his steps, and rang the bell. He opened the door wearing his uniform trousers and shirt, no tie, open collar.

I wore a different uniform; soft-peaked cap, red and white striped shirt, red trousers. The pizza box contained his usual order; I'd intercepted the delivery guy around the corner, and for thirty bucks he'd let me do his delivery, so I could surprise my good friend on his birthday.

Dayton, expecting his usual evening pizza, opened the door, gave me a smile, and I shot him in the left thigh with the Glock from underneath the pizza box; the suppressor barely made a sound.

He staggered one pace backwards. As he put his hands to his leg his eyes flickered to the wall by the door, I shot him in his right thigh. He cried out and went straight down.

I stepped inside, flicked the door shut behind me and took off my cap to let my long hair down. I paused to give him time to look at me. Then I shot him in his right shoulder. I put my hand over his mouth and waited for him to calm down.

'Do you know who I am?'

He was too busy trying to clutch both his thighs and his shoulder and deal with the pain to have a conversation. I kept my hand over his mouth, put the Glock down, opened the pizza box, took a slice out, and began eating it. Not bad, but a little heavy on the pineapple.

I looked around the room; comfortably furnished in an old-fashioned kind of way. He was starting to leak blood onto the carpet, but I could see from his eyes he was getting on top of the pain.

'Do you know who I am?'

His eyes briefly flicked towards the front door.

'They're dead.' I paused to let those two words sink in. 'Your bodyguards. The two defence contractors in the van outside? They're both dead. You think I would just walk in here for a chat with you without making sure I was safe?'

His look was still defiant. I punched him in the thigh. He moaned into my hand. I waited until his focus had returned.

'Do you know who I am?'

He nodded, so I took my hand away.

'Who am I?'

'Asian bitch, the one who…'

I didn't want to hear him disrespecting me. I covered his mouth again and shot him in his right forearm. His muffled scream went on for ages. I waited for him to quieten down. I leaned over and whispered in his ear. 'Mind your mouth.'

'That's the formalities taken care of. Let's get to business.'

I took my hand away.

'What do you want?'

'I want you to die.'

'Go to hell.'

'You know I'm here because of Flight ZJ184?'

'I said go to hell.'

'Yeah, you know what brought me here. And you talked everyone on the board of directors into ignoring the truce I offered. You convinced them to send a gunman for me.'

'Fuck off.'

I clamped my hand over his mouth and hit him on the bullet hole in his thigh. His muffled yell wouldn't have been heard outside. I leaned down and whispered again. 'I told you to mind your mouth.'

I waited for him to calm down; he was losing quite a lot of blood, but I needed to have this talk. 'So, let's chat. But I don't want to start with chewing the fat over ZJ184.'

I took my hand away again. 'I would like to talk about the whistle-blower who was on that flight. That OK with you, General?' He looked surprised.

'A Senior Airman, twenty-four months in service. A three-striper classed as "outstanding" at every assessment, and promoted to the rank early. A twenty-year-old intelligence analyst who just happened to look the wrong way at the wrong time and see the wrong information.'

He knew what I was talking about.

'And how did you repay this diligent airman who flagged up, through command, that the US Army's main defence contractor was giving intel about US troops, to the enemy? That one of our most prominent defence contractors was directly involved in events that led to the deaths of US servicemen and women? You stifled the report, General. You erased all trace of it. And then you sent three of your thugs to visit the intelligence analyst's apartment. They raped her, General. They all raped her. And then they beat the living shit out of her and left her with the clear message that this was only a warning.'

His expression changed. He was now seeing where this was going.

'And why, General? Why the grand deception in the first place? Why has Whiteland Security been feeding intelligence to the enemy on the ground? Because it's good for business. It's good for defence contractors like Whiteland Security, because it keeps them in business. Whiteland Security, the company you work part-time for, the company you are a major shareholder in. And I guess it's good for the Pentagon who you work full-time for too. Am I right?

He didn't speak so I took out my phone and played my sister's voicemail, the same recording I'd played to Charlie back in LA. Hana's description, recorded in her hospital bed, of everything she'd just been through played into the room. He started to talk; I pushed the Glock's suppressor into his mouth to shut him up.

Tears fell from my face as the recording played out. It ended with her usual 'Love you, big sister' sign-off. I cleared my throat to get my voice back.

'Her parents flew thousands of miles to be with her. They sat with her at hospital. They cared for her, took her back to her apartment and tended her physical injuries. But even though she'd been raped and beaten, she was still a fighter. She told our parents what had happened. They wanted to take her home, but she said no, didn't she, General? She said she was going to take her discovery to the highest officials in her command at the Pentagon. And that was you, General. She emailed you directly, because she didn't know who else she could trust, but she trusted a man of your position. She trusted your rank. She trusted the uniform you wore.

'My sister, General. That intelligence analyst was my baby sister. You blew up an aeroplane to stop her; you killed my sister, my mother and father and two-hundred-twenty-four other civilians to keep your dirty little secret safe, General. You had my sister raped three times to protect your name and reputation, General.'

His eyes were fire. I think he knew he was going to die this evening. But now he knew he wasn't going to die just for bringing down ZJ184.

'She was just twenty years old and just two years into the job, and you had her beaten and raped as a threat, and when she ignored your threat, you had her killed.' I knelt beside him and put the mouth of the suppressor against the underneath of his jaw.

'So here's how this is going to play out, General. I'm going to shoot you one more time, and you're going to stop breathing. Then later tonight, three men are going to visit your house at Cape Elizabeth. Just like I've done here and just like I did in Arizona, and on Long Island, those three men will kill your family's security detail. Then they'll break into your family home.

'They're going to make your wife watch while your fifteen-year-old daughter is raped three times. And when they've finished with your daughter, they're going to shoot her in front of your wife. Then they're going to shoot your wife.'

He swallowed hard. 'They've done nothing wrong in all this. They're innocent.'

'My sister was innocent. My mother and father were innocent. All of the other people on ZJ184 were innocent. What's going to happen this evening at Cape Elizabeth is the consequence of your actions. I'm just sad you won't be there to see it.'

I squeezed the trigger, and the top of his head splattered all over the far wall.

Chapter 67. Attempt 3
Home/Life

Week 51. California

I wanted to get home as quickly as I could, so I took a late-night flight that got me into LAX at 3am. The taxi dropped me outside Charlie's house; I quietly crept into the unlocked kitchen.

'If you hadn't messaged me that you were leaving LAX, I would have blatted you with a frying pan.'

'You waited up for me!'

'Of course, I waited up. We're married. That's the kind of thing that marrieds like us do.'

'Oh! Well, I have to brush up on what marrieds like us do.'

'Are we still going to gym in less than three hours?'

'We should stay in bed and maybe go swimming later instead.'

'For that excellent idea I will get us breakfast in bed.'

'Now?'

'No. Now you can have a shower. While you're doing that, I'll get you a slice of toast and some fruit juice. You can have those in bed.'

'Oh, God, I love you so much for that.'

'Just for that?'

'Let me have a shower, and then we can talk about it in bed.'

'We can talk tomorrow. For now, I've got better things to do with my mouth.'

A week later, I picked up an email. A name, a phone number, and the words 'Call me.' Nothing else. Charlie was out shopping. I called.

'You asked me to call?'

'I've got some questions.'

'Go ahead.'

'Did you have to be so brutal with him?'

'Dayton? Yes. Next question?'

'My husband wants to know how you found us.'

'Social media. Your kids are all over it.'

'Sandy too?'

'No, he had more sense. But his girlfriend's Insta was just one big signpost.'

'And Dayton?'

'Same. His daughter's social media. How is she, by the way?'

'Oh. Fine, she's fine. She's upset at the loss of her father, but otherwise she's fine. Why?'

'Just wondered. How's your husband?'

'He's a changed man. So are the others. You scared them. You scared us. You scared us all. But the company is dead and there are going to be criminal trials. What happened is going to come out, but the real leaders are gone.'

She meant dead. I was cool with that.

'Do we still have a deal? Is our arrangement still good?'

'Our deal is solid forever. But there's one thing.'

'What's that?'

'You killed eighteen men at my house. And for all that he's done, you shot my husband. I never want to hear from you or about you ever again.'

'Suits me. Suits me just fine.'

We hung up.

'What do you fancy doing today?' I asked.
  'Not much. You?'
  'I fancy doing not much too.'
  'Beach? Or go watch a film? Or watch a film and then beach? Or…'
  'Beach and then cinema?'
  'You know where we are right now?'
  'Umm, beach?'
  'You know how long we've been here?'
  'About three hours?'
  'Yeah, about that long.'
  'You want to pass me the sunscreen?'
  'We're out of it.' She replied.
  'Oh. Should we get a dog?'
  'Or we could get a dog instead of some more sunscreen.'
  'Well, maybe let's plan that a bit better.'
  'I didn't mean that for today.'
  'I didn't think you did.'
  'What kind of dog?'
  'Something we could love.'
  'You know we're talking about a child substitute?'
  'I do.'
  There was a pause in the conversation.
  'I love you, wife.'
  'I love you too, wife.' She replied.
  'You know I will never get tired of hearing that.'
  'We've only been married a month; you're still getting used to it.

'Thirty-four days.'

'Are you counting the days already?'

'I have a calendar in my head.' I said.

There was a long pause.

'I guess we should go home soon.' She said.

'Yeah, we should.'

'What about tonight?'

'Tonight, I'm taking you out for dinner. Italian. Candles. Wine.'

'Ooooh, I like the sound of this. Special occasion?'

'Yes, indeed. It's my thirty-fourth wedding dayversary, and I love my wife very much.'

Chapter 68.
Last Words/First Words

California

I woke. Curled, foetus-like. Shaking. Cold. Sweating. Aching. Stomach pain. My brain was working but my body was mostly doing its own thing.

I started crying. The start of a new cycle. I'd lost it all. I'd lost everything. I'd lost her.

An arm reached over me and held me.

'You all right?'

Charlie.

I couldn't believe it. This wasn't the damp squat in London? I opened my eyes and squinted. No, this was definitely the bedroom in Charlie's house.

I gasped.

'Are you OK?'

I slowly rolled onto my back and looked at the face of the woman I loved with all my heart. I felt tears start to fill my eyes. I had broken the cycle. For the first time in my life, I didn't know what was going to happen next.

'I'm just feeling a little wobbly.'

She brushed a tear from my cheek. 'You drank waaaay too much last night.'

Because I thought that was the last night for us, for both of us. Last night was the final night in the cycle and I should have woken up back in London.

'It's not going to happen again.'

'I kinda liked it. You were cute and funny. And you told some great stories. If even half of them are true, you've had one hell of a life.'

'Believe me. I have had one hell of a life.'

'So, what happens now?'

'I'm going to puke, maybe.'

'Nice. And afterwards?'

'And afterwards, I'm going to slow everything down and become an old married with my beautiful wife.'

'Nice again. And that sounded like you really meant it.'

'I really mean it more than you could ever, ever know.'

And I did.

The End

Brennig Jones was born and raised in the Welsh Valleys, has been around the world a bunch of times, lived in Spain a few years and is now based in the East Midlands (UK) with his wife, two step-children, four spaniels and four cats.

Tempest is Brennig's second novel.

Brennig can be contacted via his website:
https://brennigjones.com

Printed in Great Britain
by Amazon

17464679R10231